THE SIREN'S SCREAM

THE GOD SINGER: BOOK II

JACOB OAKLEY

Admittedly Bad Publishing, LLC

Copy Editor Lydia Craig
Editor at Large Keith Winkelman

First Printing, July 2022

Art by Jacob Oakley

To my wife and family, thank you for supporting and tolerating my excessive nerdiness

For my kids, don't ever stop dreaming, and write down the really good ones.

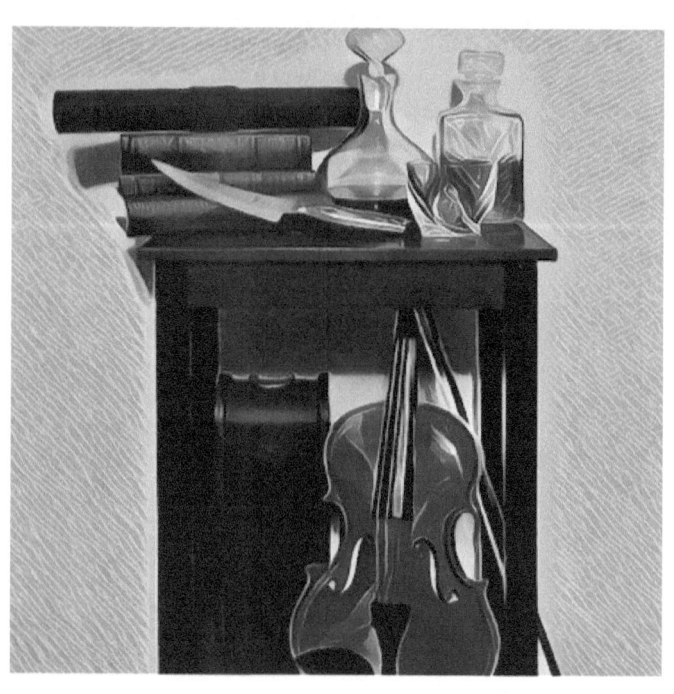

Quaf Island

The Hall

Tuath

N

The Sanctum

Lake
Gitche

Fjall

Fjall River

Mer
The Archdiocese
The College

Ravnice

Glasduille

Kalt

Lodestar Island
The Syndicate

Urylap Atoll  Aylap Atoll

Jawylap Atoll

Quaj Island

N

Lodestar Island

Huval Island

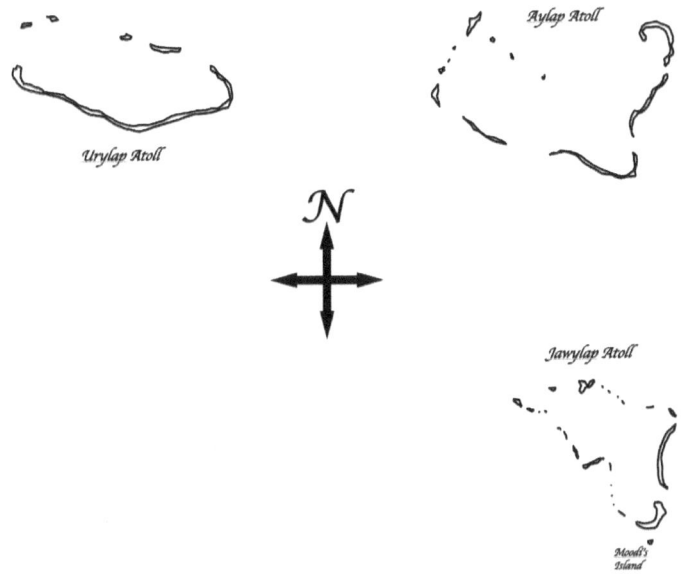

THE SIREN'S SCREAM

Prologue

Jedren Akkeri's fishing junk bobbed with the gentle coastal waves while he fought with his net lines. The chill in the air hugged the ship and the southern tip of Quaj Island under grey overcast dawn skies. The cold was numbing his hands, and the tingling pain made hauling and working his nets bothersome work. Winding the rope around a pair of wooden pegs so the net would not slip further out to sea, he paused and tried to warm his hands with his breath.

His red hair was in a knot behind his head to keep it out of his blue eyes, which surveying the distant Fjall mountain range at the island's end. Fishing the subarctic waters off the southwest coast of Quaj had weathered the man's body and corded his muscles. After almost a decade working larger fishing vessels out of Kalt City, Jedren had purchased his own small fishing boat, and he had carved the name *Muse* into the stern in memory of a one-night lover he had met on his last day in the city. Since that day, the *Muse* and its small one-room cabin had been Jedren's home.

His hands sufficiently warmed, Jedren grabbed his basket rake from the hooks that held it on the cabin wall and decided to pass the time waiting for arctic salmon to find his net by scraping for oysters and clams. His efforts with the basket rake were often fruitless, the work was like playing a tug-of-war with The Siren herself for the delicious shellfish of her seas.

Suddenly, a thick grey fog rolled in, engulfing his vessel. After a few moments, Jedren could make out the sides of something huge amongst its haze. He hauled in the basket rake and dropped it on the deck. Once it was in, he grabbed a boathook from where it leaned against his cabin and faced the mass next to

1

him.

A few seconds went by, and the fog cleared enough for him to see it for what it was. The galleon was the most massive ship he had ever seen. It was twice the length of the large brigantines that sailed out of northern Tuath harbor. The four-masted monstrosity next to his boat was over one hundred sixty feet long. The railings of its main deck were twenty feet above the sea. Jedren craned his head, gawking upwards at the still mostly fog obscured, greyish-blue painted hull.

There was a clicking sound from above, and a crossbow bolt thudded between his feet.

"Drop the weapon and come aboard, or the next one sends you to The Sleeper," said a distant and hollow voice above him in the cold fog.

It was followed by the lowering of a rope ladder down the side of the ship. Not having much of an option if he wanted to live, Jedren obediently tied its end to the stern rail and made his way up the rungs, wondering if it were the last time he would see his boat.

As he made the railing of the giant ship and climbed onto its deck, Jedren noted the presence of several men holding crossbows aimed at his chest. The bald-shaved men were wearing pale blue cloth pants and fur-lined dark blue dyed leather tunics. Looking up briefly, he noted the blue-dyed sails strung up huge masts. The door in front of him to the halfdeck was swung open from inside and couldn't help but rub his eyes in disbelief at the visage that approached him from the ship's cabin.

"Well met once again, Jedren Akkeri," the woman he knew as Tessa said. She crossed her arms, squeezing her chest together. The look in her eyes dared Jedren to drop his gaze.

For his part, Jedren could only utter her name in a whispered shock, "Tessa."

"In truth, my name is Kisa Hadjuk. Duchess, Kisa Hadjuk, and you find yourself aboard one of my ships. I never used my real name when making excursions into other countries."

Jedren felt his cheeks flush as he tried to stammer a sentence together.

"I have thought of you every day since that night. I even named my vessel muse after your memory!" he exclaimed.

"You men are purely for breeding," Kisa said, snorting in

derision and rolling her eyes,

The woman's beauty had him so overwhelmed that though he tried to open his mouth to respond he could not bring himself to speak. The memory of the night they shared was an affliction he could not escape. Yet somehow, she seemed to feel nothing for him.

As if to confirm his thoughts, Kisa glanced mischievously at the woman next to her. She ran her fingertips from the woman's ear, down her neck, between her breasts, and slipped it behind the small of her back. Kisa then pulled her in for a long kiss before separating and staring into her eyes.

She continued without turning to Jedren, "Women, on the other hand, are for pleasure."

She snapped her fingers, and a man emerged from the halfdeck doors. In his hands was a baby wrapped in a blue blanket. He walked up between Jedren and Kisa.

Still, Kisa did not look back at Jedren. Instead, she continued looking down into the almost black, brown eyes of the black-haired child.

"Half breeds such as this child you left inside me are sometimes allowed to live amongst the Tormenta. However, since the half breed is a lowly male like yourself, neither my people, my goddess, nor the queen will suffer me to keep it. Perhaps the child would be better served as a sacrifice at sea to The Siren, but I have decided to leave his fate to you."

The man offered the strangely silent and calm young baby to him. Still reeling from everything Kisa had said, Jedren took the boy and looked down into his eyes.

"What is his name?" Jedren asked, and Kisa finally met his gaze.

"We do not name sacrifices to The Siren. Return to your *Muse* and cast off our ladder. We depart now for the southern seas."

Jedren watched her walk back towards the halfdeck doors, cloaks billowing behind her and her partner as they held hands. The guards shut the door behind the women and faced Jedren grimly. He looked down at the boy in his arms.

"More a Harpy than a muse, I suppose. No?" He asked the baby.

*****

Harpis watched as his father Jedren Akkeri deeply inhale the warm, humid spring breeze that carried with it scents of blooming flowers and trees.

The seasonal warmth made it the most pleasant time to fish the southern waters and the most treacherous. The Fjall mountain range running along the back of the island funneled the warmer air from the north into the chillier subarctic winds of the south. The result was the tremendous storms that rocked the southern seas in spring.

Jedren took a break from working the handle of his basket rake to wipe his brow. He glanced over at his son, who was doing the same off the other side of their boat.

"Twenty years old lad, thinking it's time you stop suckling at the teat and get off my boat."

Harpis shook his head and continued flexing his shoulders and arms against the rake handle.

"Suckling at the teat? What would you be doing without free labor to work this miserable boat for you? You're moving a little slower lately, old man. Are you sure you could handle minding her on your own again?" he asked.

Jedren snorted at his son. "Well, boy, I will tell you what, the man with the least number of clams in his basket is cooking dinner. But first, we shall see who can and cannot work this boat."

The two men were a physical match in height and build, and both plunged their basket rakes out as far as the handles would let them. Then, pulling and flicking his basket rake handle, Jedren effortlessly cast it dancing across the seafloor.

Harpis, for his part, was straining every muscle in his body and essentially dredging the bottom with his basket. Then, as the two men finished dragging the rake heads close to the boat, they pulled them up out of the water.

Feeling how heavy his basket was, Harpis shot his father a look of superiority. However, he was sorely deflated when the basket rake came up full of mud, rocks, and the broken shell of a long-dead clam. When Jedren pulled his basket out of the water,

4

it was full of twenty clams and several oysters.

He laughed from his belly at the look of dejection on his son's face. Then, flicking an oyster to Harpis, he ate one himself fresh out of the shell before walking over and dumping the clams at Harpis' feet.

"Looks like you're cooking dinner tonight. Get to cleaning those," Jedren said, rubbing Harpis' white-streaked black hair fondly.

Looking past his son and out to sea, Jedren's gaze was pulled skyward. A black wall of clouds was moving quickly in their direction.

"Leave that boy. We ought to be hauling in our ropes and crab baskets. Those clouds look as angry as The Siren herself."

The two men positioned themselves on either side of the stern and unwound the netting ropes from the pegs that held them in place. Then, with a nod from Jedren, they began methodically and evenly pulling in the net.

Jedren marveled at the youthful strength of his son. "I tell you, Harpis, give up sea life. A young man like yourself would make a fine addition to a city militia! Out here on the water, The Siren tries at least once a day to kill you. Folk on land do not have that problem. Her waves cannot reach them away from the coast. Instead, the storms she raises from the deep renew the crops and bring water to animals!"

Harpis shook his head at his father, and both men looked up at the sky together. Jedren's face grimaced in concern as he noted how the clouds were moving toward them. He began a work song, and the two began hauling the net in earnest.

The last bit of netting held several dozen fish and was challenging to get onto the ship's deck. As the salmon flopped around, Harpis kicked them into the water of the live well. The sun disappeared, and it looked as if dusk was suddenly upon them. Jedren and Harpis made for the ropes that ran out to a crab basket and began pulling.

The air around them cooled as the front approached, causing both men's skin to prickle.

"Cut the lines, Harpis. We have to go now!" Jedren shouted above the din of the air rushing around them.

Before they could free the lines, a massive surge of wind ripped the sail from the boat's small mast.

"Damn The Siren, damn her seas, and damn this confounded shipwreck of a boat!" Jedren cursed as they grabbed the two long oars and tried to maneuver the boat inland. Torrential rain pelted the craft, with the wind blowing the drops almost horizontally. The waves were now over twice the height of a man and threatening to capsize the small boat.

After glancing towards the coast, a look of defeat filled Jedren's eyes as he turned and shouted new instructions to his son. "We're not making it inland in this. We need to keep her facing the waves."

They spent a few successful moments riding up and down the swells before the increasingly rough seas pulled the *Muse* almost vertically as it rode down the backend of waves taller than the boat was long.

The black clouds above suddenly disappeared behind an immense rogue wave. Harpis and Jedren exchanged strained looks while flexing their entire bodies against their oars to hold the boat facing into the swell.

Jedren barely had the breath to speak while his body struggled. "Gods above, I love ya boy, but your mother, The Siren, and their storms can all shove themselves up a horse's ass!"

It was only the second time Harpis had heard his father even mention his mother. He opened his mouth to respond, but the words never made it from his lips as the colossal wave sucked the small boat onto its back.

As they crested and began the almost straight downward plunge, Harpis felt weightless. The strain of steering the ship against the mountain of water snapped both men's oars, and with a last glance at each other, everything went to black as the waves rolled the ship.

Chapter 1
Unfolding

"Again!" Mahala half-shouted through clenched teeth and Harpis was glad that he was not the target of the tiny but fiery woman's ire for once. Not that he had fared much better than Bravit on his previous attempts.

Bravit picked up the cloth-wrapped mallets with a defeated shrug and began a rhythmic and soft pace on the drum that sat in front of him. As the trot of his strumming across the stretched leather drumhead sped up, the words to *Panoryla's March* rolled out in the bard's deep and robust voice. Even before the portly man wove his gift amongst his words and through the notes jumping off the drum, his song filled the small cavern they were in with a commanding force.

Harpis felt his pulse quickening and smiled at the vast improvement of Bravit's ability to wield the gift these past months. He struggled to contain an urge to jump to his feet and sing along with the other man's magic surging around him.

As Bravit ceased his drumming, his cherubic smile fell into disappointment at the frustration still painted on Mahala's face as she squeezed her forehead with her fingers.

"I think that is enough for the evening Bravit," she said in resignation while Bravit stared at his drum mallets as if they betrayed him.

Wanting to comfort his old friend Harpis tried to offer consolation.

"For my part, I was barely able to refrain from joining your performance Bravit, your ability to impart your gift has grown tenfold since you first taught me to weave magic through song," he said.

Mahala rolled her eyes at Harpis before crossing her arms and facing Bravit.

"Your volume is indeed undeniable, but you wield that hefty baritone like a hammer. If you wish to master specificity in your delivery, good Bravit, you will somehow have to master embroidering silk with a sledge for a needle and anchor chains for thread," she said.

Harpis appreciated her analogy in attempting to impart to Bravit and himself how to target specific people in a crowd with their gift amongst music heard by many ears. When the three had first started gathering months ago, she had told them to imagine a song as a blank tablecloth held by everyone in the audience. She had said that unbound weaving of the gift was akin to unfurling a specific tapestry across that tablecloth for all to see. Specificity was like forcing magic to be woven and sewn amongst the tablecloth threads, stitching the gift on the notes such that they would only reach the intended person.

Bravit placed his drum along the cave wall and laid his mallets gingerly atop it.

"I don't see the point of specificity for a song like *Panoryla's March*, meant to benefit those around the bard, but I appreciate the lesson nonetheless, Mahala," he said, a tinge of resentment in his voice.

As unrelenting as ever, Mahala gave Bravit a sharp look before answering sternly.

"Specificity has little use in benevolent composition. When performing malignance, though, one can see the utility. However, I would rather subject us to invigoration than malaise as you learn to control your clamorous gift," she explained.

Bravit offered no argument as he rose to depart. "Indeed, that is enough concentrating for one evening for me. I've still got musicians to train tomorrow," he said to Mahala before turning to Harpis with a grin.

"If you two conclude before midnight, find me for a flagon or two in the kitchens, God Singer" he offered.

Mahala stared at the cave ceiling above in exasperation before returning her gaze to the two men.

"Good evening, Troubadour," Bravit said to her as he left.

"Maestro," she responded, standing from her chair in respectful farewell.

8

Harpis watched the hefty, cloth-covered wooden door close behind Bravit. He could barely make out the sound of the second door several paces beyond it closing shut as the overweight man began his slow ascent up the curving staircase to the second basement of the performance hall stage pit above them. A brief breeze flowed through the room as the door's opening allowed the wind outside to force in fresh air off the sea from the inlets cut along the cliff face when the dwarves had created the small cavern.

Mahala looked around the cave for a moment before taking her seat in one of four cushioned chairs that sat around the small table at the center. She kicked her feet onto the tabletop, barely avoiding the stack of parchment and books atop it before turning her fierce eyes on him.

"Well, Harpis, I don't know how much more I can help the two of you improve your gift beyond simply telling you to keep practicing. I think it is time you tell me your endgame," she said.

He paused and considered her question. They had spent most nights for the past months in what the three of them had fondly referred to as The Quarry. The absolute silence afforded by a hundred feet of limestone above and the thick tapestries that lined the house-sized cavern was necessary to practice gifted song safely and in secret.

Taking the seat across from her, he met her gaze.

"I want our craft to match the efforts at research and governance for magic and science that the mages accomplished at The College of Elements in Mer. In addition, however, ours will enable unrivaled dedication to the creativity and adaptability of our unique art."

She dropped her feet back to the floor, picking up her violin and giving it a fond look as she responded.

"They've had the benefit of numerous and varied practitioners, rich history, and centuries of experience and exploration. What have we?" she asked

"We have the three of us," he answered, plucking a copy of The Treaty of Mer from the table and examining it.

"Three humans with barely fifty years of song-weaving combined between us, Stone Mage Lorkin alone has spent more than three times that dedicated to magecraft." She stopped, pensive in thought for a moment before setting her violin on the

9

table.

"Why is that the case?" she asked, sitting up straighter as she responded.

"Why is what the case?" he returned.

"Why so few, and why all humans? I mean, we have barely scratched the surface of a field whose entire body of knowledge sits before us," she said, indicating a dozen books and assorted scrolls piled at the center of the table.

"And most of those read like myth and legend, second or third hand and centuries removed. Still, none mention an elvish dwarven, gnomish, or any other such bard. Just humans," she finished.

"I have given much thought to that question. Though you may far outstrip my expertise in bardic art. I have spent the better part of the past three years in the company of elves, dwarves, and one especially grumpy gnome. I have never gotten the inclination from any of our fellow inhabitants of the mortal plane that they have the empathy necessary to affect others in the way we do," he answered, sitting up thoughtfully in his chair.

"What do you mean?" she asked.

"They just don't seem to feel like we do, emote as we do. Being around such folk day in and day out is akin to being a toddler again. You are surrounded by those who have learned to bridle and suppress the spontaneous, raw emotions that rule our short human lives," he answered.

Mahala tilted her head in consideration, her brown hair tumbling down her shoulder as she did.

"I guess that makes some sense. It must be difficult to have passion when there is always tomorrow or next week," she reasoned.

Harpis laced his fingers and set his hands atop the table, looking her straight in the eyes.

"Or next year, or a decade," he said, emphasizing the point.

"It is our adolescent zeal that lets us manipulate other beings then?" she asked.

"And you, Troubadour Mahala Shelta are the most mature of us adolescents!" he said, smirking.

Mahala snorted and shook her head.

"Such rank is chief amongst my accomplishments," she said sarcastically.

"I ask you to continue here, to keep theory crafting, experimenting, and documenting our gift with Bravit, at least until I return from my trip to the south," he said, speaking in a more serious tone.

"I will, for now, at least until the urge to wander overwhelms me again, but why must it be in this secret school of rock," she asked, motioning at the cave walls.

"Because, we are exploring, as you put it, a wildfire of magic that we barely understand which is safer gone awry down here away from unsuspecting ears. Further, until we mature and formalize the art of song-weaving, I would prefer to keep its potential and its limits a guarded secret," he answered, picking up his violin and bow.

"That whole Syndicate business made you quite paranoid, you know," she said.

"You have no idea," he said before gathering himself and attempting to weave his gift through a voiceless instrumental.

*****

As the evening chant to The Sleeper ended, Wren unclasped his hands and took a private moment of solace. Staring into the black depths of The Dreamer's Door always steadied his thoughts. When the elderly gnome looked up to the other necromancers gathered in The Sanctum's sepulcher, he let out a sigh. Before the death of the previous Herald and his ascension to her position, he had been one of her half dozen death speakers.

Sitting on the semi-circular stone bench that surrounded the well-like structure with him now, there were only three. To his left sat Zekander Kilnstoker, a middle-aged dwarf with unkempt auburn hair who had only a decade ago pulled forth a familiar from the great dream.

He looked to his right where his third cousin sat. Daugor Ikinstainfurontowry had attained the rank of death speaker shortly after Wren had first summoned Xissay. The other gnome was almost a half-century older, but they appeared to be nearly the same age given the cost of Wren's bargain with his goddess on behalf of a particular fiddle-playing human.

Looking past the dwarf, Wren gave a smile to Eileen Filenthroe. She was both the youngest of them and most likely to meet The Sleeper next. The white-haired human woman of ninety-three years clutched her necromancer scythe like a cane for support even as she sat.

Gazing down from the dais to the rows of pews that could hold some hundred worshippers, Wren lamented that barely thirty were shuffling their way out of the sepulcher to take their suppers. With a nod from Wren, Zekander rose and lent his stocky dwarven frame to Eileen as they followed the procession of acolytes.

When the human and dwarf passed out of the sepulcher, Daugor turned to him with a curious look.

"Out with it then," his cousin prodded.

"I have made my decision. As Herald, I believe that I should be trying to rebuild our ranks, not praying away the rest of my days here in The Sanctum," Wren explained.

"Do you think that wise given what drove us to this island those two centuries ago?" Daugor countered, shaking his head.

Wren paused and grimaced away the memory his cousin's words summoned to mind before speaking again.

"During our time here, there has been no indication of such prejudice spreading to this home of shipwrecks and wanderers. We've even had the likes of humans and dwarves join us in our devotion. If we can't safely grow her faith here in the middle of Nysia's vast oceans, at the precipice of The Dreamer's Door, it will fade as we do," he said

"You're the Herald, the obligation is yours, Wren, but I'll remind you that Zekander is only the second of his kin to join us. Our clan that made it here when we were children is likely to be all but gone in another generation. Half will perish in the coming five decades, the two of us included. That would leave some dozen gnomes who live beneath Fjall to carry on, and when was the last time one chose the robes?" Daugor grumpily asked.

Wren sat patiently, expecting this and other arguments and planning to hear and debate them all if necessary. Unlike Zekander, he spoke calmly, keeping as much emotion from the easily embattled conversation as possible.

"That is why our people in Fjall will be my first stop on my journey, followed by a talk with Ingar. I am aware that in the next century, the only gnomes left here on Quaj will be too closely related to each other to birth another generation. Unfortunately, our elders could not have foreseen nor prevented that issue," he replied.

"Well, it has been nearly three hundred years, and we have yet to hear from any of the others that fled Sikef. You would then entrust our hereditary duty to humans?" Daugor asked.

Wren bowed his head slightly and spoke in a heavier tone, knowing his cousin had likely already accepted the inevitability.

"We have no other choice, and she has no other option," Wren said, patting the cracked opening of The Dreamer's Door.

Daugor said nothing, simply resting clenched fists in his lap. He stared for a moment at the ceiling in obvious frustration and then back at Wren.

Standing, Wren pulled forth his necromancer scythe. There was a puff of smoke, the smell of sulfur and then Xissay appeared floating atop his purple-robed shoulders. The fire sprite familiar gave a warm smile to the other gnome before speaking to Wren.

"Is it time then, old gnome?" she asked.

"It is," he said, motioning for Daugor to also rise. The other gnome faced Wren as Xissay sped off to the sepulcher door and beckoned Zekander and Eileen to join them.

Once gathered, the three death speakers summoned their scythes and stood facing Wren. He smiled at them before speaking in a confident and unconditional tone.

"Death Speaker Daugor Ikinstainfurontowry of the gnome clan Marhohonu, I name you Rector of The Sanctum, responsible to its inhabitants and their faith."

The three bowed in unison, and Daugor replied with his head still bent.

"I accept Herald," he answered

Eileen and Zekander embraced Daugor briefly before Wren walked in front of him and put his hands on the other gnome's shoulders after dismissing his scythe.

"This old place is in good hands. I will take but one with me on my journey of evangelism. Our young acolyte, Jabruelle, will be most useful in bringing other humans into the fold," Wren said.

Above his shoulder, he heard the soft slap of a small hand on a tiny forehead.

"Do you mind?" he asked Xissay.

Floating her way in front of his face, the diminutive, undead, fire sprite crossed her arms.

"Yes, I mind!" she glowered.

13

Wren snapped his fingers and scoffed as he dismissed his familiar, glowering at her exaggerated eye roll before turning his glare to his three most senior necromancers who stood staring at their feet trying not to laugh.

"I'll depart in the morning for Fjall and Jabruelle will make his way to Mer to see what he can learn of spreading faith from the clerics," he finished.

*****

Svenus stood, rigidly tense, facing the window in his office at the unusually quiet docks of Kalt Family Timber. He could feel his pulse beat in the fists shaking at his sides as he stared across the Kalt harbor. He looked out at the city and, specifically at the home of the governor who had betrayed him. He could feel the nervousness of his nephews who stood behind him, fidgeting in the growing silence since they had reported on earnings, orders, and staffing.

He turned to the three younger men with a shrewd look, rubbing the back of his black-haired head before speaking in a feigned consoling voice.

"Does anyone have any ideas on how we move on from here?" he asked.

He looked from one pale, dark-haired Kaltese man to the next, rage silently swelling within him as each slowly lowered their eyes from his to their feet.

Snatching his wood chair by its back, he brandished it threateningly at them.

"The Siren curses my family that the three of you blundering idiots are what will be left to save this business and our clan from ruination should I die! Perhaps my rage at the disappointments you have turned out to be will spur me to immortality lest I hang between life and death in the maddening purgatory that would be your succession!" he yelled.

He swung the chair in front of their faces. Grinning as all three flinched away from him, he then turned and flung it through the window.

"It was bad enough that the northern patsy playing at Myrlman Tuath floundered his way into losing a revolution of his own creation, costing us much needed support and business," he said, sneering indignantly and pointing out at the city of Kalt.

Svenus Kalt walked to the now open window. With his hands on the ledge, his speech turned to a growl as he went on. He was seemingly unfazed or unaware of the cuts from leftover glass and the blood trickling down the wall from his palms.

"I can no longer sit idly by while these waters and this city that bear my family name are under the governance of that spineless, back-stabbing conspirator of a governor, Jaeryl Innisgrath. Worse, not one of you has any idea how to return what is ours or turn around our fortunes," Svenus continued.

"That ignorant fink sits at the council in Mer, cowing to the children of farmhands and serfs that run the other states of this five-forsaken island, ceding our lands to those worthless elves," he said, spitting out the last word as if he could taste its bitterness on his tongue.

Chapter 2

Reunion

Harpis could smell the first dry hints of chill that found their way into the dusk air as autumn approached Ravnice City. The hustle and bustle of shipping the harvest would soon take over the wharf that he and Wren were walking across on their way to the Siren's Scream. Their steps grew hasty as the sun disappeared below the horizon, and the slight chill became more biting.

The inn's hugging warmth and soft din greeted them as they stepped inside, and the brisk evening air became an afterthought. They made their way silently back into their customary booth behind the staircase at the back of the establishment where whiskey glasses were already waiting for them.

Wren took a long pull from the glass and set it down before addressing Harpis.

"Well, bard, it is good to see you. This past year since the peace has been long in passing. How fares The Hall and your fellow bards? Have they named you Impresario yet?"

Harpis shifted uncomfortably at the mention of the title. The image of the last Impresario being skewered in front of him while he was helpless to stop it still haunted him. The fact that he had been the reason Benali was there with Sirul in the first place made the pain of his friend and mentor's passing even more difficult.

The newly won peace aside, the cost to many, himself included, had been high. He ran his hand through hair which was much more white than black. Another reminder of the penance he bore for using a goddess's true name. Aged well beyond his twenty-three years, he imagined he looked like his father would have if Jedren were still living. He stopped raking his mane with his hand, and his eyes met the raised eyebrows and inquisitive

16

gaze of his friend, still awaiting a reply.

"The Bards Hall is undergoing some significant changes. The revelation of The Syndicate and my role in it while being a sanctioned bard has complicated things. In addition, the musical institution's ties to the Tuath family via Benali during the whole Sirul debacle has left the public with a poor opinion of The Hall. Bravit has met several times with the Arch Mage in Mer to discuss what we could do as an organization to regain some of that trust. For one, we plan to establish a constitution like The College of Elements," he answered.

"Seems sensible enough," Wren stated.

Nodding, Harpis continued.

"Anyone who wants to be trained and sanctioned by the Bards Hall must agree to the terms our new constitution. Any that do not and those who violate it will face expulsion. This doctrine should help assure the people of the island that our plans are to be impartial from any specific regional influence. It helps a great deal that the college has worked this way for decades, and we can lean on their established practices. At Bravit's suggestion, we will also separate the formal bard training from the pursuit of gifted song. This way, the sanctioned bards are assumed only to perform their role as journalists of the island," he explained.

Wren folded his hands together on the table and nodded approvingly at his former apprentice.

"I must admit that I am proud to say you are a far cry from the brash drunk fisherman I first met on the *Sea Goat* and later propositioned in this very tavern to join The Syndicate. What place in this grand new architecture of barding does the refined and fabled Harpis Akkeri, fit?" he asked.

"I do not," he said, giving a short shrug at the gnome's questioning expression.

"I'd have thought you were sure to become Impresario Harpis after the gifted display you put on in Tuath Bay and at the gates of the city," Wren said with his glass halfway to his lips.

Harpis shook his head slowly while staring at the glass in front of him before taking a deep sip of his own.

"That title died with Benali Tuath. Maestro Bravit will retain the academic title of Maestro, now meant solely for the headmaster of the Bard's Hall, the other instructors now being Composer or Dictum depending on their subjects. Mahala Shelta is now the Troubadour, the senior-most gifted bard, the more junior of whom we will refer to as Virtuosos, which for now I guess that would just be myself. Besides, I am terrible at reading music and mediocre at best at playing my fiddle. I'd make for a poor instructor of musicians," he said.

"It is called a violin for Sleeper's sake," Wren said vehemently.

Harpis had nothing to offer but a shrug, their conversation returning to silence as the barmaid took their empties and replaced them with full glasses of whiskey.

"That'll be going on the good gnomes tab as well, please, Kalna, my dear," Harpis said with a sly grin to the strawberry-blond barmaid who had become their usual server since their first time at the tavern.

The girl curtsied at Wren before turning to Harpis, "Obviously it is going on Wren's tab. He tips far better than you!"

Harpis' face crinkled in feigned anger, and Wren threw her a wink as she went to other patrons.

"Even if she was into purple dress-wearing gnomes, you're too old for her," he said.

Wren crossed his arms in front of him with a grin of his own, "You look too old to be her type even if she was into dating her father's friends."

Harpis wanted to counter with further clever wit but instead simply scoffed.

Wren held up a hand in peace to end the sarcastic exchange. "I'll be honest, lad, without The Syndicate to keep me busy, I'd be lying if I didn't say I was a little bored. I have been collaborating with another institution on our little island. The Exarch had much advice on spreading the word of his goddess and how the necromancy could similarly benefit. The large obstacle I see is that folks struggle to find the same reverence in death that they do for life. There are barely thirty of us. All cooped up in The Hole, and only a third of us are gifted. Worse yet, there are very few young or even middle-aged necromancers. If we don't change our ways, we will simply be a group of death worshippers living out their dotage waiting to join our goddess. Her faith will pass from the mortal plane with our last breaths," he lamented, pulling a demur face as he continued.

"I think I will use the mantle of the Death Herald to travel the island and preach her faith to others in hopes of encouraging some new and young souls to join our fold. I will leave the senior Death Speaker to carry on the traditions of the temple. I have named Death Speaker Daugor as Rector. Truthfully Harpis, I can't stand being cooped up in the tunnels of Fjall mountain despite my hereditary love for the underneath places," the gnome finished.

Harpis leaned back in his booth with a smile creeping across his face.

"Then how about you join me on my trip to the archives in Mer to look through their historical texts for other mentions of a gifted song or gifted bards before we join the Fall council," he said

The gnome returned the smile, seemingly happy for an excuse to stay abroad a while longer.

"I have some affairs to attend to regarding my shop here in town. I can meet you here tomorrow afternoon and we can head north together," he said.

Harpis raised his glass to toast the gnome.

"To another adventure then, albeit far less exciting than our last one. I promised Aanaman I would stop by tomorrow morning. Perhaps I can relieve the good governor of a bottle of his whiskey to hold us over while in Mer," he offered.

******

The past three times that Tawito had sailed past Lodestar Island, he had found it barren, burnt, and uninhabited. This voyage would be the last time he would check in on it before giving up on his old friend. The Quaji elder had promised Turin Deadeye to visit every few months. If after a year none were on the island to visit, he was never to return. Turin had a contingency for everything it seemed.

This time though, the lighthouse beacon shone as it came into view over the barely distinguishable evening horizon, and the short, white-haired, dark-skinned man let out a sigh of relief. His single-sail canoe quickly made the distance to Lodestar Island's small harbor, and he tied off at the partially repaired dock before disembarking and making his way to the lighthouse.

As he neared the front door, he smelled the sweet-salty fragrance of a seafood soup wafting out the first-floor window, and he rapped on the front door before being bid to enter. Tawito had known Turin for as long as he could remember, and though Tawito was now nearing sixty years old, Turin still looked almost entirely the same as when they had first been introduced. When the elf met his gaze, the man noticed weariness in his eyes where once there was nothing but determined purpose.

"Welcome back, Tawito, my friend. Please, sit and join me for some dinner," the elf welcomed.

Tawito did as Turin bid, awkwardly sitting in the chair opposite him at the small table in the lighthouse kitchen. He was still processing what was going on, why the island had been seemingly barren for nearly a year, where the guards were that typically saw him into the depths of the Syndicate's natural fortress inside the island's dormant volcano. Tawito spent a few moments staring at the soup in front of him.

"What happened?" he finally asked the elf.

Several hours later, he wished he hadn't known. He felt sorry for the loss of so many lives, especially for his Quaji brother and sister Arken Hester and the water mage Trilia. Since outsiders arrived from the east, they were two of only a few Quaji native islanders to return to Lodestar or Quaj in the centuries.

Turin cleared their places and returned with wine to share.

"I regret in my failure Tawito, that I was also unable to bring your people back to their home island. I needed to unify the current city-states in democratic governance before suggesting in one way or another that they ought to cede some or much of their land back to the island's original inhabitants."

"Turin, how could you possibly feel responsible for the transgressions of past generations, not even of your race, my friend," Tawito said.

"How are the three exiled tribes of Quaji?" Turin asked.

"Still not unified, despite attempts by me and others. It does not help that we have no central thread to bind us. Even our worship of The Wild is a localized thing for families and tribes alike. The mystics each have their own unique devotion to our goddess. Folk living dispersed across the atolls does not help things either," Tawito answered.

Turin sat deep in thought for a long moment.

"It always struck me that your kind did not worship The Siren too or foremost, given her control over the domain most important to your survival, it would seem," he commented.

Tawito spat on the floor like any good Quaji would at the mention of the twin sister of his goddess.

"Curse to her. The Wild and her bounty keep us alive and safe. Her ill-tempered sister is naught but a menace to my people!" he exclaimed.

Turin refilled the man's glass and slid it back.

"I understand. I have always been curious how the sisters, all four of them, have influenced the mortal plane. I have a favor to ask of you, my friend, if you would bear it," he said.

"Anything Turin, my people and myself owe you several debts that we could not possibly repay," Tawito replied, taking the glass from the ancient elf.

*****

The six-sided stone cavern resembled a large tomb, a quiet howl constantly moaned though no wind blew within it. Rock walls stained by millennia of moss echoed water dripping from somewhere above. The ceiling felt heavy, as if it were the deepest place under the highest mountain. Five of the sides looked like once open entryways, now filled with solid stone, and the sixth was bare. The stone of three of those portals began to swirl in slowly widening circles slowly.

The first portal revealed a forest scape on the other side. Through it stepped the youngest of the sisters, she would be short by human standards and though tens of thousands of years old, had the look of a woman barely come of age. Brown-haired and olive-skinned, with soft and smiling green eyes, she walked towards The Nexus center. In each spot where her bare feet left the cold stone floor behind, there were footprints of fresh moss, budding plants, and young grass tracing her path to the center of the room like small foot-shaped natural rugs. Her curvy form was clothed, barely, by a natural drapery of foliage, from ivy and wildflowers to spots of moss and leaves.

As she neared the center of the room, the thick tresses of her hair were rustled as if by a breeze and then blown forward by a gale-like wind. The portal next to hers finished expanding and showed a rocky coast with crashing waves and pitch-black clouds illuminated sporadically by forks of lightning. The wind died as

21

her sister stepped fully into the small cavern from the storm on the other side. The lady of the tempest had unblemished, almost translucently pale skin with wild red hair and piercing blue eyes. The air in the room was still. Yet, her hair and clothes rippled as if she was still on the coast and in the storm. She wore a revealing sheer gown woven from shreds of clouds that hid nothing of her body underneath. As she reached her sister at the center, they grabbed each other's hands and hugged in a tight embrace.

Before they had the chance to converse, the third portal opened, bathing the entire Nexus in radiating light that brought calm and silence with it. One of their older sisters followed that peace into the Nexus, filling the room with a soft glow. Taller and lither than her younger sisters, she strode through her portal with waist-length blond curls bouncing down her back.

She wore a gown of pure white silk, and her skin glowed like a sunrise obscured by fog. Her entire presence was warm and welcoming and nearly impossible to ignore. Reaching the center, she clasped her sister's hands in greeting and her calm brown eyes met each of the younger twin's gazes in turn, before speaking in a voice that sounded like chimes and bell tolls.

"Thank you for heeding my call, sisters. It has been too long since we last met. I have grown concerned, I felt our sister stir, and she has not awoken since last we walked the mortal plane."

The abruptness of the statement and lack of conversational niceties from their typically formal and measured older sister set the younger twins on their heels. Their faces displayed a similar concern. The elder spared a forlorn look for the portal next to hers that was still rigid stone before continuing.

"What an irony that the one who still sleeps is the first to have her true name uttered in centuries. I felt the surge of power as her influence connected to the mortal plane, even if for a moment. I wish my name were still uttered so that I could once again walk amongst my adherents."

"At least there are still many believers on the mortal plane with fervor for you, sister. Unfortunately, some of us are not so blessed," the olive-skinned sister said, squeezing her hand.

The red-haired sister scoffed at her siblings, "At least you two receive only worship. I am just as likely to be cursed by the mortals as praised by them!"

"Maybe if you were nicer to them, they'd praise you more

than curse you, sister," the brunette said with a smirk.

A sudden wind whipped around all three of them as the storm goddess seethed.

"Sisters!" the blond said calmly.

The raging wind dissipated in the quiet that followed.

"Something is not right. I feel unbalanced as I haven't since the four of us walked together to banish our brother.

*****

A smile crept its way across Enky's face at his oldest sister's statement. It always made him happy to see the sisters even though they knew not when he watched them. He enjoyed observing the mortals and gods alike in the portals that hung on his walls. Enky had been worried at first as the sisters began this meeting that they knew something was amiss, but they had made it clear they were not aware of his machinations even if they were suspicious of something yet unknown.

He was not one for plans, but this time his designs seemed to be so far unfolding as intended. His most recent attempt to influence the mortal plane had not ended at all as he'd hoped. Admittedly, he should have known better than to employ one such as Sirul Amun. The man had more than looked the part. However, his mind was one of maddeningly singular focus, beyond even Enky's ability to manipulate.

This time Enky would further his plot through a proper agent of chaos

"Another puppet on my strings, whom duplicity and disorder brings," he whispered.

Chapter 3

The Tormenta

Harpis felt like he was back south in Kalt with the whole city of Mer caught in the midst of a blustery late-fall rainstorm. Winter temperatures had yet to set in, but the stinging wind off the sea and ice-cold raindrops had many of those caught outside soaked and shivering.

The walk from the inn where they were staying to the council building was a short one, but Wren grumbled the entire way, pulling the cowl of his robe tight around his neck and cursing away the cold. Harpis tilted his face slightly skyward and nostalgically accepted the beating from the storm. The sound of the wind and the smell of rain always seemed to set him at ease despite having every reason to despise The Siren's elements.

As they neared the council building, they could hear a jovial tavern-like din making its way from the covered porch of the newly built barracks next door. There, guards of each attendee had a place to spend the day within hasty reach of their charges inside.

The contingents were much smaller than in the past. After the Tuath conflict, governors were only allowed a ten-person escort within the city limits. Further, each escort was required to serve at least four council meetings in the post. The result was a familiarity and friendliness between the soldiers and militiamen from the six city-states. The rain did not seem to impede the good spirits of the thirty-some men, four dwarves, and two elves. Most remained in the barracks and near the warmth of the fire. However, several men from Kalt and one of the dwarfs were lounging on the porch as he and Wren walked by.

One of the men noticed their approach through the pouring rain and stood to address them.

"Excuse me, sir. You'll have to take your daughter elsewhere. The council meeting is in session, and this area is no place for children," the human guard challenged.

Wren stopped mid-step and glared furiously at the man. Harpis choked on a laugh and nearly tripped, barely avoiding his suddenly halted companion. The dwarf next to the man squinted his eyes to peer through the rain and then slapped the human upside the head.

"Koenig ya daft idiot, that's the Death Herald!"

Harpis kept moving and pulled Wren along to avoid the grumpy gnome raising some corpse or worse, calling forth Xissay from The Great Dream to make the man soil himself.

"Good day, sirs, our thanks for your watchful eyes!" Harpis yelled in passing.

"Watchful indeed," Wren muttered, scowling.

Arriving at the heavy doors to the squat square building, Harpis pushed them open to enter. The two were greeted with a gush of warm, dry air from the fire raging in the fireplace at the opposite end of the single room inside. Summarily the cold air that forced its way in behind the pair garnered the attention of those already gathered and seated at the five-sided table. The orientation of the pentagon was with a pointed corner towards the doorway, so no member had to have their back to the entrance.

The new Exarch and ancient Arch Mage occupied the seats nearest that point. The bald and pudgy Bravit sat to the right of the Arch Mage, representing the bards and The Hall. Wren climbed into the seat that was open to the left of the newly appointed Exarch. Two governors each sat at the remaining three sides. With the last seat at the table filled by Wren, Harpis walked to one of the spare chairs near the fireplace.

Along the way, he paused to shake hands with Bravit and nodded a greeting to Aanaman. As he took his seat, the Ravnice councilman returned his nod with a wry smile and addressed the room.

"We may begin our council session now that his highness, Harpis the bard, is in attendance!"

There were many snorts among those gathered, and Bravit did not bother to hide his chuckles at Harpis' expense.

"Hitting the bottle before a council meeting Governor Reaper?" Harpis questioned, crossing his arms indignantly.

25

The older sandy-haired man grinned back at the bard over his shoulder.

"I've hardly any bottles left for myself after hosting you and the pious Death Herald. Thankfully it has been a good harvest, and I can replenish my stores," Aanaman returned.

"I don't see how someone of my diminutive stature could possibly have drained your whiskey barrels, good sir," Wren said with a hurt look.

"Small as you may be, I am convinced at this point that you are nearly all stomach under those robes!" Aanaman replied, raising an eyebrow at the gnome.

Governor Elliswerth wrapped the table next to Aanaman with a small wooden gavel in mild exasperation.

"I think I speak for all of us that council meetings would be more sufferable if Aanaman did indeed partake of his local commodity beforehand. However, I must now call this meeting into session before the lot of you make for one of my city's wonderful taverns with no official business handled."

The room grew silent, and Governor Elliswerth looked to his right at Ingar Hammersmith and Ceanna of Glasduille and then to his left at Jaeryl Innisgrath and Isra Rashida before continuing.

"If there is no objection, I would like to maintain the order we followed in the summer, of calling on the institutions first and the city-states after," he said.

He received only shrugs and nods of agreement from the gathered council.

"Death Herald, you have the table," Governor Elliswerth finished.

Wren brushed a few remaining droplets from his robe. The wet, dark purple fabric was soaked nearly black, and the silvery embroidery of his goddess and station shone brightly against it on his cuffs, chest, and back.

"Some of you are already aware, but I am formally notifying this governing body that I will be taking up a more nomadic posting in hopes of spreading the word of my lady across the island. As such, I ask your acceptance that one of my senior necromancers attend in my stead whenever I am unavailable."

After pausing a moment waiting for responses, he continued, "Further, in my absence at The Sanctum, I have appointed Death Speaker Daugor as Rector. He will serve as the authority for The

Sanctum whenever I am not present there. If there is no issue or questions, that is all I have."

Next to the gnome, Exarch Weksnor smiled and placed his hands on the table.

"I would like to report that some months ago, Turin Deadeye finished carrying out his sentence at The Archdiocese of Daybreak and has fully recorded the machinations of The Syndicate over the centuries. Our historians have just started examining and transcribing them. Copies will be made and sent to the diocese in each city-state and available for review by all," he said officiously.

Arch Mage Uridyll nodded approvingly at the comment and stroked his belly-length gray beard.

"I have nothing for the group," he said, motioning to Maestro Bravit to speak.

"With the help of the Arch Mage and others at the college, we have nearly finished drafting our constitution for the Bard's Hall. Upon its completion, I will present it to this group, and, if agreed upon, it will be disseminated to the city-states so that all may know the governing rules for sanctioned bards henceforth. That is all I have from The Hall," Bravit said, waving a small stack of papers.

Governor Elliswerth gave a moment for any comments before motioning at Jaeryl Innisgrath.

"I suppose we might as well start from the south and work our way up today. Governor Innisgrath, what issues would Kalt like to bring?"

The pale and weaselly-looking man from Kalt straightened in his seat before speaking.

"I have nothing new to bring up as an issue besides the continuation of problems involving Svenus Kalt and his clan. Some members of his family refused to accept the decree of this council last year in granting lands officially to the elves," he said, pausing to look at the Ceanna.

"Most of my people have received the creation of Glasduille state with noted appreciation. However, members of the Kalt family are attempting to create trouble within the elven lands as well as my state to undermine the agreement. The governor from Glasduille, Aanaman, and myself have already discussed a joint policing effort with militiamen from Ravnice and Kalt, aided by

27

the elves to capture those attempting to subvert the rule of law and formally charge them for their crimes. However, I do not foresee a reason why this won't be resolved by our next convening," Jaeryl finished.

Before Governor Elliswerth could direct the next representative to speak, the doors to the chamber were flung open. In strode a drenched Gwenolyn Amura, cloak and cowl pulled tightly about her. She was followed quickly by the dwarf and Kalt militiamen from the barracks porch, weapons drawn and clamoring for her to halt. Around the meeting table, the governors tensed, and Wren stood in his seat, scythe in hand before relaxing as all in attendance recognized the niece of Turin Deadeye. Elliswerth held up a hand to halt the guards.

"Gentlemen, I appreciate your quick response, but the elf is welcome here."

Sheathing their weapons, the guards obediently departed and closed the doors behind them.

Ceanna was the first to address the other elf.

"My dear, what brings you here? I did not expect you back on dry land for some weeks," she inquired.

Gwenolyn removed her hooded cowl revealing long tresses of reddish-brown hair and met the gaze of each in the room, returning it to Ceanna last. When she spoke, she wore a look of melancholy sadness in her blue-gray eyes.

"Turin Deadeye is with The Sleeper," Gwenolyn stated somberly.

*****

Zolga stood steady as the small sailboat carrying her and Galonica rolled heavily in the frigid southern seas. The rough waters did not bother them, and neither did the pre-dawn cold prickle their bare skin. Their destination came into view not long after their armada disappeared over the gray horizon behind them.

Huval Island was the southernmost regularly inhabited spot of land on the southern seas. Its northern harbor was just far enough north that the waters at its mouth never entirely froze over. Only about one mile wide, the island stretched nearly ten miles southward. In the colder winters, the waters would harden up all the way to Huval's southern shore.

However, it was barely discernible at this distance against the rocky forestland that rose behind it. They were bound for the only structure on the island. It was a three-story longhouse with a lighthouse tower rising from the middle. The building served the whaling outpost as a general store, living quarters, and tavern.

Zolga and Galonica both had the pale skin, blue eyes, and white-streaked black hair of The Tormenta. The only difference between them was that Zolga had a warrior's short, cropped hair, and the storm priestess had a waist-length ponytail.

Galonica spoke first, slipping off her pale blue robe.

"Come Zolga, we will be in sight of the shore soon, and we must change to blend in better. I know it is smothering and itchy, but I'll not be the one to tell Duchess Kisa we failed our queen because we pandered to our comfort. It would raise suspicion if we did not seem to feel the cold as they do," she said.

Zolga reached to her feet and threw fur-lined leathers at the other woman before pulling her tunic over her head. As she finished changing, Zolga slipped her rapier into her belt and then rummaged around in the boat's small hold before tossing a sword to her compatriot.

"If it is blending in that you're after Galonica, throw that in your belt. It would be odd for anyone, let alone two women, to be unarmed at a place like this."

The priestess looked at her haughtily and then glanced unimpressed at the sword.

"Unarmed?" she asked while lightning flickered and crackled around her upheld right hand.

"Besides, I don't have any idea how to fight with that crude thing," Galonica said, poking the handle with her finger.

"Pointy end at the enemy, may you strike them down with your unrivaled prowess," she said sarcastically.

Lightning leaped from Galonica's fingers to her sword, shocking Zolga. Galonica greeted her yelp with an unwavering glare. Deciding she had pushed the priestess far enough, Zolga pointed to the harbor that was now clearly in view.

"Look, there, a double hulled Quaji catamaran, probably the biggest I've seen. I haven't met with the northern sea tribes often, but I doubt we can expect to run into more than one crew of them down here. It must be the trader ship our contact told us of," Zolga stated.

Parked along one of the two longer docks, the cabin of the Quaji ship was large enough that she figured it likely had at least a dozen sailors, and the smoke coming from its oven chimney indicating that crew was probably not staying at the tavern.

Galonica stood and motioned towards the third, shorter dock.

"There are fewer ships at that dock, and it is distant enough for my liking. Bring us in over there. We'll make quick business of this transaction, have a meal in the tavern to give a legitimate reason for our visit and then make back for the armada," the priestess said.

"As you wish dear," Zolga answered, mocking the commanding tone her partner had taken.

When they bumped into the short dock, a grumpy man in heavy furs with a wind-burned face made his way down from the longhouse and greeted them.

"This dock is for locals. I am afraid you ladies will have to tie off in one of the slips on the other two," he explained.

Galonica raised her fist at the man as if she was about to shout him down. Before she could, Zolga quickly appeared in front of her.

"Not a problem. Is there any charge for using the slip?" she asked.

The man harrumphed and walked away back towards the tavern and responded without looking backward.

"Not if you're paying customers, I'll have a table set. Two pretty things like you two should get the blood going for most of the lads in there! Should mean more drinks sold for me!" he shouted.

After he was out of earshot, Zolga turned to speak to Galonica.

"It would be counterproductive to demonstrate our superiority over impudent males now, especially given that humans do not share our ways or know we still exist. However, there will be time and opportunity aplenty for that in the coming days if we are successful here," she said to calm the priestess.

Galonica unclenched her white-knuckled fists as they turned about and eventually tied off a few slips down the dock from the Quaji boat. Zolga was not happy about having to sneak about and play nice, but their mission came straight from Queen Oluja Vetar.

Any time they had come into contact with the former tribal residents of Quaj Island, the Tormenta inquired about knowledge of the island's layout. They had learned that there was one Quaji trader whose crew and catamaran frequented most of the ports on Quaj Island. As it turned out, each fall the trader also spent the last month before winter trading with the whalers and fishers at Huval Island.

As the Tormenta walked up to the Quaji boat, one dark-skinned crew poked his head out from the main cabin door.

"Can I help you two? If you require warmth, I am sure we can arrange something," he said with a smile.

His statement was answered by glares from the women and snickers from behind him in the cabin. Zolga clenched her sword handle, and it was Galonica's turn to keep calm.

"We come only seeking an audience with Koibaneh, and we will pay in gold for his time," the priestess replied.

An older, more wrinkled Quaji with white hair stuck his head out after pulling the younger man back inside and waved them in, shouting at his crew to get below decks. Entering the cabin, the women had to let their eyes adjust to the dim firelight before noticing the old Quaji sat behind a small desk, motioning them to sit at the chairs on the other side of it.

"The name is Koibaneh, what can I do for you here at the bottom of the world?"

Zolga remained standing by the door with her arm resting on her sword pommel. Galonica sat and produced a leather purse and dumped several coins on the desk.

"All we want is a map of Quaj Island, and to know the type of people on it, their allegiances, and where best to make port," she said.

The old Quaji glanced at them for a moment with furrowed white eyebrows.

"And for what reasons will you need this map? I do quite a lot of business at those ports, and despite your heavy furs, I've sailed the seas of southern Nysia long enough to have heard tales of tribes of sea witches with blue eyes and lightning-struck black hair that pirate in its coldest parts."

Galonica didn't flinch, but behind her, Zolga slid her rapier out of her belt. The priestess held a hand up to stay her before replying.

31

"There is enough gold here to answer whatever questions you may have. We just want the information," she answered.

"Mind you. I can't write. I can, however, count, and I think that a man with my caring disposition will probably need at least triple to forget this little exchange ever happened," the man said with a shrug.

Galonica nearly emptied the purse onto the table. Koibaneh slid the gold into a drawer in the desk and pulled out a piece of parchment. Dipping a quill into ink, he drew a rough outline of Quaj Island. Then, he drew a tree by the southern harbor, wheat by the eastern harbor, and a palm leaf by the northern one.

"Now the folks down here at this southern harbor, Kalt, they look a bit like you folk, don't spend enough time in the sun if you know what I mean. Their primary trade is lumber. Here, Ravnice is mostly farmers and the like. Up north, you have Tuath. Now those folks look a bit more like I do and primarily trade in spices and such. Mer here on this peninsula is the largest city, kind of a trade hub for the whole island, and has its own navy too," he explained.

Unimpressed, Galonica looked down at what he had drawn with her arms crossed.

"I am sure their navy will prove to be of little concern," she said.

The Quaji man shrugged again and filled in the trade paths between the city-states and made a line from the harbor at Ravnice towards the spine of the island, where he drew a few mountains and a hammer.

"And this is the river Fjall, Fjall mountain and home to the dwarven clan of Ingar Hammersmith."

Both women spit on the decking at the mention of dwarves before Zolga spoke.

"Is there anything else you can think of that might prove useful?"

The Quaji shook his head at them before blowing the ink on the parchment dry and handing it to Galonica, who took it from him and rose from her seat.

"Our thanks to you then, Koibaneh, I sincerely hope you forget we ever met," she said in a grave tone.

As they left the ship and walked up the docks toward the longhouse, Zolga questioned the priestess.

"Do you think it was wise to be so overt on our intentions towards Quaj?" she asked.

"He already assumed much, and correctly. If he happens to go as soon as we leave and sell information about what we were doing here to someone from Quaj, we have insinuated that we will move on Mer, which we will not. Further, he referred to us as tribes, perhaps it is not yet known that The Tormenta clans have unified. If he warns of anything, it would be a raiding party, maybe a ship or two strong, not the full armada," Galonica responded without turning to her.

Chapter 4

I am Sudbina

The ice-laden walls and roof of the longhouse creaked and moaned as they thawed and expanded in the warming rays of the morning sun. The familiar sounds woke Sudbina just as they had for the past month on Huval Island. The fast-approaching winter would make the island a genuinely miserable abode, and regardless of the cold, she had grown tired of her current lodging.

Winter and boredom aside, it would have been time to move on. Sudbina hadn't spent more than a month or two in the same place since she divorced herself from her mother as a child and set off on her own. As a girl, she had often taken temporary excursions away from the brothel in Kalt state where her mother worked. During her last excursion nine years ago, she had decided not to come back.

Sudbina did not know exactly how old she was at the time or even how old she was now. She guessed she was around eleven or twelve when she decided to stay gone. Barely out of adolescence she could sense a change in the way customers looked at her. They had begun sizing her up like prey, and her mother had started to look at her as if appraising potential profits. When her mother and the madame sat her down and asked how long until she'd like to start working, Sudbina decided it was probably best to try her chances on her own. She had found herself haphazardly wandering ever since.

Sudbina flipped the thick fur blankets from her petite nude form and sat up, swinging her legs off the edge of the bed. Sitting for a moment, she let the morning chill finish waking her fully. Then, dismissing her prickled skin with a shiver, she stood and pulled her high collared tunic and leather britches from the floor.

34

She laid the tunic on the bed, slipping on the pants, and then her calf-high leather boots, patting the small blowgun slid in a sheath along her right shin.

She reached into her travel sack for one of her wigs, but her hand came out holding her chest wrap instead. Sudbina smirked and shrugged. Today she would be the man then. Though in her twenties, she appeared barely out of childhood. The youthfulness of her facial features and a short, slight build accentuated her ability to come across as both a young man or woman.

Her hand went deep into the single-strapped pack again and pulled forth the unmistakable form of her folded razor. She sat back on the edge of the bed and spat in her left palm. She alternated wiping her moistened left hand over the stubble atop her head and then running the razor over it with her right.

The rhythmic sound and feel of the razor sliding across the stubble put her in a near meditative state until there was no more vibration from the razor and her scalp was smooth. Finally, she slipped the folded razor into her other boot and began wrapping her cleavage tightly against her chest before donning her tunic, buttoning it all the way up to the collar.

Striding to the polished brass mirror, she gave herself an approving look and blew her reflection a kiss from plump lips. With no hair to frame her features, her dark eyebrows, and green eyes stood out strikingly against the backdrop of pale skin. She left her heavily furred winter cloak on its hook, retrieving instead her hooded shawl, pulling it over her head and bunching the hood behind her neck.

She made her way out of the small room she had paid extra coins to secure on the third floor. The upper level was where the permanent residents of the whaling station and a few other customers stayed. The circular stairwell took her past the second story of entirely visiting tenants and to the first that was a tavern and general store and where most folks spent their day if they spent it on land at all.

As she took her last step to the ground level, the short and stocky tavern keeper greeted her. The odd little man was always doing his best to come across as grumpy. He looked her up and down before raising his eyebrows.

"Another fine Huval morning to you, Sudbina. Peculiar as you may be. I cannot complain about the unexpectedness you

35

bring each day to this dreary place at the end of the world," he said, as he had each morning during her stay.

Standing on the other side of the bar from the man, Sudbina put her hand over her heart and gave a slight bow.

"Change is the only certain thing, Ernal," she said in her ever provocative and flirtatious sounding high-pitched voice.

Sudbina had long ago noticed that men and women alike always seemed enamored when she spoke. A byproduct of learning to talk in a brothel, she assumed.

"That may be. Change as you may, though, the depraved lot that calls this place a home still sees you as a nice piece of meat," Ernal said with a snort.

Sudbina reached over the counter, putting her finger under Ernal's chin, pulling him close.

"A tasty piece of meat on a nice and sharp hook. Do not worry for me. None of these men have sight good enough to see or wits sharp enough to sense the hook," she whispered in his ear.

She released his chin from her finger and his captivated eyes from her gaze. Then, she placed more than twice the necessary coins on the counter and left him with a kiss on his cheek.

"Break my fast if you please, and do you happen to know the next departure from Huval? I think I'll be booking passage," she asked.

"I'll have one of the lads bring you over some porridge. Where are you looking to get to?" he asked, with a hint of disappointment.

"It matters not, just somewhere. Speaking of something else that could use changing, do you have anything besides porridge this morning?"

Ernal crossed his arms and scoffed as she walked away towards the small table near the exterior door that she had occupied each meal since arriving.

"I'll have a few dried berries thrown in your breakfast for good measure then, your highness. I wouldn't want the bottom of the world to be a culinary disappointment," Ernal replied sarcastically.

The man turned and shouted into the kitchens before looking back at her.

"I believe the Quaji tribesmen depart in a week bound for one or another of their atolls, I presume. You might see about finding passage with them, but they rarely make their way in here, so you'll have to find them at their boat," he said.

As she wove her way slowly through the tables and patrons, she noted that many of them glanced warily up at her or pulled in cloaks tight. A couple instinctively put a hand on their purses or tabletop coins as she walked by. Perhaps it was a good thing she was moving on. She hadn't any need to relieve others of their currencies and other small items, but old habits are hard to cease, and this old habit had become more of an impulse. The risk was well worth the fun, the value of the bounty not-withstanding.

Sudbina settled into her usual wobbly chair. She decided she would grab her cloak and make her way to the docks to talk with the Quaji after her belly was full. Sitting at the table waiting for her food, she couldn't shake the sensation of having come downstairs for a specific reason besides her breakfast and inquiry of travel, but for the life of her she could not remember what it was.

The doors to the tavern opened behind her. The winter air from outside sent a shiver up her spine. Glancing at the two that entered, Sudbina decided this might be an exciting day after all. She eyed the two attractive women up and down, happy for a change in the scenery. The women scanned the room methodically but paused for a moment longer when their eyes met hers.

The longer-haired one sat at a table halfway between Sudbina and the bar while the short-haired one made her way over to Ernal and ordered food before turning back and walking towards her seated companion. Sudbina shouted to Ernal for a cup of warm rum with her meal to rid herself of the chill from outside.

One of the kitchen staff walked out with her bowl of porridge and placed it down while standing directly in her line of sight with the newly arrived women.

"Who are those two?" she asked quietly.

"No idea, they just pulled in this morning. Ernal ran out when he saw them sail in and made them port at the visitor docks. Why he bothered going out in the cold for that is beyond me, plenty of slips available here as the cold comes in," the man replied.

Sudbina picked up her spoon and pulled a face at the porridge before speaking to her food as much as to the departing server.

"Probably because poor Ernal has nothing better to do," she

37

said.

As he walked away, she bit her bottom lip while contemplating the newly arrived women. She immediately abandoned her mischievous thoughts when Ernal waved at her behind the bar and held up a steamy mug. She scooted her chair back noisily and rose to retrieve her drink. The two women huddled close as she strode past, and she noticed they were discussing a piece of parchment on their table.

She made sure her eyes did not linger too long on them or their table. Best not to make potential targets leery. She would probably have a better view over their shoulders of whatever they were looking at on the way back to her porridge anyways.

Taking the mug off the bar, she gave Ernal a wink and headed back to her seat on a path that would take her right past the two women. She distractedly peered over its rim at the table in front of the women as she walked. Then, she yelped in pain at the scalding of her lips and tongue. In her haste to pull the burning liquid away from her mouth, she sloshed some steaming rum on the back of the shorter-haired woman's neck.

The woman cursed loudly and shot up out of her chair, knocking Sudbina's elbow with her shoulder and dumping the entire contents of the mug on the table. Steaming rum drenched the other woman's lap as well as the table and the parchment map that lay on it. The two were now standing, glaring furiously at the shorter Sudbina.

"Watch it, boy, lest you find yourself dead where you stand," The dryer of the two growled, gripping the handle of her sword.

Sudbina smiled and apologized playfully to the drenched woman in her most sultry voice. She inched closer and tried to brush her hip against the other woman's while attempting to put her arm around her back, fishing for something to pilfer. The seething and scalded stranger stepped away from her before she had a chance, and her companion's rapier tip appeared barely an inch from Sudbina's throat.

Sudbina completely ignored the sword, drawing an exasperated look from its owner. Her focus was instead on the ink running down the rum-soaked parchment.

"What are you two beautiful ladies so interested in Quaj Island for?" she asked them.

They shot each other curious looks, and the sword tip was

lowered some.

"What do you know of Quaj, boy? Or is it girl?" the longer haired woman asked.

Sudbina smiled at the question and answered, staring at the sword wielder and not the one who inquired.

"It is Sudbina, and I grew up there."

A smile crept across their faces, and the women nodded after a glance at each other.

"Well then, Sudbina, I am Zolga, and my companion here is Galonica. We were sent to take back information of Quaj Island to our leader for trade purposes, information which you have just destroyed. Perhaps you can make up for your clumsiness by telling us about the place you were born," the woman threatened.

Galonica held a finger to her lip in pensive thought, and her eyes narrowed.

"If you would like to come with us, we can pay you well for information regarding your home," the woman with long hair stated, her features softening.

Sudbina decided today was going to be very exciting indeed. "I'll tell you whatever you want to know about the place if you take me off this dismal frozen rock when you depart," Sudbina offered.

Zolga responded while curtly sheathing her sword, "Agreed, but we leave now."

Both women were taken slightly aback at the gleeful look that took over Sudbina's face.

"In that case, I'll come for free!" she said and ran off to get her winter cloak and travel sack, stopping at the bar on the way to grab Ernal by the front of his shirt and pull him in for a final kiss.

"Farewell, Ernal!" she said on her way back down after shoving everything she owned into her satchel.

"Fare thee well, wandering vagabond," the old man called after her as she departed with the two visitors.

The three hastily headed to a small, single-sail vessel and once they pushed off, quickly made their way towards the horizon. Once Huval Island was out of sight, Zolga and Galonica stripped out of the heavy furs, and Zolga bent next to Sudbina to retrieve her thin blue leathers. As the short-haired Tormenta woman grabbed the clothes, Sudbina cupped one of her bare breasts with a smirk.

39

Not bothering to straighten, Zolga angrily kicked at Sudbina's crotch, hoping to punish the impudent groping. She straightened with a confused look on her face.

"So, you are a woman then, playing at being a boy?" Zolga asked as she donned her clothes and buckled the belt holding her rapier.

"I told you, I am Sudbina. I am playing only as myself," she corrected, turning to gaze longingly at Galonica.

Galonica finished getting dressed and pulled her fur-lined cloak around her shoulders to cover herself.

"You are a puzzling one, Sudbina. However, I expect your information regarding Quaj Island should be less of a riddle," the cloaked woman said.

It occurred to Sudbina that she was being told and not asked and that these strange women who seemed not to feel the cold had very specific purposes for accommodating her wants for travel.

Any worry she had was soon replaced by a peculiar feeling that she was right where she was supposed to be.

"With the women of the sea, go capricious and free," she whispered to herself in a wistful voice that surprised even her.

Her curiosity towards her hosts was steadily increasing, though, and she was always one for speaking her mind.

"Does the cold not bother you? Not that I mind the views of your flesh compared to the furs that covered you back on Huval. The two of you look so similar. Are you sisters? Cousins? Wives?" she asked hopefully.

"All of The Siren's people look like us. Neither her cold, nor wind, nor waters bother us. We are the Tormenta. We have sailed the southern seas of Nysia for most of this age," Galonica answered, looking down at Sudbina with an air of superiority.

Chapter 5
A Death & Four Funerals

Harpis tried not to shiver as the small contingent finished making their way through the volcanic tunnel on Lodestar Island. The crater-turned-courtyard that was once the soul of The Syndicate was bitterly cold despite the shelter it provided from the island's constant howling wind. Winter in the southern seas was a consistent demur grey and he thought it especially appropriate today given the sullen occasion.

The day after Gwenolyn had burst in on the council meeting to announce Turin's passing, the funeral attendants had made Lodestar Island by late afternoon. Harpis, Wren and Gwenolyn had sailed on the *Open Ocean* while Ingar and Ezera arrived shortly after on the dwarf's ship. Only five had made the voyage to bid the old elf farewell because only five had been summoned. Pry as they might during the day-long sail, Gwenolyn would reveal nothing of the intended ceremonies.

They walked to the courtyard's center, and Harpis felt a heavy responsibility as he looked around the crater. Black soot from the long-burning funeral pyre of those lost during Sirul's naval raid coated the grounds as well as the stone walls around them. The enormity of what was given by those no longer with the living was immeasurable and ever-present on Lodestar.

Harpis could not dismiss feeling like an imposter amongst those gathered. It was only two years ago that he had left Lodestar and his new family after his indoctrination. Ezera had served for over a decade and the elf and gnome had spent centuries in service of the greater good. Seeing the stain of their companion's death on the courtyard where he had trained tore fresh sorrow from his heart.

41

Gwenolyn Amura walked before them into the center of the mass grave and looked down solemnly at the soil for a moment before addressing them.

"Friends of Turin Deadeye, thank you for joining me here at his request," she said quietly.

Ingar Hammersmith crossed his arms over his chest before speaking in an unusually soft tone for the burly dwarf.

"Well spit it out lass, what is with all the secrecy? Is the old elf here and alive?" he asked.

"In truth, Turin had died six days ago, at least that's when I discovered his corpse frozen solid, sitting cross-legged and clutching a leather scroll to his chest where I now stand. After dragging his body to the cellars to thaw, I followed the instructions he left on that scroll," Gwenolyn answered.

She paused to look from Ingar to Ezera and then Wren, finally stopping with a sympathetic look at Harpis.

"I sailed immediately for Fjall to notify Ezera and Ingar. There I waited a day for Ingar to make his way to Mer for the convening council meeting that your and Wren were attending before bursting in as Turin asked. In death as in life, timing was of the utmost importance to my uncle," she explained.

Wren blew out a low whistle, and Ingar uncrossed his arms as she continued.

"The humble spymaster has asked for four funerals. One from each goddess and then parting guidance for the five of us will follow. But first, Ingar, I require your assistance in the cellars," Gwenolyn explained.

Ingar followed her down the tunnel across from them with a bewildered look. The two reappeared in the courtyard a few moments later, Turin's corpse, slung across the stalwart dwarf's shoulders was lowered onto a hand cart and pulled to the middle of the crater. Ingar Hammersmith, governor of the mountain city, showed considerable mental and emotional strength as he gingerly walked to the center of the more recently turned soil and laid the elf's body down on its back.

In Gwenolyn's hand was the rolled leather scroll she had spoken of but left hidden on the island. She unrolled it and looked up at the other four as Ingar went again to stand by Ezera, Wren, and Harpis.

"The following are the parting words of Turin Deadeye," she

said as she unwound the string and held up the scroll, and Harpis could almost hear the old elf's voice in hers.

"Thank you, my friends, for once again answering my call. You are all that yet live of our life's work, and it remains unfinished. I have chosen to enter The Great Dream because it was necessary. I had the privilege to witness the final transition to democracy amongst all the Quaj city-states. However, the final leg of this journey must be completed without my hand on the helm. Without my passing, the governors and the people would be looking for puppet strings with every significant happening that transpired since the activities of our organization were brought to light."

Gwenolyn closed her eyes and drew a long breath before finishing.

"I ask that you remember me as I would have wanted, with the oldest barrel in our cellars, and celebrate what we have done, mourn what it cost, and steel yourselves for what is to yet to come. I regret not being there to help or witness the culmination, but I have already seen it in my mind as I write this. I tell you all, Harpis, Ezera, Wren, Ingar, and my dear Gwenolyn, I have seen it," she finished.

As she read her own name, Gwenolyn choked for a moment, shaking her head to regain her bearing.

"Honor me with a ceremony to each of your goddesses and mine."

With that, Gwenolyn reverently returned the tie around the scroll and lay it on the ground next to her as she knelt beside Turin's corpse.

"First, I will present him to my goddess, The Wild," she said, drawing a skinning dagger from her belt.

She used it to cut through the thin layer of permafrost in the ground at the center of the mass grave and dug a small hole with it. Next, she stabbed the dead elf in the chest, making quick work of cutting around his heart. Finally, she stuck two of her fingers into the wound that was slowly filling with molasses-like, recently thawed and heavily coagulated blood. She wiped two lines of blood from above Turin's eyebrows, over his eyelids, closing them forever, and down his cheeks to his chin. She then took more of the blood and did the same to her face.

With a stoic grimace, she then plunged her hand into his chest

43

cavity and withdrew the elf's heart while whispering soft elvish prayers to The Wild in hushed tones for only her goddess to hear.

Harpis struggled to keep his own emotions in check as he looked upon the scene of the elf wearing her uncle's blood.

Placing the bloodied heart into the hole, she reverently pushed dirt over it. Then, she bowed forward on her knees and put her forehead on top of her hands. She wept for a moment as she whispered goodbye to her uncle.

Gwenolyn sat back on her haunches and sheathed her knife, finally looking back at the others.

"The part of him that still belonged to my people is with The Wild now. We have less than an hour until dusk. Wren, will you give him to the one who sleeps?" she asked of the gnome, tears rolling down her cheeks.

Wren walked to her, placing a hand on her shoulders in comfort before she stood and joined Ingar, Harpis, and Ezera. Wren stared at Turin's body pensively for a moment before beckoning Ezera to his side, exchanging fervent whispers and gestures.

With a final nod at the blond woman, Wren questioned Gwenolyn.

"I assume since he is also to be given to The Siren that his final funeral will be a burial at sea?" the gnome asked.

Collecting her emotions, she responded with only the slightest crack to her voice, "Yes, I have prepared a canoe with a makeshift sail and pyre that we will place his body on at the end. It is on the shore near the lighthouse."

Wren then looked to Ingar. "Governor Hammersmith, would you be so kind as to place his body back on the cart and bring it out to the canoe? I think we can make the final three farewells a joint affair."

*****

Wren clung to his robe, holding it tight around him. The wind constantly blew across the island and out to sea, unimpeded as if the rocky coasts were just another set of swells in the south seas. The gusts would conveniently push the funeral boat rapidly out to sea. Still, the gnome decided it did indeed make for an incredibly uncomfortable and frigid experience even though he wore every bit of clothing he had brought with him when they set out from Quaj.

Turin's body still lay atop the wagon with Ingar, Harpis, Gwenolyn, and himself looking out at the relentless tumult of The Siren's bosom. After a quick prayer over the elf's corpse, Ezera had made for the top of the lighthouse, where she now stood ready to follow his lead.

"Mind you all, I have only ever heard of this channeling. Apologies if this doesn't go as I intended," Wren said with one last glance up at the lighthouse.

He had long ago read the ancient funeral rites that were found in the oldest religious texts kept at The Sanctum. He wouldn't have believed that *The Dance of Death* ritual was real at all save for his predecessor mentioning several visions of similar rites in the memories that floated about The Great Dream.

Death Herald and head of The Sanctum or not, typically Wren or any other necromancer could only beckon the readily available spirits and undead to their call. However, when one such as Turin had gone to The Great Dream days or even weeks ago, it was akin to a personal favor from one of The Sleeper's handmaidens. Such a favor was necessary to connect the caller to the intended spirit in the great dream and thus convey true command over the remnants of their mortal form.

The result of such a connection was that the memories of the spirit would assault their focus. These memories would pose a challenge to their control over the deceased form. This assault made a successful ritual quite challenging, especially since the most recent memories that would pour forth would likely be those of death. Such memories were rarely peaceful.

Wren's necromancer scythe appeared in his right hand, and he snapped the other, summoning forth the acrid sulfuric smoke from the belly of the world and the undead fire sprite that came with it. Xissay raised an eloquent eyebrow at Wren before looking at Ingar and Gwenolyn with a quick bow and giving Harpis a lascivious grin. Her typical coy snark was replaced with genuine sorrow when her gaze came across the cart and Turin's corpse.

"He is with her now, Wren. I am sorry he no longer walks with those that wake," she said.

"I have a role to play, as do you. I am going to attempt one of our oldest rituals, and you will complete the final rites by lighting the mooring lines and his pyre to give him The Siren's farewell," he said in a voice both stern and pleading.

Understanding his request, she floated her way to the canoe and sat where the rope tied to the stern. The old gnome necromancer slowly began his chant, and the visage of the sea before him greyed, revealing the slowly approaching wispy white form of one of his goddesses' handmaidens. As she neared him, he spoke the name Turin Deadeye, his voice nearly faltering as he uttered it. The feminine form faded from view, and after a moment, he felt his attention drawn to the elf's corpse and saw its limbs twitch at his connection.

He had hoped that he would meet with the fleeting memory of his centuries-long friend in carrying out the ritual. But, instead, there was nothing, a connection devoid of any clue or intimation. His eyes still shut while he prayed, Wren spared himself a sad smile at the appropriately silent link he had with the former spymaster.

The elf's corpse rose from the wagon where it lay and eerily walked itself to the one sail canoe. The long-dead body of Turin deadeye unfurled the sails before then sitting itself at the canoe's stern, hand on the rudder, and went still. Wren opened his eyes and gave Xissay a nod.

The fire sprite stood, giving Wren a deep bow. She grasped the taut rope holding the canoe to the coast against the constant winds and lit it ablaze with her reddening hands. The floating death pyre of Turin sprang to life and sailed out to sea. As it did, the unheard prayers of Ezera began at the top of the lighthouse. Her gift gathered and focused the fading light of the setting sun into the lighthouse mirror, where she then aimed it in a hallowed spotlight that followed the sprinting canoe out to sea.

Xissay made her way to sit with the now rigid corpse. Then, placing her hands amongst the kindling of the pyre, she set the canoe ablaze. Wren watched as the canoe and its sails lit in a reddish-orange glow. It continued out to sea illuminated by the same hues from the setting sun as it quickly approached the horizon.

Wren smiled when Harpis began *The Sleeper's Serenade* with his fiddle. The gnome watched as the flames of the canoe sank into the sea at the exact moment that the sun set below the horizon, and Ezera's spotlight faded. With the end of Turin's final funeral, Harpis played the last note of *The Sleeper's Serenade*, and the mournful fading note seemed to die off the same way as the light and flames while dusk grew on the frozen coast of Loadstar Island.

Wren walked to Harpis' side and clasped the man's hand for a moment as Xissay returned to her usual position floating above his shoulder.

"Thank you for that, my friend," he said.

Once Ezera had made her way to them from the lighthouse, Wren looked to the party with a smile.

"I can think of one last thing the old elf would have wanted us to do!" he said in a cheery voice unbefitting the circumstance.

Gwenolyn gave the gnome a knowing nod and led them back into the quiet, vacant Syndicate fortress. Making their way through the tunnels, they finally arrived at the kitchens, where Xissay floated from Wren's shoulder to face him directly.

"Don't even think of dismissing me and denying my participation in the old elf's wake," she said threateningly.

"I wouldn't dare," Wren responded.

"Grab some wood from the rack on the far wall if you would please. Xissay can do the one thing she is useful for and light it ablaze to get some warmth down here." He said, looking at Harpis.

"Shall we fetch the final toast?" he asked Gwenolyn.

"No need for secrecy Wren, I think it would surprise no one that Turin hid a barrel of his favorite vintage below the cellars of his spy castle to guarantee the toast to his life was a good one," Gwenolyn laughed.

With the fire already blazing in the oven, Gwenolyn lit a torch in its flames and took them all down to the cellars below the kitchens. There, she began inspecting the tiled stone floor with Wren as the others looked on in mild confusion.

"Here," Wren said, pointing at a tile with an eye symbol etched in it, "Harpis, come here and stand on this tile," he said, pointing.

Gwenolyn similarly motioned for Ezera to stand on another one she found that had a hand-etched on its corner before herself going to the one with a ship's helm carved in it.

Wren sat tapping his chin in thought as he looked over the rest of the unmarked tiles before doing some quick math with his

47

fingers.

"Ingar, over here, please," he said, motioning at a nondescript tile by the stairs.

A few moments after the dwarf stood on the tile, there was a scraping noise of stone sliding on stone as the tiles each of them were standing on slowly sunk into the ground, and in the middle of the cellar floor rose a four-tile square section. The counterweight tiles they each stood upon fell only a little, but the section in the middle rose high enough to reveal a small barrel of whiskey, which Wren then walked up to and shouldered so that it rolled off the platform.

As the barrel left the hidden dais, it revealed a leather scroll that curved slightly after the barrel's weight left it. Snatching the scroll from where it sat, Wren motioned for them to join him, and as they left their tiles, the sunken and the risen stones returned to an even level, appearing again as a normal cellar floor.

"One last riddle?" Ingar asked gruffly as they all stared at the seemingly random sets of numbers and letters written in several columns on the scroll. Finally, at its bottom was a plainly written request.

Light the tower and await a native visitor the night after my farewell.

Squinting in the candlelight, Ezera spoke first after a shared moment of thought.

"The second column looks like the codes we use at the dioceses to catalog the location of texts in the libraries," she explained.

"No riddle then, but a key," Gwenolyn answered.

"I'd wager my life that in carrying out his council-sentenced recordings of The Syndicate's histories and schemes that Turin left us a new one to take up," Wren responded while still staring at the writing.

Harpis, who had been unusually quiet amongst the somber and respected party, cleared his throat.

"Or an old one to finish. Perhaps this native visitor will offer clarification," he offered.

"Our questions will not be answered this evening. Let's leave this tomb-like cellar and celebrate my uncle's life together, warmed from within and without," Gwenolyn suggested.

*****

Harpis squeezed heavy eyelids around eyes that felt oversized in their sockets from a lack of sleep against the grey light of the winter morning at Lodestar's dock. Turin's tiny wake had lasted late into the evening, and the night's celebrations were an experience he would never forget. He had the privilege of listening to the war stories, tales of espionage and recounting of spy craft spanning many centuries and wars. Ingar, Gwenolyn, Ezera, and Wren's stories were more enthralling and just as challenging to believe than any fiction or legend he had heard before.

As the wind interrupted the still morning peace and whipped their fur-lined cloaks around, Ingar and Ezera boarded their vessel.

The dwarven governor faced them while the crew that had remained aboard during the previous day's ceremonies untied their lines and pushed away from the docks.

"I'll be expecting some summation of whatever Turin's contact tells you at your earliest convenience, if you don't mind. I was ever available to the old elf in life, and I'll not stop supporting his efforts now," Ingar said with a gruff wave before heading below decks and out of the cold.

Brushing her blond hair out of her face, Ezera gave the three of them a curt nod before turning towards the stairs.

"Ezera," Wren shouted over the wind, halting the woman mid-step.

"The game is still afoot. We will be in touch as soon as we are able," he yelled.

Her face grew stern, and she gave a slight bow in acknowledgment before disappearing below.

"Well, Navigator, what next?" Gwenolyn asked the gnome.

Standing slightly behind the shorter elf and diminutive gnome, Harpis couldn't help but chuckle at the question and title pinned on his friend.

"Seeing as how I was but a babe when you had seen your second century, perhaps you should be the one navigating," he retorted.

49

Gwenolyn laughed before answering the gnome's accusatory statement.

"I feel more like I am lashed to the mast instead of having my hand on the rudder," she replied.

As the squat dwarven ship shrank on the horizon, Harpis turned towards the lighthouse.

"While you two decide who is steering the ship, I am going to do as the dead bid and get a fire going in the lighthouse and take my frozen body away from this five-forsaken wind," he said.

Chapter 6
The Flotilla

Though she was rarely overwhelmed, Sudbina could not help but look around in wonderment when the small ship Zolga, Galonica, and she sailed in approached the Tormenta armada. She struggled to make out vessels within the clouds and fog that seemed as much a part of the flotilla as the ships themselves. As they got closer, a huge galleon appeared from the mist to their far left and sailed along a path that took it between them and the other vessels.

All the hulls were a blueish grey that was somewhere between the color of the fogbanks and the seawater they floated upon. The sails were a paler blue that seemed to blend with the clouds and blue of the sky alike. The galleon slowed while passing by them, and as Zolga pulled in their own sail, Sudbina could make out several stern-faced men aiming crossbows at her chest.

Galonica waved up at a similarly unfriendly woman who was cloaked like her.

"What's that you two have brought back with you? I wasn't aware we were expecting a foreigner?" the woman shouted down at them.

"She has information the Queen needs to hear," Zolga yelled back, stabbing her rapier in the air towards Sudbina.

The woman aboard the galleon crossed her arms and raised an eyebrow.

"Hold there," she said as they drifted nearer.

Sudbina watched as a man climbed to the top of the galleon's center mast with a lantern and seemed to signal to someone on one of the other ships. He covered and uncovered the lantern in a series of long and short pauses before sitting in wait, peering hard into the distance.

The man nodded as if in conversation and then yelled down.

"You are expected at the throneship, tie off at Duchess Hadjuk's ship and make your way from there!"

The cloaked woman looked down and waved them on dismissively before gesturing with a flip of her hand towards the steering deck. Then, all at once, the galleon's sails snapped tight and caught the wind. The hull seemed to leap partially from the waves, and it headed off in a path patrolling around the back of the flotilla and back into the fog. They were left bobbing in the water while Zolga found the wind again with their lone sail, and they set off straight for the flotilla.

Trying not to shiver at the dampening air, Sudbina looked from the distant galleons to her escorts, who stood unbothered. She smiled hungrily again at the sight of Galonica who was barely covered in her sheer blue robes. The longer haired Tormenta scowled when she noticed and pulled her cloak around her.

"Who is your duchess, and do I get to meet her?" Sudbina asked.

Zolga ignored her question and continued to focus on minding the rigging and rudder.

Galonica narrowed her eyes for a moment before relenting to the question.

"Duchess Kisa Hadjuk. She is our commander, and her duchy consists of four galleons. She is in most regards the third most powerful Tormenta behind the Queen and High Priestess."

"And is this Duchess as fine a specimen as the two of you?" Sudbina asked, unable to help her curiosity.

"We all look similar if that is what you mean," Zolga replied.

Sudbina licked her lips, and both Tormenta rolled their eyes. She looked from them to the galleon they had pulled alongside, craning her neck to look up at the massive vessel. She barely dodged out of the way in time as a weighted rope ladder was thrown down from above and secured to the deck.

"Up you go," Zolga said, pointing at the ladder before tying two ropes thrown down from above to the stern and bow of their small sailboat.

Galonica motioned for her to proceed first, and she awkwardly climbed the slightly swaying rope rungs to the ship's railing above. Then, shimmying herself over it, she stood face to face with a cocked crossbow held by a nervous-looking man in blue leathers. The bald-shaven man looked beyond her to Galonica as the priestess gingerly came over the railing. Sudbina almost flinched as the Tormenta woman put her hand on her shoulder and spoke to the man sternly.

"That will not be necessary. Sudbina is our guest," Galonica said.

The man lowered the crossbow, and Galonica walked in front, beckoning for her to follow. Sudbina reached out and touched the man's cheek softly with her finger, sliding it down under his chin and tugging it slightly to pull his gaze directly into her eyes.

"Hello there, handsome," she said with a smirk to the man who was clearly bewildered at the interaction.

"Back to your post!" Galonica shrieked at him, and he recoiled away in terror, scurrying towards the bow of the ship.

Sudbina rushed to catch up to Galonica as the woman briskly walked towards the stairs to the helm on the far side of the deck. Looking at the robed woman with flowing black and white hair she was following, Sudbina decided she needed at least one more question answered.

"Why are the men all bald?" she asked, glancing back behind her at the males who were winding a windlass to bring the canoe up to the ship's railing.

Galonica stopped when they were at the railing of the raised steering deck and turned toward her.

"Men do not deserve to wear their manes. The right to display the banner of our exalted lineage is for women alone. They should be grateful to be considered Tormenta at all," the priestess explained.

Rubbing a hand over her freshly shaved scalp and looking down at her suppressed cleavage, Sudbina found the irony of her current situation an exceptional curiosity. The disgust the two had shown her at their initial meeting finally fell in line with her newly enlightened understanding of the Tormenta's feminine power structure.

She watched on in surprise as Galonica jumped atop the ship's railing and grabbed at a rope slightly above her head that stretched into the distance. Then, stepping onto a rope tied to the banister, she began slide-stepping her way out across the water.

Sudbina finally looked around her and out at the floating city the Tormenta called home. She saw at least ten ships moored together around their current destination. The colossal catamaran had an expansive deck that connected the hulls of former galleons. In the middle was a wooden, fortress-like structure that sat three stories high with a giant figurehead carved in the likeness of The Siren protruding from its front, leaned out over the waters below.

She let out a long breath and climbed onto the railing. Then, after wobbling and reaching out to snatch the overhead rope to support herself, she started putting one foot in front of the other at a pace much slower than that of Galonica. Nearing the middle of the rope bridge, she felt sail-like herself as a gust of wind blew into her, swaying her backward for a moment. Looking down at the choppy and deathly cold sea below her and then at the galleon and catamaran on either side of the rope bridge, she wondered if she had perhaps finally gotten herself into a situation she could not sneak or persuade her way out of.

*****

Harpis had been sitting huddled with Wren and Gwenolyn near the fire in the lighthouse tower since they had finally gotten it lit in the late morning. The weather around Lodestar Island had grown angrier and colder as the day had passed, and he wondered if this supposed native visitor would make it to the island or be able to dock at all.

The three of them had hours ago given up the endless debate of who they would be meeting or why. They at least found themselves agreeing that they would probably meet with a Quaji of one of the tribes that fled from their namesake island.

"I am going to get some more wood so we can get the beacon glowing at nightfall," he said, rising from his seat between the gnome and elf with a groan.

Gwenolyn shivered once, clutching her fur lined leathers as she got as close to the flames as she could without catching on fire.

"Let's just hope this visitor decides to show up before long, and we can make a fire in the kitchens. The thin wooden walls of this three-story shed don't seem to slow the southern winds at all," Gwenolyn complained.

"Get to fetching more wood before we freeze to death up here and find ourselves asking Turin himself the answers to our questions," Wren said, pulling his robe collar against his neck and looking up at Harpis.

Harpis scoffed at his friend and made his way down the creaky steps. He gasped at how quickly the warmth from the third-floor chamber faded as he descended. He felt noticeably slowed as his body stiffened against the cold while he forced his muscles to obey his commands and gather as many logs as he could carry before trudging his way back up.

Shutting the door to the stairwell behind him, he threw a few logs into the pit below the burnished bronze mirror. He stared a moment and smiled at the tongues licking their way up the fresh fuel before depositing the rest of the wood on the floor. Then, looking up, he noticed his two companions were squinting at the growing dusk.

With a spyglass to her eye, Gwenolyn spoke in a surprised voice.

"How in the world did that boat sneak into the harbor without us noticing?" she asked.

Wren took the glass from her and shrugged after a moment before handing it to Harpis and answering the elf.

"It looks like a Quaji vessel," he stated.

Harpis grabbed the small telescope from the gnome and looked through it in time to see the bundled figure of their guest tie off the boat bouncing in the heaving harbor waters and head their way.

A few long moments later, the bell that hung on the first floor rang as the person outside tugged the rope for entry. Wren stood, and his scythe appeared in his hand, and Gwenolyn unslung her giant crossbow and walked to the far end of the beacon room.

Wren answered his confused look with his typical caution.

"Can't be too careful," the gnome said.

Harpis drew his dagger with a dubious look at both of them and opened the door to make the chilly descent once again to the first floor.

"I am coming," he shouted as he went, though he assumed that the person outside could hear the creaking stairs even above the din of the winter winds and crashing seas.

Reaching the bottom, he turned to unbolt the door and then opened it, struggling to keep it from slamming when the weather outside forced its way in behind the short, dark-skinned man who stuck out a gloved hand in greeting.

"I am Tawito, pleased to meet you," he said in a voice muffled by the scarves around his neck. Tawito helped him slam the door shut and gave a skeptical look at the dagger in his left hand.

Embarrassingly disarmed by the other man's calm demeanor, Harpis sheepishly slid the knife back into his boot as the white-haired Quaji removed his scarf and gloves, tucking them into pockets and motioning for him to lead the way.

Reaching the top of the stairs, Harpis opened the door. He closed his eyes for a moment of respite as the warmth washed past him and down the stairs. As Tawito entered behind him, Gwenolyn lowered her crossbow and Wren's scythe disappeared back into The Great Dream.

Calmly surveying the room, he gave them all a big smile and was the first to speak.

"The hallmark of Turin Deadeye's influence is a wake of paranoia," he said in a throaty accent perpetuated by the over-mouthing of common tongue words by one who preferred to speak in their native tongue.

Gwenolyn and Wren glanced at each other side-eyed in response to the statement and visibly relaxed. Harpis came to stand beside Tawito as the shorter man introduced himself.

"As I told Harpis downstairs, I am Tawito, a longtime friend and part-time accomplice to Turin Deadeye," he stated.

"I am his niece, Gwenolyn Amura, and this is Wren, The...." the elf stammered into silence as Wren punched her thigh before she could utter his title to the newly arrived company.

Tawito sat down by the fire and motioned for the others to join him. The firelight dancing off the faces of his friends and Tawito, Harpis listened on as the man consulted them.

"I am here, as you three are, at the bidding of the now-dead elf. Turin chose his own time to leave the living. He used that journey as he used everything to further his agenda. I met with him months ago as I did on a specific cycle. At our last meeting, he revealed to me some of what he had kept compartmentalized within the Quaj arm of his Syndicate," Tawito recounted.

The three friends sat straighter at the mention of Syndicate goings-on that none of them had been aware existed.

For his part, Tawito smiled at their apparent surprise before continuing.

"Turin was trying to unite the three bickering Quaji tribes through other agents and me, just as he was trying to guide folk on Quaj towards democratic rule. He made it plain that his ultimate intention was to bring us all together, unified and resettled. Not just on Quaj but the surrounding atolls and islands too," he explained.

Wren pulled the rolled leather scroll from his robe and showed it to Tawito.

"Does any of this mean anything to you?" the gnome asked, pointing to the columns of numbers and letters.

Tawito scrutinized them for a moment and shrugged. "The first column looks like the Quaji dating system. For instance, today is the nineteenth day of the tenth month, year forty-six of the eighth millennium," he said while placing a finger on the scroll he pointed at the top left number *80461012*.

"That is the day Turin died, the twelfth day of the tenth month, this year," he indicated.

Sliding his finger down to the bottom entry on the scroll's first column that read *76810307,* Tawito continued.

"The seventh day of the third month, year six-hundred-eighty-one of the seventh millennium, I believe that date would be just after Turin founded his little organization. I imagine the rest is instructions he left for you all as the other number and letter sets in the following columns mean nothing to me," he said.

Wren rolled the scroll back up, slid it into his robe, and shrugged.

"At least we have a little more information to work with then. Tawito, how can we stay in contact as we figure out our roles in Turin's final plans?"

Tawito held his leathery hands nearly in the fire for a moment before rubbing them together.

"I will circle back here from the atolls as I have every third new moon and look from a distance to see if the beacon is ablaze," the Quaji replied.

Gwenolyn crossed her arms and looked thoughtfully into the flames before staring hard at Tawito.

"You traveled from the northern atolls in the dead of winter to say just those few words?" she said accusingly.

"You came all the way here from Quaj and sat in the miserable cold of this lighthouse all just to hear those few words?" Tawito responded with a chuckle.

Wren snorted at seeing Gwenolyn taken aback, and Harpis decided he liked the old Quaji man.

Tawito stood and pulled his gloves and scarf back out before facing them. "We are, the lot of us, following the instructions of a now-gone puppet master. It is solace enough to know that we are not alone in our task, is it not?" he asked with a pause before continuing.

"I look forward to our next meeting after you have learned the rest of his intentions for you, and I am to share my own machinations at that time. Only then can we jointly plot to unify the Quaji and the peoples of Quaj," he said.

Before wrapping the scarf back over his mouth, a grave expression made its way across Tawito's face.

"I tell you this, friends of Turin Deadeye, there are greater threats to us all than our divided selves. There are worse things across Nysia than an exiled people and the infighting of those that forced their emigration," he warned.

"Nysia?" he asked, frowning in confusion while looking at Tawito.

It was Wren, though, that answered before the bundled man had a chance to.

"The ancient name of this world, lad. The name given in the first age. Before even those that ascended walked amongst the mortals," the gnome answered.

Wren's explanation did little but create more questions in his mind as Tawito and Gwenolyn nodded in agreement.

Reaching his gloved hand to the door, Tawito gave them a parting smile.

"May The Wild keep you," he said, turning and heading down the stairs.

*****

Queen Oluja Vetar lounged unimpressed, sprawled on her throne as the gawking Sudbina was escorted out the antechamber's double doors to the main deck of the catamaran. She sat with her left leg slung over the chair's arm and her right

58

dangling off the seat in front of her. The front of her sheer gown spilled between her legs. Waist-high slits kept her long pale legs uncovered from the tops of her thighs to her bare feet.

She ran her hand back over the tufted crest of her hair until she reached the base of her waist-length ponytail. Then, grabbing the bundled hair in her hand, she pulled it from behind her back like a whip as she stared down the gathered duchesses.

"Well done by your operatives Kisa, the information this Sudbina has provided will prove most useful to us," she said.

Kisa smiled tightly and bowed her head in acknowledgment of the compliment.

"I am glad, my Queen," she returned.

"Especially given the inability of our agents to gather intelligence in Kalt or on Quaj in general since your last outing there decades ago," Oluja said in a more demeaning tone.

When Kisa looked back up, her face was granite. Oluja raised an eyebrow and looked down at the duchess without relenting. After a moment, she forced herself to smile before addressing her charges.

"Duchess Zeln, your ship will join Duchess Vana's, and under her charge, your three vessels will scout and patrol this Lodestar Island ahead of our arrival. Let none who see you live lest they ruin our surprise," Oluja said threateningly.

The two women she mentioned nodded, and Oluja dismissed the six duchesses with a wave. "That will be all, ladies."

Kisa briskly departed ahead of her compatriots, and as the last of them latched the chamber doors behind as they left, Oluja rose from her throne and turned to the woman standing to the side of it.

"You were abnormally quiet through that whole thing, Spavati," she said, looking down at the older, blue-robed woman.

"Do you think it wise to prod Kisa so? Her rise to prominence during the joining of our tribes would do well to worry you. She has considerable sway amongst our people," Spavati said, unclasping her hands where they had rested respectfully at the small of her back and crossing them in front of her.

"You keep to the running of our religion, High Priestess, and I will keep to managing the politics that drive our people towards greater glory," Oluja said.

"All in the name of The Siren," Spavati said as both a

suggestion and a question.

"Of course, why else would I have bonded my flagship and your temple-galleon into this twin hulled barge of a throneship if not to represent the joining of our people and their ambitions, hand in hand with our faith," she replied dryly.

Spavati did not argue the point, and Oluja kept to herself the added benefit to her influence and control that had come from lashing the religious leader's vessel to her own.

Walking in front of the throne, she looked the High Priestess up and down.

"Kisa's rise amongst the unification of our seven tribes was my own doing. Supplanting her over the ignorant chieftess who had ruled her clan was better for all involved, and the debt she owed allowed me leverage and the majority I needed to bring the other five tribes and their nine ships in line with my vision. So now we journey as one. With no sigils on our sails to divide us," she explained.

"You are yet to produce a female heir despite reaching your fourth-decade next winter. Perhaps you should be more careful with how you handle your most powerful underling," Spavati countered, looking unconvinced.

"Kisa is almost ten years older than me and heirless as well. She should be looking over her shoulder at the ambitions of one Duchess Morel, who commands three ships of her own. I will produce no heir. My legacy is the only progeny I choose. I dare not risk offspring inheriting and tarnishing it, I will bring our people to their rightful place, ruling over all the southern seas of Nysia," Oluja sneered, spitting at Spavati's feet.

"I meant no insult, Queen Vetar," Spavati apologized, holding her hands up in appeasement.

Oluja strode to the throne, snatching up a pike pole that was as tall as she was, and pointed it menacingly at the High Priestess.

"We are joined, you and I, in the advancement of our unified peoples. Judge not the way of the warrior or the politician, and I will judge not the weakness your ilk created for our kind when The Siren's priestesses snuffed out the practice of magecraft to protect their own sway over the gifted Tormenta!" she threatened.

Spavati took a step back from the statement as much as from the weapon.

"Who did you learn that from?" she asked.

"I can read the histories just as you do, High Priestess. How else do you think I steered seven rival tribes into what we are today?" Oluja asked.

Spavati's shoulders sagged as she seemed to fully realize the implications of Oluja's statement.

The High Priestess looked down the pike pole with barely controlled anger in her eyes.

"That specific history was in a singular text kept in my vault. One that I saw there even this morning," she said accusingly.

"Indeed," was Oluja's only response as she dismissed the other woman in the same contemptuous manner that she had shown her Duchesses.

Chapter 7
The Chase

Harpis had spent most of the night staring into the oven's dancing flames in what had been The Syndicate kitchens with Wren and Gwenolyn. He felt as though the Quaji man Tawito, and Turin through him, had simply pointed them towards more questions without providing any answer.

Come morning, the three of them had mostly thawed, but barely slept. He was glad at least that the weather had abated, even if the chill had not. They made their way out the front of the lighthouse, latching the door behind them and boarding the *Open Ocean* a short walk later.

Harpis untied the boat and pushed it off the docks before tightening the rigging while Wren steered them out of Lodestar Island's small harbor. Noticing Gwenolyn staring sadly at the island, he tried to distract the elf.

"What do you think we will learn when we look through the histories indicated in the scroll?" he asked her.

She did not respond at first, simply sighing at the receding island's shoreline before turning to Harpis with watery eyes.

"You know what? That Siren-cursed old elf makes closure little more than an ever-fleeting hope. Will there ever be an end to the breadcrumbs he has left us, or will I unwittingly find the last of them without realizing it? How would I know? Will I spend the rest of my days wondering if we have fulfilled his final agenda or if I had simply failed to solve the latest riddle?" she asked.

He tried to think of a witty response, but the enormity of her questions gave him pause as well.

"I envy you for your short life, Harpis the human," she said sincerely.

"I think maybe you'd have a different opinion if you learned to cherish days over centuries, Gwenolyn the elf," he answered sarcastically.

He made his way to the bow and joined her as Wren turned the boat out to sea.

Looking due south with her, he noticed what seemed like a tiny cloud on the water's surface, barely in view.

"That seems a bit out of place," he said as she spotted it too and asked Wren for the spyglass.

The gnome lashed the rudder in place and walked to them.

"Are the two of you up here seeing ghosts on the sea? There isn't a cloud in the sky, and barely a wind is blowing," he exclaimed.

Instead of handing the looking glass to them, he put it to his eye and pulled a frown. Then, tossing it to Gwenolyn, he pointed to the rigging.

"Get as high as you can and tell me what you think it is," he suggested.

"What is it?" he asked the gnome, whose only response was to hold up a finger while they waited for Gwenolyn's opinion.

He looked up to see her legs wrapped around the top of the mast and crossbar leaning forward intently, looking through the monocular.

"Foreign," was all she said before dropping it into Harpis' waiting hands.

When he looked through it, he saw the now much closer wispy blotch was a greyish painted vessel with blue dyed sails devoid of any marking.

"It is a ship. One we can surely outrun if necessary. What's so bad about that?" Harpis asked.

Wren did not answer him. Instead, he looked to Gwenolyn as she landed nimbly back on the deck.

"How big would you say that ship is?" he asked.

"Probably close to twice the length of a Tuathian brigantine and much wider," she replied.

"That is roughly my guess as well," Wren said, heading back to the rudder.

He sharply turned them away from the splotch and on a northern track around the back of Lodestar.

"I still don't understand," Harpis said in frustration, looking

63

from the gnome to the elf who was now dancing along the riggings, trying to maneuver every bit of wind possible into their sail.

After uttering a curse in gnomish that Harpis did not understand, Wren looked at him with obvious concern.

"Are there any ships sailed by the people of Quaj bigger than a Tuathian brigantine?" the gnome questioned.

"No," Harpis replied.

"Then a ship twice that size would be from somewhere else, wouldn't it?" Wren stated as much as asked.

"Oh," He answered, realizing that the other ship, which was closing on them, was of an unknown and potentially unfriendly origin.

With the sails as full of wind as they would stand, Gwenolyn looked at their pursuer and then at her crossbow. "I reckon a ship that size could have close to four hundred aboard, and by the looks of it, we will be overtaken by evening. Well before we could reach Kalt."

Wren beckoned them to join him at the stern, speaking without looking away from the other vessel.

"I think the right thing to do is to make a run in a direction that takes them away from Quaj and hope this vessel does not stumble upon our home lest it brings whatever friends it has there as well," he said.

For the second time in as many years, Harpis looked at the deck of the *Open Ocean* and considered whether or not he would die on it.

"We do not know if they are hostile, Wren," he stated with false hope in his voice.

"How about we determine that as far from Quaj as possible," the gnome retorted.

*****

Queen Oluja Vetar flung open the double doors and strutted out onto the expansive balcony that stretched the entire width between the hulls of the catamaran throneship. Usually, she would have looked down from the higher observation deck as a stately ruler should. Today though, the warrior queen wanted to look her duchesses and their captains in their eyes as she addressed them.

Behind her followed High Priestess Spavati and the captain of Duchess Vana's second ship, which had arrived and reported only an hour before. She stopped paces away from the gathered women. The four duchesses whose ships were still with the flotilla stood immediately in front of her.

As she had at every other formal gathering, she looked first at the left and senior-most, staring Kisa in the eyes. Behind the older duchess were the captains of the woman's four ships, standing at rigid attention.

Oluja continued moving her gaze to her right. First, Duchess Morel and the captains of her three ships stood together, and then Duchess Emni and the captain of her second ship. Next was the much younger Duchess Lorent, who captained her lone ship as Zeln did. Lastly, she nodded approvingly to her commodore and the seven captains that piloted her own ships.

"Today the Tormenta take the first step in expanding the reach, power, and dominance of our unified tribes. Today we seize the island before us," she said, pointing to the small blotch on the horizon that was Lodestar Island.

She lowered her hand and waited for their eyes to return to her before speaking again.

"The flotilla will anchor just offshore. Duchess Kisa, your forces will secure the island," she commanded.

The older duchess gave her a grin and nodded her acceptance of the task.

"It would be our honor to claim the first parcel of land for the Tormenta Empire," she said before turning to her captains to issue orders.

Oluja drew their attention to her one more time, raising her right fist in the air.

"Tonight, we dine somewhere none of our ancestors ever have. On our own land. Tormenta land. Return to your ships and relish the beginning of our glorious rule over southern Nysia," she stated.

While the others departed across the webbing of rope bridges that connected the ships of the flotilla, she turned to her right and addressed the High Priestess.

"Well, Spavati, let's go and speak with your storm priestesses," she said, motioning for the other woman to proceed.

Spavati turned and led the way towards the left hull of the

65

catamaran that at one time had been her own ship to captain.

"They are not my storm priestesses, nor yours, Oluja. They are The Siren's. As am I," she said as they descended into the cavernous middle section.

Oluja silently scoffed behind the religious woman. Reaching the landing below, she took in the worship hall. It always felt odd to her to be in such an expansive space onboard a ship. In her own, and all other Tormenta vessels, the many rooms were cramped and the ceilings short to accommodate more decks and as many crew and family members as possible. Even on those configured more for families than warfare, the rooms were mainly for sleeping.

But here in the temple hull, that was not the case. Instead, the middle section they now stood in was a full three stories tall and open save the many cross beams. The forward section was the quarters of the priestesses and their male curates. The aft was where they kept religious artifacts and texts and was where Spavati lived and worked.

With her union of the tribes had also come the luxury of using the throneship as a residence. There, the old and young were out of the way of those who sailed and fought. Something that had previously only been available to those with larger fleets who could spare an entire vessel as a sanctuary while others fought.

Spavati walked ahead and stopped as the forty storm priestesses and four times as many male curates turned on their benches to face her. Oluja took a striding step to stand imposing behind her with arms crossed over her chest as the High Priestess greeted her blue-robed congregation.

"While we do not share the political or military aspirations of our great queen and the duchesses, all Tormenta share The Siren's divine lineage. Though conquering islands and their peoples are not directly in alignment with the tenets of our faith, Queen Oluja Vetar believes it is the best way to ensure the spread of our beliefs and the safety and growth of our people," she began.

Spavati stopped and turned back towards her with a bitter look in her eyes before continuing.

"Thus, we will pray for the success of the coming campaign, and we will use our Siren-given gifts where possible to aid in the efforts of our people. May she sweep away our enemies!" she finished.

As the last words echoed off the wooden walls, Oluja smiled as she mouthed along while the chamber resounded with the worshiper's emotional response.

"And may we hold her breath in our sails!"

*****

Harpis stood at the stern of the *Open Ocean*, straining his eyes in the moonlight to see individuals moving about the giant galleon. It was barely a thousand feet behind them and closing that distance with each passing moment. Looking up the mast, he shook his head at the statuesque visage of Gwenolyn perched precarious and unmoving atop the riggings. She had been there for hours, taking in every detail of their pursuer. After chasing them into the middle of the sea for the better part of a day and night, he no longer questioned their intentions.

Turning from their hunter for a moment, he looked down at the grim-faced gnome steering their boat.

"Putting Lodestar between them and us to hide our due east turn as long as possible gave us another half a day of running, but it looks like our doom will come before dawn. Any more tricks up the sleeves of that purple dress?" he asked his old friend with as much optimism as he could muster.

Wren craned his neck to look at the galleon for a moment and then shouted up to Gwenolyn, "How much time do you think we have, lass?"

"Less than a quarter of an hour, and we will likely be within range of their crossbows," she stated flatly from above.

Wren nodded his head in agreement and answered Harpis' question.

"One more trick and perhaps another if things become desperate," he said.

Snapping his fingers, Xissay was soon floating above his shoulder.

"This does not appear to be The Sanctum, Death Herald," she said sarcastically to Wren while looking up at the moon for a moment before noticing the giant ship behind them.

With an exaggerated point of her arm, she continued her questioning.

"Where on The Siren's seas are we, and who is following

67

you?" she asked.

With one hand still on the helm, Wren finally spoke to his familiar.

"We are almost a full day and night sail due east of Lodestar," pointing at the galleon, he continued, "and that is someone who felt it worth pursuing us that far into the middle of nowhere. How about you go have a look and perhaps set a sail or two of theirs alight to slow them down," he answered.

Harpis smiled to himself as he watched the undead fire sprite take off, cackling gleefully, while Wren turned back to face the bow and grabbed the helm with both hands again.

Harpis gasped as he watched Xissay near the vessel before seeming to run into an invisible barrier right as she reached it. She fell towards the water with little blue flashes of electricity tracing across her tiny form, illuminating her descent. He nearly jumped as he heard a thump next to him where Wren had fallen to his knees. Clutching the wheel to steady himself, the gnome hung his head for a long moment.

Putting a hand on his friend's back, Harpis spoke softly to the gnome while looking concernedly at the ship that was moments away from being within range.

"Wren, what happened? Where is Xissay?" He asked in a desperate voice.

Wren shook his head and blew out a long breath to gather himself.

"I was almost mind-lost when she ran into that magical barrier. She is back within The Great Dream, but I dare not try summoning her again until we figure out more about the abilities of our pursuers. I nearly lost my control over the binding that keeps Xissay on our plane," he said worriedly.

Rising again to his feet, Wren motioned for Gwenolyn to join them on the decking.

"That galleon can sail faster in a straight line with the wind, but it can't out-steer us. I will cut in against its path as soon as it is close enough for its crew to pose a threat, and maybe they'll lose the wind. The two of you tie yourselves to some rigging and get ready to stand as a counterweight when we make the turn," he said.

Gwenolyn stood at the corner of the stern with one foot on the railing across the back of the boat's steering deck and another back on the side where she tied a rope to her waist and unslung her crossbow.

Harpis made his way closer to the bow on the same side, wrapped rigging around his waist, and waited as Wren held up one hand to warn them of the turn. The ship appeared to be almost on top of them, and he could hear crossbow bolts plunking into the water all around, but Wren stood motionless for another long moment. Finally, a bolt thudded into the stern railing not far from Gwenolyn's foot, and he dropped his arm. Grabbing the helm with both hands, the gnome spun it rapidly, turning it to the right and putting them on a near-collision course with the giant galleon.

The *Open Ocean* was nearly on its side, and Harpis leaned back, looking almost straight down across the deck into the water as it sprayed them each time the side of the ship hit choppy seas. He looked back in awe as Gwenolyn steadily aimed her crossbow as they lurched through their turn. A robed figure looked down from high above them on the galleon's decking, and she loosed a bolt that took the grim-faced woman from the mortal plane.

More crossbow bolts landed in the waters around them and slammed into the decking for a moment before they were once again out of range, and the galleon began its own lumbering turn to follow. Gwenolyn fired once more as the *Open Ocean* steadied back into its centerline, hammering a crossbowman who stood at the rails in the chest where he fell back out of sight.

The three shared a half-crazed laugh, drenched in seawater as the sails of the galleon hung empty with its turn out of the wind. Their own were stretched to their limits as they began their run, once again with the wind. Harpis looked around in confusion as the hair on his arms and neck stood up, and he smelled an odd burnt scent. He was nearly blinded and then deafened as a lightning bolt streaked from the galleon and slammed into Gwenolyn before everything went black.

He was shocked awake by the cold sea and coughed up the water he had swallowed while regaining consciousness. Nearby he heard sputtering and cursing from Wren. Looking behind him, he saw pieces of the *Open Ocean* all around them. He began swimming to Wren, where the gnome clung to what was left of the mast, still attached to a chunk of decking. Looking off into the distance, he saw the galleon turn away from them and head for the horizon with the setting moon.

69

Panting as he reached Wren, Harpis struggled to speak, "Gwenolyn?" he asked with desperation in his voice.

"She's gone lad," the gnome said, choking as he spoke, with tears in his eyes.

"Wren, what Siren sent evil was that? Who in this world can control lightning like that?" he asked.

"Honestly, I am not sure. But now, we have more pressing matters to attend to than answering that question. Be glad we sailed so far from the arctic waters, or we'd be dead from the cold already."

*****

Zolga smiled as she surveyed the seas around the island in front of them from Duchess Kisa's second ship. Anchored a thousand feet off the west coast of Lodestar Island, its lighthouse was in her direct line of sight. She relished this moment that she and many others had anticipated for so long. This was to be the first, unified exertion of force from the Tormenta people.

To her right, she could see the entire flotilla, including their duchy's family ship, moored together in the waters off the island's southern tip. In front of them was Kisa's flagship, and unseen on the opposite side of Lodestar was their third ship, both of which were configured for the landing and disembarking of assault forces with dozens of landing ships hanging from their sides, just above the water.

Hand resting on the pommel of her rapier, Zolga glanced behind her at Galonica and Kisa's four other storm priestesses. It was rare for their duchess to place them all on the same ship, but today was a special occasion.

"What's wrong, Zolga? Are you sad you're not on one of the assault sculls?" Galonica goaded her with a wink.

"I am a bit old to be rowing an eight-oar boat half a mile to shore only to jump off and assault said beach under cover of lazy crossbowmen who were along for the ride, thank you very much. I'll happily sit here and watch your display," Zolga said to the priestess.

"Stand by!" the captain shouted, interrupting their banter.

Zolga looked up to the mast tip where a lookout clung to rigging with her legs. The woman had a spyglass to her eye, looking for the black signal banner on their flagship no doubt. Her other hand, held up in warning, suddenly swung downward.

"Now!" the captain yelled.

Zolga heard the five priestesses behind her chanting slowly. After a few moments, she felt the hair all over her body stand on end a split second before a giant lightning bolt streaked across the sky to slam into the lighthouse on the island, crumbling the beacon tower and taking down most of the front walls.

A moment after the bolt had struck, she could make out the sculls plopping into the water as the lines that held them slung over the flagship's side were let loose. The narrow boats sprang towards Lodestar's harbor as eight oars swept angrily in and out of the waters, propelling each toward the island.

Within minutes all twelve assault boats from their ship had made the docks or shores across the south end of the island and deposited seven of their raiders while one crossbow stayed with each boat. If the raiders died and the assault was a failure, no sense losing so many vessels as well.

Zolga knew the same thing was happening on the distant side of Lodestar. She knew that between the two beachheads, some two hundred of the most practiced of all Tormenta warriors, Duchess Kisa's raiders, were rapidly making for the dormant volcano fortress. She had no doubt they would be ready to dispatch any resistance they might face.

So it was that Zolga's hungry eyes and tight smile turned to slight disappointment at the anticlimactic completion of the assault. Moments after disappearing into the lighthouse, the warriors walked nonchalantly back out, and the crossbowmen atop the volcano crater unwound and unloaded crossbows.

She was nearly startled when Galonica quietly spoke from beside her.

"Well, that went smoothly," the priestess said.

"Perhaps next time there will be someone to fight. Nonetheless, we have our foothold," she replied.

A whistle from the lookout drew everyone's attention and the woman shouted down her report.

"The command ship lowered the black flag!"

The captain nodded and directed the helmswoman to turn their ship towards the harbor.

Chapter 8
Moodi Shen

Harpis clawed his way up the small beach in agonizing exhaustion until he felt his feet no longer lapped by the waves. His elbows collapsed, and his face fell to the sand. He was thankful for the cooling sensation on skin that had been burnt by the sun as they bobbed in the open ocean for an entire day. Late in the morning they had spotted the speck on the horizon and had spent all their effort steering the flotsam they rode towards it.

After a few moments spent embracing the sand to make sure it was not a hallucination, he rolled over and looked up at the stars above. The monotonous cadence of the waves crashing and then racing back out across wet sand was interrupted when Wren sat up next to him and coughed several times before letting out a long sigh.

He looked at his half-naked friend, who was barely a silhouette in the starlight.

"It must be almost morning. The moon has been set for hours now. I can't believe we made it to land, Wren. Maybe The Siren no longer has it out for me," he said, speaking in a raspy voice.

"Don't be counting your blessings yet. We may still die from lack of water or starvation. Maybe the goddess of the sea and storms just wanted to see you suffer longer. We may find ourselves wishing for a death like Gwenolyn's," Wren scoffed.

Harpis painfully sat up and looked behind them at the tiny island covered in trees with a small volcanic crater rising above the canopy on the far end.

"Your cheerfulness is infectious, my friend," he said to the gnome and laid back down.

"Live as long as I have and see how much optimism you cling

72

to, young bard. Pass me that storm goddess engraved dagger of yours if it's still in your boot, I'll take the first watch," Wren said, holding out his hand.

Still lying on his back, Harpis bent his leg, pulled the filet knife from its sheath along his calf, and handed it, handle first, to the gnome.

Wren turned it over, examining the edge and handle before pointing it at him.

"If you start snoring, I'll be sticking you with this" he said threateningly.

Harpis rolled on his side with a halfhearted wave and was almost immediately asleep.

*****

Harpis' eyes flitted open to the grey of dawn as he heard soft moaning and whimpering. He nearly cried out at the pain of his muscles seizing and cramping as he tried to straighten from a fetal position. His extended legs were immediately soaked by the risen tide, and he sat up in frustration.

It was then that he noticed the sounds were coming from Wren, who lay several feet from him, shivering and straining. Suddenly the gnome sat up screaming, gripping the filet knife and swinging it about madly. Harpis let out his own surprised shout, which startled and woke his nightmare-tormented friend.

"Gods above Wren, what were you dreaming about?" he asked the gnome.

Panting, Wren closed his eyes again and slowly gained control over his breathing, seemingly ignoring the question. Harpis was going to ask it again when he paused at the visage of the gnome's body in the morning light. He had never seen Wren without a robe or shirt until the night before when the gnome had shed it in their final swim to shore.

The sunrise revealed what faint starlight had not. Marks from poorly healed cuts and burns almost entirely covered Wren's chest, and there were scars from crude stitch marks that went all the way around his elbows, shoulders, and stomach. Wren stood and turned from Harpis to face inland revealing his bare back that was calloused and marred by hundreds of lashings.

After dropping the knife to the sand, the gnome spoke so

73

quietly Harpis barely heard him over the waves.

"Wars are violent, brutal, and ugly. What is done in the shadows to start, end, or prevent them, though, often involves unrivaled horrors and atrocities," he whispered.

The gnome then turned to him with hollow eyes that stared through him, over the seas and into the past.

"Without the whiskey to drown it, my mind went to places best forgotten. Sorry that I woke you, lad," he apologized.

After a moment, Harpis noticed Wren seemed to be once again fully in the present, looking him directly in the eyes instead of beyond them.

"Continue looking at me. We are not alone on this island," the gnome whispered.

Keeping his gaze from wandering, Harpis walked to him and picked up the filet knife. Taking a knee to obviously sheath it, he leaned in closer to Wren.

"A threat?" he asked.

Wren pulled his necromancer scythe from The Great Dream and closed his eyes in prayer before opening them and giving Harpis a confused look.

"What?" he asked the gnome.

"I don't know if that has ever happened before. There is nothing that has died on this island to reanimate."

"That seems odd," Harpis said in confusion.

"It doesn't exactly give me much to work with," Wren agreed.

Harpis scratched his head in thought. "What about summoning Xissay?" he asked.

"I am weak already and would risk losing the binding and my mind. That will be our very last resort. How about a song? Got any tunes you could hum to help us now?" the gnome asked sarcastically after shaking his head.

"I'll try singing around the cotton in my mouth if it looks like it would be beneficial. However, I am not sure I could hinder our opponent without also hindering you," he answered honestly.

Clutching his scythe with both hands and holding it like a club, Wren looked at the trees.

"Go ahead and grab your knife then, I suppose. We are going to rush whatever it is. Stab it with the silencing blade if it tries to call forth a spell or enchantment," he said.

Drawing the knife, Harpis looked down at his tattered clothes and then at his diminutive, bare-chested friend.

"That's not much of a plan," he accused.

"I am too tired, thirsty, and hungry for a plan," Wren responded.

"They will sing tales of our glorious deaths for millennia!" Harpis laughed.

With that, the two charged the tree line, dagger and scythe held high, screaming with their last breaths.

When they were paces from the shadow of the palms, they heard a bellowing scream from within the foliage, and out rushed a lean-muscled, loincloth wearing mountain troll. It was head and shoulders taller than Harpis and easily half again as heavy.

Still screaming, the troll raised both hands at them. Thinking it would be wise to stay out of its grip, Harpis stabbed the troll's right palm with the dagger. A look of shock came to the troll's face as he grabbed his wrist with his other hand and stared open mouthed at the dagger blade sticking through it. While he was distracted, Wren tucked into a roll to the left behind him and swung his scythe as hard as his slight frame would allow, sticking his scythe blade halfway into the troll's calf-muscle.

Harpis watched the troll hop around in agony, mouthing exclamations of pain, all in surreal silence afforded from the dagger's enchantment. After another awkward dance, the troll seemed to realize it was making no noise and fresh terror took hold in its eyes as it looked around confused. It then fell to the sand alarmedly, glancing from the scythe in its calf to the dagger in its hand.

Looking behind the greenish-gray-skinned behemoth, he saw Wren standing with his hands on his hips, eyebrows raised in astonishment.

"What do you make of this then?" he asked over their writhing victim.

"I think if he wanted us dead, he could have done it last night, or even now," Wren said, and then dismissed his scythe.

The immediate disappearance of the blade piercing his calf incensed the terrified troll who looked wide-eyed at where the weapon had been.

Harpis stepped closer, holding his hands up in peace. The troll recoiled, his hands held up defensively, and Harpis pulled his

75

knife from his hand and took a seat with the troll.

"Sorry about that. We thought you were hunting us. My name is Harpis. That centuries-old, bearded child is Wren."

The troll seemed comforted by being able to hear again and at no longer being a pincushion.

"So-kay hair piss. Me are Moodi Shen. Is all-ratty fixing," the troll said in a guttural accent. Moodi then held up his hand for Harpis to see the wound that was already healing from the troll's natural regenerative ability.

Feeling less guilty for stabbing the well-meaning troll in the hand, Harpis questioned Moodi further.

"Why were you hiding here in the trees while we slept on the beach?" he asked.

"Hide from the mean red-haired lady with the fire whip," Moodi answered, pointing a thick gnarled finger at Wren.

Wren gawked in stunned bewilderment at the troll's statement before silently shaking his head and walking over and sitting down with them.

"Moodi, where in the five-forsaken world are we?" Harpis asked.

"Home!" Moodi answered cheerfully.

Harpis exchanged a worried look with the gnome before pressing the troll further.

"How did you get here? When?" he prodded.

The troll crossed his legs and sat facing them both while tapping his upper lip and furrowing his brows in thought. His eyes widened as if someone had whispered the answer he was trying to think of into his ear.

"Moodi walked. Ninety moons ago," he said matter-of-factly.

Wren buried his face in his hands, but Harpis decided to play along.

"How did you walk here then? And why?" he continued.

The troll crossed his arms and gave Harpis a knowing wink and smile.

"Walked on my feet, hair piss. She told me her sisters would be sending me friends! Did not for thinking you arrive same day!" the troll said, laughing and slapping his thigh.

"Her sisters?" Harpis asked, deciding it couldn't hurt to ask.

"Aye, the dreamer, and the screamer!" Moodi said, nodding sagely.

Wren stared at Moodi with his mouth hung open, and even Harpis was beginning to question the troll's sanity.

The troll stood and waved for them to follow.

"Come, they must be thirsty. Awata wouldn't forgive me if I were a bad host to our friends," he offered.

Moodi led them on a short walk through the trees, arriving at the foot of the small volcanic crater with a gaping entrance. He beckoned them inside to a small camp set up next to a pool of fresh rainwater in the middle of the crater. The troll grabbed two coconuts from a pile next to his hammock and deftly cracked the tops open on the rock wall, handing one each to them.

"Drink up! Moodi will be right back!" he said, disappearing back out of the crater for a moment.

Harpis paused before putting the coconut to his lips.

"Do you think he is completely insane or maybe just half-insane?" he asked.

Wren had already begun drinking and did not respond until he had finished, putting the coconut down and wiping its water from his beard.

"Completely insane," the gnome answered as Moodi came back, a bunch of bananas and several papayas in his hands, giving both several pieces of fruit each.

Harpis grimaced as he watched the troll eat the banana whole without peeling it.

"Moodi, do you have any way of leaving? A boat? We need to warn our friends about the ship that attacked us," he asked hopefully.

The troll grew a sad look on his face at the mention of them leaving.

"They have boats. We can walk there later. Let me ask Awata what she thinking about you leaving," he said, nodding to himself.

Moodi then got up and headed around the edge of the crater floor, skirting the small pond in its center. He sat on a small patch of shaded moss and gazed intently at what looked like a group of miniature orange and purple water lilies in the water in front of him. He plucked one from the water and examined the mushroom-like fungus before sticking it in one of his cheeks. Then grabbing a tuft of moss, he stuck it in the other side of his mouth and closed his eyes.

The troll sat unmoving and silent while Wren and Harpis

77

finished their food and drank water from the pond. Finally, he opened his eyes and smiled.

"Ok, she says you should be going. Be getting some resting up, tonight we long walk!"

"Moodi, we need to leave the island, not walk around it," Harpis said concernedly.

Nodding, Moodi beckoned them to follow as he walked out of the crater and took them up around the side of the hollow mound, talking as he went.

"Only be leaving at night, long walking to Rawylap!" he said.

When they came around the side of the crater twenty feet above the sea, Harpis finally understood what the perplexing troll had meant.

"The screamer retreats under the dreamer's light," Moodi said, pointing at the submerged coral bridge that ran several miles away from the north of the island towards a much larger island that was the bottom of an atoll chain of islets and islands that stretched to the horizon.

"This must be one of the Atolls settled by the Quaji tribes. I did not think we had made it that far north and east. We might be able to make it back to Quaj Island after all," Wren said, letting out a sigh of relief.

"The Rawylap be living on dem islands! Long walk though, time for resting," Moodi said, shaking his head up and down vigorously.

When they returned to his small camp, he dug around a pile of things and pulled out a leather waterskin. Uncapping it, the troll sniffed the contents and grinned.

"We no napping with that mean lady around," he said, filling one of the empty coconuts with the cloudy brown water from the skin and handing it to Wren.

After taking a snip, the gnome pulled a face and then guzzled the rest before throwing the husk to the ground.

"It isn't Aanaman's finest barrel of whiskey, but who am I to be picky or rude to our guest? Thank you, Moodi," he said, laying down with his back to the crater wall and closing his eyes.

Moodi offered Harpis the skin. After a quick smell of the acrid fermented liquid, he almost gagged.

"No, thank you, Moodi," he replied.

The troll shrugged and took a deep gulp before climbing into his hammock. Harpis sat next to Wren and similarly closed his eyes as the weariness of the past two days and comfort of a full belly set in.

*****

Harpis was yanked from his slumber by the sound of distant screaming. The crater was bathed in the reddening-orange light of sunset, and he saw Moodi sitting up in his hammock looking around in confusion. Wren was no longer with them, and when the sound of another shout reached them, they both ran out of the crater and through the trees.

A few moments later, they made it to the beach where Harpis and Wren had spent their first night on Moodi's island. The gnome was standing, hands in the air holding his necromancer scythe and madly yelling in gnomish at the sinking sunset. Wren's chanting reached a crescendo as the last of the sun disappeared.

Out of the sea snaked two half-rotten tentacles as thick as a horse's body. Harpis almost gagged at the fishy scent of the recently dead sea creature, and Moodi looked on in dumbfounded silence. Then, a third tentacle appeared, rising into the air from the waters before slamming into the sand so hard it knocked Harpis from his feet.

Moodi let out a childish scream of terror, causing Wren to spin around and point his scythe at the troll and man. A split second later, Xissay appeared in the air, screaming before streaking straight at Harpis and Moodi with flames flying from her hands.

Moodi recoiled in terror, and Harpis stared stupidly at the fire sprite as she came to a halt floating in the air in front of him. The flames around her hands disappeared as she put them on her bare hips.

"Sleeper below! Harpis, what is going on!" she shouted at him. When he did not immediately answer, she looked at Moodi.

"Who are you," she demanded.

The troll waved cheerfully, "Moodi Shen!" he said before screaming in terror and running into the woods as a fourth decaying tentacle slammed into the island.

Harpis' mouth fell open, and he pointed at Wren, who again had his back to them and out to the water of the sea.

79

"What in all The Siren cursed seas is that?" he asked.

A wave formed far out from the beach as something immense pulled through the water towards them.

Xissay spun about to see what he was pointing at, "What in the world is he doing?"

"I think he's hallucinating that we are under attack and has reanimated the largest corpse he could find to defend himself," Harpis shouted.

When the wave crashed into the beach, behind it, the gaping maw of a colossal leviathan crested from the water. Under the strain of pulling itself towards them, one of the more deteriorated tentacles snapped with a grotesque rubbery ripping.

Xissay snatched Harpis' dagger from his belt and sped towards Wren, stabbing the gnome in his backside. The immediate peace created by the knife's enchantment ended Wren's chanting as the castle-sized corpse slipped back into the sea, and the three tentacles that were still attached slid loudly against the sand and disappeared.

Wren was glaring furiously at Xissay while rubbing his behind. The undead sprite returned the look, still clutching Harpis' dagger. The gnome then looked in surprise at Harpis.

"What's wrong with you, and what is that awful smell?" the gnome asked in confusion.

Before Harpis could respond, Moodi walked back onto the beach and inspected the cart-sized tentacle piece that remained in the sand. Then, the peculiar troll sniffed it, shrugged, tore some of the flesh, and started eating it.

Harpis fought to keep the contents of his stomach from spewing all over the beach at the spectacle. Wren closed his eyes and shook his head as if trying to dismiss the visage of the troll eating.

Xissay floated over and hung above the gnome before addressing him.

"Any reason you felt the need to resurrect the corpse of a sea monster from The Siren's depths and attack this nice little beach with it? Been drinking more than you should have again?" the sprite questioned.

After a confused look at the scythe in his hands, Wren dismissed the weapon and looked to the troll apprehensively.

"Moodi, what was in that drink?" he asked.

The troll strolled over to them and bent down, putting his face close to Xissay before straightening and giving them a huge toothy grin.

"Vision tea!" he said proudly.

*****

Several hours after nightfall, they had begun the four-hour trek towards the rest of Rawylap Atoll. The enigmatic Moodi Shen bid them farewell halfway and had told them they had three hours to finish the two-mile journey to the far side before the tide came back in and submerged their land bridge.

Harpis had a hard time keeping his balance on the perilous algae-encrusted and still wet rocks. Wren struggled now that he was not riding the sinuous shoulders of the troll. After a few slips, he had finally accepted Harpis' steadying hand, grumbling about appearing as though he was a human child on a late-night walk with their father.

They made the beach on their destination island with an inch of water already gathering over their boots. The sky was painted orange by the not yet-risen sun, and they were quickly spotted and greeted by a Quaji fisherman casting a net into tidal pools trying to catch trapped fish before the tide rose any further and took them back out to sea.

Dropping his net, the fisherman looked the beleaguered pair up and down.

"The Wild keep me! Where in The Siren's seas did you two come from?" he asked incredulously.

Bending at his waist to gather himself after the journey, Harpis pointed his thumb back over his shoulder and answered the man in between gasps.

"We washed ashore on that island behind us after shipwrecking out at sea," he said.

Straightening, he looked the surly Quaji in the eyes.

"A troll named Moodi Shen found us there and showed us how to get here," he finished.

The fisherman simply shook his head and furrowed his eyes pensively.

"I am Harpis. This is Wren, and we need to get back to Ravnice city on Quaj. Could you help us find a Quaji named

Tawito? We could compensate you well once we get back home," Harpis asked, too tired for niceties.

"Why would I help parasitic non-natives return to the island you took from us? Or in finding some apparent commiserating Quaji with a Urylap sounding name?" The fisherman asked with crossed arms after spitting at their feet.

Harpis held up a staying hand at Wren before the gnome reanimated the man's catch to frighten him into helping them.

"Look, sir, we could really use your help. The same ship that attacked us out at sea is a danger to your people as much as it is to ours. We just want to go and warn of its presence and hopefully chase it from the southern seas," he pleaded.

Harpis looked away from the man and down at Wren, who was giving him a perplexed look. When he looked back to the Quaji, the man's features had softened some.

Speaking with a chuckle, the man seemed to shed his grumpiness.

"That old troll is nice enough. Our shamans seem to think that crazy Moodi can talk to The Wild herself. Just don't go drinking his tea if he offers it. Our last Oracle did and went raving mad, dug a hole and climbed in it and cut out his own heart with a fishing knife while screaming about being unworthy!" he exclaimed.

Wren blew out a long whistle, and Harpis looked over his shoulder at the distant island in astonishment.

The fisherman sighed as the tide finally came in enough for the trapped bounty in the tidal pool to flee and threw his net to the ground behind him before addressing them again.

"All right, Harpis, I'll go and see if anyone here knows a Tawito, though I suspect given his name he is of one of the other exiled tribes. Probably Urylap, maybe Aylap. If not, maybe one of our merchants will take you up on the offer of reimbursement for being taken back to the lands we surrendered," he said.

As the man walked away, Wren smacked the side of Harpis' thigh.

"What was that?" the gnome demanded.

Harpis shrugged unknowingly at his friend.

"I didn't just hear you. I actually felt you ask him. Sleeper below me, for a moment there, I wanted nothing more than to find you a boat myself so you could get back to Quaj. When did you learn how to do that?" he asked.

"I wish I knew," was his only response as he stared in shock at the departing man.

"Mahala had mentioned that our gift could be more than just song and music. Perhaps that is what she is talking about, but honestly, Wren, I did not purposefully use my gift just then," he said.

"Maybe figure out how to be specific when you are doing that sort of thing, would you? I'd hate to be the poor fool around when you accidentally do it to some woman you're trying to swoon and end up with an entire tavern clamoring for you," Wren replied.

Chapter 9
Incipience

Ezera found sailing back with Ingar and their night spent in Ravnice dining with Governor Aanaman pleasant enough. Still, she let out a sigh of relief as her diocese came into view around the river bend. The ferry from Fjall sliding across river stones pulling into the dock to her diocese was music to her ears. Brushing her blond tresses behind her shoulders, she smiled at Ingar.

"Thank you again for letting me ride along with you these past few days, Ingar. You did not have to see me back out to the diocese, I am sure the Fjall Governor has better things to do," she said, stepping off the boat.

"Nonsense, I am happy to see you safely back home. Mind if I join you inside for a moment?" Ingar asked, following her off the boat and motioning for his armed escorts to disembark.

She was surprised that he hadn't simply left her at her docks and headed back into the mountain city.

"Ah well, then can I get you something? Tea or anything from our cellars?" she asked.

"Sure," was the dwarven governor's only response.

Grabbing the key from her robes, she unlocked the door and held it open, inviting them in.

"I believe your workers left a barrel of ale in the cellar after they finished carving it out. Feel free to have as much as you like," she said.

He beckoned her in after several dwarves headed down into the cellars, and another eight roamed around the diocese grounds with a purpose.

She followed him down the central aisle of the worship hall

and sat with him after he took a seat and patted the bench. Before he could begin talking to her, one of the dwarves who had disappeared into the cellar stairwell at the back of the hall returned carrying several mugs of ale. He handed one to Ingar and Ezera each.

"Out with it, Jovan," Ingar said, after raising the mug in thanks.

"Well, sir, the additions look rather straightforward. We will have to dig away from the river to avoid erosion and cave in concerns as we go deeper. They're finishing a couple of drawings so we can return with appropriate bracing and digging equipment tomorrow," the dwarf answered.

Ingar seemed happy with the report and dismissed the other dwarf. Ezera gave the ale a smell and wrinkled her nose, setting the mug down on the ground near her feet.

"Additions?" she asked, with an eyebrow raised at the dwarf.

Ingar gulped the ale down and put his mug down. Reaching around her, he grabbed the cup she had set aside and took a sip.

"Aye, additions. The two rooms on the left side of your hall should stay yours and Dobry's and the others for any sick who need attending. However, I will be digging a barracks big enough for twenty dwarves off your cellar and expanding that and the kitchens as well, enough to accommodate that number," he responded.

The statement caught her unprepared, and she took a moment to gather her thoughts. Though she felt she probably knew the answer, she asked anyway.

"My thanks as always for your support of this diocese, but why?" she questioned.

Crossing his arms, he looked up to the shrine to Daybreak and then spoke.

"If Turin was worried about threats from abroad, then it would be wise for us to worry too. Also, if there is more meddling to be done by you lot, you'll need a new, unknown, and safe place to orchestrate said meddling. We will dig a hidden third basement below the cellar as an office and meeting room," he said.

Seemingly on cue, the dwarves emerged from the stairwell and nodded to Ingar before departing. The last of them held the door open as eight dwarves from outside came in.

"These lads will patrol and keep watch until the work is

85

complete and you've room for more. Do send word once my sunrise-loving son returns from his training at the hospital in Mer," he said, standing and clasping her hand in his before turning to go.

Ezera stood and bowed her head slightly in respect.

"Of course, and thank you, Ingar. I truly appreciate it," she replied

"No problem at all. Let's hope this is simply an unnecessary precaution," he said over his shoulder as he pushed his way out the door.

*****

Oluja stood at the wide windows of the long office carved into the Lodestar volcano rim, gazing out at the circular courtyard below. She had so far resisted the urge to strike Spavati across the face for the impudence she showed while stalking behind her like a trapped animal.

She felt the High Priestess pause her pacing and turn towards her to speak.

"How many more days are we just going to sit here while you turn this little island into your new castle Oluja? It is unnatural. Our people belong on our ships, at sea!" she complained.

No longer able to resist, Oluja spun around and slapped the other woman. While Spavati clutched her face in shock, Oluja stared her down, daring her to continue. With the High Priestess sufficiently cowed, she turned back towards the crater.

"Address me as anything other than Queen again, and I will find a more obedient replacement from the ranks of your priestesses. Her first act as High Priestess will be saying the burial rites while your body is lost to the sea," she warned.

The crackle of electricity and the smell of burnt air caused her to look back over her shoulders. She calmly took in the view of a seething Spavati, making sure to seem unimpressed by the arcing and dancing flashes of lightning tracing the woman's body.

"Go on then, High Priestess, strike me down. Leave me nothing but ashes and black, burnt stone. Then you can die a slow death along with the rest of our people, dwindling out at sea, a husk of our former glory and an embarrassment to our own potential," Oluja challenged.

86

The door to the office swung open, and Oluja turned to see Duchess Kisa Hadjuk. After glancing at the calming Spavati, she faced the woman she had earlier summoned.

"Your assault on this island was flawless, Kisa," she said placatingly.

"It was easy enough. Even Zeln's meager forces could take a vacant island," she answered, seemingly insulted by being given the task in the first place.

"I would expect nothing less from the admiral of my naval forces," Oluja said, watching as a look of surprise made its way across Kisa's face before it returned to a more military bearing.

"I am more than honored, Queen Vetar," the duchess responded in obvious surprise at the promotion.

Oluja embraced the woman for a moment before stepping back towards the crater window and continuing.

"The children and the old will stay here, as will the throne ship and family ships of the other Duchesses and several galleons to keep patrols around this island. However, our military armada will be under your full control. Return to me tomorrow morning with a full assembly of the captains who will be under your command, and we will formalize the appointment," Oluja explained.

Kisa snapped to attention and Oluja dismissed her, closing the door after she left.

Oluja then faced Spavati, who was glaring at her suspiciously through narrowed eyes.

Unfazed by the look, Oluja stated her intentions to the religious leader of her people.

"We will make our initial assaults on the larger island of Quaj the morning after tomorrow. Based on the information from Sudbina, the southern port of Kalt seems the most appropriate," she explained.

"And have you given your most powerful potential rival command of our forces in hopes that she will die in the taking of Quaj or so that you can blame her if we fail?" the priestess said, taking a step towards the door.

Smiling coldly, Oluja waved a hand to dismiss the other woman.

"That will be all High Priestess. I expect a list of which storm priestesses will be joining the assault come morning," she said.

*****

Sudbina did not take to cages well. Even when those cages were luxurious quarters aboard the Tormenta throneship. She snuck about in the darkness just as she had each other night since being brought on board and was beginning to wonder if she would ever be able to leave the relative confinement of the flotilla. During each outing she was sure to don her black-haired wig to appear as akin to the Tormenta as possible.

She had waited until the late hours of the evening to go on her current adventure. Walking softly down the stairs into the worship hull of the throneship's temple area, she gazed in wonder at the surprisingly open, vaulted expanse of the Tormenta's chapel. The shrine to The Siren's visage on the far wall seemed nearly alive, bathed in moonlight from the tiny skylights cut into the ship's deck above. Smiling at the soft snores from the room behind her, she made for the intricately carved door to the side of the shrine.

Reaching the handle, Sudbina tried slowly turning it and felt the catch from the lock. She ran her hand over the nude carvings of The Siren around the keyhole before digging out a flattened nail from where it was stuck in her wig.

"Interesting doors hide interesting things," she said to herself with a grin as the lock quickly gave way to her efforts. She slipped inside, latching the door again behind her after softly shutting it.

Looking around the lamp-lit chamber, she found herself in wide but shallow quarters that had a bed instead of the typical hammocks she had seen in almost every other cabin.

She prowled between the tables and shelves that held talismans, scrolls, and books, looking for something to pique her interest when she noticed a pedestal with a locking mechanism at its top. Tapping her knuckles on the pillar, she heard a hollow report. Excited at another challenge, she produced her makeshift lock pick once again. After considerable application of skill, she was rewarded with the click of the lock opening to reveal a small, ancient-looking book laid open.

Gingerly she picked it up from the pedestal and quickly glanced around. Finding a similarly sized text, she put it in place of her recently acquired prize before closing the pedestal and making her way to sit on the bed near the lamplight. She closed the book and turned it over in her hands, admiring the dark blue leather cover and its beautiful fish-scale patterned embossing.

A jiggle at the door lock to the quarters startled her, and she hurriedly rolled beneath the bed to hide. From her position lying beneath the mattress, she made out the robes of a woman she quickly identified as the High Priestess by her voice.

"Quickly, Dejan," the woman said, and Sudbina spotted a pair of boots enter before the door was closed again.

"What's got you so worked up?" a man's voice asked playfully.

"Our deranged and self-important queen has named Kisa as her admiral. They will make their assault on Quaj the day after tomorrow," the woman answered.

"A risky proposition for both women, I imagine. Perhaps, as risky as your opinion of our glorious ruler," he said, standing near enough the bed that Sudbina could see the salt brine on his boot leather.

"That is High Priestess to you, Dejan," Spavati returned flirtingly.

Sudbina smirked as the woman's light robes fell to the floor, the oil lamp was doused, and lovemaking began in earnest above her. Tucking the peculiar book in her waistline, she lay patiently silent for a while enjoying the lustful symphony. A short while later, with the couple snoring, she made her way out and back to her room where she began concocting a way to stow away aboard Kisa Hadjuk's flagship before it departed as Spavati had mentioned.

*****

The wind faded behind her as the pale, red-haired goddess joined her olive-skinned twin and their older sister in The Nexus. The stony room seemed to grow lighter as the blond looked her way with a smile.

"Hello, sister, what have you found?" Daybreak asked.

Lacing her elegant fingers together, she gave them a strained look before speaking in a disgruntled voice.

"After my twin sister was kind enough to check on our banished brother and found him still peacefully dormant, I

89

thought I would look for the influences of Enky," The Siren said, nodding in thanks to The Wild.

After a moment of startled surprise, Daybreak pressed the stormy goddess.

"And did you stumble across out-of-place disorder?" she asked.

"That I did. It appears he has found another marionette, and she has birthed disorder on Nysia's southern seas, though I have yet to discern his purpose." The Siren said in frustration.

"I don't know what he is up to, but if it has caused Lilynth to stir in her great dream once already, it is cause for concern," Daybreak answered.

The olive-skinned goddess put a comforting hand on both her sister's shoulders and spoke to them.

"I have done what I can to counter what I perceived to be entanglements of his influence where they should not be, but I fear further involvement." The Wild stated.

Daybreak was taken aback again and admonished her younger sister.

"You should not have at all," she warned.

"I wouldn't consider what I have done as a direct influence, more like curated phantasms among hallucinations innumerous," The Wild chuckled.

Daybreak silenced her with a stern look and clasped their hands.

"Perhaps it is time we pay the unruly interloper a visit," she said.

Chapter 10

Foray

Zolga had hours ago given up her pacing on the deck of Duchess Hadjuk's second ship and she now sat perched in rigging above the helm, staring impatiently at the Kalt harbor before them. She had not yet been of age when the Tormenta stopped sending operatives into lands and cities such as the one before them. The practice of such excursions ended when her duchess created the now infamous incident in this very city. Having never seen one before, she tried not to be impressed at the sprawling expanse of buildings before her.

Their ship was joined by nine others in the most significant Tormenta assault force ever deployed. Kisa's flagship, second and third ships made up the central portion of their blockade of Kalt harbor. Flanking it to the north were three of the queen's galleons. To the south were two of Duchess Morel's as well as Vana's and Emni's fighting vessels. Zolga wondered if the Kalt citizens and their militia were itching for a fight as much as she was. She had not been in a real battle in the years since Oluja Vetar had unified their warring tribes and named herself queen.

"Officers!" the captain shouted at the helm below.

The command interrupted her mental walkthrough of their eventual assault on the wharf ahead, and she dropped nimbly from the rigging. After landing, she quickly adjusted her leathers and tugged her rapier handle to ensure it was still fully sheathed. She waited in silence at attention while several other officers and the priestess Galonica joined the captain and her at the helm.

With the ship's senior leadership gathered, the captain crossed her arms and looked them up and down.

"Today, ladies, we open hostilities with the island before you.

91

Our goal is total domination of this southern city of Kalt, and eventually the subjugation of the entire island of Quaj to our rule!" she said in a near shout.

Zolga shifted slightly and let out a frustrated sigh, earning her a severe glare from the galleon's captain.

"What is it that so frustrates the great warrior, Lieutenant Zolga?" she said with her hands on her hips.

Ignoring Galonica's snicker behind her, Zolga looked towards Kalt as she spoke.

"I do not understand why we sit here like gull hens waiting for mates when we could already be ashore," she complained.

"You'll get your chance for bloodshed soon enough," the captain said, easing slightly before continuing.

"Admiral Hadjuk shared intelligence provided by the recently missing Sudbina with me before we left. Kalt has no formal navy but does employ some two or three thousand militia. We hope that they decide to take to the waters and attack us where we are strong before we assault a numerically superior force in their own home," the captain explained.

"We've three thousand Tormenta in their harbor, nearly three-quarters of that experienced and tried raiders. So how are we considered the inferior force?" Zolga scoffed proudly.

Before the captain could respond, a hand rested on Zolga's shoulder from behind.

"They also don't have The Siren's priestesses," Galonica said as tiny fingers of lightning flickered around her.

The captain held up her hands to stay the officers, and her voice became increasingly stern.

"Trained or not as their militia might be, that city holds tens of thousands of citizens, and we have no idea what their stomach for rising against invaders might be. So, we will be deliberate for now. If you have a problem with those orders, I'll throw you over the rails myself, and you can swim over to the admiral's flagship and ask her in person why we are doing this or that! Get to your posts and ready your forces!" she threatened.

*****

Svenus anxiously plucked the steaming cup of coffee off the serving tray just as he had the previous three throughout the morning. After a long sniff of the dark brown contents, he smiled to himself.

"Those tan and perfumed northerners in Tuath are good for one thing, I suppose," he said to himself before taking a sip.

He dismissed the server with a wave for the fourth time since his watchmen had woken him at dawn. He had initially thought the man had been drinking his shift away with the description of ten impossibly huge ships sitting just outside of Kalt harbor. It was nearly noon now, and he had observed keenly and calmly from his dockside office as they sat motionless and did nothing while the city sounded alarms, scrambled about, and panicked.

"What do you think they are doing?" he was asked, for probably the hundredth time that morning.

Svenus silenced his youngest nephew with an upheld hand as one of the Kalt merchant ships made its way slowly towards the blockade in an attempt to leave the harbor. There were several gasps behind him, and he raised an eyebrow as the attackers enveloped the ship with their slim canoe-like sculls being rowed impossibly fast from no less than four of the galleons.

Through his spyglass, he watched as the female crew of the small boats threw grapnels up and ascended the ship under cover of crossbows aimed threateningly at the vessel from all angles. At once, the ship's anchor was dropped. Its Kalt banner was ripped from the topmast by one of the attackers and its surrendered crew were bound, and the sails brought in.

"By The Siren's bosom that was quick" he exclaimed.

Not long after his proclamation, he spotted a ship beyond the blockade, and he put the lens to his eyes to view the distant vessel. The vessel, flagged out of Mer, was turning about and hastily letting out every scrap of sail it had, trying to make a run from the foreign ships.

Svenus nearly fell out of his chair, and there were screams of terror behind him, as a huge lightning bolt snaked from the southernmost galleon in the blockade and blasted the center mast of the fleeing ship clear in half. The top section tore down most of the sails and rigging as it crashed to the deck, and he could just make out the forms of the ship's crew attempting to abandon it, swimming towards the shore. Unfortunately, they never got there as more of the fast attack sculls rowed out in haste, and the entirety of the crew was shot dead by crossbow bolts.

Lowering the spyglass slowly, he let out a slow whistle as scared murmuring grew in volume behind him.

Snapping his fingers, he waited for a moment for the serving boy to appear at his side.

"Grab me a flask of rum and have two of the lads rig up one of the tender dinghies so that I can sail it myself. Lower the Kalt flag and grab a white tablecloth or something and string it up above the sail!" he ordered.

The boy bowed slightly and ran off, and Svenus stood from his chair and turned to his sister's sons.

"Uncle, are we to flee? Board up the lumber yards? Why do you dare sail into such obvious danger?" the youngest inquired, unable to stop fidgeting.

"While I appreciate the feigned concern for my livelihood, Vikt, I think of it more of sailing into obvious opportunity and not certain death," he scoffed, turning an unimpressed glare upon each of them.

With that, he walked out the door and left the stunned silence behind him. He grabbed the flask from the boy, took a long pull, coughing at the fire from the dark rum.

"That should be enough courage, I am hoping. Too much and bravery turns to idiocy! You tell my simpleton nephews to gather the senior members of our company, the chief of our watchmen, and whatever senior Kalt militiamen we have in our pockets for my return," he said to the boy.

Throwing him the flask with a wink, he cut the mooring line, and the wind-filled sail blew the dinghy out into the harbor, the white tablecloth snapping in the breeze above him.

*****

Confused and terrified silence turned to well-known, and oft-exercised, rage as Jaeryl Innisgrath's mouth went from hanging agape to angrily clinched.

"What does that horse's ass think he is doing, surrendering our city?" he yelled.

He heard shifting behind him and called out to the guards he knew were similarly staring out the windows.

"What do you think, Lazar?" he asked the older guard who had been at his side since he took office.

94

"Maybe he is surrendering himself, Governor," the older guard replied with a shrug.

"We should be so lucky. I am guessing that snake Svenus Kalt is trying to find another ally by offering his help or docks to our attackers," Jaeryl said, unconvinced.

Jaeryl turned away from the harbor view and his windows to his desk, grabbing a parchment and pen he wrote vigorously for a few moments before folding and sealing three letters and waving them at Lazar.

"Find our fastest six horses and riders and send these with two of them each to Governor Aanaman of Ravnice, Governor Ingar of Fjall, and the elven chieftess as quickly as possible."

The older man nodded and hastily departed.

"Captain Valdik!" he yelled out the door, shaking his head in bewilderment.

A moment later, the leader of the Kalt militia poked his head into the room.

"Yes?" he asked.

"Call up all our reserves and prepare to defend the harbor docks. Evacuate all civilians possible from the wharf and waterside areas and send a small patrol to the Kalt family dock offices to see if they are willing to share with us their crazed patriarch's intentions," he commanded.

The captain snapped to attention to salute and was quickly gone from the governor's office.

Jaeryl squeezed his face between his palms for a moment while staring in frustration as Svenus' boat continued towards the flotilla.

"May The Siren do us all a favor and take you from the plane of the living Svenus Kalt," he pleaded.

*****

Enky leaned back in his chair and put his arms behind his head, relaxing as he surveyed the scenes unfolding in the picture frames hung on the wall of his small planar home. Kicking his bare feet onto the desk, he wiggled small toes before turning his attention to a particular visage, framed in stone instead of wood. He did his best to hide his grin and force his attention to the frame that sat on his desktop as the stone-filled portal to his right gave way to a view of The Nexus, and through it stepped three of the sisters.

He stopped drumming his fingers and dropped his feet, swiveling to face his guests.

"Oh, my, but what a pleasant surprise! It has been too long since I have seen you all!" he said.

"How have you been, Briny, Blossom, and Sunshine?" he asked, standing and running to the sisters and hugging each of them in turn.

After embracing the blustery redhead and her olive-skinned twin, he nestled the welcoming warmth of the eldest of the three. However, when he went to pull away, she held him firmly by his shoulders, and a stern and questioning look replaced the disarming smile her face usually wore.

"We know you watch us as you do the mortals and others, little brother, no need to pretend at surprise," the blond said, dropping her hands from his shoulders.

Enky grinned. Standing on his tiptoes, he pinched Daybreak's cheek. "Now, now, sister. According to our mother, I was born first!" he admonished.

The Siren put her hands on her hips and glared at him, responding tartly before her blond sister had a chance.

"And yet you appear always as a child," she reminded him.

Enky sat back in his chair, reclining and crossing his arms before addressing his angry half-sibling.

"It isn't my fault I ascended so quickly, and it took you old hags longer," he said, laughing.

Lightning flickered in The Siren's eyes. The Wild and Daybreak clasped her hands in theirs to calm her.

Daybreak stepped between the younger twins and him before speaking again.

"You are playing a dangerous game, brother, one that looks to break the rules of your ascension," she warned.

He opened his mouth to respond but was interrupted by the steady voice of The Wild.

"We have found your marionette and watched the ripples and repercussions of her actions," she said.

Trying not to reveal his surprise at The Wild's claim, he spoke directly to Daybreak.

"You seek to blame me as the cause when I am merely the

96

effect. Or, perhaps, I just, am. Certainly, I haven't done anything worthy of bothering mother. It's just a little havoc here and there," he said, trying to sound as innocent as possible.

The Siren snorted and rolled her eyes at his statement.

"Are you sure you aren't our father's son?" she asked.

"Interfere if you like, sisters. That is if you think you can do so without breaking the rules yourself and being cast down amongst your flocks again," he said defiantly.

Daybreak walked up and sat on his desk, looking down at him with concern.

"Why the havoc? You are rarely so direct," she accused.

"I am just doing a little reminiscing, Sunshine!" he exclaimed before looking past her to his other sisters.

"I thought you two would understand that most of all since he is your father's son!" he exclaimed.

Daybreak held her hand up in peace and softened her voice before continuing.

"We miss him too, but you know as well as we do why he was banished. He had no intention of ascending. Keep going, and you may find yourself similarly imprisoned," she replied.

It was Enky's turn to scoff in disbelief.

"Perhaps you three should be worried about issues beyond me missing our brother. I, too, felt Lilynth stir in her sleep. Maybe you should be more worried about her dwindling devotion amongst the mortals and the awakening its disappearance would cause. Or concern yourself with the fact that the mortals seem to have found the voice to call to us again," he finished.

*****

The not quite warm, but still humid, air of autumn in the northern tropics reminded Harpis of his time training at The Hall. Though not the elevated balcony found hundreds of feet above the water in Tuath, his perch on the bow of the Quaji catamaran afforded an equally splendid view of the ocean stretching as far as his eyes could see. He smiled as he heard Wren curse and looked over his shoulder to see the gnome awkwardly carrying a large leather canteen.

With a huff, Wren made his way to the edge of the bow, standing next to Harpis. The gnome's head was for once at an

97

even height to his. Looking back over the waves, Harpis shook his head at the sight of beautiful oranges and reds painting the clouds ahead before dancing their way into deep purples as the sun finished its descent.

"It is a mystery how her domain is so captivatingly resplendent and yet savagely vengeful," he said to the sea as much to his small friend.

"Some mysteries are not worth knowing, lad, such as what it was these Quaji sailors put in that stew we had for dinner," Wren grumbled before uncorking and sniffing the contents of the leather skin.

"Perhaps they are better at making rum," Wren said hopefully.

After a long sip, the gnome sighed and smiled before handing him the canteen.

Looking Wren up and down, Harpis tried to hide his amusement.

"What?" the gnome asked, casting him a glare

"Oh nothing, I just was thinking how much I liked your new wardrobe. Quaji children's clothing is much more befitting a person of your station than that purple dress was anyways," Harpis said before taking a mouthful of black spiced rum.

He struggled against coughs from the burn of the fiery drink when the necromancer smacked him hard in the gut mid-swallow with his summoned scythe.

"I thought you were against summoning Xissay or that thing to avoid startling the crew?" he asked after regaining his composure.

"What thing?" Wren asked snidely, the scythe disappearing from his hands as he grabbed the rum skin back.

Rolling his eyes, Harpis looked back out at the gathering dusk.

"I wish I could pull a new fiddle from the air as you do your scythe, Death Herald," he said.

"That poor violin is better off in The Siren's hands than yours anyway," the gnome chuckled.

He thought of shoving his friend overboard for a moment but decided he did not want to add any unnecessary delays to their three-day journey from the atoll to Ravnice. They had been lucky enough that one of the few Quaji merchant vessels that made regular trips to Quaj island still was docked in Rawylap's main harbor. Even more so that the merchant who owned it was willing to accept the promise of gold and silver as payment.

"The past few weeks have been quite the adventure indeed, old friend," he said, patting the gnome on the shoulder.

"Certainly, more than I was expecting when I decided to leave the boredom of The Sanctum," Wren said sarcastically before growing more somber.

"More death than even I care to see as well. We owe the people of our island a warning about our assailants. We also owe it to Gwenolyn to repay whoever they are in kind for her death," he said mournfully.

Harpis hung his head as he reflected on the passing of both Turin and Gwenolyn.

"Our hard-won peace is beginning to feel more like something else," he said.

Chapter 11
The Calm Before

Svenus was increasingly agitated from waiting with no idea when, if ever, he would leave the small cabin he was locked in. While waiting on others was something he was unaccustomed to, he had little choice. He was, for once, in a situation almost completely out of his own control, locked below decks by his hosts with his hands bound snugly behind him. His irritation showed no signs of abating as the burlap sack over his head brought complete blackness and made breathing difficult. His anger made him breathe harder, and he struggled to maintain calm to avoid sucking the rough, moist fabric against his nose and lips.

He heard a latch click and he turned on the rickety wooden stool towards the creak of a door opening.

"Get up, land-born," a feminine voice said sharply.

Before he could react, he felt slim but strong fingers grab his arm and tug him from his seat. Though there were men on the eight crewed boat that rowed out to meet him from a ship at the center of the blockade, he had so far only heard female voices speak. Serious men with blue tunics, crossbows, and sword-wielding women in dark blue leathers were the last thing he had seen in hours.

The woman pulled him along narrow wooden corridors and up several stairs.

"Where are we going?" he demanded.

"To your death if you do not show some respect. Impudent male," his guide answered right before purposefully leading him into a door jam.

"Siren's tits that hurt," he cursed.

He felt the sack pulled tight on his face as the woman grabbed it from behind. He let out another curse when she slammed his head into the wall again.

"Blaspheme like that again and I'll throw you overboard and let her reward you for your insults herself!" she growled in his ear while holding him against the bulkhead.

Despite the pain, he smiled to himself and caressed the muscled thigh pressed against his bound hands. With a shriek of rage, she spun him around and punched him square in the nose so hard he felt the crunch of cartilage breaking. In the blackness of the burlap sack, he saw stars for a moment and then felt the front of the burlap covering turn warmer and wetter with blood. Svenus decided he had done enough antagonizing, for now, happy with what he had learned about these odd foreigners. They had a thing for The Siren and had something against men, or at least him.

They went through the door, whose frame he had just spent several intimate moments inspecting the sturdiness of, and out into the cooler autumn air. After being led up a final staircase, they went into another cabin. His escort turned him towards the door they had just passed through, and he felt an additional set of hands hold him in place.

After a long moment of silence, he decided he might as well attempt his proposition.

"Do you treat all of your guests this way? It's no way to welcome an ally, really," he said as confidently as he could and was rewarded with a slap.

Behind him, another woman spoke in a more steady and commanding voice than that of his escort.

"You would have to have received an invitation to be considered my guest, and the Tormenta have no need for allies," the woman commented.

"Suit yourself then, girl. Best of luck doing whatever it is you came to my city to do on your own then," Svenus said, shaking his head dramatically for added effect.

He heard hissed breaths sharply sucked in by the women holding him before they kicked the backs of his legs, sending him crashing to his knees.

"Enough," the calmer woman said.

"Clearly, your arrogance is not limited to your decision to row out to us on your own. Who are you, and why did you come here to your death, man of Kalt?" she asked.

101

"I'll not parlay further blind and bound," he said in muffled defiance.

He tried not to obviously sigh in relief as he was answered by being hoisted to his feet and spun around. A crossbow cocked to his left before a blade freed his hands from his bindings pricked him threateningly in the back.

Without warning, the cloth over his head and accompanying darkness disappeared, replaced by the blinding light of the sun pooling in through small windows. The fresh air he hungrily inhaled almost fled in astonishment as his eyes finished adjusting to the sunlight and he caught a glimpse of the woman who had questioned him. He closed his mouth and lowered his raised eyebrows after a moment of staring at the white-streaked, black-haired woman wearing nothing more than a sheer gown and fur-lined blue cloak.

Svenus was rarely taken aback by beautiful women, but the alluring sculpture of feminine power before him was a far cry from the provocatively voluptuous flesh of the Kalt brothels.

"What happened to him?" she asked.

The wielder of the sword tip in his back gave him a slight prod before speaking.

"His mouth happened to him," she answered.

With a thin smile, the woman rose from her seat and stood with her hands clasped in front of her.

"Your name or the next words you utter will be your last," she said sternly.

"Svenus Kalt," he proclaimed, straightening proudly.

"I see," she said with a bemused expression.

"Head of the long-deposed Kalt family for whom this city gets its name, I presume?" she inquired.

Having killed men for lesser insults, it took all the discipline he had to bury his rage.

"And you are?" he growled, ignoring her question.

"I am Duchess Kisa Hadjuk, Admiral of the armada blockading your harbor, Svenus Kalt," she answered, looking him up and down with an unimpressed expression before continuing.

"I sure hope you have something worth trading for your life. Otherwise, you personally rowed yourself to your own burial at sea," she concluded with a smile.

"I can give you the city that bears my family name if you can allow it to be mine again, humbly and under your rule, of course," Svenus said, looking her in the eye.

Kisa tapped her finger on her lip pensively for a moment before sitting back in her chair.

"What makes you think I need you to give it to me?" she asked.

Shrugging, he took a moment to look around the room at the silent, grim-faced women in the cabin with them before resting his gaze back on the duchess.

"You can take it from many thousands of folks, fighting tooth and nail, motivated and infuriated with their backs against the walls of their homes with their children screaming scared inside. Or you can have it as a submissive colony of whatever you lot call yourselves, The Tormented, is it?" he countered.

Frustrated by Kisa's silence and her lack of reaction to his insult, he played his last bit of leverage.

"Why don't you tell me why you are really here. What you really want, and I will tell you how I can help you." He stated flatly.

Kisa tilted her head to the side, seeming to consider his offer.

"I want the entire island," she answered.

"Lady, the whole island is what you're going to get if you send tens of thousands of refugees fleeing from this city and rouse the other states against you. They'll march in force right down here and push you back into the sea," he replied.

Despite his efforts, he could not read the beautiful woman and hoped divulging further information might pique her interest.

"It won't be long before Mer and Tuath, those would be the only two states with formal navies you see, sail their combined hundred vessel fleet down here to see what all the fuss is about," he continued.

With a nod from Kisa, he was escorted to the table and shoved into the chair across from hers.

"And?" she asked.

"And, you have got about a day or two until messengers reach Ravnice and Fjall to warn about your little show this morning and two or three more at most before a welcoming committee heads your way," he said, hoping his over-exaggeration of Quaj's ability to unify and respond would not matter.

Kisa slid a parchment, inkwell, and quill across the table to

103

him and sat back, crossing her arms.

"Draw me a map of this island and tell me how you will hand me the city, Svenus Kalt, and you may yet outlast the day," she demanded.

Clutching the quill in his fingers, he watched as a drop of ink dripped from its shaky tip onto the parchment while he desperately thought of how to cling to what leverage he could.

"Seems like I should be having this discussion with your leader, Duchess Hadjuk. Maybe I'll wait for him instead," he said smugly.

Searing pain exploded in his midsection when Kisa kicked him square in the groin under the table. Between gasps of breath, he bit his tongue to stave off the urge to vomit and held up his hand in peace.

"Right now, on these waters, my authority is absolute. That is the last warning I will give to an insolent, insignificant, land-born male," she said through clenched teeth.

*****

Kisa sat silently, deep in thought, looking at the map and notes from Svenus on the parchment she held in her hands before looking up at the gathered captains and officers. The commodore of the queen's vessels stood before her with arms crossed angrily while she impatiently waited to be addressed.

Kisa raised the parchment to completely block the woman while allowing the awkward quiet to continue longer before letting go of the map, which floated down to the table next to her. She stared past the angry captain to the other woman whom she had cause to be wary of. Duchess Morel, leader of the third strongest Tormenta clan, stood with her hands impudently on her hips, staring right back. Morel's ships and the three commanded by the queen's chief lackey made up half of the assault force.

She decided she would crush them both now instead of risking being undermined further.

"Duchess Morel, who is in command of this armada?" she asked.

"We are all aware the queen put you in charge, Kisa, but working with that man is ridiculous!" Morel answered with narrowed eyes.

Kisa calmly held up a single finger to silence the belligerent woman.

"Admiral Kisa. You may address me as Admiral Kisa or remain silent." She said before turning to Oluja's pet.

"And you! Another word from your mouth, captain, and I will kill you where you stand and take it up with Queen Vetar when she sees fit to join us at the front instead of lounging at Lodestar Island," she warned.

She then rose from her chair and stepped up to the indignant captain. She slowly looked the younger woman up and down, stopping to sniff her. She then spat on the deck boards at the woman's feet. She put her finger under the captain's chin and raised it so that she was looking directly into her eyes.

"Your leathers smell with the sweat of your toil, commodore. Do not ever forget that you are a worker, not a ruler. An accomplished commoner, but a commoner, nonetheless. You are not the queen, and to question me as if you speak for her will get your tongue cut from your mouth," she threatened.

Letting go of the woman's face, she ignored the fierce look in the officer's eyes.

"If you disagree with my decision, then cut loose one of your sloops and sail back to Lodestar or into exile. Then, you can return in disgrace with the queen to a conquered Kalt. Maybe then she'll kill you herself," Kisa said hopefully.

She smiled as defiance faded from the eyes of the commodore and other duchess.

"We must take Kalt while not exposing ourselves to immediate recourse from the other city-states of this island. Whether Svenus' claims end up being true or not, we must strike fear into the naval forces of Tuath and Mer," she explained.

Kisa returned to her seat and motioned for the others with practiced calm. They joined her, huddling at the table. Then, smoothing the parchment, she pointed at where Svenus had drawn the cities of Tuath and Mer.

"Queen Oluja's three ships will sail for Tuath, which allegedly has the largest fleet, while Duchess Morel, your two ships will make for Mer," she said, indicating the cities.

Kisa paused to look up at the two women and ensure they nodded in acceptance and to make sure she watched their reaction to her next order.

"You are going there as a distraction. You will transfer most of your forces to my three ships as well as Duchess Emni and Duchess Vana's vessels."

"You send us to our deaths, Kisa," Morel said plainly.

"Your disobedience will send you to your deaths before our enemies get their chance. Our galleons are much larger, and the ships of this island do not have near enough sail to catch them. You won't be battling. Instead, you will be performing hit-and-run raids to keep them in their harbors while damaging as many of their ships as possible," she replied.

"How long do you want us to keep them engaged?" Oluja's commodore asked.

"If they are feeble, then until you destroy their ships. If you don't find their navies at port, return here as quickly as possible. If they prove problematic, do your best to give us three days to establish our hold here before you ultimately return. Morel, you will sail up the east coast, commodore, up the western," she finished.

"When do we depart?" Morel defeatedly asked.

"As soon as you offload your raiders and their longboats. The queen's forces will come aboard my ships, Morel's on the other two. We will plan to make our assault the day after tomorrow. Dismissed," she answered.

Kisa grinned as she watched Morel shove aside the similarly cloaked Emni and Vana on her way out of the cabin. Oluja's commodore was more measured in her departure, waiting for the Duchesses to leave before heading through it without a word. As Zolga and Galonica followed, she held up a halting hand.

"Galonica, I want you to stay on the flagship. Send for our other priestesses to join you here. Lieutenant Zolga, I have a task I can trust only to you and your most experienced raiders," she said, staying the other woman for a moment.

She paused and dismissed Galonica with a nod. After the priestess bowed and left, she rose and laid a hand on Zolga's shoulders.

"You are like a daughter to me, Zolga, and so I am reluctant to send you on this mission. However, you are the best boat commander I have, and that is what I need."

The steely-eyed Zolga gave her a slight bow before looking her in the eyes.

"What do you need from me?" she asked.

"Handpick your crew, six of the best, for an excursion into Kalt once darkness falls," she responded.

Zolga looked at her questioningly for a moment. "Only six? Who is the passenger on our scull?" she asked.

"Svenus Kalt. You will follow him while he sets his plan in motion tonight, and you will come back first thing in the morning. Observe as much as you can of the man, as well as our enemy. Wear heavy cloaks and cover your hair as much as possible to blend in while ashore," Kisa explained.

"Of course," Zolga answered, turning for the door.

"Zolga, I will be sending nearly two thousand raiders to shore on your word. So, make sure you're confident in it," Kisa warned her favorite officer.

*****

Sudbina quickly bored of staying hidden and stowed away on the assault armada. She found it ironic that in resolving herself to move on from her floating adventure, the ships would erupt in a frenzy of activity. With her uniquely varying appearance and atypical disposition, it easy to go unnoticed when she needed to. The mass movement of people and supplies that began just after sunset afforded so much distraction, she could have probably walked nude and gone overlooked as the Tormenta urgently went about their tasks.

With the intermingling of crews, she was sure her black-haired wig, pale skin, and tight leathers were enough akin to many of the Tormenta that if she appeared as busy as they were, she would pass for any of them. Still, she was constantly on the lookout for the few women amongst the armada that might recognize her. Zolga and Galonica from Huval Island were the most problematic. However, the Duchesses present during her interviews with the queen might also be able to identify her.

Thoughts of the women fled, and she froze dead in her tracks. A voice that had not assaulted her ears in over a decade floated over the water from the blockade's flagship.

"And why can't I sail my own boat back to my docks?" Svenus shouted from amongst a handful of hooded and cloaked Tormenta.

107

Sudbina turned in time to see him get shoved towards a rope ladder at the railing.

"Because we want your people to think you are still our guest for as long as possible, simpleton," one of the women said before Svenus begrudgingly made his way over the railing and climbed down.

She spit in his direction, which caused a passerby to stop and face her.

"I know, the land-born male is more disgusting than even our weakling men," the woman said and kept on going.

Sudbina grabbed the wooden railing next to her and took several trembling breaths to stop her pulse from pounding at the fear of being caught and the anger the sight and sound of Svenus Kalt brought her. After gathering herself, she watched the whir of activity up and down the line of galleons.

Tormenta crews were lowering the two-sailed sloops from where they hung off the backs of the larger ships. The big longboats lashed to each side of the ten galleons were also cut loose and dropped to the water. On the decks of every ship, hundreds of raiders were unstacking the eight-crew sculls and disembarking larger long boats, loading them with oars and then lowering them into the water where others tied them to long lines of rope.

As darkness enveloped the harbor, she struggled to continue scanning the growing flotilla. Amongst the mass of small and medium-sized boats spread out behind the armada, she paused when she spotted a Kalt dinghy with a small white flag hanging over its single sail.

"That might be the first useful thing you've ever done, Svenus," she said out loud, smiling at her newly identified means of escape.

Chapter 12
Paying Debts

Svenus clutched the boat sides with both of his hands. He watched in quiet wonder as six sets of oars methodically slipped above the surface, snap back towards the bow, and then silently plunge back into the water, pulling them ever forward. The only sound he heard was the soft rhythmic dripping of water droplets liberated from the harbor in between each surge of speed.

Turning from the quickly approaching shoreline, he glanced at Zolga. She was perched like a hawk, her body unmoving as her eyes peered around them for potential threats to their stealthy advance. Looking back at the crew of the eight-person scull, he shook his head in wonder at the hardened discipline of the seven cloaked and hooded women. He was quickly gaining an appreciation for the fact that his offer of assistance was far more a convenience than a necessity for the Tormenta invaders.

Moments later, they reached the rocky beach just out of view from his own lumber company docks at the southern end of the harbor. The crew expertly positioned the boat on a wave just cresting a dozen feet from shore before pulling in their oars and exchanging them for weapons. When the wave pushed them onto the beach, there was no splashing of boots to indicate a landing. Instead, the six Tormenta women in front of him pounced one after the other from the bow while behind him, Zolga held the boat in place with her oar jabbed into the harbor bottom as a makeshift anchor.

The first three fanned out in different directions into the edge of the coastal pine forest under cover of the others who lay motionless on the beach with crossbows at the ready. Seconds later, the others reappeared and nodded at Zolga.

"Your turn Svenus, try and maintain some semblance of stealth while jumping to the beach," she said in a doubting whisper.

As he awkwardly made his way from the narrow boat, it took all the balance and instincts of his life near and on the waters to not capsize the scull as he crouched on the bow before more falling then jumping to the smooth stones. Gathering himself, he followed Zolga to the cover of the trees while the other six picked the boat up and hauled it into the foliage next to them.

"You sure you don't want to just conquer the city tonight with these six?" he asked, only mostly joking.

Rolling her eyes, Zolga pointed at two of the crew and then the boat. The one with a crossbow nodded and began climbing a tree after shedding her cloak. The rest did likewise and covered the vessel with the black garments.

"Lead on, Svenus," Zolga ordered, following at his side as he picked his way through the woods towards the lumber company complex.

He glanced around, looking for the other four women but could no longer see or hear them.

"Where'd the others go?" he asked in a whisper.

"Watching out for us and scouting your city, worry not," she answered without stopping her constant scanning.

They reached the clearing where his buildings sat, and she followed him out of the cover without pause or showing any concern for her own well-being despite being out in the open in an enemy city.

"Zolga, I think you overestimate the abilities and dedication of our humble militia here in Kalt," he chuckled, stopping for a moment.

She crossed her cloaked arms and looked like some hooded and draped specter of death in the moonlight.

"It is Lieutenant Zolga to you, male. Only the soon-to-be-dead make habits of underestimation or overconfidence. Traits you land-born men seem to have in common with ours. Perhaps it is your need for genital measuring and brashness that similarly holds you back," she said.

Still unused to being talked to in such a manner, he decided it best not to confront the woman as his instincts told him to. He assumed crossbow bolts would pincushion him from the tree line if he had. Looking at the rising sliver of a moon, he glanced around at the few windows with candlelight.

"It is nearly midnight. We should make for one of my company guard huts to avoid raising the alarm by being otherwise spotted," he said and waved for her to follow him again.

Rounding the corner of a large storehouse, he coughed loudly in the direction of a small watch hut and heard surprised cussing and a short commotion before two of his men rushed out brandishing spears and shields only to come to a skidding halt at attention.

"Sir, sorry we did not know it was you!" one of them shouted.

Cringing, he silenced the man with an upheld finger.

"You weren't supposed to know it was me, you daft idiot. I am trying to go unnoticed. I am taking my friend here with me to my office. Go wake my nephews, senior company staff, and the rest of our guards," he said.

Zolga pulled the large hood lower and the cloak tighter around her shoulders before walking to his office.

Once inside, he drew the blinds shut and lit only a single candle, motioning for her to take his seat behind the desk.

"I think not. You sit. I will stand behind you. I am not as confident as it would seem my Duchess is in your motivations or your trustworthiness," she said, leaning against the wall behind his desk.

"Oh, you probably shouldn't trust me, but you can assuredly trust my motivations," he replied.

No sooner had he sat down and calmly laid clasped hands on his desk did his door burst open as three of his nephews and the leader of his guards flooded in. Recognizing the sound of a rapier whipping out of its sheath behind him, he quickly put his hands in the air for calm.

"Don't skewer them. These men are a waste of breath and space most of the time, but no threat to you or anyone else," he said, nodding at the others but mainly meaning his sister's sons. Deciding that he'd rather not end up killed by Zolga or some other Tormenta woman because one of his people blabbed their plans, he kept his knowledge of what was to come to himself for now.

"What have we heard from our contact?" he asked the leader of his guards.

"He says the governor has put the entire militia on alert and has stationed ten men in his home and another ten patrolling the grounds and streets near it at any given time, all of them handpicked and loyal to him as far as he knows," the man answered.

Tapping his teeth in thought for a moment, Svenus crossed his arms.

"As far as you know, and anyone better say, I am still aboard that ship in the harbor. Me and my friend here are going to run an errand this evening. In the meantime, I want the watch standing on our properties doubled with foot patrols. Detain anyone you don't recognize that I am not accompanying. I want every employee and family member we have assembled here on the grounds by dawn. We have some important work to do in the morning," he said.

"What kind of work?" one of his nephews asked.

Svenus' knuckles cracked as he clenched his hands into fists before grabbing a ledger from the top of his desk and chucking it at the man's head.

"If I wanted you to know, I'd have told you, now get out and do as I've asked," he ordered.

When the three left, he rose from his seat and looked at the lithe warrior woman who eased her shoulder from the wall once he stood.

"Maybe I see what you mean about my fellow man," he said, squeezing his brow before staring at the now empty doorway.

"Thank the gods they did not curse me with the embarrassment of offspring like the lot that just left here. Sometimes I try not to think of what will become of this business and city when I am gone," he said in frustration.

"What now?" Zolga asked quietly.

"Now we go get this whole thing started. We could probably use help from your raiders in the woods to do so. I have a debt to collect that will greatly aid our currently aligned causes," he said.

After a moment of thought, she nodded in agreement.

*****

It had taken Svenus, Zolga, and four of the raiders almost two hours to make their way shadow by shadow until they were across the street from Jaeryl's mansion. With only a few hours until dawn, Svenus shook his head at the supposed militia foot patrol of ten men. Two sat awake playing dice by lantern light while the other eight snored with their backs against the wrought iron fence that stretched around the home. He turned to Zolga, unsure of his plan despite the calm in her eyes.

"You think the five of you can deal with those inside and then these poor excuses for militiamen out here and hide them all inside while not raising alarms all over the city?" he asked.

The only response was Zolga and the others unsheathing long filet knives tucked in their boots and one of the women producing a rope and grapnel.

"You'll have to forgive me if I stay out of the way for most of this. There is a grey-haired guard with a long beard named Lazar that I'd prefer you left alive, and the governor I will handle myself when the rest are dead," he said hopefully.

He paused before pulling the sizable black pearl pendant necklace from under his shirt and handing it to Zolga.

"Show the older guard this. He will know you are here with me and obey your commands willingly," he suggested.

Zolga raised a sarcastic eyebrow at him after taking it before tucking it in her leathers. She held her hand up and made one last scan of the area. As soon as a cloud drifted in front of the crescent moon. They made their way to the stretch of fence furthest from the gate and the militiamen.

Svenus caught himself nearly whistling aloud as the five women were at once over the fence and scaling the rope grapnel to an open second-story window. Time stretched on in agonizing inactivity as he tried to keep control of his excitement at finally precipitating his revenge on the insolent governor he had put in office. It had not been even half an hour when he saw three women descend back down the rope. The moving shadows made their way to either side of the gate. A second later, the front door to the mansion cracked open and the other two filed out in a hasty crouch.

He looked up and down the street, seeing no one. By the time he turned back to the mansion, the gate had swung open. The two guards who were awake glanced up from their dice game and were each struck in the throat by crossbow bolts. Svenus could hardly hear their gurgled gasps from where he sat before everything across the street was lost to shadows as they doused the lantern,

113

and the gurgles went silent.

When the moon peeked from behind the clouds a second later, he couldn't contain his gasp as he watched ten bodies dragged two at a time into the house. Zolga strode to the edge of the street and motioned for him to join them.

He walked briskly across the empty street and followed the last of the corpses into the mansion. He saw one dead guard face down at a small table at the foot of the stairs to the second level.

"Where are the others who were supposed to be in here?" he asked Zolga.

"They are dead. We killed them where they slept in disregard of their duty. Your warriors are feeble and undisciplined," she answered without emotion.

Familiar with death as he was, he couldn't help but shudder slightly at the efficiency with which his city's militiamen were sent to The Sleeper.

"To be fair, the Kalt militia is mostly responsible for breaking up fights between sailors and fishermen in the bars and on the wharf. You may find those from Tuath and Mer more ready and willing. What about my man inside?" he questioned.

Zolga motioned for him to follow her around toward the kitchens, where he sighed in relief at the sight of the old guard bound and gagged. She cut him free, and he stood suspiciously from the chair.

"Is it our time after all these years, cousin?" the freed man asked.

Svenus nodded, embracing him quickly and then passing orders in a hushed tone.

"Lazar, get a bunch of the wine this pathetic excuse for a governor hoards in his cellars. Dump it at the gate and on the walkway to wash some of the blood into the grass and streets and then make for the lumber yard after telling some of the militia loyal to us to post watch outside here and make sure no one enters."

With a wary look at Zolga, Lazar left to set about his task.

"Where is the governor then?" Svenus asked.

"In his room sleeping," she said, pointing up the stairs.

Svenus undid his belt with a grin and quietly made his way up to the second floor with Zolga as his shadow. When he entered the room, he signaled for her to wait at the door and walked around the far side of the bed clutching his leather belt like a garrote. After making a shutting motion with one hand, Zolga obliged him and slammed the door shut. When Jaeryl Innisgrath sat up in his bed staring at the door, Svenus wound the belt twice around the man's neck, pulling with all his might.

As Jaeryl kicked and squirmed, Svenus whispered in the man's ear, "This is how I have decided to thank you for all you've done for the people of my city, you spineless, unfaithful coward."

Svenus looked up as the kicking slowed to see Zolga approach like a phantom. She crouched in front of Jaeryl, pulling off her cloak to reveal her cropped hair, its white streaks, and her pale skin seeming to glow in the moonlight.

"Look upon the face of your conquerors. Look upon the face of the Tormenta," she said in an eerie calm, staring at Jaeryl's face until the man went still and then turning the look to Svenus himself.

He shivered away the chill and prickle of skin the look in her eyes gave him as he wondered if her comment was more for his benefit or Jaeryl's.

Releasing his grip on the belt around Jaeryl's neck, he spat on the corpse and turned to Zolga.

"Give me the day tomorrow to prepare the city for your arrival. Attack at night. I will light this house ablaze to signal that I have secured the wharf for your ships to land," he said.

Zolga walked to the window and stared over the city, speaking to him without turning his way.

"We will come whether you signal or not. The day after tomorrow. We will not fight in an unknown place while it is dark," she replied.

"Do as you will then, I'll tell the folk it will be tomorrow night, all the same, that way those who don't want to fight you or stay with me in charge can leave and not cause either of us issues. Further, those that do want to fight will have spent the whole night awake in anticipation," Svenus said to her back.

She faced him, the promise of death in her eyes, and pulled her hood back over her face.

"I will find you in two days, Svenus Kalt. It is on you now to decide whether I will be the last thing you see or not," she threatened.

115

Chapter 13

Signals

With a soft tug of the reins, Aanaman guided his horse into the last turn towards his home after a long slow ride from the wharf on the other side of Ravnice city. The fall air had long since cooled what had once been warm sweat on his tunic. Though dry, the cloth still clung to his back, and he tried not to grimace as each plod of the mare's hoofs sent a twinge of pain up his spine.

With his house in view, he pushed down on the pommel of his saddle, arching his shoulders backward until he felt the satisfying pops of his back cracking. Ignoring the chuckle from the militiaman riding behind him, he attempted to ride tall in his saddle as his mount took the final dozen paces to the front gate.

After a brief pause and a heavy breath to steady himself, he swung out of the saddle. Patting the horse fondly on the neck, he handed its reins to the still mounted militiaman.

"My thanks for babysitting me this morning. Turn these two out in the stable and grab yourself lunch and an ale at the tavern across the way," he said, throwing several silvers to the smiling militiaman.

"Of course, sir," the man responded after a short salute.

As the militiaman turned to go, Aanaman took in the bustling city they had just passed through.

"Oh, and no need to repeat the whining and complaining you heard as we rode back here!" he shouted after the other man, turning to walk stiffly through his gate.

"I don't recall hearing anything at all, Governor Reaper. Good day" the man yelled back as he headed towards the stables.

Aanaman smiled in appreciation at the parting response and did his best to hide the discomfort of his screaming joints and weary muscles while he made his way inside. He had taken the first step on his way up to his office and the comfort of his chair when his wife's voice halted him.

"You stink like a sweaty farm boy I once dated," she said with her arms crossed.

"Shanowen, for the life of me, I wish I still felt like the sweaty farm boy you once dated," he replied, begrudgingly.

She smiled and handed him a waterskin before waving him up the stairs.

"Go on then, dear. Your mistress is obediently waiting for you in your office," she chided.

He rolled his eyes and laughed, "Aren't you supposed to be out with the girls?" he accused.

She raised one eyebrow and looked him up and down as he grasped the railing and took measured, slow steps up the staircase.

"What and miss the spectacle of you coaxing your nearly fifty-year-old body into pretending it doesn't have a century's worth of wear on it after abusing it like you were twenty again for an entire morning?" she said with a laugh.

He wanted to say something clever in return but was too busy focusing on putting one foot in front of the other as he pushed his way into his office.

"You look like a steamy pile of horse dung!" Captain Kilannry said from his typical seat at the small table in the corner of his office.

After lowering himself gingerly into his desk chair, Aanaman took several long pulls from the waterskin before addressing his old friend.

"Your exquisite powers of observation never cease to impress me, Captain Cormac Kilannry," he retorted.

"You smell like a steamy pile of horse dung, too," the older man laughed after exaggeratedly waving his hand in front of his nose.

"I am getting too old for this, Cormac," he said, rubbing his neck.

"Too old for what? Sitting behind a desk, running the city and state?" his friend asked with a smirk.

"It's the height of harvest, and it serves me well for the people to see me out and about as we export our crops and livestock to the rest of the island. And it serves me well to take the pulse of the city as it thrums through the cobbles and docks at our harbor," he said proudly.

"And how does it serve your aging back, old man?" Kilannry asked, rising from the table to hand him a glass of whiskey.

His shoulder ached as he took it, raising his arm in a slight toast of appreciation.

"Ask me after one or three more of these if you don't mind," he answered.

As he sat back in his seat at the small meeting table, it became apparent Cormac was not done having fun at his expense.

"Let's have it then," he prompted the gruff captain of his militia and decades-long friend.

"Every autumn, you take your aging bones down to our wharf and help lads young enough to be your sons chuck sacks of grain and corral hogs and cattle aboard our merchant ships from dawn until lunch. You do know those hoofed critters won't be here to vote for you next election. Doubt they would anyway with you helping send them to their slaughter," Kilannry laughed.

"If I am honest, sometimes I wish they'd all stop voting for me and let me go back to my crops and distillery," he said with a sigh.

He scoffed at Kilannry's feigned bafflement. After a sip from his glass, he leaned back in his chair and threw his boots on his desk.

"And how did the former farmer, turned governor, find the harvest season at the wharf?" Kilannry asked.

He couldn't help himself but smile. "It looked good. The summer was long and mild, and I didn't run into a single cropper that complained of not getting in their fields before the first frost. The livestock was as plump and healthy as ever too. With trade more normalized in the peace following the Syndicate debacle, there were ships from every city tied off in our port ready to take on our goods," Aanaman said happily.

"To the harvest!" Kilannry toasted, lifting his glass.

Raising his own glass in kind, Aanaman nearly fell backward out of his chair when horns started blaring and bells tolling alarm from the direction of the harbor. Slamming his feet to the ground to keep from falling, he sat straight in his chair.

"You didn't tell me we were running any drills today," he asked halfheartedly.

118

Kilannry shook his head in disbelief as he grabbed his sword from where it leaned against the wall.

"There are no drills today, Aanaman," he said as he flung open the door.

*****

Svenus' eyes were puffy and pained by the late afternoon sun as he stood cross-armed at the gate to the Kalt governor's mansion. His muscles were weary from being awake for nearly a day and a half without rest, but he did his best not to show it. He was on the precipice of accomplishing the reclamation of his family's pride and place, leading Kalt city. Not from behind the shadows with puppets like the recently deceased Jaeryl. Instead, he would be in the open, acknowledged by those who lived in the land that bore his name.

He had not eaten, but vengeance nourished him, and the moment of Jaeryl Innisgrath's long deserved death would sustain him for as long as necessary.

"Unfit to rule your own life, let alone my city," he said, glaring back at the empty mansion.

A large commotion approaching down the cobbled street drew his attention back to the moment at hand. He smiled in greeting as his watchmen, and other loyal enforcers herded a group of Kalt City's more influential citizens to him. The crowd included wealthy merchants, heads of powerful families, and lower-level local politicians, as well as a particularly surly captain of the Kalt militia.

"Greetings everyone, especially you, Captain," Svenus said with flippant congeniality.

He knew the captain was his only genuine concern. After the blustery man was dealt with, the others would fall in line one way or another.

"What is this about, Svenus? Get bored commiserating with our invaders out there in the harbor? Why are we here at Governor Innisgrath's house, and why is he not out here also?"

Svenus almost laughed aloud at the predictability of the aging militiaman but instead he spoke in as grave a tone as he could muster.

"You are here, Captain Valdik, because of the answers to

119

your other questions. Yes, I finished parlaying with the Tormenta. That would be the folks blockading our harbor," he stated.

He waited a moment for theatrical effect as they all obligingly looked out towards the harbor with curiosity and fear.

"Since our benevolent leader, Governor Jaeryl Innisgrath, sought fit to sit here in hiding while an enemy encroached on our waters, I took it upon myself to act for the city that still carries my name. I came here to tell the governor their demands and what I learned. I found the grounds vacant, and the mansion abandoned by that coward," he said, looking back at the building.

There were scoffs and snorts of derision and murmuring from the crowd before him, but it was Valdik who crossed his arms and challenged his statements. All as Svenus had expected.

"That all seems just a bit too convenient for you, Svenus Kalt. Let me guess, you've allied with these Tormenta, and you sold them our city for a sliver of power?" Valdik asked.

"I don't need aid taking power in a city protected by the likes of you, Valdik," he said sarcastically, causing the other man to stiffen angrily. He held a hand up in peace, a gesture that caught his entire audience off-guard.

"I tell you truly. the Tormenta will take this city tonight. They do not need my help, or anyone else's, to conquer us with ease. I simply asked for a chance to let it happen without further bloodshed and that we may keep some semblance of our lives intact," he said.

He glared at the house before them before snapping his fingers and holding out an outstretched hand to receive a lit torch from one of his men.

"In the absence of our cowardly Governor to accept the terms, I will do so myself. Look!" he said, pointing at the wine still staining and covering much of the walkway and cobbles in front of the mansion.

"Jaeryl did not dare forget his precious wine as he fled our city but not one word to any but his closest cronies as he left us all to die, fleeing north to his allies at the council!" Svenus shouted in disgust.

He then threw the torch right through Jaeryl's house window before facing those in front of him again.

"You're insane, Svenus Kalt, and a traitor. I'll not hear another word of this nonsense! I have a city to defend, and you'll be lucky to not be arrested when this is all over!" Valdik warned.

The militia captain spit at his feet, but Svenus did not flinch or react in anger. Valdik stared him down, seemingly waiting for support from the others. When it was apparent none would come, the captain turned and stormed off down the street.

After a moment of awkward silence, one of the older seafood merchants spoke up.

"Tell us how to keep our families safe and preserve our businesses and homes, Svenus," the man asked, and nearly all the others nodded along in agreement.

As wood began crackling and popping behind him, Svenus relished the heat that was radiating on his back. He bowed his head in acknowledgment of the request, hiding his smirk. After spending years working through how to manipulate the very folk before him, he found the task an almost out-of-body experience. Once the flames engulfed the mansion, he turned away from it and motioned for the others to follow him. As he walked towards the grounds of his family business, he felt no weariness, only the raging thrill of a long-awaited vindication.

*****

Enky ran his childlike finger around the lone frame sitting atop his desk and sat back with an accomplished sigh. A smile growing on his face, he shook his head at the visage of a cowled and cloaked Sudbina making her way north out of Kalt under cover of darkness.

Everything was unfolding more perfectly than he could have hoped. Conflict looked all but certain in the southern city on Quaj Island, and he suffered the anticipation as a long-delayed elation and protracted misery all in one. Despite his tens of thousands of years, patience was something that he rarely attempted and never accomplished.

Oh, how deliciously unpredictable his marionette was. Even as he exerted all his attention and influence, her actions appeared purposeless and of a higher level of disorder than his own turbid designs. Still, feckless as she was amongst his manipulation, she was invariably on the fringe of every precipitation. The waves from the wake of her uncharted passage seemingly crashed on the shores of his ambition, yet he could not see them.

121

Earlier, he had watched scenes play out on the frames of his walls as the Tormenta women, and this Svenus, had set the stage in Kalt for unavoidable calamity. He knew she was there, amidst it all, his conduit to the mortal plane, but how she was entwined remained a riddle even to him.

He leaned forward, resting his elbows on his small desk as he watched the beguiling mundanity of her trek toward Ravnice, relishing the mystery of it all.

"How is it that I wish for a thing, and it is achieved through you, yet at times, I haven't a clue as to how. Go north then, my enigma. I know not the reason for your travels, but your mystery is a delicacy I have not enjoyed for millennia," he whispered.

Chapter 14

Trespasses

Arch Mage Uridyll sat back in his chair with a satisfied grunt. Wiping a few of breakfast's escaped egg yolk drops from his long white beard, he paused as the unwelcome sound of warning horns echoed around the city outside.

"At least I got to enjoy my breakfast," he said quietly.

He spent a few breaths just staring at the empty plate on his desk and hanging his head. He had thought the battles in Mer and Tuath and the heinous acts of Sirul Amun would have scared the people of his island into sensical peace for more than two years.

"Apparently not," he said to his coffee after taking a sip and rising to see what the fuss was.

Only half out of his chair, he nearly fell over as the door to his quarters burst open, and behind it came to the panting lone apprentice of the Tower of Wind.

"Arch Mage, come quickly! The harbor is under attack! You must see this!" the apprentice shouted.

Uridyll moved as quickly as his eighty-three-year-old muscles and joints would accommodate across the courtyard to the Tower of Wind, whose north-facing windows afforded the best view of the Mer Wharf.

"Who is it that has decided to break the hard-fought and well-earned peace? Tuath? Kalt?" he asked, assuming the dwarves of Fjall and farmers of Ravnice were not to blame.

"Neither, sir," answered the young man as they took the stairwell and made for the tower's third floor.

"Pirates?" Uridyll asked in confusion.

"Not unless pirates learned how to make ships two or three times bigger than a Tuath brigantine and hurl magical lightning from them!" the apprentice said, pointing out the northern window at the mayhem unfolding in the Mer harbor.

For a moment, Uridyll stared at the back of the man's head, struggling to make sense of what the apprentice had said about magic. Then, more frantically blaring horns drew his attention to the harbor. A flurry of activity signaled the departure of the Mer naval ships, all heading towards a giant, blue-sailed galleon that had crossed into the harbor while a second sat further out to sea.

Uridyll abruptly straightened as he felt the budding tug of immense magical summoning and began searching from one galleon to another to see where it was gathering. Several long moments later, a lightning bolt arced across the sky from the galleon in the harbor, blasting away a large portion of a pursuing ship's bow.

Uridyll and the gathering crowd of students and staff in the tower gasped and cringed together at the damage and the thunderclap that followed. The Mer vessels turned in unison to flee, and another bolt struck the stern of the slowest.

The second galleon made its way into the harbor, joining the destruction. Bracing himself with his hands on the stone windowsill, Uridyll whispered to himself as worried and scared college members began frantic discussions around him.

"Hameki, old friend, I am glad you did not live to see this new terror. This may be the end of the college, and of peace. I just hope it will not be the end of us all," he said sadly.

"Arch Mage," the wind apprentice said, tugging his robe.

Turning to face the young man, Uridyll noted his clenched fist and hardened features.

"Yes?" he said, knowing full well what was to follow.

"We need to go to the aid of our people. We need to help them!" the apprentice demanded, and Uridyll noted murmurs of agreement from some of the mages and apprentices as well.

Uridyll's shoulders sagged under the burden of his responsibility for the first time in decades. Still, he stood tall and stared down the rage, fury, and fear in the eyes of those around him.

"Who among you knows the source, potential, or limits of the magic ravaging the Mer naval ships and harbor?" he asked while alarms and shouting grew from around the wharf and harbor.

"I do not." He stated harshly after there was no response. His point was punctuated by the lengthening silence from those around him and the thunderclaps of more lightning strikes from the harbor.

"I will not involve this college in the battle unfolding nor whatever else may come. Firstly, I abstain because all of us swore to impartiality and pacifism. But most of all because none of us, myself included, have experience using our gift in combat. We will send for Lorkin and see what he thinks is appropriate. Further, we will not reveal to the enemy our own gifts before necessary. It would be a wasted advantage and put a target on all your heads," he cautioned.

Without waiting for a response, he headed back down the stairwell.

"I want every Mage, Sage, and apprentice in my quarters now!" he shouted over his shoulder as he reached the door to the courtyard.

*****

Zolga squeezed her eyes shut and shook her head to clear cobwebs of sleepiness. Looking down the length of her eight-crewed scull, she clutched the pole of her bladed trident and gave her raiders a tight smile as they bobbed with the waves of the incoming tide. She longed for a good battle, especially one where she would be able to wield her three-pronged harpoon. Unfortunately, neither the previous night's activities, nor the visit to Huval Island, had afforded her appropriate environments for its use.

She had only been back to the flotilla long enough for a short nap when one of her crew had come to her quarters and told her that Admiral Kisa wished to see her. Reaching the top deck and standing next to her duchess, Zolga was glad to see the Kalt governor's mansion blazing like a beacon in the early evening, signaling Svenus had prepared the city for them.

Kisa had offered her well-earned rest, but she refused. Her place was here on this boat with her raiders, assaulting the Kalt shores amongst the tide of Tormenta. But, if the signal was a lie and they were betrayed, she had a promise to keep with one Svenus Kalt.

In the slowly fading darkness of pre-dawn, she could make

out the more prominent smudges that were the line of galleons anchored across Kalt harbor to her left and right. Near to them, she could make out other raider sculls and a few of the larger assault vessels. Each galleon was its own capable attack force. They carried a shallow-hulled landing boat lashed to each side capable of holding a crew of forty with half of those rowing. A two-sailed command sloop hung off each stern, used by the advance officers to manage the assault. Finally, there were two high-walled long boats with a crew of twenty each for their landing cover and ten or so sculls like her own.

While she had been on land, the entire flotilla's assault contingents had been lowered and staged in the water. In the earliest morning hours, the crews made their way across the diverse web of tied together vessels and waited. As the grey took over from the blackness around them, Zolga could make out hundreds of boats. Then she began to hear soft tapping around her, barely audible from the boats closest to hers. She gave a slight nod to her lead raider, and the woman hastily undid the roping at the bow that tied them to the rest of the boats.

She did the same as the others around them, softly tapping her trident butt against the side of her boat, watching as others repeated the same process across the blockade line. In short order, the waters were once again silent, and she could feel her crew tensing in anticipation. A quick whistle was blown only once from Kisa's flagship, and as soon as it faded, the officers on each command sloop began blaring three long whistles of their own, and all at once, hundreds of boats sprang to life and began sprinting from the line of galleons to the shore.

She reveled in the pure discipline of her people. There were no more whistles, no screaming or yelling, only the rhythmic sound of hundreds of oars cutting into the water in unison. She could make out the wharf and its docks and spat at the sight of at least four thousand armed men lining it from its far northern end all the way to Svenus' lumber docks to the south.

She was about to curse Svenus aloud and order her scull to turn south towards the lumber yard to hunt him down when she saw his trap sprung. A quarter of the Kalt forces, the entirety of those at the southern end, turned north and began a wild and screaming attack on their fellow citizens. the Tormenta landing crafts split, disembarking their forces at the two opposite ends of the wharf under cover of crossbow fire while raider sculls assaulted the center.

The sloop behind her began blaring new signals, and though the landing ships maintained their course, the longboats carrying twenty crossbowmen each now all turned to the north end of the wharf. Once within range of the northern wharf's edge, the longboats turned as one and began peppering the Kalt militia with devastating effect. At the same time, hundreds of fighters charged from landing boats, hitting the northernmost defenders, and bolstering Svenus' attack to the south. Seeing the hopelessness of the situation, nearly a third of those who had stood ready to defend their harbor fled back into the city.

By the time her scull, along with the others, made the wharf's edge, the battle had turned. As their boat reached one of the docks, four of her crew sent their crossbow bolts at the nearest enemies. While they reloaded, Zolga and the other three leaped aboard the dock and joined the fray.

Two Kalt militiamen headed straight for her, and she hurled her trident, completely taking one of them from his feet as it buried itself in his chest. With a scream of ecstasy and rage, she charged the other, who did nothing but cringe at her before her rapier disemboweled him. Smelling death and enveloped by the din of battle, she shrieked again, snatching her trident from the first man's chest, and leading her raiders into the fight.

*****

Svenus could only shake his head at the ruthless efficiency of the Tormenta. Within minutes, hundreds of Kalt defenders had died on the wharf, taking very few of his forces or Tormenta with them to the grave. Outnumbered by Tormenta and those loyal to him three to one, the thousand or so left fighting at the wharf fell back. After a few short skirmishes, they wisely threw down their weapons and surrendered.

He picked his way to the front of the lines, finding Zolga and who he assumed were several other officers standing before Captain Valdik. The Kalt militia captain was holding his sword by the tip, offering it, handle first, to one of the women. Svenus quickly shouldered his way between them. He ignored the glares of the warrior women, hoping they wouldn't kill him for his actions. He held up a hand to silence the defeated crowd before him.

"You fought poorly and surrendered like cowards. However, your lives will be spared and the lives of your families and your homes as well if you raise no further aggression towards our new rulers, the Tormenta," he shouted, motioning his arm to indicate the attackers behind him.

Valdik spat at his feet. Still holding his sword by the tip, he growled at Svenus.

"I can't believe I am surrendering to the likes of you, Svenus Kalt, betrayer of the city that tragically bears your name. The people will not forget what you've done here today!" he growled.

"I hope that they do not, Valdik. I accept your surrender, he said, looking behind the man to the militiamen.

"But you," he said, looking back at Valdik, "your surrender I do not accept."

He quickly grabbed the outheld sword handle and pushed the tip deep into Valdik's heart. The man collapsed to his knees staring in surprise at the blade protruding from his chest. Svenus kicked him over and stepped on the still gurgling man's back as he died.

"Hear me well, people of Kalt. This city was, is, and will always be protected by my family. Captain Valdik would have endangered you and your families if he were allowed to live. He would have perpetuated civil unrest resulting in harsher treatment from our new guests resulting in the destruction of this city," he said, pointing beyond the wharf.

"The Tormenta are not here to kill us or destroy the lives you have built. They are here to expand their dominion, and we are now their most important and loyal colony. Do not fear the ferocity you witnessed here today. Embrace its strength and protection," he said, turning to Zolga.

"Kalt City, as promised," he stated.

With a flick of her wrist, the point of her trident scratched his throat.

"You killed a warrior who had given up his arms in surrender. You have no honor Svenus Kalt," she said, sneering at him.

Slowly pushing the trident tip from his throat, he looked Zolga in the eyes and tried to match her intensity.

"No, lady warrior, I do not," he said, turning away from her and heading to his lumber yard. After a few steps, he turned to face the glowering Tormenta officers.

"I'll be in my office when your boss arrives. I'll gladly entertain her there and organize the occupation and operation of the city with her. In the meantime, if you would like, I can have some of my men take some of your forces out on horseback to scout the borders of their new territory. The militiamen you faced on our wharf here today are not your only enemies on this island," Svenus finished.

*****

Bravit happily licked his fingers as he munched the last of his blueberry scone breakfast while looking out over the eastern sea from his perch on the balcony. Glancing down his chest, he smirked and gingerly plucked a large leftover crumb and winked in thanks at his belly for thoughtfully preventing its fall to the floor.

The creak of the balcony doors from the attached quarters drew his gaze to a glowering Mahala. He had come to realize that her features did not always reveal her true mood. Despite her rarely changing expression, the petite woman did indeed feel emotions other than the rage, discontent, and disgust commonly painted across her face.

"Good morning to you, Troubadour, could I offer you a scone?" he asked, rising from his seat.

Mahala stopped and stared out across the waters, seemingly ignoring his question.

"What sort of Siren's nightmare did those monstrosities come from?" she said, pointing an accusing finger at the sea.

Spinning around, Bravit looked in shock at what had been empty waters but now held three enormous blue sailed ships heading southward towards Tuath. His fingers fidgeted nervously for a moment before he calmed himself.

"Fetch our two fastest horses and meet me out front. I will leave Dictum Olimir in charge. Those might just be an advance party. We have to warn the city," he said.

"Bravit, we have no hope of reaching the city before them," Mahala responded as she headed down the stairs ahead of him.

"We might if horses find that beguiling voice of yours as

129

enlivening as men do!" he shouted at her, trying not to stumble.

*****

The fifty-mile ride from The Hall to Tuath City typically took seven hours on a good horse. Bravit and Mahala had made the trip in just under five with the bards singing *Panoryla's March* to their mounts at the top of their lungs the entire time. When they reached the gate of the Tuath Governor's mansion, the horses nearly collapsed, and the bards could hardly talk above a whisper.

With sadness, Bravit glanced out at the smoldering wreckage in the harbor of what had once been Tuath's navy. He was grateful at least that no additional ships had joined the galleons and that no invasion force had landed on their shores. One of the enemy vessels listed heavily and seemed to be missing many sails and a mast. The attackers tied it to one of the other vessels, at the edge of Tuath Bay.

The gate to the mansion opened and Mahala tugged him inside. Looking up, he saw the grim-faced Governor Isra Rashida, who beckoned for them to join her on a balcony overlooking the city. When they made it through the office doors and saw her silhouetted against the afternoon sun, he also spotted the captain of the Tuath militia and the commander of the naval forces standing behind her. All three faced the bards when the doors creaked shut after they entered.

The look in the Governor's eyes and clench of her jaw showed the strain she was under to maintain her composure.

"Governor, how can we help? We spotted the ships early this morning and did our best to try and warn the city," he said in a strained voice.

Her features became almost motherly, and her voice was oddly comforting, "Maestro, Troubadour, thank you for your attempt at warning and offer of aid. I have already called up all militia and reserves, and the city is on war footing unseen since the ill-fated battle against the dwarves. Thankfully this enemy seems content to own the seas for now," she said.

"How did they decimate our fleet with just three ships?" Mahala asked from beside him.

The naval commander visibly slumped before shaking away his frustration and speaking.

130

"They are more than twice the size of our ships, and with much more sail, we could not catch them in a straight line, and they easily rammed through several of our vessels. We never got a good opportunity to board them and do battle," he reported.

"Worse still, they seem to command lightning as if they were The Siren herself. They struck most of our ships into smoldering wreckage within an hour of arriving," she added, putting a hand on the commander's shoulder.

Bravit couldn't believe what he heard from the commander of the strongest navy on the island and his governor.

"Then we are under attack from foreign forces?" he asked, afraid for the answer that would confirm his suspicions.

"It would appear as such," the militia captain answered sternly.

"Our sailors and ships were able to overwhelm one of their vessels in a brave attempt and hobbled it, setting fire to many of its sails and killing some of its crew before being decimated by the other two galleons. They are not invulnerable, but they are clearly beyond our capabilities," the naval commander said.

The governor silenced them all with an upheld hand.

"It is fair to assume that they are probing us for invasion. It is also fair to assume we are not the only targets on this island. I depart in the morning for Mer with two thousand militiamen," she stated.

Bravit could not help but interrupt, "What of the city? The Hall?" he asked.

"You, kind and worldly Maestro, will balance the opinions of these two military men, and the three of you will govern the city and state and protect this harbor with the rest of our forces while I am absent. I have thought long on our options, and I won't delay a unified response of this island by refusing to leave the north. I will travel to Mer and hope some of the other Governors have decided the same," she said.

Bravit could not argue the woman's logic as he turned to Mahala.

"Go with her, seek out Harpis. If he is not there, ask the Fjall or Ravnice governors if they have seen him. He and his former associates may know something of these foreigners or how to counter them," he instructed.

Mahala and Isra nodded in agreement.

Chapter 15

Homecoming

After three days at sea, Harpis was weary with anxiety when Ravnice harbor came into view, and anxiousness turned to dismay.

"Looking like we will be providing one less warning and adding a few more counts of revenge owed," Wren said beside him.

Harpis could find little argument as he looked at a harbor without a single floating ship in it and no docks left standing. To his left, he spotted a dozen or so vessels scuttled at the southern end of the harbor, making the mouth of the Fjall River impassable. He then noticed the wharf itself and the buildings of Ravnice within his view were wholly intact and became hopeful as they slowed their approach to the wharf wall.

"It looks like it did when I convinced Aanaman to make the harbor less vulnerable to an attack by Sirul's navy, though as to the ships scuttled at the river, I do not have a good answer," he said hopefully.

Even without docks to tie to, the Quaji were expert mariners and deftly leaped from the catamaran to the wharf wall, tying the boat off without the slightest bump. With the docks destroyed, Harpis had to lift the gnome to one of the Quaji crew members who had already climbed the seawall.

Placing his hands on the wharf, Harpis heaved himself onto the cobbles. He had barely gained his footing when militiamen carrying lanterns and weapons swarmed from a nearby building and surrounded them with cocked crossbows and menacing sword tips.

"Hold fast, men of Ravnice!" he shouted with his hands up.

One of the closer militiamen sheathed his sword and stepped forward, shouting at the others almost immediately.

"Put down your weapons! Do you not recognize the bard and gnome as our own?" he said.

He turned to face Harpis and extended a welcoming hand before looking Wren up and down.

"Where's your robe, Herald?" the man asked.

Ignoring his friend's grumbling and snickers from the Quaji sailors behind him, Harpis turned to the owner of the catamaran.

"Sir, we will pay you double if you can deliver a message to one of your people, a trader named Tawito? If he can find his way safely to Ravnice, we would like to discuss the terms of reconciliation and repatriation for your peoples," he asked.

The Quaji nodded, and Wren set off to his house to get the payment.

"Gentleman, I will wait here until Wren returns and see our friends here off, but would you mind sending someone to Governor Reaper so he can be expecting us shortly?" Harpis asked, turning back to the militiamen.

The man who recognized him nodded and sent another running to where the mansion sat on the far side of the city. He also motioned for two of the men to go with Wren.

"If it is all the same to you, we would prefer to wait with you until the Quaji set off. No offense to you lot, but we are under strict orders regarding foreign folk at the wharf," the militiaman said.

*****

It had been almost an hour since their arrival at the wharf when they reached Aanaman's home. The eerily quiet streets of what should have been a bustling Ravnice celebrating and exporting the goods of an autumn harvest were unsettling. Lantern-bearing guards greeted them at the mansion's wrought-iron gate, giving grim, silent nods as they let them through.

The house was quiet and dark. Harpis assumed the governor's daughters were fast asleep, so he whispered to Wren as the gnome awkwardly climbed the stairs behind the two guards who took them inside and led them to Aanaman's office.

"I am glad you took the time to change. I much prefer the

133

purple dress to the Quaji garb," he whispered to the gnome, who glared at him as they reached the door.

One of the guards softly rapped on the door and quietly announced them before opening it and motioning for them to enter.

Harpis could not help but breathe a sigh of relieved comfort upon entering the familiar office. It had been ten long days since he had last seen Aanaman at the council chamber in Mer, where they had all learned of Turin's fate. It seemed like it was both yesterday and another lifetime altogether on the other side of the week-long adventure since being attacked after leaving Lodestar.

He strode quickly across the office and embraced the governor before turning to Captain Kilannry, who rose from his typical seat and clapped him on the shoulder.

"Gods, but it is good to see you bard!" he said before sitting back down.

"It is indeed good to see you, bard," a weary Shanowen said as she stood from Harpis' usual seat across the small circular meeting table from the captain. She hugged him tightly, holding on a moment longer than he expected.

"He needs you, Harpis. The Wild keep us, we all need you," she whispered in his ear.

She let go and gave him a tight smile before turning to Wren and extending her hand.

"Well met, Death Herald. I am sad to say we have not been formally introduced before," she said.

Wren took her extended hand in his own and placed his forehead on the top of it in a formal greeting Harpis wasn't sure he had ever seen the old gnome make.

"More than well met, Missus Reaper," he said sincerely.

Shanowen gave a slight curtsy to the gnome before facing her husband.

"I'll leave you, gentleman, to the frightful discussion I am sure will soon follow. Bard, Herald, see to it that the people of Ravnice are protected, these two drunks included," she said as she departed.

After his wife left through the door, Aanaman waved at one of the guards in the hallway.

"Get an extra chair for the Death Herald, if you would, before the gnome flirts his way into my wife's chambers," he laughed.

134

A moment later, the guard returned with one of the children's chairs. Harpis could not help but double over as he watched Wren's mouth hang open in outrage. He heard Aanaman's hand slap his forehead, and Captain Kilannry hit the table before shouting at the poor man.

"He's not a child, you horse's ass. The gnome is older than the four of us combined. Get him a proper chair before he turns you to ash where you stand!" he yelled.

The guard ran off, and Wren bowed in thanks to the captain.

"Might as I'd have liked to, it is beyond my abilities to turn your man to ashes, Captain," Wren corrected.

Kilannry sat back in his chair with a snort, "He doesn't know that!" the captain laughed.

The guard swapped the child's chair for one from the dining room and hastily closed the door behind him after bowing in apology to Wren.

Aanaman kicked his bare feet up onto his desk and took a long sip from his whiskey glass.

"Before we discuss the problems I already know about, what fantastical events bring the Death Herald and the God Singer home to Ravnice aboard a Quaji trader catamaran, and why are you dressed like a pirate?" he asked, pointing at Harpis.

Ignoring Wren's laughter, he recounted the events that transpired after Turin's funeral, including the meeting with Tawito and the dead elf's wish to return the Quaji to the island and that he sent word for Tawito to head their way.

Captain Kilannry pointed a finger accusingly at Harpis.

"Just once, bard. One time, could you show up here to visit us out of the blue and when we ask how you have been, might you just answer with normal nicety and not world-altering news?" he asked.

Harpis shrugged at the man before looking at Aanaman, who looked pleadingly at the ceiling for help before raising an eyebrow at the captain.

"What?" the captain asked innocently in reply to the governor's look.

"Every time it is some epic apocalyptic tale, it'd be nice if, for once, we could simply visit and talk about the weather or something. I am just saying!" Kilannry exclaimed.

"For once, we also have something of grave consequence to

share. Nearly three days ago, an armada of ten ships, matching the description of your pursuer, blockaded the Kalt harbor and sank several ships," Aanaman stated.

Wren sat silently in thought for a moment after Aanaman mentioned the vessels.

"Ten more at least then, and by my guessing, those ships could be carrying nearly four hundred crew and fighters each, even if that is all we face, it is quite the force given their abilities we have witnessed," Wren said, shaking his head at Harpis.

With a nod, Aanaman continued.

"Governor Innisgrath sent riders to the elves, Fjall, and here. Four Kalt riders made our ferry station at the Kalt river crossing where Ravnice, Kalt, and Glasduille states meet. Two were given fresh horses and sent sprinting to Fjall. The other two rode a sailing ferry south on the Kalt river before heading north to our harbor. Word of what happened reached us at noon that next day."

Captain Kilannry leaned forward and looked Harpis in the eyes.

"We followed the same advice you gave us two years ago, lad, and made ourselves a harder target for an assault from the sea. We destroyed the docks, moved the harvest and livestock out over the land, sent all the ships in the harbor up the Fjall river to Lake Gitche, and scuttled enough of them across the river to prevent pursuit or use of the waterway against us," he said.

"Wisely done, Captain," Harpis said to the older man before turning to hear Aanaman's response.

"Wise indeed. The next day, elven messengers arrived to tell us that Glasduille would not be drawn out of their borders to support any conflict but also assured me that we could count their border as safe. No enemy will be allowed to traverse their lands," Aanaman answered.

"Well then, Governor Aanaman, what next, and how can we help?" Wren asked.

Aanaman dropped his feet from the desk and sat up, looking from the gnome to Harpis.

"As we have received no further messengers or word from Kalt, I must assume the worst, that they were unable to resist whatever aggression beset them. We now consider our border with our southern neighbors along the Kalt river as hostile. I have sent nearly half our militia regulars to patrol it lest they make it to our lands unnoticed and unabated," the governor concluded.

Harpis nodded in acknowledgment of the sad but sound logic and looked to Wren, who was again deep in thought.

Looking up, the gnome nodded at the governor.

"According to The Syndicate's last assessment, Kalt had maybe two thousand militia, perhaps half that in reserve. Even if it were only the ten ships, the numbers would be at best even, and that isn't counting for this lightning magic and whatever else they have at their disposal," the gnome reasoned.

Aanaman walked around and sat on the front of his desk before continuing.

"By the gods, I don't know why we have yet to see enemy ships here," he finished.

*****

Three days after leaving the soon-to-be embattled Kalt, Sudbina had left her stolen horse to graze on the southern shore of the Fjall river a few miles from where it ran into Ravnice harbor. It was the narrowest the river would get for many miles, and with the autumn sun rising, she knew she wouldn't freeze to death after she swam to the other side.

The water was frigid yet refreshing, and she angled herself rather than swam as the current pulled her down the river and across to the northern edge. Squeezing as much of the cool water from her clothes and satchel as she could, she shivered for long moments until the sun's warmth heated her bald head enough for her skin to stop prickling.

Bathed in the dawn light, the plains that stretched in all directions looked like a carpet of gold. She reached into her satchel with a sigh, pulling forth a reddish-blond wig that would make her appear more local than her others. She began walking towards the city's edge, not putting the damp wig on until it was dry and warmed.

A heavy quiet permeated the city as the dirt road she walked turned to cobbles. She had been to Ravnice during harvest season several times and enjoyed the whir of activity that usually would allow her to weave her way unnoticed as she pleased. Instead, she felt as though she was the only one in the entire city until two militiamen patrolling toward her held up their hands to halt her.

137

"I have never known the streets or men of Ravnice to be so unwelcoming, gentlemen," she said in a sultry voice and smiled as she watched the militiamen exchange bewildered glances.

"Have you not heard, lass? Kalt was attacked several days ago, and our own city is on the watch for threats from the sea and the south," the older of the two stated.

She shook her head in feigned surprise.

"Where might you be heading from?" the other asked.

"I am but a wandering soul, friends. I had always heard Ravnice in the autumn was amongst the most beautiful wonders of Quaj Island, and I can tell you both, your fine state did not disappoint," she said, hoping her compliments would enhance acceptance of her explanation.

The younger guard still looked her up and down with some suspicion.

"And why are you nearly dripping wet walking about all by yourself? You aren't some vagabond on the run, are you?" he probed.

"Good sir, you embarrass me with accusations of such naughtiness," she said in her most playful voice, adding a wink for good measure.

"Leave the poor girl be," the older guard said, shoving his companion into continuing their patrol.

"Find your way to The Siren's Scream at the wharf if you're looking for a nice fire to dry your clothes and a warm meal. Welcome to Ravnice, young lady," he said as they walked past.

"My thanks to its gallant protectors," she said, blowing the older man a kiss. She smiled as he blushed in response and headed for the wharf.

*****

Enky leaned back in his chair with his feet on his desk, gazing at them as he wiggled his toes. The next thing he knew, his tiny domain was home to the winds of a raging gale that blew him from his chair and into the wall across from his portal to the Nexus. He frowned in dismay as forks of lightning surged around him, blasting viewing frames from his wall and desk.

His surprise was short-lived as he got to his feet and looked across his tiny abode at his seething sister.

"Enky!" she shrieked at him, clenching her fists as lightning flickered across her milky skin, and its static had her red mane standing on end.

"Yes, sweet sister?" he asked, standing and brushing wooden frame fragments from his vest.

"You leave my people out of whatever pandemonium you are plotting for the mortal plane!" she shouted, looking down her angrily pointed finger.

He defiantly tucked his hands in his pockets.

"Your people? The Valar haven't made themselves known in Nysia for millennia. I would hardly call the distant descendants of the sea elves that call themselves Tormenta, your people," he said.

"I know your marionette was among them, Enky," she accused.

"Your devout and fervent worshippers don't need my help in seeking out conflict, embracing as they are of your most admirable attributes," he said with a shrug and a grin.

Her hands were shaking in tight fists in front of her. She screamed in unbridled rage, unleashing more gusts of wind and lightning, causing Enky to cringe even though he knew they couldn't harm him.

"Yes! Just like that!" he shouted excitedly as her storm let up.

As she opened her mouth to respond, the stone wall behind her became a portal again, and Daybreak and The Wild walked through it.

"Enough," Daybreak said in a voice that twinkled like tiny bells.

"I, too, am troubled by his actions, but he has not broken the rules, and there is nothing we can do about it here," the blond goddess finished.

He gave a fond smile to the eldest, and she raised a suspicious eyebrow at him as she departed through the portal with her younger twins, and his wall once again became stone.

"It's no wonder the Tormenta are such a miserable and angry bunch!" he said to the wall.

Rolling his eyes, he sat back down in his chair that was once again upright at his desk and happily went back to looking at the scenes playing out in the frames that were once again intact and in place on his desk and wall.

Chapter 16
Keeping With Tradition

Danaeyra roosted like a hawk in the top boughs of a massive pine at the edge of her people's domain. Around her, unseen and unheard in other trees, were the elves of her watch. Word spread throughout the elven state that they should direct unarmed folk fleeing from Kalt north to the border with Ravnice. Armed folk from the south were now considered hostile and in league with the invading foreigners.

As such, she assumed the odd, short-haired, blue-cloaked woman pointing at the tree line and her leather-wearing female escorts were probably invaders. She had free reign to dispose of the mounted women and the armed men who rode ahead of them. Not that she needed more of an excuse to execute the men as they wore the colors of the Kalt family and the uniform of its lumber business. At the formation of Glasduille state, Governor Innisgrath had assured that any of the Kalt family or its employees venturing into their lands were doing so illegally and could be dealt with at the discretion of the elves.

She cupped her hands and made a soft bird call. A moment later, two arrows streaked from other treetops and struck the two men leading the scouting party in the chest. The horses startled, and the foreigners clumsily fell from their saddles. She aimed at one of the women brandishing a crossbow when she saw the cloaked woman hold her hands outstretched while staring skyward with her eyes rolled back in her head.

Danaeyra loosed her arrow and took down the warrior with the crossbow, but as she drew her next arrow, she nearly fell from her branch when lightning surged from the woman's outheld hands and into the trees near her, blasting its top into charred debris. She tried to hold her ear with one hand and plug the other with her shrugging shoulder as the strike, and ensuing thunder, rumbled through the woods.

A second later, a thud from the ground saddened her eyes as she realized it hit a member of her party. She quickly loosed an arrow at the robed woman who was already in the act of summoning another strike. In her haste to shoot, the arrow did not fly true, and it struck the woman in the shoulder instead of mortally wounding her.

The woman collapsed to her knees, screaming hysterically, eyes still rolled back in her head. Instead of grabbing for her wound, she erratically clawed at her temples so hard that blood began pouring down her face.

Stunned as Danaeyra was by the display, she recoiled in further horror when one of the foreigner warriors drew a filet knife from her boot and shoved it under the woman's chin, ending her screams with a gurgle.

*****

It was almost morning by the time Harpis had left Aanaman's home. He walked with Wren to the gnome's house before heading to The Siren's Scream to rent a room. He was so exhausted he slept until noon, waking only when the Kalna had brought him lunch. With food in his belly, he drifted off until the early evening, waking and enjoying the quiet familiarity of the room where he made perhaps the most crucial decision of his life two years ago.

He almost fell from his seat on the bed's edge when a knock on the door interrupted his reminiscing.

"Come on then, your bardliness, we have an obligation concerning some whiskey at our customary table downstairs," Wren said from the other side of the door.

"Coming dear," he muttered, taking his dagger from the nightstand.

Sheathing the weapon in his boot, he opened the door and bowed low to the gnome.

"After you, your holiness," he said, motioning for the gnome to lead towards the stairs.

As they reached the bottom and turned to their table, Harpis noticed the typically empty back section of the tavern was unusually crowded as a young red-haired woman held court over several tables full of hopeful suitors in various stages of drunkenness.

Sliding into their seats, he smiled at Kalna as she placed bread and stew in front of them, followed by two glasses of whiskey.

"Food first, boys, or you'll be too quick to bed, and I won't make as much money off ya," she said with a smile.

A particularly exaggerated laugh from one of the tables drew his attention.

"This place is a bit livelier than I have seen it in quite some time," he said while glancing at the other tables near them.

Kalna looked over her shoulders for a moment and turned back, rolling her eyes.

"That pretty little thing booked a room here this morning, and I don't think a single customer that has come in and seen her has left yet. Who am I to complain, though? If half of Ravnice wants to puff out their chests while guzzling mead and whiskey for hours on end trying to impress her, I'll happily sell it to them," she laughed.

"Would you like me to move you two to the front where it is quieter?" she asked, noticing they didn't share her merriment.

Wren scoffed at the notion.

"Here is a fine, lass. This is our table, and it is where we celebrate surviving another ordeal," the gnome answered.

She raised her eyebrows at Wren.

"And what sort of adventure was it this time? Fighting some huge kraken while at sea or perhaps battling these ghost ships everyone keeps saying will show up and kill us all?" she asked.

Harpis opened his mouth to tell her how close to the mark she was when men started shouting for more drinks behind her.

"If you'll excuse me, duty calls!" she said sarcastically, turning to the other tables.

Looking past Kalna, he noticed the red-haired woman was staring right at him. However, instead of looking away when he met her gaze, she simply smiled and kept on staring.

Wren slouched down and kicked him under the table. "Hey! I think she has plenty of attention already," he said before sitting up and holding up his glass.

"To Gwenolyn," Wren toasted, and Harpis raised his glass in kind.

142

Even as he closed his eyes and took a deep sip of dark Ravnice whiskey, he could feel her still staring at him. By the time he set the glass down and opened them, she had turned back to her attentive admirers. When she began speaking, her unique voice floated above the general din of the tavern.

"Where was I," she asked, holding her finger to her lip pensively.

"Ah yes, there I was in Kalt three summers ago, throwing knives for money with this rough crew of pirates. I didn't have any coin to wager myself, so I told them I was good for the money since I was the captain of this rickety old boat with some stupid sounding name that I'd spotted docked outside. It was called *Sea Goat,* I think. Would you believe I swindled every bit of silver and gold those drunken brutes had! Oh, they were incensed by the time I slipped out of there! They even threatened to hunt down and sink my ship" she said, laughing along with her audience.

Harpis sat in shock, staring at her. He was dumbfounded and in disbelief of hearing the name of the very boat where he first met Wren. Harpis sat unmoving until he was startled by Wren dropping his own spoon, slowly turning to look at the woman as well. She stared unnervingly right back at him for a long moment before tilting her head and looking at Wren with distinct interest and then addressing her audience.

"Well, gentlemen, it has been quite the entertaining day, but it seems my friends have arrived, and we have some private matters to discuss," she said with an apologetic bow.

She then dragged her chair noisily around to sit on the open end of their table.

Harpis felt naked as she looked him up and down before speaking in a voice more intoxicating than the whiskey he had just finished.

"A lady might take offense to being stared at like that by a man who won't introduce himself," she said accusingly.

He could feel his cheeks flush as he stammered in response to her statement.

"I am Harpis. My friend here is Wren," he said, leaving out the details of their positions despite desperately wanting to impress her.

Wren grunted in acknowledgment, picking up his spoon and eating while looking at the woman with unveiled suspicion.

"I am Sudbina," she said, turning to Wren. "I've never met a gnome before. Are you a girl or a boy, Wren?" she asked sincerely.

Dropping his spoon again, Wren stared dumbfounded, mouth agape. Harpis could not recall the last time he had seen the unflappable gnome, a spy for over a century, and chosen of The Sleeper, caught flat-footed in conversation. Harpis snickered at his friend, who looked from Sudbina to his twice dropped spoon as if it betrayed him and then back at the woman.

"I meant no offense, some dwarven women proudly wear a beard, and you are wearing an embroidered dress after all," she explained in an innocent, disarming voice while smiling sweetly.

Wren slowly closed his mouth and narrowed his eyes before going back to eating without answering her.

Harpis did his best to save Sudbina from herself.

"He is over two hundred years old, so I don't know if he would necessarily qualify as a boy, and that is not a dress. Those are the robes of a necromancer," he explained.

"What male wouldn't want to worship a voluptuous nude woman who can't wake up?" she asked rhetorically with an understanding look.

Seeing the rage in his friend's eyes, Harpis made another effort at distraction.

"Sudbina, do you find yourself in Kalt often?" he asked, unsure if she would survive further prodding of the surly gnome.

Before she could answer, Kalna arrived back at their tables with another round of drinks.

"Ah, Sudbina, I see you've met our most famous patrons!" the barmaid said, placing two whiskeys in front of Wren and then him before handing a cup of mead to Sudbina.

"Don't worry, beautiful Kalna, you're still the most interesting person in this tavern," Sudbina said, taking Kalna's hand and the cup in both of hers, lightly caressing the other woman's wrist as she took the mead. Kalna blushed and curtsied before hurriedly going to another guest.

Harpis shook off an unfamiliar feeling of jealousy from observing the exchange. The strange emotion fled when she returned his gaze to him.

"I was born in Kalt City," Sudbina said, finally answering his question.

"What a coincidence! I was born in Kalt too, though in a fishing village near the Fjall mountains, not the city," he said, genuinely pleased to discover their shared history.

Noticing Wren was almost done angrily eating his stew and had already finished his second glass, Harpis decided it best to give him more time to simmer.

"What brings you to Ravnice, Sudbina?" he inquired.

"After the savagely exquisite Tormenta queen rudely had me locked up. I decided I should make an escape and stowed away on one of their galleons they sent to Kalt from some island called Lodestar, and I then made my way out of that state before they got to the business of conquering it," she said casually.

Wren dropped his spoon for the third time, though this time it was purposefully into his empty bowl before slamming his fists on the table and interrogating Sudbina.

"You were aboard the armada that attacked Kalt?" he asked incredulously.

"They hadn't attacked the city while I was there, just a couple of ships like I told you. I left while they sat in the harbor," she said.

Harpis exchanged a look of disbelief with Wren before the gnome continued his questioning.

"How many of them are there? Why are they here? Where does the lightning come from?"

She sat in thought for a moment and then spoke, "They sent about half of their ships to Kalt. The rest are still at that island, for all I know. Their priestesses seem to be able to summon lightning. I am not sure why they came to Quaj, but I can tell you they worship The Siren above all else."

Turning from Wren, she placed her hands on top of his, and Harpis could feel the beckoning warmth of her skin as much as he could see the hunger in her eyes.

"If you want to know more about the wicked women of the sea, I'll be in the room at the end of the hall," she purred.

She stood and gave Wren a short bow.

"Well met Wren, the gnome necromancer," she said before heading up the stairs, accentuating the sway of her hips by slowly taking them one step at a time.

When she was finally out of view, Harpis looked across the table at Wren, who looked just as confused as he felt.

The gnome turned his glass upside down on the table and sat back in his chair.

"By The Sleeper and her dreams, what just happened," he said.

"Do you think she made it up? How could she know about us and the *Sea Goat*?" Harpis asked his friend.

"I've been watching people lie for more than a human lifetime, and I am certain she wasn't. I also did not sense her calling on a magical gift, and she carries no enchanted items. So, she is no more or less dangerous than any other alluring young woman," Wren said with a shrug.

"I should probably do the professional thing and gather as much information as I can from her," Harpis said with a smirk before rising out of his chair.

"Are you sure that's wise?" the gnome asked with a raised eyebrow.

"I think she is as interested in me as I am in her Wren," he responded almost hopefully.

"I think that's just the way she talks to people, lad," Wren said while sliding out of the booth and leaving ample payment on the table.

"Go on then, spymaster Harpis Akkeri, find out what you can. I'll meet you back here tomorrow, and we can take her to see Aanaman," his friend said dismissively as he walked towards the door.

*****

With her clothes puddled at her feet, Sudbina squinted in the candlelight as she bent over and rummaged through her satchel bag.

"So that is the infamous God Singer and his powerful friend The Death Herald," she said to her wigs in feigned fascination.

Normally she clung to information and secrets as one should to such powerful tools. She couldn't resist the temptation, though, and now found herself on the precipice of being in the godlike position of having the power to tip the scales of favor for hundreds of thousands of lives on her own whim.

There was a soft knock from the hall, and she smiled mischievously to herself.

"Took you long enough, get in here!" she called to the door.

*****

Harpis tried not to seem overeager as he flung the door open. He immediately lost all hope of discipline when the light from the hallway spilling into the room revealed every inch of Sudbina's flesh as she bent over a bag on the far side of the room.

"Close the door and get out of those clothes," she commanded.

He quickly closed and latched the door behind him before kicking off his boots and dropping his trousers to the floor. He paused with his tunic pulled over his head to look at her again. Expecting her to have faced or approached him, he was confused at the sight of her still bent over. Her upside-down face had a small blowgun to her lips, and she threw him a wink between her spread legs before her wig fell off as she puffed. He felt a stick in his neck before the room began spinning, and then everything went dark.

*****

Sudbina shook her head as she walked to the snoring Harpis.

"It turns out the hero of Quaj Island is just another predictable man like the rest of them," she laughed.

Crouching next to him, she turned him on his side to make sure his nose wasn't bleeding and propped him up with a pillow from the bed. She then gingerly placed the book she had stolen from the Tormenta in front of his face. Inspecting his belongings, she noticed a knife handle protruding from one of his discarded boots. Drawing it, she admired the engraved depiction of The Siren in its handle.

"A fair and fitting trade, I think," she said to the unconscious bard.

After gazing appreciatively at Harpis' tattoos and muscled frame for a moment, she gave his bare bottom an approving slap and rose to get dressed.

*****

In his apartment above the mortuary, Wren locked the door behind him and walked straight for his comfy chair. He grabbed a bottle, whiskey glass, and shot glass from his eating table and sat them on the arm of the chair before throwing several logs into the empty fireplace. Sitting deep in the human-sized chair, he sighed in satisfaction at the feel of the soft cushions.

Glancing at the unlit wood, he looked at the ceiling hopelessly before snapping his fingers.

"Oh good, we're home," Xissay's nasally voice called out as she floated from a cloud of sulfuric smoke in the air in front of him.

"Get that lit, and I'll pour you a glass," he said, tilting his head in the direction of the fireplace.

"I live to serve," she said sarcastically as she sat amongst the wood that was ablaze within moments.

He rolled his eyes at her and handed her the smaller glass as she sat cross-legged on the arm of the chair.

"I regret to inform you, sweet Xissay, that I may have finally met a female more dangerous than yourself," he said, making a toasting motion at his familiar.

"And where is this devilish demon-lady now?" she asked with an intrigued expression.

"Spending the night in a tavern room with Harpis," he answered with a huff.

The sprite sat back as if appalled.

"And are you not afraid for our fool of a friend?" she gasped sarcastically.

"Bah, he is a grown man, and I am no longer his keeper!" he said, pouring himself more to drink.

"Oh my, you really are worried," she said with sincere concern in her voice.

"Oddly enough, she may be the very reason I met the bard in the first place," he said, still struggling to come to terms with the evening's events.

Xissay stared at him skeptically over the rim of her glass.

"Oh?" she asked.

He shrugged and leaned forward, holding his hands out closer to the fire to warm them.

"There are few alive that could place the bard and me on the ship called *Sea Goat* several years back. I can't concoct a reason for the puzzling young Sudbina to have gone through the lengths of finding that information. Let alone fabricating a situation that let her haphazardly divulge her involvement in the pirates attacking us," he said, scratching at his bare scalp and pouring himself yet another glass.

"I've never known you to believe in coincidence, old gnome," she said with concern.

He slumped back into the chair in frustration and sipped his drink.

"Perhaps I am just not clever enough to divine them, but for now, the machinations that brought her across our paths are beyond my mortal comprehension," he said begrudgingly.

"There, there, Death Herald, I still think you're plenty clever!" she tittered sarcastically.

Chapter 17

Accession

Oluja had not sailed for any length of time away from her two hulled throneship in the years since unification, and she forgot how much she enjoyed the feel of rolling seas afforded by the sleeker galleons. After receiving word of Kalt's surrender from Kisa, she ordered her own four captains that remained at Lodestar to take her to Kalt. She left Duchess Zeln and Duchess Lorent to preside over the seven galleons and throneship at Lodestar, secure in the belief that the two were incapable of undoing her designs, especially while also bickering with each other in her absence.

With dawn rising over the waters of the Kalt harbor, she stood proudly on the steering deck of her senior-most captain's ship, taking in the view of her newly acquired city and the fourteen Tormenta galleons that loomed intimidating at the edge of the harbor.

She turned to the three women behind her and addressed the High Priestess first.

"Impressed, Spavati?" she asked the one woman she made sure not to leave on Lodestar to cause trouble while she was away.

"It seems we had The Siren's favor in battle, and all of our ships still sail," Spavati said, partially dodging the question.

Deciding to deal with the intractable robed woman later, she turned her gaze to her commodore who had been leading her three ships and then to Duchess Morel who had arrived with the rising sun.

"Why were you two with half our assault force when I arrived last night?" she asked, staring down Duchess Morel.

"Why don't you ask your pet admiral that?" the duchess sneered.

Oluja resisted the urge to kill the woman and have her officers throw the body overboard. She had a plan to deal with her list of problematic women, and Morel had several names ahead of hers yet. Best to eliminate enemies from within one at a time to keep the infighting from getting too brutal and messy.

She stepped towards the shorter woman, putting her chest in Morel's face, and forcing her to look up awkwardly.

"I am not asking Kisa, I am asking you, Morel. Forget your place again, Duchess, and you may be forfeiting your Duchy, if not your very life. I am sure the others would be more than happy to divvy up your ships," Oluja cautioned, keeping herself out of directly having to deliver on the threat.

After Morel finally nodded in acceptance of the warning, she stepped back and motioned for a response.

"Kisa sent me with both of my ships to the city of Mer on the eastern coast and sent your three ships to the northern city of Tuath. We went with a minimal crew and some priestesses. We offloaded all our fighters and boats in Kalt for the assault," the duchess complained.

Ignoring Morel's tone, Oluja then turned angrily to her commodore.

"Did you not contest weakening the assault force that I sent to take our people's primary objective?" she asked.

"I did initially, as I also questioned Kisa bringing that land-born rat onboard and hearing him out in the first place, but his information proved correct. We did find fighting ships in both city's harbors and prevented them from surprising our assault forces," the captain answered.

"Land-born rat?" Oluja asked, caught off guard.

"His name is Svenus Kalt, apparently his family once ruled the area. He told us Mer and Tuath cities had the only formal navies and showed us where to find their harbors," Morel explained, spitting at the mention of Svenus.

"It seems Kisa and I have much to discuss," Oluja said, looking across their blockade at her recently promoted admiral's ship.

"And how challenging did you find their naval ships?" she asked the other women.

"They are an embarrassment to the sea they sail upon. We destroyed every ship floating in Mer's harbor and suffered no damage or casualties. They had no stomach for fighting after the first lightning strike. Though it did take several hours, and the priestesses were exhausted," Morel laughed.

Oluja raised an eyebrow at her commodore after Morel finished.

"What of Tuath?" she asked.

The captain shot Morel a glare before answering, "We found around twenty brigantines in the Tuath waters and dealt with them easily. They did put up a fight and damaged the mainmast of one of our ships after ramming it and attempting a boarding. We lost several sailors, but it was more of the same. The priestesses were able to turn the battle quickly."

The news was more than she could have hoped for, and Oluja felt more confident than ever in her plan.

"It would seem our campaign has The Siren's blessing," she said, giving Spavati a cynical smile.

"Duchess Morel, send your ships out to begin patrolling the southern coast of the island. Commodore, signal to Kisa that she has an hour to ensure the wharf and harbor are secure and meet me there. Tell her I plan to berth all seven of my own vessels at the docks to send a message to our new subjects, and I expect her to do the same with her own. Duchess Emni and Vana will face out to sea and intercept any attack should it come," she commanded.

*****

While the crews were busily tying off her seven vessels to the undersized docks of Kalt's wharf, Oluja stood at the protruding bow tip of the one she rode, holding a lone rigging line to keep her balance. Now that she had joined Kisa's vessels at the wharf's edge, the open cobble space looked completely ringed with the railings of many galleons standing several stories high above it, almost entirely blocking the view of the harbor.

She could make out thousands of gathering Kalt citizens trying to catch a view of her arrival from the streets. There were more still in the windows of nearby buildings, but not on the wharf. Kisa had deployed half of their fighting force to ring the waterfront. The scene of a thousand Tormenta raiders projecting their power brought a genuine smile to her face that grew almost feral as she spotted Kisa making her way off one of the docks and onto the wharf with a dozen guards. Throwing a tied-off coil of rope from the bow, she leaped and slid down its length until her boot heels hammered into the flagstones.

She strode forward determinedly, showing her people and her new subjects that she felt no need for personal protection in Kalt. Meeting Kisa's contingent at the center of the deserted wharf, her own guards scrambled to catch her. She stopped and accepted Kisa's bowed greeting.

"Our new city conquered and still largely intact, you have outdone yourself, Admiral Kisa," she complimented.

"It was my honor to deliver it to you and our people," Kisa responded.

"What was the cost of our victory here?" she asked.

"Seventeen dead, most of them men, another thirty wounded. Those too injured to fight are licking their wounds aboard Duchess Vana's ship. The Kalt militia was poorly trained and badly led, and there were no gifted amongst those that joined the fighting, just as Sudbina said. The dead were sailed out to the deep waters and burial rites performed yesterday as the sun set," Kisa answered.

Oluja nodded at the older duchess, honestly impressed.

"Not so much to pay for what we've gained," she stated.

"I would agree. Unfortunately, we did lose a storm priestess and several raiders late yesterday. They were struck with arrows while scouting the border of this state's border with elven lands twenty miles to the northeast," Kisa said, pointing inland.

Oluja tried to keep her surprise and concern from showing across her face.

"Real elves?" she asked.

"Based on what our priestesses know and what the folk here have said, yes. We assume them to be direct descendants of the Walar bloodlines, children of The Wild. Svenus Kalt says they have never cared about human wars and that if we avoid the woodland state that they should not concern us," Kisa said, nodding.

"Ah yes, Morel mentioned that you had found a local pet. I do hope the fraught dalliances of your youth in this very city aren't making you nostalgic, Kisa," Oluja said accusingly.

"I take no ownership over the land-born, nor do I trust him.

But, for now, his needs and wants align with our cause. That is the only reason I suffer for him to live. He sailed out to our blockade the day we arrived, offered to help us take the city. He made good on that, killing the governor, aiding in the assault, and dealing with the loyalist militia captain and his supporters," she replied, seemingly unfazed by the indictment.

"He sounds like an unusually enterprising male specimen indeed," Oluja observed.

"I can have him summoned here if you would like," Kisa offered.

"Do that. You and your guards are dismissed. My thanks for your initiative, Admiral Hadjuk," she finished.

*****

Svenus had observed the morning's dramatic arrival with interest through his office windows. With the return of the five ships that he knew were sent north, he wondered what the state was of the harbors in Mer and Tuath. Worse than his own, he reasoned with a smile. He heard a commotion from the adjacent room followed by long-awaited knocks and what he had come to expect as the typically irritated voice of a Tormenta having to suffer the inconvenience of speaking to a male.

"Let's go, land-born, Queen Oluja Vetar demands your attendance," came the command from the other side.

He opened the door and held up a calming hand to the guard who had knocked on the door and mostly failed at halting the two Tormenta women that were to be his escort.

"After you ladies," he said sarcastically with an obnoxious bow, walking after them as they stormed out of the building. He waved a hand at his men that started to follow.

"If they wanted me dead, boys, I'd have been worm-food long ago."

As they made their way from the far end of the wharf, he whistled at the emptiness of the usually bustling area. Trying to keep up with the briskly marching escorts, he shook his head at the impressive display the blue sailed galleons made while moored to the docks with their bow tips shading the sea wall. The queen stood proud and alone at the center of it all, dressed in the same revealing gown and white fur-lined, blue cloak Duchesses

Hadjuk wore.

His two female escorts knelt when they were a few paces from her. He involuntarily joined them on his knees when one of them noticed he still stood and slapped him in the groin. They dragged him back to his feet after she motioned for them to rise, and he kicked his heel into the ground to stay the pain in his belly and crotch while doing his best not to wince.

"You are dismissed," she commanded the other two women, who looked at each other and then to Svenus questioningly.

"If the land-born were to attack me, the short moments of his death would be the most fun I've had in years," she said confidently.

The two bowed and joined the forces around the wharf, well out of earshot. As Queen Oluja faced him, he hoped that the same methods that had worked well with Kisa would prove effective with this woman. Those in positions of power only acknowledged those that lived with the same arrogant confidence. Where the petite Kisa had been the visage of disciplined martial beauty, he found the queen, who was perhaps even taller than he, to be the embodiment of feminine authority.

"You went through a lot of trouble to claim some of the very land you so disdain," he said, clasping his hands behind his lower back, hoping to appear unafraid.

"My disdain is for weak people, coddled by the comfort of living far from the reach of the sea and her temper," she answered, looking him up and down.

"You're the big fish then," he said unimpressed, inwardly wondering how far he could push her.

While he was still learning how the Tormenta operated, he needed no lessons on hierarchy. Hierarchy he understood completely, and he knew full well that his borderline disrespect would have already resulted in physical abuse had her inferiors still been about to witness it.

"No, Svenus Kalt. I am the biggest fish," she said matter-of-factly.

"What does that make me to you then?" he asked.

"Useful. For now," Oluja replied, taking several steps to stand almost nose to nose with him.

"How would you assess my position in this city and beyond?" she asked, crossing her arms.

Svenus knew when he was being tested. He also knew that this was likely his only opportunity to prove his worth. Lesser men would have averted their gaze and gushed over the irrefutable dominance of the Tormenta to their queen. Svenus had pursued power for decades, both within the shadows and directly. For this task, he was more than ready.

He looked at the sky thoughtfully for a moment before looking back into Oluja's piercing blue eyes.

"You have your city, its wharf, and harbor. The governor that would have resisted you is dead, as is his problematic militia captain. Most of those left in this city answer to me loyally or begrudgingly and simply want to carry on with their miserable lives whether you lot were here or not. Some folks want to leave. So far, they are being kept in line by my patrols and the presence of your fighters. If I am honest, though, I think you should allow those that wish to flee to do so," he stated.

She took a step back, considering what he had said with a curious look.

"Why?" was all she said.

"Let them leave as refugees, spreading fear of your people to the rest of the island. In addition, it might make it harder on the leaders of the other states to convince their people they should jointly respond to your presence here, and you'll have to spend less energy policing disgruntled citizens," he answered.

Oluja nodded at his logic, and he sighed in relief.

"What of these other states? And the elves?" she pressed.

"The elves live a thousand years. They have no problem waiting for you, me, our children, or grandchildren to die. They'll not suffer war on their lands if we don't force them. The only border you need to worry about if you control the seas is the one with Ravnice along the northern thirty or so miles of the Kalt river. There is a stone bridge at the southernmost point of that border where most trade flows. I'd send a show of force there to make them think twice about a response," he recommended.

"Should I be concerned about the forces boasted by this Ravnice?" she said, intrigued.

Svenus chuckled, "I don't know if boasted is the right word. Governor Reaper is a former farmer and advocates for pacifism before anything else. Their militia is maybe as big as what you have here under my leadership. The dwarves could be a problem, and they would be allowed to march through Ravnice and cross into your lands, but as of, yet I doubt you've done enough to motivate that sort of response from them," he answered.

"By all accounts, and my own observation, you would have made quite the woman, Svenus Kalt," Oluja said without taking her eyes off him.

He opened his mouth to respond, but she cut him off.

"Retire to your people and continue your patrols. I will summon you again soon to aid in fortifying the city and the borders you mentioned, as well as loading several of my ships with supplies," she said, dismissing him.

Chapter 18

Abetment

With The Syndicate gone and her service to the organization an afterthought, Ezera would have felt completely safe with her Daybreak-given gift and her wits to protect her. She had even more reason to feel at ease, given that she was traveling with Governor Ingar Hammersmith and Stone Mage Lorkin. However, the news of the blockade in Kalt had set Fjall on war footing and it seemed like every blind bend in the river potentially held unknown enemies.

Every available river ferry had been loaded and launched under cover of darkness that following evening. It had been a surreal experience floating in silence down the Fjall river for two days with two-hundred-fifty armed and armored dwarven warriors. Even with the considerable guard escort, she constantly scanned for threats and the dwarves were ever checking weapons and armor.

As the small flotilla came around the final bend and the Ravnice river portage came into view, she let out a sigh of relief.

"That was a surprisingly and thankfully uneventful journey," she said quietly to herself.

"I am thinking there will be surprising events aplenty in the coming days, lass," Ingar said gruffly, walking to the bow with Lorkin to stand beside her.

"I fear the people of this island may soon lament that their watchers in the shadows are no more," the mage said, patting her shoulder.

"I wish Turin were still here," she said, and both dwarves nodded in agreement.

"Might be a good idea for you and your former associates to

meet," Ingar suggested.

"If any of them are in Ravnice, I plan to," she stated.

Lorkin grunted a laugh, "That death worshiping gnome may have left The Sanctum on a mission to spread the word of his sleeping goddess, but I'll be a goat's uncle if he isn't spending harvest season at his home here. Never known him to miss the barreling and bottling festivities," the dwarf said with a smile.

As they were thrown ropes from dockworkers and militiamen crowding the river's edge Ingar turned to her.

"I'd imagine Gwenolyn will have found her way here as well once Kalt warned her people. Go on ahead of us and see if the gnome is about and meet us at the governor's" he said.

*****

Rubbing the sleep from his eyes and donning his robes, Wren headed downstairs to answer the knocking at the door of his long-shuttered mortuary office.

"Have any luck seducing the young vixen and revealing her secrets then?" he sleepily asked as he opened the door.

He stopped, mouth still open in surprise as he looked from the white cleric robes and black vicar stole to the smiling face and raised eyebrow of the blond-haired, blue-eyed former Syndicate Hand in Mer.

"I am afraid not Wren, seducing young vixens was never really my thing," Ezera laughed.

"I don't think it's Harpis' thing either, but I'll be damned if the lad wasn't keen on trying," he said.

"Harpis is here too?" she asked, her face brightening.

"He was when I left him last night at The Siren's Scream anyways," he replied.

"Has Gwenolyn arrived too? I imagine she would have headed this way as we did upon hearing about the Kalt blockade. The four of us should join Ingar and Aanaman."

Wren hung his head for a moment before looking up at the sun and realizing that it had been dawn for some time already.

"Gwenolyn is with Turin and The Sleeper now, Ezera," he said sadly, squeezing her hand.

The constant threat of death from their former occupation may have dulled her to the surprise of such news, but he saw and

159

shared the heavy burden in her eyes.

"How?" She asked.

"Walk with me to the wharf so we may collect the bard, and I'll tell you all that has happened in the two weeks since Turin's funeral," he said.

Locking his front door, he motioned for her to follow. It took almost the entire walk to tell her of the meeting with Tawito, how they had been chased and attacked after leaving Lodestar and how they had met the deranged troll and made their way back from the eastern atolls.

Her blond curls tossed around her shoulders as she shook her head in amazement.

"I have a thousand questions, but I am guessing Ingar will too, so I will save them for our little council," she said, opening the door to The Siren's Scream.

"Age before beauty," she said in a grinning attempt to lighten the mood.

"Such respect," he replied with a snort and entered the dimly lit tavern, waving in greeting to Kalna.

"Good morning, a table and breakfast for two?" she asked.

"I am afraid we are in a bit of a rush, but if there are any fresh loaves, I will take one, please and thank you. Has the bard been down yet?" he replied, looking around the nearly empty bar area.

"I have not seen him or Sudbina since they went up together last night," she answered with a laugh as she headed into the kitchens.

"Sudbina?" Ezera asked, following him up the stairs.

"Hard to explain, that one," he answered honestly, kicking the door to Harpis' room.

When there came no reply, he tried the handle and was surprised to find it unlocked and swung the door open to reveal an empty room.

"I believe she said hers was the one at the end of the hall," he said.

When they reached it, he placed his ear against the door and heard snoring from the other side.

"Harpis! Wake up, ya daft idiot!" he shouted while knocking on the door. When the snores continued, he tried the handle and found it locked. Looking over his shoulder, he fished in his robe pockets for his lockpicks.

160

"We'll make quite the pair of criminals, The Death herald himself and the Vicar of Daybreak's Diocese in Fjall, locked up by the local militia for burglary," Ezera said, laughing and crossing her arms.

"Keep watch then if you're so concerned," he said grumpily and turned back to the door, making quick work of the lock.

"There," he said, giving her a smug look and returning the tools to his pocket.

"I bet your friend the barmaid would have just given you the key," Ezera said with a laugh.

"Bah," he said, turning the handle and swinging open the door.

They both startled in surprise when the door was halted with a thud only halfway open and heard Harpis groan from the floor.

"You all right, lad? Have a bit too much fun last night?" he asked.

Walking into the room Wren immediately burst into laughter.

"What's so funny?" Ezera asked, following him in.

"His bottom is as white and pale as Daybreak's dawn," she laughed with a raised eyebrow while looking upon the nude bard.

"Ezera, when did you get here? How long have I been asleep?" Harpis asked, lifting his face from a puddle of drool.

He then confusedly rolled towards them before easing into a sitting position, pulling his trousers back on and then his boots.

"Where is my knife?" he asked before turning his head to look around and grabbing his shirt.

Wren walked up to the sitting man and stared hard for a moment before pricking what looked like a tuft of feathers from Harpis' neck. He examined the dart with amusement and ran his finger down its length and licked it. He quickly spat and wiped his fingers off as his tongue immediately began tingling.

"I'd say your assailant has made off with your knife, lad," he laughed.

"I am starting to recall visions of a nude blowgun wielder now that you mention it," he said drowsily, "and I think she was wearing a wig."

"What gave that away, Spymaster? I thought all red-haired women had dark brown eyebrows," he chided.

"My intuition tells me that eyebrows are not the features of this mysterious woman that he was observing," Ezera said,

161

bending down behind him and picking up a blue-dyed leather book from the floor.

"What's that," Wren asked?

She turned it over in her hand and flipped through several pages.

"It looks like a religious text. The first section is titled Tormenta, Daughters of the Valar," she said

"Tormenta? That is what Sudbina said the foreigners called themselves," Wren said, taking the text from her.

"We can read it while we walk. The Governors of Fjall and Ravnice are expecting us across the city, that is, if his lordship, Harpis the bard, is ready to go.

*****

When Aanaman's house came into view, Harpis let out a whistle at the sight of a quarter of Fjall's army clogging the entire street in front of it. As they passed through, they greeted and embraced several of the warriors they recognized before being let through the gate by a local militiaman and entering the mansion.

Shanowen greeted them with a smile and pointed towards the dining room before shooing her daughters back upstairs. Harpis nodded in thanks, and the three of them headed towards the din of gruff dwarven voices.

"Nice of you three to decide to join us," Ingar joked before becoming more serious.

"My condolences on the loss of Gwenolyn. Aanaman caught me up on your trials at sea," he said sincerely.

Aanaman disappeared into the hall and came back bearing two more chairs. They joined the Governors, Captain Kilannry, Lorkin, and another dwarf Harpis did not immediately recognize at the now crowded table.

"Apologies for the cramped space. I usually don't hold council meetings in my dining room," Aanaman said, retaking his seat at the head.

Captain Kilannry laughed at the statement.

"It might as well be a council chamber. We have got a mage, vicar, bard, the Death Herald himself, and two out of six Governors," he said.

Ingar silenced the table with a raised hand.

"I think most of you have met Stone Mage Lorkin. Beside him is Commander Shatter-Hand. He leads First Company, that'd be our escort outside. He is my most senior commander, second to General Shieldborn. I would have brought Okliff, but he is overseeing Fjall while I am gone. The Sleeper help them. Ezera is vicar of our newly built diocese and often represents the interests of the few scattered human communities across Fjall state," he said, motioning to each as he introduced them.

Captain Kilannry gave Ezera an odd look.

"How did a nice lady like yourself fall in league with Wren and Harpis?" he asked jokingly.

Harpis tensed, and he could feel Ezera and Wren do the same. He exchanged a glance with her and addressed the room.

"It should go without saying that what we discuss here today should, with the utmost discretion, be kept amongst ourselves," Harpis stated.

Turning to Ezera, he spoke more quietly, "I trust Aanaman and Kilannry with my life," he said comfortingly.

She nodded and calmly placed her hands on the table and answered the captain's question.

"In truth, good sir, I was a member of The Syndicate, its senior operative in Mer."

"Perhaps not so nice a lady then, eh? All the same, if I am honest, it would be nice to have more than the three of you left at a time like this," Kilannry said, taking the surprise in stride.

Ingar looked across to Aanaman and brought them back on topic.

"Governor Reaper, it appears we have both received the same troubling news of the blockade in Kalt by lightning hurling, blue-sailed galleons. That was made worse by the news you received from riders from Mer that their ships and harbor were destroyed by a pair of the same sort of ships," the dwarf stated.

"What is also troubling is that there has been no information to follow from Jaeryl Innisgrath and no Kalt citizens seen fleeing into our lands. I assume the worst, that Kalt has fallen. I received word this morning passed to our patrols by an elven scout yesterday. She said that the foreigners and some men from Kalt rode out to their border. A robed woman among them called forth lighting and killed one of their groups before being struck non-fatally with an arrow while attempting to do so again. The elf said

163

the woman screamed as if she'd gone mad and her companion killed her, perhaps out of mercy. That is the only information we have," Aanaman said, nodding.

Wren kicked his leg under the table, and Harpis coughed to interrupt the discussion.

"What is it, bard? Aanaman asked.

"We have come across some information from a source that was previously in Kalt and among the foreigners. They call themselves the Tormenta. They worship The Siren, and their ten ships in Kalt harbor are perhaps half their full armada. Allegedly the other half is at Lodestar Island. The method in which I gathered this information is, a, uh, long discussion for another time as I do not want to detract from the business at hand," he said, trying to ignore Ezera smirking next to him.

Wren then produced the leatherbound book and tossed it to Lorkin.

"It would seem their magical gift is goddess-given and not inherited, so they are more akin to Ezera or me than a mage. I flipped through that briefly. It appears they consider those born with gifts a corruption and do not allow them to conjure or enchant with elements under penalty of death. According to them, the only acceptable gift is the one their goddess bestows. Based on what the elves told Aanaman, they would seem to have the same danger as any of us in actively using our gifts," he said to the orange-robed dwarf.

"Yet another thing to be discussed in Mer," Lorkin replied, examining the book.

"What is in Mer?" Harpis asked.

Aanaman smiled at him from across the table.

"Before you decided to grace us with your presence, we had been discussing how to proceed in protecting our border. It goes without saying we need to meet with the other governors if possible. With Mer sending word asking for a meeting, I assume they also sent riders north and that we should have many of the island's representatives at this emergency council. Stone Mage Lorkin intends to consult with the Arch Mage about temporarily suspending the laws of the college," he answered.

Ezera looked across to the dwarves with great interest.

"I would like to come with you and talk with the new Exarch about the involvement of the clerics in whatever is to come as well," she asked.

"Of course, Ezera. We leave tomorrow morning. We will ride with Aanaman and a small guard escort. Commander Shatter-Hand will stay here with most of our warriors and assist Captain Kilannry. They will help the Ravnice militia train, drill, and watch the border along the Kalt river, north of Glasduille. I agree with Aanaman's assessment that we can count on at least no attack making its way at us from along the elven border," Ingar stated.

Captain Kilannry nodded at the dwarven governor before explaining.

"Our primary concern is the trade road bridge. It is big enough for them to move forces into our lands quickly. Perhaps the most suitable way for them to invade since we blockaded the river and sent our ships to the lake. When the governors head out tomorrow, we plan to go up there in force and see what we may see of the enemy and secure it," he said.

Aanaman drummed his fingers before speaking to the three of them at the end of the table.

"Which brings us to the last thing. Ingar and I can't speak for the other states and certainly not for all the people of the island. Still, at least until we rid ourselves of these invaders, we would like to sanction you to operate as you once did, with impunity and with our blessing within the borders of Ravnice, Kalt, and Fjall if necessary," he said gravely.

"You'll have to figure out a new place to operate from with these Tormenta folk at your old island and the seas no longer safe. The three of you talk it over tonight, and Ezera can debrief Aanaman and me on our way north," Ingar suggested, looking directly at Ezera.

Looking from Wren to Ezera, Harpis decided he might as well bring up the Quaji to the Governors now.

"Speaking of speaking for people, there is one other item that needs discussing at your council meeting. One that may allow us to have allies that are still sailing the seas, allies that these Tormenta would not know we have."

"Get on with it then, Harpis the diplomat," Aanaman said, bidding him continue.

"At Turin's funeral we received a message to meet one of his contacts at Lodestar. Ingar and Ezera returned the morning after the burial rites, but the late Gwenolyn, Wren, and I stayed. The man we met is a Quaji native named Tawito. Unfortunately, when we left that meeting, we were tracked and attacked by an advance ship of the Tormenta. Tawito was an operative of Turin's around the island and off on the eastern atolls where the three Quaji tribes now live," Harpis said, trying to gauge Aanaman's reaction.

"And?" the governor prodded

"And Turin was working to unite the three exiled Quaji tribes for almost as long as he tried shifting the states of this island to democratic rule. He had the eventual hope of bringing the Quaji back to this island. If the Tormenta prove to pose a mortal threat to this island, then allying with the Quaji to defeat them at the cost of bringing them back to the island they once called home seems like a fair price and a strong proposition for all concerned," he said with as much confidence as he could.

Captain Kilannry slapped the table, startling everyone.

"The silver-tongued bard talks more like a politician than either of you ever have!" he said with a laugh at Aanaman and Ingar's expense.

Aanaman sat back in his chair with his arms crossed, waiting for his militia captain to stop laughing at his own humor before speaking.

"Discussions with this Tawito, your newfound knowledge of the Quaji tribes, and your yet-identified source from Kalt with information on the Tormenta. It seems to me that you haven't been waiting for our blessing to continue your work in the shadows," Aanaman said with a raised eyebrow.

"It was more accidental and opportunistic stumbling into information than spying, to be honest," Harpis replied.

"We will propose this as an option in Mer if Ingar also agrees," Aanaman stated.

"I do indeed," the dwarf answered.

Harpis noticed Wren sitting back in the chair beside him and looked down to see his friend smiling.

"Harpis and I will join your little excursion to the border tomorrow then, if you don't mind," the gnome requested to no argument.

Lorkin stood from his seat and handed the book across the table.

"Before the three of you have your little gathering of puppet masters, I think it would be prudent for the four of us to spend

166

some time going through this before we head north. I'll need as much information about them as possible before I have a hard conversation with the Arch Mage."

Wren took the book and tucked it into his robe before answering the mage.

"We can meet in my apartment after we finish here," the gnome agreed.

Captain Kilannry was the next to rise and gave the room a slight bow.

"If our gracious host and revered guests will excuse us, Commander Shatter-Hand and myself have some military matters to attend to and some troops to find barracks for," he said.

After the two of them left, Harpis met Aanaman's gaze across the table.

"I wasn't aware we had enough spare barracks to accommodate two hundred or so dwarves," Harpis said in mock concern.

"Oh, I have a feeling that these new barracks Captain Kilannry speaks of are likely to resemble many of the taverns and inns across the city," Aanaman said, turning to Ingar.

"I not only appreciate the military assistance you have brought to my city but the economic contribution as well," he finished with a smirk.

"The lads are bad enough when there is only ale around, but if they get enough of that corn whiskey of yours in their bellies, we may return to a city in ruins, I fear," Ingar chuckled.

Chapter 19

Retribution

Harpis had been part of several gatherings of the island's most impressive and influential folk. From strategizing with Wren and Turin on how to undo Sirul Amun, to the council he had just participated in, he felt like he was more observer than participant.

This afternoon in Wren's small apartment, though, he represented magically gifted bards everywhere. He hoped his three years of experience, and the twice-sung name of a goddess, made him useful in the coming discussion. Wren and Lorkin both had centuries of experience in using their gifts, and Ezera was held in Daybreak's highest favor.

The four of them made their way up to Wren's apartment, and the gnome ushered them in. He shut the door behind them before walking to his small table and picking up a bottle.

"Welcome to my home away from The Sanctum, Lorkin. What is it that you need us to tell you about our gifts before you head north to Mer?" he asked while searching for glasses.

"I was hoping we would do more than simply talk, and I am thinking we ought to forgo the whiskey until later," the dwarf responded.

Wren set the bottle back on the table and gave Lorkin a curious look.

"Meaning what exactly?" he asked the dwarf.

"Meaning that we face an enemy with unexplored and poorly understood goddess-given gifts. During The War of Magi, it was only a mage's gift that wrought destruction and devastation. I am the only mage left living who has used my inherited abilities in battle. Not just to fight, but to fight other mages," he said, pausing, "and unfortunately to kill," he finished.

Harpis was beginning to understand the gravity of what they were discussing, and it was apparent Wren and Ezera had too. Wren walked over to one of the shelves next to his fireplace and grabbed a few tomes.

"You are wanting to see how the inherited gift of mages feels and works amongst and against goddess-given powers such as my own and Ezera's," the gnome reasoned.

Lorkin nodded in agreement and pointed at Harpis.

"I'd like to see how your performances might interact as well if there is anything you can think of that would be appropriate, bard," he requested.

What Benali had said about *Clario's Cacophony* came to mind, and Harpis smiled.

"I do, but I don't think you'll enjoy it. Even if it doesn't work, it sounds awful. I am afraid too that my fiddle was lost when the Tormenta attacked us at sea," he said sadly.

Wren walked over to the door, awkwardly holding the hefty tomes.

"We are certainly not destroying my tidy apartment with magical sundering. We can do that down in the basement. I have a violin you can use, Harpis," he said and bid them follow.

When they arrived back on the first floor and Wren had him unlatch the door down into the first level of the basement where the gnome prepared corpses for burial, Harpis paused for a moment, realizing the potential source of the instrument.

"Wren, I don't know if I would feel comfortable playing something you filched off one of your dead customers," he said.

They took the stairs with Ezera's laughter and the gnome's grumbling curses echoing off the stone basement. Reaching the preparation room, Harpis saw only a small workbench and a table meant to hold bodies in the middle with several old coffins leaned against the far wall.

"Lorkin, Harpis, if you wouldn't mind taking the table upstairs, so we have some room," Wren requested.

Putting the tomes on his workbench the necromancer climbed onto the stool.

When Harpis followed Lorkin back into the preparation room, Wren pointed at the coffin in the far corner.

"The violin is in there," he said, pointing and not looking up from his texts.

169

Harpis hesitated for a moment, and the gnome grumpily slammed the book he was perusing.

"It's not from the deceased, you thankless singing idiot. I had it made for you months ago and hid it there until I had the chance have it enchanted!" he said gruffly.

Walking over to the coffin, Harpis slowly opened it and reverently took the instrument and bow out, examining them in the growing glow of candles Wren and Ezera were lighting and placing. It was made from the purest black ebony wood, and as he turned it in his hands, the candlelight danced and flickered off dozens of tiny pearl inlaid stars across its top plate, and along its neck was an inlay of The Sleeper.

"Wren, it's stunning. I don't know how to thank you," he said.

"Stop calling it a damn fiddle and consider us even," the gnome said with a huff.

After hopping down from the stool, Wren walked to face Lorkin.

"Unfortunately, the closest thing to these Tormenta priestesses, if their gift is from The Siren, would be a druid or shaman who worships her twin sister The Wild. However, theirs is a singular faith, without congregation, rules, or specific holy sites. Aside from a troll several days sail from here I don't know about quickly finding another or convincing one of the elves to join us. So, it would seem you have only myself and Ezera. What did you have in mind?" he asked.

"Before Ezera and I go and see about our fellow clerics and mages joining in fighting, I need your help with something. I would like to see how the elements and a cleric's Bulwark fare against each other and similarly a necromancer's gift," Lorkin said, walking to the other side of the room and bidding for Wren to join him.

"What about me?" Harpis asked.

"We will get to know your peculiar abilities later, but for now, stand behind Ezera. You're going to be our target, so leave your new toy on the workbench so it doesn't get broken. If her bulwark does not stop our efforts, she should have an easier time concentrating and unweaving her connection to it as you will be the one experiencing our effects and not her," Lorkin explained.

With a resigned look, Harpis made his way behind Ezera, and

the blond woman winked at him.

"Don't worry your pretty head, Harpis. I won't let the big bad dress-wearing dwarf and gnome hurt you," she laughed before closing her eyes. Slowly she brought her hands in a circle from her side and then straightened them before her with her palms out and facing Wren and Lorkin. Where he could usually feel a faint tug at his senses when others used their gifts, he felt nothing.

"Ready, lass?" Lorkin asked her with a grin at Harpis.

She gave a slight nod, and Harpis watched as the orange-robed dwarf dropped to one knee on the stone floor, put his palm on the ground and began muttering an enchantment. A moment later, a small pillar of stone rose beneath his palm until it was waist-high, and then Lorkin placed his other palm vertically on the pillar. The stone bent and flowed slowly towards Harpis and Ezera like a miniature battering ram.

Despite its slow approach and small size, Harpis still cringed as it closed and then winced as he felt the stone contact an invisible barrier in front of Ezera like a hammer striking a gong.

"Good for more, lass?" Lorkin asked in a slow and distracted voice.

"Much more," she said in a similar tone through gritted teeth.

Lorkin then pulled his hands apart, and the vertical portion of the manipulated stone grew as big as a tree trunk between them. The increased width surged forward from that base and over the narrower initial formation. Finally, it slammed into her bulwark like an avalanche with much greater speed than the first time.

Harpis stared in wonder at the display, and after a moment, Lorkin opened his eyes and took his hand from the stone, which retreated like melting ice back into the basement floor. Ezera relaxed her hands and looked back at him confidently.

"See," she said, turning to Harpis, "nothing to worry about."

"How did it feel?" Lorkin asked her.

"It was intense, but not overwhelming. Still, if something were to distract me from holding the barrier together, I can tell I would be in a race to pull my mind from it before it shattered," Ezera answered.

"That is similar to what I felt. It is also my experience when I have sparred against the elements of other mages. It would seem the older texts may be right about some of the uniformity between gifts of devotion and blood," the dwarf said.

171

"Care to try again?" asked Wren before taking Lorkin's place directly across from him and Ezera.

"Surely," she said.

"I'll first try sending my familiar through your barrier at the bard, and then I have another experiment I want to try," the gnome said, drawing forth his necromancer scythe and snapping his fingers.

"I won't say this is the oddest company and situation I have been summoned forth into, Wren, but it is close," the undead fire sprite said, looking around the basement.

Ezera resumed her palm out position, and Wren pointed across at Harpis.

"Fly straight at the bard and burn a hole in his trousers and I will let you finish the whole bottle of Reaper vintage we stole from the Governor's cellar all by yourself," the gnome said, pointing at Harpis before closing his eyes himself.

Harpis cringed again as Xissay sped towards him, cackling madly, her tiny hands ablaze.

She bounced off Ezera's bulwark with an undignified thud and then turned to Wren, who had his eyes back open and was smiling.

"That is a dirty trick, old gnome," she said, floating over towards him threateningly. Wren dismissed Xissay and she said several curses in a language Harpis did not understand as she faded.

"I'll be right back!" the gnome said, disappearing down the second set of stone stairs into the deeper basement where he had once stored corpses. A moment later he reappeared carrying a jar the size of his chest. Walking it over and setting it in front of Harpis' feet with a grunt, he unscrewed the lid and walked back over to the other side of the room.

Harpis looked down into the liquid-filled jar and could make out fur and paws.

"Wren is that a dead cat?" he asked, afraid of the answer.

"Unless cats can breathe embalming oil, then yes, I presume it to be dead. All right Ezera, once more if you please," he asked.

When Ezera had raised her bulwark, Wren closed his eyes and began murmuring while clutching his scythe in both hands. After a few moments of palpably building magic, the cat remained unmoved.

Ezera relaxed as she let go of her bulwark and looked curiously behind her at Harpis and the unmoving cat.

"I did not sense anything passing through or touching my bulwark," she said in surprise.

"It was almost as if I could not sense the corpse on the other side," Wren said, closing his eyes again as if in thought.

Harpis screamed in surprise when the feline corpse came to life and leaped from the jar at him. Without thinking, he kicked it into the wall before glaring around the room at the laughter of the other three.

"So, cleric's bulwarks can also stop goddess-given magic from being channeled through them. Let us hope that applies to Tormenta gifts as well," Lorkin said after scratching his beard and then walked over to the workbench to retrieve the violin and bow and brought it to Harpis.

"All right, lad, how about you give us a performance," Lorkin asked.

Taking the violin, he looked from Ezera to Wren and then to the dwarven stone mage.

"You're not going to like this, and if it works at all like Benali thought when he taught it to me, there is a chance it could destroy your ability to maintain control over your gifts," he cautioned.

Ignoring their scoffs, he continued.

"I will begin playing, weaving my gift through the song from the first note. I'll play for a few verses and give you three ample opportunities to try summoning your bulwark, reanimating your cat, and manipulating the stone," he said.

Giving them a nod, he placed the bow across the strings and clenched his jaw against the awfulness to come.

He began sawing the violin strings with the vigorous and jarring motions required to dictate the disorganized and haphazard notes of *Clario's Cacophony*. As he played, he could not resist grimacing at the awkward rises and falls of his wailing violin strings. When he stopped, he noticed all three of his companions cringing and shuddering.

"Don't you dare use that beautiful thing to make such ugly raucous ever again, bard!" the gnome threatened.

"It worked!?" he asked them excitedly, looking down to see the cat's corpse lying where he had kicked it against the wall earlier.

"I could not shape stone," Lorkin confirmed, and Ezera also gave him a nod.

Wren rummaged through his workbench for a moment before producing some gauze and handing it to Ezera.

"Shove that in your ear and try shielding us from the bard's abuse," he said, and she joined him and Lorkin across from them.

When he saw Ezera's palms, he played again and smiled despite the auditory assault of his song when he saw the dwarf and gnome were obviously frustrated.

"That is enough experimentation for now," Wren said before looking up at Lorkin to explain.

"When the Tormenta attacked us at sea, Xissay crashed into a sort of lightning barrier, and I was so surprised I almost went mind lost. It appears gifted barriers, at least those of Daybreak's clerics, cannot defend against the songs of bards," Wren stated.

"Let's just hope they don't have an abundance of gauze. I had no issues maintaining the bulwark and did not feel anything," Ezera said with a grin.

Lorkin chuckled and headed for the stairs.

"I leave you three to your talk of espionage. Ezera, I will meet you just after dawn at the Governor's house for our departure to Mer. We can discuss our plans for persuading the Exarch and Arch Mage while we ride north," he finished.

*****

Harpis appreciated the reprieve before the coming storm as Wren, Ezera, and he sat around the gnome's fireplace in the late evening hours enjoying supper and now a drink together.

Ezera stared thoughtfully into her glass before looking up at them.

"That was quite interesting using my bulwark to stop the magic of others. We first learn how to stop things like arrows and weapons. Halting the flow of magic was more theory than anything else until now. It was easy to construct the single face of its panes, like a wall of windows in my mind. I wonder how I would fare if I had to construct a dome of glass and protect from all directions," she said thoughtfully.

"Let us just hope that we don't need you to try," Wren said, sipping his own glass in a toast before continuing.

"I know you must leave, but before you do, I just wanted to make sure the three of us agree on our priorities. We are now the hands, eyes, and navigators all at once, and there are only the three of us. As far as I see it, we have three missions. We need to find out what Turin's messages in the archives say. We must learn more of our enemy, and we should ultimately try and help bring the Quaji back to Quaj Island," he stated.

"I will do my best to find out that information in Mer while we are there if we have time, but Turin's final words may have to wait for safer times," Ezera said.

Harpis did not disagree with what his friend outlined, and it appeared Ezera did not either.

"As for the Quaji and potentially defeating this enemy, hopefully Tawito receives our message," Wren said.

"Any thoughts on additional members? Unfortunately, I usually only meet with the sick and work with Ingar's son Dobry. I doubt he would approve of us enlisting his son as an operative, but he did have his workers build us several sub-basements in the Fjall Diocese from which we can operate," Ezera said.

"Mahala has wandered pretty much every foot of this island. She might just be sick enough of Bravit's pestering to work with us in the shadows," Harpis said, looking at the pensive Wren.

"Ezera, if you run into Acolyte Jabruelle Kalt in Mer, he may be of use to us as well. He has been attempting to increase the worship of The Sleeper across the towns and cities of the island. He much prefers adventure to The Sanctum," the gnome said.

"Sounds like another certain goddess worshiper I know," Ezera said with a laugh.

"That accusation is a bit hard to stomach coming from yourself, Ezera," the gnome responded.

"Jabruelle would be very helpful as long as he is more loyal to your goddess and you than his family name," Harpis said.

Wren spat into his fireplace, and there was a slight flare as his wasted whiskey caught fire.

"That boy was disowned long ago and has never had a love for his family or the state you and he were born and raised in," Wren said, pointing at him.

Harpis raised his hands in peace at his friend, and the gnome filled his glass and went on.

"Ezera to Mer then, and us two will join the excursion to the

175

trade bridge tomorrow. We will grow our ranks when we can and codify our operations when this is over. Namely to prevent the compartmentalization and abuse of power that would lead to another Sirul," the gnome said.

Ezera stood and gave them a slight bow.

"On that, gentlemen, we agree. I wish you safe travels tomorrow. I shall see you in a few days," she said.

"You as well," Wren and he echoed in unison as she left.

*****

Sudbina ran a hand through her short and stiff hair and checked the button at the top of her tunic collar. Better to travel as the boy, she thought, at least until she made it out of the state of Ravnice. She had liked Wren and Harpis, there were not many individuals she enjoyed enough to seek to come across in her wanderings, but she truly hoped she would meet with them again one day.

"I guess that means I do have a preference on what the winning side in all this ends up being," she said to her stolen horse, patting its neck affectionately.

"I suppose that since you will be my only company for some time that you'll need a name. How about Stormy? Good name for a horse if you ask me. Your coat is the dark grey of angry clouds and your mane as black as the deepest sea," she said, fingering several strands of the darker hair.

The horse continued its slow walk north and east, and she decided that the silence was the horse's agreement.

"I tell you the truth, Stormy. I have never met a folk as provocatively stimulating as those Tormenta. If it weren't for the malice in their hearts, they would be as irresistible a temptation as The Siren herself," she said, closing her eyes for a moment.

She drew Harpis' filet knife from her boot and gazed appreciatively for a moment at the storm goddess's depiction in its whalebone handle.

"But not as tempting as the opportunity provided by the disorder and unfamiliarity that they have brought with them," she reasoned to the horse.

With a slight tug of the reins to her left, she set stormy on a westerly route towards Kalt.

"There is a long-overdue debt I may finally be able to repay," she said quietly.

The horse gnawed the bridle bit and gave a sighing whinny at the release of her pull.

"I am glad you agree, Stormy," she whispered.

Chapter 20
Taking Measure

When Emni and Vana had returned from their supply run to Lodestar, Oluja had the duchesses moor on the northern end of the wharf. In turn, she moved her senior captain's vessel, which was acting as a temporary throneship, to the end closest to the lumberyard. She had her crew pull it in stern first so that she could use the aft rails of the higher steering deck like her own floating castle balcony.

Flanked by four of her six Duchesses and High Priestess Spavati, Oluja looked upon the thousands of Kalt citizens that filled the wharf to hear the first address from their new queen. She was not worried about being attacked by the crowd. The cobbled area closest to her was filled with Tormenta raiders far enough out that a crossbow bolt or arrow would be helpless to reach her. Beyond that, among the crowd that he had helped gather, were hundreds of men loyal to Svenus Kalt to put down any dissent.

If that was not enough to keep order, the bows of the twelve galleons completely lining the sea wall to her left were bristling with crossbowmen and storm priestesses. Raising her hand, she waited for silence and then took a step forward, her hands gripping the deck rail.

"My name is Queen Oluja Vetar of the Tormenta Empire. An empire that you are now a part of as the first and most important colony," she shouted, looking from one end of the wharf to the other to let her words sink in.

"That means that you are under my rule and the rule of my Duchesses," she continued, motioning towards the women.

"They, like me, will be respected under the penalty of death. The same goes for The Siren's High Priestess Spavati and her priestesses," she said, pointing towards the blue-robed woman.

She again paused for effect before continuing in a less stern tone.

"The requirement for respect is absolute, as is our rule. However, being part of the Tormenta Empire also means you are under our protection. As we speak, I have sent patrols to this state's northern borders to protect our territory and now aligned interests. This city and its harbor will be our fleet's primary base of military operations as we move to conquer the whole of this island and unify it as the first nation to become part of our expanding dominion in the southern seas," she stated.

She waited as several grumblings were silenced at the end of swords and clubs threateningly brandished by Svenus' men.

"The people of Kalt will be the benefactors of being the capital of that new nation and for being loyal to our cause from the start. My people respect lineage and hereditary rule. As such, Svenus Kalt will serve in a governing role, carrying out my orders in this city and beyond," she continued.

She thought for a moment of personally informing the people of Kalt that they had a single day to leave the city if they did not want to be part of the greatness to come, but she decided the risk of it being seen as weakness was too great. A task for Svenus then, she decided. After all, it was the man's idea, and she could blame any fallout from it on him if necessary. With a final look at her new subjects, she spun and walked down the stairs of the steering deck and into her makeshift quarters beneath it.

She could hear the tenseness of Spavati's muscles in her steps as she angrily clomped down the stairs after her. The High Priestess followed her into the quarters and locked the door behind her. Unconcerned, Oluja sat in a fur-covered chair and sprawled out. She held up one finger to pause the coming tirade from Spavati.

"I'll only warn you now, this once, about the tone you take and the way you speak to me," she said softly before lowering her finger and looking at the other woman expectantly.

Spavati shook for a moment with rage before trying to calm herself and opening her mouth to speak.

"Subjugating the land-born? An entire city and state? A Tormenta Empire of many nations? Unification of this whole island under our rule?" Spavati asked incredulously.

Oluja answered her with silence and a questioningly raised eyebrow.

"These are not the campaigns on behalf of The Siren and our people we originally discussed!" the High Priestess hissed.

"Has The Siren spoken to you, Spavati?" Oluja asked her.

When the woman looked at her confused, she continued her point.

"Do you, in fact, speak for her? Or for that matter, know that she is or is not displeased?" she asked.

It was Spavati's turn to remain silent.

"I thought not. If you could talk to The Siren as our High Priestesses once had, I would be bowing down to you and the other robe wearers instead of the other way around," Oluja said matter-of-factly.

"Now, it is obvious you disagree with my plans. So, you can go about sowing doubt behind my back amongst our people through your priestesses if you like. However, I will be the first to condemn it as treason and lean on the obvious victories so far achieved as a clear sign of our goddesses blessing my actions. I think we both know the way our superstitious and bloodthirsty people would react," she said, staring the woman down until Spavati averted her gaze.

She waved in dismissal, and as Spavati reached the door, she gave her a parting warning that made the priestess pause.

"Do not make me threaten you. If I do, then there is the potential for you forcing me to make good on it. I do not believe that is in the best interest of our people or yourself, High Priestess Spavati," she said coldly.

The robed woman never turned back to look at her as she left, but the fact that she did not slam the door as she departed was enough for Oluja to know she still held enough sway over her.

*****

Lazar Kalt had been one of his cousin Svenus' most trusted family members and operatives of the wider business and oft-times criminal endeavors. As such, he had received important roles such as babysitting Governor Jaeryl Innisgrath. Lazar hadn't minded that job. It came with comfortable quarters as one of the governor's trusted confidants. Or so the governor had believed anyway.

Lazar had been more than happy when the knife-wielding foreign women had bound and gagged him instead of sending him to The Great Dream with the others. As such, despite wanting to complain when Svenus had asked him to take some men and babysit a Tormenta scouting party, he had dutifully accepted the task.

That did not stop him from complaining during the entire day-long trek forty miles north to the center of their border with Ravnice along the Kalt river the day before. His old joints creaked in the southern autumn chill when he woke the party of thirty Kalt men, a dozen Tormenta raiders, and one particularly self-entitled priestess to ride east towards the trade bridge.

He raised a hand, and the line of riders came to a halt behind him. He tried not to chuckle at the commotion as the Tormenta struggled to control their horses. He planned to share a laugh with his cousin at the expense of the Tormenta's woeful ability to stay in a saddle when they returned this evening.

"What is it?" the priestess snapped at him after awkwardly guiding her horse beside him.

Lazar pointed to the distant bridge and then across the river, where the smoke of several cooking fires drifted into the sky.

"It would seem our northern neighbors had similar thoughts on scouting the border. I'd recommend we don't get much closer. The elven border is about a mile further down the river, at those treetops you can barely see. We had planned to turn back to town at the bridge road anyway. It is hard to tell from here, but it certainly looks like they easily outnumber us three or four to one," he explained.

"Your people have proven to be poor warriors. Being outnumbered does not worry me. They will scamper like rodents when my lighting scorches the first of them," the priestess scoffed at him.

Lazar sighed and narrowed his eyes as he tried to pick out details of the distant camp.

"I only see a few horses. However, if I am not mistaken, it looks like there are close to a hundred dwarves and a similar number of men, probably Ravnice militia," he said with obvious concern.

"The ignorant dwarves worry me no more than the weak and

cowardly humans," she said.

"Lady, I'll give you I have never met a dwarf I would accuse of being an intellectual, but I can tell you that if we engage with them, you'll have to kill them all to stop their advance," he said.

"The Siren's thunder shakes all that oppose her," the priestess said confidently, waving to the raiders before heading towards the bridge at a gallop.

One of his men was quickly at his side as soon as the thirteen Tormenta were out of earshot.

"Sir, are they mad? The dwarves will cut us to pieces," he said.

"Let us hope it does not come to that. If that priestess is wrong and the dwarves and militiamen don't turn and run at her little magic display, tell the boys we are heading home as fast as possible. Warning of so large an advance force already at our border and the dwarven involvement is more valuable than this woman's power trip," Lazar said, kicking his horse after the Tormenta.

*****

Harpis diligently watched as Wren and Commander Shatter-Hand discussed battle planning while pointing at various locations on detailed maps of Kalt and Ravnice. They were sitting at the center of the makeshift encampment. Their supply wagons from Ravnice were parked in a protective circle before the horses were tied off to nearby trees.

Their discussions were interrupted when a red-faced dwarf came to a noisy halt and saluted Shatter-Hand.

"Sleeper below us lad, what's the matter?" the commander asked grumpily.

"Sir, a patrol of about fifty riders is heading south along the river's far side!" he said between gasps.

After clonking the dwarf upside his head, Shatter-Hand grabbed the horn that hung around his neck and sounded the alarm.

"Form up. I want a fifty-wide shield wall a few paces off the bridge, crossbows, and bows behind it!" Shatter-Hand shouted before turning to the officer in charge of the Ravnice militia.

"You lot fall in behind ours and just listen and do as we say if you don't mind," he said, and the man nodded before quickly leaving to get his men formed up.

Shatter-Hand shoved the messenger before him as he made his way to the formation.

"Ye tell me this before sounding the alarm ya moron?" he shouted.

*****

While the dwarves and men fell into formation, Wren climbed to the driver's seat of the nearest wagon, standing on it to get a better view across the river. He watched with interest at the disorganized arrival of the mostly female group of foreigners followed by at least twice as many men.

"What are you planning?" he asked out loud to himself, scanning the much smaller group across the river for clues as to their intentions.

Surely, they wouldn't charge across the bridge to certain death. He watched a lone woman rider in a blue robe walk her horse in front of the group. She halted halfway across the bridge, still far enough away that the dwarven crossbow bolts would not reach her.

When she held her hands straight out at her sides, palms up, he felt the slow-building tingle he had experienced on the *Open Ocean*. He knew there was no time for their forces to interrupt her summoning. His scythe instinctually materialized in his hands, and he allowed himself to be pulled fully into the grey between the living plane and his goddesses.

"Take her!" he commanded, pointing his scythe at the priestess, desperately hoping his goddess would heed his call.

*****

Lazar gawked in horror as the priestess's scream turned to a gasping rattle. Her body fell limp while what looked like a white wispy feminine form floated away from her and faded into the air. Her lifeless form fell into the horse next to her before hitting the ground headfirst with a sickening hollow sound. The dead woman's horse spooked, jumping twice before charging right at him, dragging the corpse behind.

183

"Run!" he yelled at his men while he tried turning his horse unsuccessfully out of the way. Her mount slammed into his own, sending him flying from the saddle. He had the good sense to keep hold of the reins, but he felt a hot burn from his ankle and heard what sounded like snapping carrots when he attempted to land on his feet.

*****

As the color returned to the scene before him, Wren shook in awe as he watched the priestess fall dead and most of the others turn and flee. He spun around to the sound of thundering hooves in time to see Harpis speeding past him and towards the bridge.

"By the gods, what are you doing?" he shouted.

"Collecting intelligence!" Harpis shouted back at him, leaning in close to the horse's neck as it stretched out into a full sprint around the formation.

He heard Shatter-Hand order the charge but realized the dwarves would be too far behind, and he cursed when he saw several of the Tormenta riders turn back towards the man.

"You are going to end up as intelligence yourself if you keep carrying out idiotic stunts like that," the gnome said, snapping his fingers. Before the smoke even finished fading, he was pointing at the distant shore.

"Has he gone insane?" Xissay asked, looking at the charging bard.

"Get over there and scare off those stragglers," Wren shouted, and the sprite sped off screaming, engulfed in her own flames.

*****

Lazar Kalt had just pulled himself back into the saddle when the Tormenta raiders flew past him and towards a lone pursuing unarmed man on horseback. He nearly fell from his saddle again in surprise as what looked like a woodland sprite turned torch streaked ahead of the horseman and into the knot of Tormenta riders. It burned the backsides of several horses and lit a few of the longer-haired Tormenta's manes ablaze with impossible speed. The result was a chaotic mess of terrified horse screams

184

and the painful shrieks of women trying to put out their burning hair. He laughed to himself as the Tormenta fell from their mounts and then shook his head as they fearlessly faced the charging dwarven front.

The rider was almost upon him, and Lazar tried to draw his sword and urge his horse to faster speeds. He did not even get the blade entirely out of its sheath when the man was upon him. For a moment, he thought he heard singing before everything went black.

*****

Harpis quickly grabbed the reins of the other man's horse and kept him propped up, snoring in his saddle. He looked curiously at both mounts as they also seemed to shake off drowsiness.

"It seems Benali was right to think anything with ears might hear us," he said.

Harpis got down from his horse and lowered the other man to the ground after relieving him of his sword. He then took the bridle and reins from the Kalt horse to bind the man's hands behind his back.

The man woke, and Harpis held the sword tip at his throat and held up a hand to halt him.

"Hold fast, friend, do as I ask, and you may yet survive the day," he said.

Before the older, bearded man opened his mouth to respond, their attention was drawn to the carnage at the bridge as the unarmored Tormenta warriors were riddled with crossbow bolts before their reckless charge even reached dwarven shields.

Harpis looked down as the man sighed and shook his head as Wren, Shatter-Hand and several dwarves and militiamen made their way towards the two.

"I told them that would happen," the man stated.

"And you are?" Harpis asked.

The man's only response was to spit at Harpis' feet and remain silent.

Wren halted a few feet away and glared at Harpis before speaking.

"That might be the dumbest thing I have ever witnessed you do, lad, and that is the top of a long and well-recorded list of dumb

185

things to include talking with the goddess of death herself. Who is this?" the gnome asked, pointing at his prisoner.

"I don't know, he won't talk," Harpis answered his friend.

"Oh, that won't be a problem," the gnome said with a hollow laugh and a distant look.

Shatter-Hand clapped Wren on the shoulder from behind and pointed at Harpis.

"I have never seen such a mad thing, a man riding into battle with no armor or weapons. Nothing but a fiddle strapped across his back!" the dwarf laughed.

"It is a damn violin," Wren said, sighing.

"How'd you get him from his horse?" the dwarf asked Harpis.

"I sang him a song. A lullaby he couldn't resist," Harpis answered.

"I am glad I was out of earshot this time, bard," the dwarven veteran of the battle in Tuath said.

"Let's get our new friend here back across the river and ask him some questions," the gnome said.

Harpis nodded in agreement and untied the man so the dwarves could take him. He loosely put the reins around the man's horse and led both their mounts back across the river behind them.

*****

Harpis stood with Wren and Commander Shatter-Hand, watching as the dwarves finished tying the man, arms outstretched, to the wheels of one of the wagons.

"I may be the military commander here, but what would you two like to do with yonder man from Kalt?" Shatter-Hand asked them.

Wren summoned his scythe and stared at the man for a long moment.

"I'll see what I can get him to divulge, and then we will send him home with a couple useful bits of misinformation," the gnome said in a whisper so that Kalt man could not hear.

"What are you going to do to him?" Harpis asked, somewhat concerned at the look in the gnome's eyes.

"Don't worry lad, if I fail to get him blabbering, we'll leave him tied there, and you can use that violin I got you to serenade him with the sounds of dying cats until he is raving mad and ready to talk," the gnome said.

"I'll leave you two to your business then," the commander said after a howl of laughter at Harpis' expense.

Wren stopped a few paces in front of their glaring captive.

"Who are you?" the gnome asked sternly, but the man remained silent, shifting his eyes angrily between the two of them.

"Do you know me, human? Know what I am?" Wren continued, holding his scythe in one hand, its butt on the ground.

When the man refused to reply, Harpis watched Wren close his eyes and clutch his scythe in concentration. There were several screams from surprised men and dwarves when the bolt-riddled corpse of a dead Tormenta raider began crawling its way across the bridge and towards wagons.

The corpse ended its writhing inches from the man's boots and folded itself into a sitting position. Its lifeless eyes opened, and facing him, it began pulling crossbow bolts out of its chest, legs, and neck and laying them in a neat line. A wet sucking sound followed the removal of each bolt, and partially clotted blood began to ooze out from the holes like syrup. Finally, after ten bolts lay next to it, the body collapsed forward into the man's legs. He grunted in pain from the sagging weight of the corpse pressing on the ankle they had splinted.

Wren opened his eyes and rested his scythe back on the ground.

"Do you know what I am now?" the gnome questioned again.

"You are a necromancer," the man said with fear in his eyes.

"I am The Necromancer, Herald to The Sleeper herself, and if you do not wish to talk, I will have this corpse slowly press each of those bolts into your body until you comply. If that does not work, I will have one of The Sleeper's handmaidens pull the soul from your body into The Great Dream. Once it is there, I will force it into cooperation and have my questions answered anyway. Or you can cooperate, provide us the information we ask and be sent on your way back to Kalt atop the very horse you rode here," the gnome promised.

The man glanced in terror at the corpse and then the gnome before looking towards Harpis with desperation in his eyes.

"I would just talk," Harpis suggested.

"Who are you, why were you out here, and are there more

187

patrols or a larger army camped nearby that we should worry about?" the gnome prodded impatiently.

"My name is Lazar Kalt. My cousin Svenus ordered me to bring the Tormenta out here to show them the border with Ravnice that will need to be secured," he answered quickly.

Wren narrowed his eyes at the man for a moment before closing them and muttering words to himself as if casting a spell, though Harpis felt no tug at his gift.

"Thank you for your honesty, Lazar. Unfortunately, if my magic detects you are lying to me, I will be forced to converse with your deceased spirit instead," the gnome said before turning to Harpis.

"Harpis, have the commander send word to the elven army that they should send at least half their force north to bolster our encampments east of here and to watch for incursions from the Kalt river," he said, casting Harpis a severe look.

Harpis walked his way around the wagon behind Lazar. For a minute, he pretended to murmur to a messenger that was not there.

When he walked back around, Wren was just staring at Lazar Kalt.

"We may have to get word to our fleet to hit Lodestar sooner than we thought if Svenus is in league with the invaders. I would guess he has used them as an opportunity to return your family to lording over the city and state named for them," he said with a raised eyebrow at the man.

Lazar Kalt nodded in agreement.

"And what of Governor Innisgrath?" Harpis asked.

"Dead," was all Lazar said, looking up at him.

Wren clapped his hands at Lazar to get the man's attention again.

"Now, last I knew, Kalt had a militia of two or three thousand men at most, including its reserves. I would guess not all were loyal to your new friends, so between the lives lost and Svenus' security forces and dock workers, I would assume the number of Kalt fighting men is about the same?" Wren pried.

Lazar nodded again.

"Last question Lazar and you may be on your way, without your sword, mind you. How many fighters and priestesses do the Tormenta have?"

188

"I've seen around two thousand fighters, not including the crew they keep on their ships. I don't know how many priestesses, but it can't be more than fifty," he answered.

Harpis watched as Wren pretended to cast his spell of truth again, this time glaring at the man in betrayal when he opened his eyes.

"Get him on his horse and sent home," the gnome shouted to some nearby militiamen before motioning for Harpis to follow him away from the camp.

"How convenient that necromancers can divine between a man's truth and lies," he said, smiling down at his friend when they were far enough away not to be overheard.

"Lazar told us the truth, but I could tell he was unsure on the number of priestesses, and I wanted him to know I could sense it. Magically or otherwise did not matter how I knew, just that I did. Let's hope they chase their tails for a bit watching the elven border and ours and worrying about an imaginary fleet attacking their forces at Lodestar," the gnome said with a grin.

Chapter 21
Consolidation

Arriving late the night before, Ezera felt her eyes heavy with sleep as she and the others gathered first thing in the morning at the council chamber in Mer. Ingar had told her Lorkin would serve as scribe for himself and her for Aanaman, assuring them the seats that they currently occupied at the back of the squat square stone room. On the edge of the five-sided table directly in front of her, sat the ancient Arch Mage and Exarch Weksnor.

She had never been a fan of the former Kalt Diocese Vicar and now Exarch. In both instances, the man wore his titles like a cloak of excuses at arrogance and self-entitlement. However, she had to admit that his political prowess was undeniable and almost entirely responsible for his being named Exarch. Like those that preceded him, he was ungifted, but unlike his predecessors, he had gone on a crusade of sorts to make all vicars that ran a diocese similarly lacking in devotion given magic.

Ezera had thoroughly enjoyed last year when Ingar told the newly appointed Weksnor that he would only tolerate a diocese in Fjall so long as Ezera or a dwarf ran it. It was not surprising that the man had repeatedly peered over his shoulder at her in discontent while the room filled. There were the notable absences at the side furthest from her where the governors of Kalt and Glasduille normally sat.

She did not know the young man who sat in Wren's seat but assumed him to be Acolyte Jabruelle. She guessed the woman who had walked in with Governor Rashida of Tuath was the Troubadour Mahala Harpis had spoken of. After Ingar and Aanaman took their chairs on their shared side, she gave a wave to the former Mer militia captain turned governor. Elliswerth then shut the doors and stood behind his chair, giving her a warm smile before addressing the gathering.

"Welcome, all. I wish we found ourselves joined under better circumstances. However, as that is not the case and given the threat that seems to be looming large over our island home, I will forgo any typical decorum and courtliness and jump right into things," he said, taking a seat before continuing.

"Two of the foreign galleons sailed into our harbor five days ago and laid waste to our ships that were in port and destroyed our docks. Our neighbors to the north saw a separate three galleons engage them in Tuath bay. They fared slightly better, hobbling one of the three, but their ships and harbor were ultimately destroyed as well. Two tuath brigantines out on patrol, several trade vessels, and three Mer naval vessels have returned since then. All sit currently anchored in the middle of our harbor, awaiting our joint decisions here today," Elliswerth finished, indicating it was Governor Rashida's turn to speak.

Isra Rashida sat stately in her chair with her hands resting on the table. The only indication that she was not a tan olive-skinned statue was the turn of her head and flick of her intense eyes around the room before she spoke.

"I came south as soon as the attack had ended with two-thousand members of my militia. I am willing to commit them to whatever course we set. I will also remind the table that we all have commitments in our own lands. Not just to keep our people safe from this new enemy. We must also keep them safe from hunger, crime, and poverty. Those challenges are only made worse by an overworked militia and the economic impact from the loss of ships and docks," she stated with much emotion.

Governor Elliswerth nodded his agreement at her statement before turning to Aanaman.

"Mer is also prepared to dedicate two-thousand militiamen for potential deployment south. What news have you two gentlemen brought us?" he asked, turning to Aanaman.

Ezera listened in, not needing to take notes as Governor Reaper recounted their previous discussions and divulged what had been learned through experience and from Sudbina about the Tormenta. As they had agreed on the ride north, he left out the revival of espionage practices. After a few moments of murmured discussion regarding their revealed foe, Aanaman quieted them

191

with an upheld hand that he then motioned towards the two empty seats.

"The elves have refused to get involved. To their credit, they have sworn no invasion force will survive crossing into or through their border to get north. This guarantee at least enables us to keep the enemy bottled up in the south if we can defend the remaining thirty or so miles of the Kalt river. We have dispatched an advance force to scout the border as we speak. If we lose that position, we could fall back to the Fjall river as another natural divide, but one much wider and more difficult to defend. If that happens it would also endanger the Ravnice ships we were able to save and hide at Lake Gitche," he said.

Exarch Weksnor interrupted Aanaman with a cough and a stern look.

"Yes, Exarch?" he asked.

"What of Governor Innisgrath, what of the people of Kalt?" Weksnor questioned.

"For now, Ingar and I agree that the border with Kalt is hostile, whether because those left living in Kalt are unable to resist the Tormenta or are in league with them. Once we have countered their ability to expand north over land, we can decide how best to liberate our southernmost neighbors," Aanaman finished.

Weksnor sat back without further comment, seemingly dissatisfied with the answer but unwilling to press the issue.

Aanaman turned to Ingar next, and Ezera's own surprise matched the look on Aanaman's face at the dwarf's response.

"I'll save my piece for last if it's fine by the rest of you," the dwarf stated before motioning respectfully for the Arch Mage to speak.

Uridyll turned in his seat to look back towards her and Lorkin.

"Regarding any role the mages will play in the coming days and battles, Lorkin and I have much to discuss. Whatever we end up deciding will be brought forth for consideration and perhaps approval by the political leadership of the island," he said with a nod in their direction.

Ezera felt Lorkin give a slight seated bow next to her as Uridyll turned back to the table and Exarch Weksnor took in the room.

"My clerics will provide medical assistance and faith leadership necessary to see the people through the coming struggles. Nothing more," Weksnor said, speaking as if she was not even in the room.

Ezera decided this was not the place nor the forum for the discussion she hoped to have with him.

Everyone looked to the young necromancer next, and Jabruelle squirmed under the attention.

"Good morning, your highnesses. I am Acolyte Jabruelle, but I, um. I am not. Excuse me, I cannot speak for The Sanctum or his eminence, The Death Herald," he stammered, stopping and looking her way as Lorkin snorted and buried his head in his hand.

"Finish your piece, lad," Ingar said patiently.

"However, I will take this news to my brothers and sisters. We will ensure The Herald learns of it as quickly as possible," Jabruelle said, sputtering.

"The gnome is currently in Ravnice," Aanaman told the acolyte.

"Oh, most wonderful, then I shall head there instead!" Jabruelle said excitedly.

The demeanor of the petite brown-haired bard next to the acolyte could not have been a harsher contrast to Jabruelle in a person's ability to exude confidence.

"I am Troubadour Mahala. Maestro Bravit has instructed me to inform the council that the bards and their hall stand ready to assist, whatever you decide. For my part, I would like to head south with your company if you'll have me. I need to speak with Harpis, and if Wren is in Ravnice, the bard is probably there as well," she said with a look to Aanaman.

"You are more than welcome to," Aanaman replied before turning towards Ingar.

"I did not know you to be one for dramatics, Governor Hammersmith, but I do believe the table is yours," he proclaimed.

"It is too little, and it will be too slow, and you will lose the coming battles and eventually this island," Ingar said sternly, looking across the table to each other attendee one at a time in the surprising silence that followed.

To Ezera's surprise, it was Governor Elliswerth that addressed the statement and not Aanaman.

"While I, maybe more than the others, trust your assessment

193

of our ability to defend ourselves, Ingar, I will have to ask you to elaborate," he said.

"You'll send four thousand militia from Mer and Tuath to join a similar amount from Ravnice, and you'll head to the Kalt river, and perhaps I will send most of my army as well. Who commands them?" he asked, once again surveying the table while there were murmured opinions as to the answer to his question.

The dwarf pounded his hand on the table like a gavel to silence them again.

"Pretend you do agree on a commander, say there is a bloody battle at the river with two or three thousand superiorly trained Tormenta warriors and ten thousand or more militia from Kalt. What if our forces win the day? Do we wait a week or longer to gather here again and decide whether to advance to the south and break their backs so we can push them off the island for good? They'll have boarded their ships and gone after another city," he said with determination.

Only stunned silence greeted his rhetorical questions and the statement that followed.

"Your enemy has a singular purpose and a ruthless disposition. They are more decisive and own the seas. They can communicate faster and maneuver their forces more quickly than we can. They will only be forced from our lives if we do so completely and undeniably. I'll commit the full resources of my people to that end. However, I will not waste lives supporting efforts that will only prolong the inevitable," he finished.

Exarch Weksnor crossed his arms and shrugged.

"If you are correct in your analysis, Governor Hammersmith, why do we not spare thousands of lives and acquiesce to the demands of these Tormenta?" he asked.

"I am not talking of surrender lad, I am talking of electing a singular leader and directing a singular command that will allow the people of this island to survive through unification," Ingar said with unveiled contempt.

"Would it be King Ingar then?" Weksnor asked snidely.

Ezera shook her head at the man's gall and spared herself a smile as Uridyll elbowed the younger Exarch into silence while Governor Elliswerth interrupted.

"As you have stated, Exarch, you and your clerics will have no part in the response. So, instead of offering opinions outside your station, perhaps you should start preparing hospital beds and digging graves," he said.

Ezera wondered if Weksnor would get up right then and leave. However, he did not, and Elliswerth turned back to the dwarf.

"So, you are recommending we elect a chancellor of sorts to make our actions more efficient and effective?" he asked.

Governor Rashida turned to Elliswerth before Ingar could answer.

"I cannot commit to this vote, even if it is unanimous. My utmost obligation is to the people of Tuath who elected me," she said almost apologetically.

Everyone turned to Ingar when he stood from his seat.

"Governor, if I were the Tormenta, and I were mired in the south, unable to press north by land, I would load every armed body I could fit on my ships and deposit them in Tuath harbor under cover of lightning strikes. I say this not to scare you, but because it is a fact that with control of the seas and control of the northern and southern fronts, this island would be hard-pressed to fight on in what would become a generations-long war of attrition across two fronts," Ingar said softly.

Elliswerth glanced at Aanaman, who still wore a much-bewildered look on his face and back to the governor.

"If I were in their place and still a military commander, it is what I would do as well, Rashida," the former militia captain said sadly, shrugging in apology of the truth.

"Call it chancellor or whatever you like," Ingar said, sitting back down, "I vote you call it Aanaman Reaper,"

The shock on the Ravnice governor's face was absolute. Then, after a long moment, he pointed an accusing finger at the dwarf.

"We did not discuss this at all!" he said, nearly yelling.

"That is because you would have refused it and refused even bringing it up," Ingar responded.

"You are by the gods right I would have refused. I do not want to be in consideration for such a position. I agree with the sentiment, but I vote no regarding myself. I don't even like being governor!" he exclaimed to several understanding chuckles.

Ezera was surprised that the Tuath governor was the first to respond to Ingar's proposition.

"But that is exactly why it should be you, Aanaman," she said in a sympathetic tone.

"I am all for giving up some political responsibilities," Elliswerth said with a wink.

Aanaman's shoulders sank, and he stared at the tabletop for a moment looking at Ingar and throwing his hands in the air.

"Fine! As chancellor of Quaj Island, I order you to tell me who you think should lead our unified forces and where from!" he ordered the dwarf.

"Promote the now governor and former captain of the Mer militia to field marshal and send him to Lake Gitche where my dwarves are already building a military base and docks for the boats there," the dwarf answered quickly.

Aanaman seemed almost taken aback by his friend's fast logic.

"You were planning this before we even started this council meeting, weren't you," he said to the dwarf with a suspicious look.

"The whole way here, Chancellor Reaper," Ingar replied, smiling.

Aanaman turned to Elliswerth next.

"Do you accept your promotion, Field Marshal Elliswerth?" Aanaman asked.

"Only if Ingar can spare General Shieldborn to command our southern army. Mer and Tuath will send fifteen hundred additional militiamen each and send them to Lake Gitche to meet up with Ravnice's forces and what dwarves Ingar will commit. It is a good location and far from any shore, making it a good command hub against our new foe. I recommend each city identify which remaining forces would be committed to a northern army if necessary. For now, keep them as part of local policing and militia efforts," Elliswerth said, exchanging head nods with Ingar.

Aanaman looked next to Isra Rashida, "Mer has always been the island's economic hub, and I'll need a voice for the people's bellies and pocketbooks to counterbalance the military ones. Would you move with a selected staff here to Mer as minister of civil affairs? If so, I will send harvest and livestock to Mer and Tuath as planned over land. Given and not sold, for you to distribute as you see necessary. I am sure the people of Ravnice

196

would consider the army arriving to safeguard them as fair compensation," Aanaman proposed.

"I think the people of Tuath will find that more than acceptable," she said.

Aanaman sighed in noticeable relief at her willingness.

"Troubadour, can you see about sending word via a rider to Maestro Bravit to send his bards to Lake Gitche. I would like to centralize their message board system there. When I return to Ravnice, I will send horses and riders to support communications efforts around the island by stationing them at key distances and locations between the cities and the lake," he said.

"I would be happy to," she replied.

Aanaman surveyed the room, deep in thought until his eyes met Ezera's for a moment and then went to Lorkin.

"Arch Mage, I will use this chamber as an office for the rest of the day. Please send word of what you and Lorkin decide. Further, make sure each of you designates a mayor to keep your cities in running order. They will report all non-military issues through Minister Rashida. Any last concerns before we get to it?" he asked the room.

"Yes, Elliswerth," he said, acknowledging the man's upheld hand.

"I would like it if Tuath's naval commander would join us at Lake Gitche as our admiral. The ships in the harbor here should set out in a three-day sail to the mouth of the Fjall river. We should try to temporarily unblock the river and get them up into the lake as well, if we can," he implored.

Aanaman did not answer himself. Instead, he looked to Rashida.

"I will inform him of his promotion. He and what sailors made it out of the harbor or were already ashore during the assault will head south with our second group of militia," she said, standing from her chair.

"I will head south in the morning to Ravnice and then likely to Lake Gitche myself," the chancellor finished, standing with the others.

Aanaman then made his way around the room to speak personally with the other former governors after giving Ingar a shove in jest.

"And you, my fine dwarven friend, I promote you to Chief

197

Political Advisor Hammersmith," he proclaimed.

"That's no position befitting a dwarf!" Ingar complained.

"Reap what you sow, my friend," Aanaman said with a laugh.

As she watched the room empty, Ezera could not help but wonder if Harpis and Wren had had anywhere near as interesting a day as she had.

Chapter 22
Rules Old and New

Ezera walked up to the wide stairs of The Archdiocese of Daybreak and looked upon its immense main doors for the first time since attending Exarch Hameki's funeral. She lamented seeing it once again under the guard of militia, something that had happened only one other time in her life. Still, she was glad that the city had posted armed watches to keep an eye on the healers and scholars of Daybreak's clergy.

She briskly made her way up the steps to the pair of militiamen, and one of them gave her a knowing salute.

"Welcome back, Vicar Ezera," he said.

"Is the Exarch in?" she asked, though she assumed he had slunk back to his seat of power after being embarrassed in the council chamber.

"He arrived maybe half an hour ago, didn't seem very happy either," the other militiamen said.

"Are there men posted at the hospital school and the archives as well?" she asked.

"The hospital, yes, but the archives have been largely unoccupied since the harbor was attacked. More pressing matters at hand than research and history keeping of late," the first man answered.

"Thank you both for protecting my fellow clerics. Daybreak keep you," she said and strode past them and through the doors.

She walked down the center aisle of the main worship hall, trying not to cringe as her riding boots hammered off the polished marble floor. Daybreak and the Exarch would have to forgive her for not wearing the typical sandals of the clergy. The resounding echoes of her walk were made worse by the sheer emptiness of the building. Usually, various clergy members were always present on the grounds and in the worship hall, praying or training or even just gossiping.

Reaching Daybreak's altar under the soaring central dome, she bowed her head in a moment of reverence for her goddess. She heard shuffling sandals come around from behind the altar and recede behind her, followed by the creaking of the front pew as someone sat. Finishing her prayer and respects, she turned around gave a tight smile and short bow.

"Good afternoon, Exarch," she said.

"I presume you are here to see me, Vicar Ezera," he replied in a manner that seemed to question not only her motivation for being there but her title as well.

"I am indeed," she answered.

"Come, sit with me," he said disarmingly, motioning towards the bench.

Trying to keep her steps quiet, she practically shuffled the few paces to him. They sat together in silence, both looking up at the altar.

"Your opinions went over about as well as flatulence at a funeral mass today," she said after the silence became awkward.

"Oh, I just try to keep them challenged and honest, something politicians do not always appreciate," he said.

She smiled at the irony of his accusation as he performed his customary deflective navigation of the conversation.

"What of you then, Weksnor? Are you not a politician? One with constituents across the island and no borders to bound your influence," she challenged with blatant disrespect.

"Of sorts, I suppose. I use my skills to keep our people's best interests safe," he said, finally turning to her.

She calmly met his gaze and laced her fingers, laying her hands on her lap after running them down her vicar stole.

"The answer is no," he said, cutting her off.

"I haven't asked anything," she said, surprised at his directness.

"I am many things, Ezera, but do not take me for a fool. You came here to convince me to let you involve our clerics on the front lines, if not in general than specifically the ones gifted by Daybreak like yourself," he said.

"You are a coward," she accused, surprising even herself. She clenched her fists in resentment. She was as frustrated at his ability to get her off balance as she was at his answer.

"You are caught up in the moment and consider only the present. However, I must worry about the consequences of our actions for our faith and the people it supports for years and decades to come," he calmly responded.

He turned fully towards her on the bench, placing his arm along its back, and continued.

"Beyond just this denial of your unasked question, I will be removing your title and the sanctification of your diocese in Fjall also. We have the tenants of the clergy and its medicine, Ezera. We are healers, scholars, scribes, and historians to all the people of this island and beyond. Having the gifted amongst our ranks, such as yourself, is a distraction that can lead to false hope and misconceptions about our abilities at large. Those sorts of misunderstandings impair our ability to give what aid we can," he said in the same steady voice.

She wanted to strike him. She wanted him to be wrong, and she wished Hameki was still Exarch. However, his statements recalled the memory of the dead baby girl in Hjalmstad two years ago and the look of betrayal on the mother's face when Ezera could not resurrect it.

"I understand," she said in almost a whisper, barely believing she agreed with the man and still stunned by his decree.

"I do not question Daybreak's favor for you Ezera, by all accounts, your devotion and gifts are unparalleled. I have a proposition for you," he said.

"I am listening," she said, turning back to look up at the visages of her goddess.

"I name you Luminary. The diocese in Fjall, which you and the dwarf Dobry Hammersmith call home, will be consecrated as Daybreak's Temple. I will not schism our congregation, not in this time of need. The twenty-some gifted currently in our order will remain for now, but you will take those gifted by our Lady in the future as brothers and sisters at your temple. Under your purview and with my full blessing and support," he finished, standing and walking in front of her.

She knew the title for Daybreak's most gift-blessed had been used centuries ago. That was back before the widespread organization of Daybreak's faith. She appreciated his well-

201

researched proposal. She was also smart enough to know that if she denied him, the struggle between the two of them would do irreversible damage to the clergy at possibly the worst possible time. He had her cornered, and she knew he knew it. Ezera was just surprised he had put her in a position where she was happy to comply despite being practically forced to do so.

"Not a fool indeed, Exarch Weksnor," she answered.

*****

Uridyll shuffled down the stairs from his quarters and through the library and communal areas of The College of Elements' central square hall with a forlorn determination. Usually, the library was host to sages and mages busily studying the science of elements at all hours, but instead, it was dark and empty. The only light was that which spilled in from the afternoon sun.

He squinted his eyes for a moment against the sunlight as he walked out into the courtyard and pulled his heavily embroidered orange robe tight around his ancient body to ward off the relative cold of late autumn in northern Mer. He had hoped to leave a legacy worthy of his title. A title that he had worn for longer than many of his predecessors. His longevity did benefit from not having to risk his life in a spell duel or at war. He had guided the college through the invasion by Tuath and ensuing battles, ensuring its continued non-bias and the safety of his students and staff. Sadly, he knew his actions in the previous days, and his discussion with Lorkin today, would be the end of a long career.

As he reached the small gathering of mages in the center of the courtyard, they all paused their murmured conversations and turned to give him a slight bow. When he slowly straightened his aching back from returning their courtesy, he gave a smile and extended his hand to Lorkin as the dwarf walked up to him from the crowd.

"Well met, old friend," he said to the dwarf, silently cursing himself for already needing to battle back a falling tear.

"You looked a lot younger the last time I was visiting within these walls, Arch Mage," the dwarf joked.

"The years are not as kind to me as they are to you, good dwarf," he said, chuckling despite himself.

"Oh, the passage of time is just as meaningful to me as it is to you. Humans should be thankful for their short lives and limited suffering," Lorkin laughed, patting Uridyll on the back.

Uridyll placed a hand on the dwarf's shoulder and turned to the rest of the mages.

"Students, friends, and peers, I lament to state that this will be my last official act as Arch Mage," he said with sadness in his voice.

At once, the mages of the four towers and their eleven gifted apprentices went silent in surprise, and he continued.

"As you already know, the trainees, gifted or not, as well as the ungifted apprentices and sages, have been sent back to their homes if they have them. Maestro Bravit has welcomed the rest at The Hall to stay there until this is over. The court mage of Kalt hopefully yet lives and has sought sanctuary at the diocese as has been the standing protocol. I am happy too that Stone Mage Lorkin of Fjall and Fire Mage Lyrnah of Tuath's court have joined us today," he said, nodding at the two.

Despite himself, he did cry. He looked at his feet and watched several tears fall to the grass of the courtyard. He took a steadying breath and turned slowly in a circle, taking in the entire college. Then he walked behind Lorkin, who he bid to turn and face the other mages. Uridyll unclasped the gold chain that hung across the top of his chest and bound the waist-length cloak of the Arch Mage atop his shoulders. He held the black cloak so that most of the college's symbol, a gold embroidered lit candle, could be seen.

"I, Arch Mage Uridyll Vatra, order that The College of Elements be closed and remain so until war leaves our island. With no guilt, pressure, or remorse, I request that each of you decide here and now to join those at The Hall or return home. If instead, you are willing to put your sanity and your life at risk to help protect this island we call home and its people, then remain and become bound to the dictates of Arch Mage Lorkin," he finished, clasping the cloak on the dwarf.

Lorkin turned around and gave him another bow.

"I am sorry it came to this. I had hoped not to outlive the constitution created following The War of Magi that bound us to pacifism and peaceful scientific research," Lorkin said sincerely.

"I know, my friend. For myself, I do not have the strength to lead elementalists in battle or to lose them to it. I know they are now in the best hands. I plan to stay here and live out my days in my quarters. Perhaps when this battle with the Tormenta is over, you can come clean what's left of my bones from my chair and re-open the college," he told the dwarf, only partially joking.

"Neither are tasks I look forward to," Lorkin replied.

"If we mages survive this, maybe the allure of battle magics will draw more to become students of the elements. I leave that problem to you though, Arch Mage," he said with a bow of his own at the dwarf.

Lorkin turned to those that remained and held up the blue-leather tome from the Tormenta that he had spent the trip north examining.

"Before you all jump at the chance to sling elemental magic at our enemies, let me tell you what I have learned about them," the dwarf said and tucked the tome back in his robe.

Uridyll genuinely hoped what Lorkin was about to tell them would sway many from joining in the fighting to come.

"Their magic is akin to that of the others gifted by the favor of the sisters. They are priestesses of The Siren, and women rule their culture and religious order. They have three conjurings taught and expected at their different ranks. Any of their gifted can surround themselves in a magical fog that visually obscures them. Once trained, priestesses can summon a sort of lightning ward that protects them, and most impressively, they can send lightning from their hands to even distant targets," the dwarf said, giving those gathered time to quiet.

"Thankfully, like our own gifts, while maintaining the fog or ward, or while summoning lightning, they can fall victim to the same spell madness of our gifts. However, unique to these storm priestesses is their ability to collectively channel summonings. This ability means that they can work together to maintain larger wards and call forth greater lightning strikes. That is something they do, for instance, as recorded in their texts here, to obscure their entire armada or specific ships, when necessary," he finished.

Uridyll strode forward and interrupted the growing clamor of conversation.

"We will be in my quarters upstairs if you have any questions. Make your decisions with your own mind and heart and commit to them fully without shame. I expect you all to be gone in the morning. Either headed home, north to The Hall or south with Arch Mage Lorkin at dawn," Uridyll said.

*****

Svenus stood awkwardly behind the desk in his own office and to the side the frustrated Queen Oluja Vetar who currently occupied the room's lone chair. His new benefactor had been incensed at the loss of one of her priestesses and another dozen warriors. He had not intervened when she put his men that had fled to death, though he planned to discuss the matter and future punishments for other transgressions that may come further when she had calmed some.

Lazar Kalt had ridden to the lumber yard and hobbled his way into Svenus' office several hours ago. The only reason his cousin still stood living before them was that Svenus had promised Oluja she needed to hear what he had to say. Svenus had felt the information was sensitive, so he kept his cousin locked in his office and under guard while they awaited the arrival of the queen. She kept her contingent outside at his urging, but only after Lazar was bound to a chair, and her guards searched the both of them.

He was unsure that Lazar would survive this meeting, and he almost sighed aloud in relief when Oluja finally spoke after staring down his cousin in silence since she arrived.

"Let us see if the information you have brought will prove useful enough to allow you to live despite your cowardice," she said, beckoning him to speak.

Lazar looked at him pleadingly.

"Tell her what happened and then tell her who interrogated you and what was discussed by all parties," Svenus said, trying to calm the man.

Lazar gave him a nod.

"We were heading southeast along the river and spotted an encampment and fires in the distance at the trade bridge. I urged the priestess to turn and head back to warn of the force and not engage. It was at least a hundred warriors from the dwarven army and easily as many Ravnice militiamen, not good odds for a patrol of not even fifty," he said.

Svenus cringed when Oluja laid back into him.

"I have seen a single storm priestess kill more than that with the wrath of our goddess. So why is it that there was not a single casualty amongst our enemy!?" she yelled.

"That's just it, your highness. Your priestess began her spell, and not a moment later, she started a scream that will echo in my memory until my last day before slumping over dead and falling off her horse. I swear it looked as if you could see her spirit leave her body. The lads took off at her scream, and your raiders charged the enemy. I regret to tell you that as fine as your fighters are, leather armor doesn't stop the rain of fifty crossbows," Lazar answered nervously.

"She just fell dead?" Oluja asked incredulously.

Lazar shrugged helplessly, and Svenus reminded him of the task at hand.

"Tell her about the interrogation," he prodded.

Lazar gave him a nod and then looked back to the queen and continued.

"Right, so, I broke my ankle when the priestess' horse slammed into my own. By the time I could regain the saddle, a rider from the other side of the river was upon me. Then, everything went black. I must have gotten knocked out or something. Now I'll tell you, I had never met a gnome, nor did I expect ever to be intimidated by a being the size of my four-year-old grandson," he said, shaking his head.

Oluja looked like she was ready to leap out of the chair and kill the man, so Svenus leaned in so only she could hear.

"I bid you, Queen, please hear him out and then let me explain," he pleaded.

She shot him a glare but motioned for Lazar to finish and his cousin swallowed hard and spoke.

"They bound me and asked me some questions. However, what was odd is that they already knew what you lot were called and seemed to know a decent amount about your forces. On my life, I only confirmed information they already had, and only after that robed midget reanimated one of the fallen raiders and threatened to torture me with her corpse!" he proclaimed.

"Tell her what you heard them saying," Svenus urged.

"Ah yes, I heard them say there was a need to send word to their fleet. That they might have to make a move on some island called Lodestar that I've never heard of, but they also spoke of contacting the elven army. I wouldn't have expected the elves to join with them, but that's what they said," he finished.

Before Lazar could say anything else that might get him killed on the spot, Svenus walked to the office door, opened it, and motioned for two of his men to drag Lazar out and unbind him. Once the door shut again, he walked and stood before Oluja, who was sitting rod-straight in his chair.

"I wouldn't worry too much about the elven army bit, Queen Vetar. I am guessing that it is a bluff by the former spy turned Death Herald," Svenus said.

"They know we have boats at Lodestar Island. How could they possibly know about that?" she asked.

All he could do was shrug.

"I would be more concerned that Fjall and Ravnice are already working together at our northern border and are worried enough to have already sent an advance party. Especially one that included The Death Herald," he said, trying to calm her.

"The Death Herald?" she asked.

"A gnome named Wren. He is the leader of the necromancers that worship The Sleeper at their sanctum. He used to spy for an organization called The Syndicate, it is a long story, but I had some familiarity with one of their least pleasant operatives. I wouldn't worry about The Syndicate or him much, though. You all have settled on the ruins of their former base at Lodestar Island," he answered, unsure why this seemed to make her more concerned.

"What is a gnome?" she questioned, her eyes narrowing.

It never occurred to Svenus that someone wouldn't know what a gnome was, but he supposed sailing the seas for generations might limit interactions with certain folk.

"They're longer living, shorter, distant relatives of dwarves," he replied.

"Maelar," she said softly to herself and then looked him in the eyes.

"Where is this sanctum where the evil worship The Sleeper?" she inquired, almost leaning over the desk.

He walked around and pulled a map from one of his drawers, pointing to its location in a section of the Fjall mountain range.

"If you want my opinion, though, it might be wise to try and keep Mer and Tuath scared and distracted in their own cities if you don't want to have to fend off an invasion from the entire

207

island across the Kalt river. I imagine Ingar and Aanaman have already sent word north asking for support," Svenus reasoned.

Oluja sat back, deep in thought for a moment, before standing from his chair.

"Find Admiral Kisa and tell her I want to be briefed first thing tomorrow on where our fortification efforts of the city and harbor are. I also want the status and numbers of our fighting forces, the people of Kalt included," she said, departing the room and slamming the door behind her.

Chapter 23
Fruition

Oluja had left Svenus' office the night before, doing her best to keep her emotions and thoughts from painting themselves across her face. Returning to her makeshift throneship and locking herself in her quarters, she had hardly slept as she plotted the path to victory for herself and her people.

Despite little rest, her eyes were wide with the excited hunger of a predator that finally had its jaws around the neck of its still-living prey. She gazed out at the dawn-lit city of Kalt through the aft windows and touched the glass almost gingerly.

"One by one my obstacles tumble, and opportunities appear," she said to herself as the door behind her opened.

"I came as quickly as I could. The priestess that woke me said it was urgent," Spavati stated, joining her at the windows.

Oluja turned and put her hands on the woman's shoulders, trying not to smirk when Spavati flinched at the unexpected action.

"I have something for you, High Priestess Spavati. It is an opportunity to do something that generations of priestesses before you would have given their life to accomplish," Oluja said.

She then warmly clasped the other woman's hand and walked her out onto the main deck of the galleon, where she went to the rail and climbed over and down a rope ladder to the two sailed schooner tied off below.

Reaching the smaller boat, she glanced at the confused Spavati, who looked around suspiciously before following.

Once the crew of four had untied from the ship and guided them into the harbor, she took Spavati below the cabin and into the boat's small hold.

"Lead me in prayer, High Priestess," she said, kneeling.

Oluja could feel the trepidation in Spavati's steps and movements but knew the woman would not pass up the opportunity to lead a queen through the oldest prayers to The Siren. When they finished, Oluja sat back, resting her shoulders against the hull so she could feel the slap of each wave as they headed towards the horizon.

"I have a story to tell you, Spavati," she said, recounting to the other woman the fate of the scouting party but saving the most exciting information for the end.

"Do you want to know what killed your priestess? What was able to pry our secrets from Svenus' cousin?" she asked.

When Spavati shrugged, she sat forward from her lounging position and whispered even though the crew above could not possibly hear them.

"A Maelar was there. He struck the very life from the priestess as she summoned The Siren's wrath," she said, answering her own question.

"There has not been a deep elf seen since the cleansing of the last age, and their followers have been hunted to the ends of Nysia ever since," Spavati said in disbelief.

While she did not necessarily believe this gnome was indeed a deep elf, she did think they were descendants from the old bloodlines.

"What else would you call a much smaller distant cousin of dwarves who worships The Sleeper and practices necromancy, Spavati?" she prompted.

She could see the excitement on the woman's face and motioned for her to follow back onto the deck.

Behind them, the Kalt harbor was barely visible, and less than a mile ahead was a galleon.

"You're giving me a ship?" the woman asked with a raised eyebrow.

"I am lending you a ship, one that already has a good sailing crew on board as well as a quarter of your priestesses, brought out here while you slept. I am giving you this," Oluja said, producing the map Svenus had given her the night before.

She opened it and pointed to the mark indicating The Sanctum of the necromancers.

"Here, Spavati. Here necromancers still worship the one that

210

sleeps, and they are led in this vile effort by several of these Maelar who call themselves gnomes. The Siren's daughters are sworn to eradicate the worship of The Sleeper and the architects of her nightmare faith. I give this task and its glory to you, Spavati. The pass over the back of the mountains will be treacherous, but you will be unbothered. The people of this island cannot withstand the cold and the wind of the mountaintops like we can. You will catch them in their hole completely unaware," Oluja explained.

Spavati looked from the map to the ship several times before turning to her.

"I am thankful that you are willing to divert some of our forces upon discovery of this revolting cabal Queen Vetar," Spavati said sincerely.

"It would not be right to let this evil go unanswered. I fear The Siren would lose favor in our cause if we knowingly let the influence of deep elves remain unchecked. I sent word via another schooner as soon as I learned of this. The galleon is Lorent's from Lodestar. I did not want to let on to our actions," Oluja told her.

"I will cleanse Nysia of these Maelar and their followers, and The Siren will bless us for it, Oluja!" Spavati shouted in excitement.

Oluja decided to ignore being called by her first name this once and instead joined in the exaltation the other woman felt.

*****

It was the first time Svenus had been in the same room with Kisa and Oluja, and only the third time he had been allowed onboard one of the galleons. The tension was evident despite the outwardly visible respects and niceties passed between them. To him, they were like two old hunting cats from the highlands around the mountains, circling and stalking each other, waiting for a sign of weakness to pounce.

His feline fantasy was interrupted when Oluja took her seat behind her desk. Her chair wailed against the decking as she slid it in. Then, crossing her arms on the desk, she motioned with one hand for Kisa to speak without inviting them to sit in the chairs in front of them.

"Good afternoon, Queen Vetar," Kisa said without bowing

before following with her report.

"At present, the assault force in Kalt includes ten galleons tied off here at the wharf, made up entirely of your seven and three of my own. In addition, Duchess Morel patrols the southern seas and guards the entrance to the harbor with two of her ships which I do not include in our forces. With the fighters you brought after the city fell, we now have two and a half thousand raiders, to which another thousand could be added if the ships were left minimally crewed," Kisa said.

"What about fortifying the city?" Oluja asked.

"We have nearly completed barriers and fencing off the perimeter of the city besides a single main road and posted watches on many of the taller buildings at the city's edge. If our enemies attack by land from the north, it will be costly for anyone to retake the city. We have done the same in the south, essentially walling off the harbor and wharf from the city, save for the now gated road that empties into its center. We could easily fall back to the wharf and hold it while making our ships ready to assault a different part of the island," she answered.

Oluja nodded approvingly and then looked to Svenus. He decided it was wise to glance sidelong at Kisa and ensure the woman had finished speaking before beginning his report.

"With those of the militia who are loyal to you, and the men I already employed, as well as those whose confidence has been bolstered by your very presence here, we have three and a half thousand militiamen. If fighting came to the city itself, you could probably add another fifteen hundred to that as far as reserves and the more elderly retired folk who would rise to defend their homes, if necessary," he replied.

"Have your men had to put down any widespread dissent?" she asked him.

"No, policing activity has been easier than before your arrival. Fear is a strong keeper of the law, as it turns out," he said.

"Tell me about our border concerns then," she requested.

"It is currently being patrolled in five-mile sections. The men have orders not to engage and fresh horses to send a warning back here. However, I strongly recommend we do something to keep the northerners worried about the home-front and not support Ravnice and Fjall by sending their forces to the south. I would think that between your raiders, the militia, and the lightning of

212

your priestesses, we could easily keep quite a large army on the other side of the Kalt river," he answered.

Oluja seemed satisfied with their answers and rose from her chair to stand face to face with Svenus. He tried not to fidget while she looked him over like a hog at a harvest auction.

"Svenus, I have two major projects for your people. First, you will send workers out to these border camps and begin constructing a line of forts to watch over the river. Make them close enough to use signal fires to alert each other. It is much faster than your horseback messengers. Here in the city, I want you to maximize lumber production. I will begin a rotation of galleons from Lodestar to here and back to take lumber out to what will become our new shipyard. Gather the best craftsman you have, and I will take them there to begin the expansion of our fleet with the Tormenta shipbuilders," she said, walking from him to Kisa.

"Admiral, I relieve you of your rank," she said, staring at the woman, and Svenus stiffened in anticipation of the coming argument.

"I proclaim you General Hadjuk instead. You will take two thousand of our raiders and two thousand of the militia within quick reach of the trade bridge. Establish supply and communication lines back here. Begin training the militia on how to handle their weapons properly and identify the best way to employ large land forces. I want to lure them into committing a large army to the south. Our expanded armada could then sail north to Tuath. We will wear the people of this island down trying to fight the same Tormenta army on two fronts, all the while expanding our naval force and fortifications," she ordered, and Svenus noticed Kisa relax somewhat.

She dismissed Kisa and turned her eyes unnervingly on him again.

"Svenus, you will return to me tomorrow with your recommendation of commanders to place at Kisa's side to help her. If you happen to decide that the information about my intention towards Tuath might financially benefit you if divulged to your fellow islanders, know that I am watching you always, Svenus Kalt," she said with a cold smile.

*****

213

Tawito had found a rare respite lying quietly in his hammock, watching the daylight grow through his catamaran's small circular porthole. It had been a tiresome undertaking, sailing back and forth across the three Quaji atolls these past weeks trying to get the chiefs of the Urylap, Aylap, and Jawylap to start agreeing to contingencies of cooperation.

"I don't know how you managed to keep all the strands of your web in order, Turin," he said with a sigh. He sat in silence for a moment, waiting to hear the old elf's voice give him a cynical answer, but there were only the waves outside. A knock came at his cabin door, and he gave the peaceful image in his porthole a forlorn parting look as he hopped down from the hammock and opened the door.

"Yes?" he asked the Quaji he did not recognize and then looked beyond the man to his shrugging crew member that had been standing guard.

"You Tawito?" the man asked

"I am," he replied.

"I have a message from a man named Harpis Akkeri," the Quaji said.

Tawito tried not to look too surprised that Turin's agent on Quaj had been able to get word to him.

"Spit it out," he said impatiently.

"The man and his gnome friend said that if you can make your way to Ravnice that they want to discuss something about reparations and reconciliation. That's it, not much of a message," the man said and shrugged.

Tawito was as shocked at the timing of the offer from Harpis as he was at hearing it on his home atoll, several days sail away from Quaj Island. Maybe he finally had what he needed to stir the chiefs to joint action.

"Do you mind telling me of how you came across the man and his peculiar, short friend?" Tawito asked.

"I don't mind at all if it comes with some coin, drink, and dinner," the man replied.

*****

Ezera nudged her horse until she was next to Aanaman and

Elliswerth near the front of their procession with Lorkin and Ingar. She turned in her saddle to look behind them at the four-wide, thousand long columns of Mer and Tuath militia behind them and gave the former governors an impressed look. Then, with a horn blast, they headed south and out of the city.

Lorkin came up beside her, and after a few moments, he broke the silence.

"How was your meeting with the slippery Exarch Weksnor?" the dwarf asked.

"He took my title and removed the designation of Fjall's Diocese," she said, laughing at his surprised look.

"That well, eh?" Lorkin scoffed.

"I'd say so, he gave me autonomy over the future generations of Daybreak's gifted, and I am free of the rules that might put my participation in this struggle with the Tormenta at odds with the rules of the clergy," she said with a shrug.

"How about you? How did your meeting with the Arch Mage go?" she asked.

"Oh, he closed the college and sent most of them away but let stand the offer for those mages that wanted to join us to head south with me. He also retired and named me Arch Mage," he answered with a shrug and smile of his own.

"Seems we are surely doomed then, Arch Mage Lorkin. Congratulations! How many decided to join us?" she asked.

"Not many. I am honestly glad for it. The last thing I want is to see every bright-eyed islander who has been born with the gift lose their mind or their life under my tutelage and protection. An apprentice from the Tower of Wind, Fire Mage Lyrnah from Tuath as well as Water Mage Helki and one of his apprentices who was born in Kalt will join me and one of my apprentices from the annex" he said, counting on his fingers.

"Let's hope we are right in assuming that these storm priestesses are unfamiliar with elemental magics. Maybe they are as inexperienced as us at fighting gift against gift," she said with some concern.

"I'll teach the two mages how to fight, and maybe the apprentice from the Tower of Wind, that lad has been studying for over a decade and is damn-near a mage himself. The other apprentices, though, they are coming to learn, not to fight, if I have anything to do with it," he said.

215

Chapter 24
Collusion and Conspiracy

After the second knock on his door, Harpis groaned and rolled out of his bed at The Siren's Scream.

"I am coming," he said as he slipped on trousers and cracked open the door to see a smiling Kalna.

"There is a woman here to see you," she said, raising an eyebrow and looking over his ink-covered, bare chest.

"I wasn't expecting anyone," he said, turning back to his room and picking up his blouse and leather tunic from the floor.

"Those are quite the tattoos she said, still smiling as he covered up the giant fishhook on his chest and kraken that covered his back and shoulders.

"I learned three things growing up on my father's boat and in a Kalt fishing village. How to fish, drink, and that it is necessary to get tattoos," he said with a tinge of mourning at the memory of getting the markings along with his father.

"I see," she said, still smiling, "Then where did you learn to sing?" she asked.

Harpis paused for a moment, realizing that this was the first time in years he had talked of his life before The Syndicate.

"The singing was more accident or desperation, I suppose," he said, shaking his head and opening the door fully.

"Is she bald or wearing a wig?" he asked in an almost nervous voice.

"No, it is not Sudbina," she said with a smirk.

He tilted his head in confusion.

"Is it the blond woman that came here with Wren several days ago?" he inquired.

"No. Also, if the number of ladies calling on you at this

establishment continues to grow, we will have to send you south to Kalt to continue operating your one-man den of iniquity, sir. The Siren's Scream is not a brothel," she said with a wink and a laugh before turning and heading downstairs.

"Always a pleasure to converse with you, Kalna!" he called, slipping on his boots, and heading after her.

The mystery of who had come to see him quickly revealed itself as he made it to the first floor of the tavern and caught a glimpse of the unbound chestnut curls hanging down to the waist of the small woman sitting with her back to him. She did not need to be facing him for him to know that she wore an expression somewhere between impatience and resentment.

Instead of heading to the table, he tiptoed to the bar and leaned over to whisper to Kalna.

"An ale and a warm loaf please," he said, and she disappeared for a moment to get the bread from the kitchen.

"Ale for breakfast, eh?" she asked, handing him the loaf and then a mug.

"I probably should have asked for whiskey," he said, raising the cup in thanks and walking to the table.

"Good morning, Troubadour, how may I be of service," he said with a bow.

He lowered himself into his chair and took a sip of his ale, noting the look of barely contained exasperation on Mahala's face over the brim of his mug.

"Thank you for finally coming down and joining me. I do like your home away from home. Of course, it isn't as private as the cave the dwarves dug you below The Hall, but it seems more fitting of your station, God Singer," she chided, rolling her eyes.

"Oh, please, you may refer to me simply as Virtuoso," he said, in feigned humbleness.

"Bravit and I decided it would be best if I tried to seek you out regarding the attacks on the ships and harbor in Tuath Bay. However, it would seem no longer necessary upon attending the emergency council. So instead, I come because as much as I care for Bravit, and as much as I loathe to admit it, he cannot weave the gift as you can, and I want to show you what I discovered after much research," she responded.

"That sounds interesting. I heard it was quite the eventful couple of days up in Mer. I spent most of last night exchanging information with Aanaman and the others before they set out north to Lake Gitche this morning. I'll be heading that way with some others tomorrow," he said.

"Is there a place we can play that would keep others safe from our gift?" she said quietly, leaning in over the table.

Truly intrigued, he finished munching on the piece of warm bread he had just bit off.

"I happen to know just the place. It is a short walk from here. I'll fill you in on what happened at the Kalt border along the way," he said, standing and finishing his glass before walking to the bar and tipping Kalna.

*****

Once they reached Wren's building, Harpis beat on the door heavily.

"Open up!" he shouted towards the second-story window. He smiled as he heard the muted sound of the slamming door at the top of the stairs, followed by growing gnomish curses.

"You took me to see a mortician?" Mahala asked, pointing at the faded business sign in the window.

He did not get a chance to explain as Wren flung open the door before he could reply.

"What lad, we aren't supposed to meet until this evening," he said, leaning to the side to view Mahala.

"Find yourself another tavern-girl at The Siren's Scream?" the gnome asked.

Harpis laughed nervously and raised a finger to quiet the gnome and explain, but before he could speak, he was wincing in pain as the petite woman slapped his ears with both her hands.

"I am Troubadour Mahala Shelta of The Hall," she said with indignantly crossed arms.

Wren gave her a low bow.

"I am Wren, Death Herald and keeper of The Sanctum, and just as you, I am an unfortunate acquaintance of this bumbling idiot," the gnome said, pointing at Harpis.

"Wren, can we use the basement?" he asked.

"If you would like to join us, Wren, our research could truly benefit from your help," Mahala interrupted behind him.

"All right then, head on down while I grab my coffee from

218

upstairs. Can I get you anything, lady bard?" he asked.

"No, thank you," she said sweetly to the gnome before turning a glare back on Harpis and bidding Wren lead on.

He showed her to the first basement level and tried not to laugh as she looked around with some concern at the coffins, preparation table, and embalming supplies.

"Don't worry, the acoustics are quite nice down here," he laughed.

Wren returned and made his way, grumbling, to the stool at his workbench and sat sipping his drink. Mahal pulled a rolled up, thin leather book from her tunic and laid it on the preparation table.

"This is *Illia's Ode to the Sea*, by Mia Kespeare," she said, reverently turning over leather pages one after another.

"It is undated but quite old, one of only a handful of texts solely dedicated to gift-woven music that I have ever come across," she finished with evident excitement in her eyes.

Harpis walked over to the table and gazed down at the page she had laid open while she unslung her violin case from her back and placed it on the table.

"*The Dissonance of Bacoj*?" he asked, reading the title of the music.

"Don't worry, God Singer, I know you can't read music to save your life. I will play it so that you can learn it, but I warn you, you might not enjoy it. According to the notations on the back of the page, the song resonates in structure of the ear, causing extreme physical pain," she said with a smile.

Harpis glared at Wren as the gnome almost choked on his coffee, laughing.

Mahala placed her violin under her chin and readied the bow. Then, looking at Wren, who had plugged his ears with his fingers, she began to play very softly.

Harpis at first felt a warm sensation in his ears that became hotter as she gradually increased the volume and speed she was playing. The song quickly became a quick back and forth of angrily shrieking bird calls, and Harpis fell to his knees, clutching at his ears in pain.

"Gods, that's awful," he said, shaking the pain from his

ears.

"Bravit thinks so as well. Unlike our cherubic Maestro, I have found this song particularly suited to the targeted weaving of our gift. Wren, you may happily keep your ears unplugged. I will cause you no pain," she stated.

Wren seemed unconvinced. However, after Harpis gave his friend an encouraging look, the gnome waved for her to play again.

After a few slowly burgeoning verses, he experienced the same expansion of warmth to heat to pain in his ears. Wren was cringing but not in any obvious physical pain.

"Quite the thing, that. It is assuredly an unpleasant song, but I did not experience the agony that our beloved friend here has seemed to endure," the gnome said to Mahala.

"At the expense of several unfortunate students, we found that when the gift is woven into this song and played with a percussion instrument, Bravit's specialty, it is much more effective. There are even riddles on the last few pages that hint at using the gift to play certain actions," she said, excitedly turning to the back of the leather page.

"See here, notes on what instrument and key work best with the song. Mia Kespeare's booklet is the only text I have seen with such information. Still, it seems our gift can be very specific and augmented to certain notes and instruments to allow for greater or more precise effect," she said passionately and turned the page with a smile, slowly running her finger across the lines of the next song.

"*Nyv's Threnody*," she said, pointing at the title before clearing her case and the music from the table.

"Harpis, lay on the table, please. Wren, if you would plug your ears up just in case and come and keep track of his pulse," she asked both of them.

Against his better judgment, Harpis lay on the table and stared up at the stone ceiling of Wren's basement. The gnome slid his stool over and shoved half-melted candle wax into his own ears before picking up his wrist and pressing a thumb into it. When the gnome nodded at her, Mahala readied her violin.

"The notes on this say that it is written for the violin," she said with an eagerness he was unaccustomed to in the woman.

220

With nothing to focus on but her movements and music, the beautiful woman's masterful ability to move hypnotically in tune with her songs was entrancing. The song was simple. She would slide the bow upward, producing a long slow increase in pitch before pulling it downward and dragging the note back into a low and resounding hum. The way her hand skittered up and then down the neck of the violin reminded him of a spider dancing around its web, only pausing for brief moments as the slide of her bow on the strings changed direction.

Normally, he felt the familiar strong pull of her gift when she wove it, but instead, he noticed only that the speed of her movement continued to slow with each back and forth of the bow until he could no longer sense the movement of the spider, and the room around him seemed to grow dark. Then, after a few more moments, the encroachment of the dark stopped, and he became more aware of the room around him again in the silence that followed.

Mahala's eyes were closed as she stood frozen, clutching the violin for a moment before opening them while she exhaled, gingerly placing it on the table.

"Sleeper below us, lass. I think you could have killed him," Wren exclaimed, turning to look at him as he sat up on the table.

"She had your heart beating so slow I might as well have pronounced you dead," he said in surprise.

"It is a wordless song written for that very purpose. It allows me to take over the heart's rhythm and once entwined, I can simply slow it down until I stop it. It is a terrifying thing. I believe that if I did not unweave my gift from the music before I finished playing that his heart may have stopped," she said with a smile.

Harpis looked at her expression and shook his head in amazement.

"It is good to see you have finally found something to be excited and happy about, even if you find that joy in songs of pain and death," he said with a laugh, noting her face had quickly returned to its typical demeanor.

Wren hopped down from his stool and walked over to him, "Try to not give this pretty lady a reason to kill you before our meeting tonight. We have much to plan before we leave tomorrow," he said, heading up the stairs.

Harpis looked to Mahala, who had picked up his violin and

221

was appreciatively examining it.

"Such a tragedy to see such an exquisite tool in your abusive, clumsy hands," she said, handing it to him with a grin.

He smiled back at the usually abrasive woman, thinking about what he had discussed with Wren and Ezera days ago.

"Mahala, if you are not bound immediately back to The Hall, would you consider joining us this evening? I think we could use your help," he asked.

"Unlike Bravit, the kitchens have not been able to keep me from missing the nomadic wandering. If it is an adventure you are offering, I will happily oblige," she replied.

*****

It had been decades since she had rowed a raiding scull to shore, and Oluja was still rubbing her shoulders and biceps as she reached the perimeter of the Kalt lumber yard with the two closest and most trusted members of her personal guard. The three of them slipped amongst the shadows until they were outside Svenus' bedroom window.

She crouched outside with the remaining guard after hoisting the smaller woman up and through to clear the room. The light taps of a filet knife tip on the glass of the window signaled it was safe for her to enter, and she used the other guard's thigh like a step to get through and into Svenus' room. The more diminutive guard made her way back through the window once Oluja was inside.

She looked down at the confused and shirtless patriarch of the Kalt family in the moonlit room and for a moment allowed herself the fantasy of taking him as a plaything. Indulgences would have to wait, though. She needed the conniving land-born to aid her in disposing of one of her most significant challenges.

"You are going to do something for me, Svenus Kalt. It will forever tie our fates and cement my rule over my people. If done well, perhaps that rule might be with you at my side," she said, sitting on his bed.

"We couldn't discuss this in the morning without me waking to a filet knife held to my throat?" he asked with a bewildered look.

"You are going to pick someone you trust, one of your close

222

family, for this task. They will go with your other commanders to support the efforts at the border. They will kill Kisa Hadjuk, and they will make it look like it was undeniably someone from the north," she said quietly, and he attentively sat up.

"I wouldn't trust my close family to do anything important. On the other hand, my cousin Lazar I would trust for this task, and given his experience with the enemy and at the border, he is an obvious recommendation to send out with her," he said.

She gave him a lascivious smile in the pale light of his room and placed her hand on the blanket over his thigh.

"Perhaps he can earn back the right to live through this mission. You will not tell him this came from me. You will tell him this is your idea, that you see Kisa as a threat to your ability to be my second in command here in Kalt," she said, squeezing his thigh.

"I find you quite tolerable for a male, Svenus Kalt," she said, turning and heading back out of his window.

If the man was not already motivated by greed and fear to aid her, she figured having his virile urges added to the list might prove beneficial and perhaps enjoyable.

*****

Harpis rose from the small wooden chair in Wren's apartment to open the door for Mahala. She walked in front of him and stopped to scan the room while he motioned for her to take his seat, and he sat atop Wren's table.

"This is Troubadour Mahala. She is the most talented and studious gifted bard The Hall has ever had. Mahala, meet Ezera and Jabruelle. Ezera was the Vicar of Fjall, and Jabruelle is one of Wren's acolytes. You have already met his exaltedness, the Death Herald," Harpis said, introducing them.

Wren rose from his comfy chair by the fire and waved a dismissive hand at him before handing Mahala a glass and pouring her a drink.

"Well met again, Mahala. Harpis says he trusts you with his life and said you are willing to help our little excursion on behalf of this island's people. I'll ask you just once then, in front of people whose lives will directly be in your hands, can you keep our secret, lass?" the gnome asked.

223

She nodded soberly and shot Harpis a curious look.

"I can and will," she replied.

Wren settled back into his chair and continued.

"The Syndicate is no more, but the need for information, spying, and espionage remains. We three are the last remnants of that clandestine group and have asked you, Mahala, and you, Jabruelle, here to assist us in establishing a presence behind enemy lines in Kalt city. If the war is short, you will aid in assuring it is as quick and as painless as possible. If it is long, you will assure we stay one step ahead of the enemy. Do the two of you accept this risk?" he questioned.

Jabruelle did not even let Wren finish before nodding his head vigorously, and Mahala affirmed her intention.

"Now, Harpis and Jabruelle are from Kalt, and look it, so they should pass easily enough, and Mahala, you are pretty enough that no man will think to ask why you are in their presence. Under Harpis' lead, you will establish a base, identify Svenus Kalt's role in all of this and see if there seems to be a way to sow disorder between the people of Kalt and their new rulers. Take on the role of a performing troupe, play at the bars and taverns, and listen to what people say," Wren finished, taking a sip of his whiskey.

Harpis walked in front of Mahala and looked from her to Jabruelle.

"If it comes to open fighting, we will make sure we are wearing the uniform of our troupe. It is how the northern forces will identify us as friendly," Harpis said.

He then handed Jabruelle and Mahala a white tabard with a black fishhook as well as a floppy white cloth cap with a thin black fur rim and large black feather hanging from its side.

"We will claim we are from the village where I was born. No one in Kalt city will be able to argue any different, I assure you," he said, sitting back down.

Jabruelle obediently took the garments and sat back on the ground by the fire.

Mahala looked from the hat to the tabard and then at Wren.

"I am beginning to rethink my original thoughts of adventure," she said.

"Come now, Mahala, that is not the attitude I expect from a member of The Sea Goats!" he said, dodging the hat thrown his way.

"The Sea Goats?" she asked.

"Yes, that is the name of our traveling troupe! We will swoon our audiences in every drinking establishment in Kalt!" he said.

Setting down her empty glass, Mahala blew out a long and frustrated breath.

"This is a terrible idea and that is the worst name I have ever heard," she said and picked up the bottle Wren had poured her drink from, taking a long pull from it.

"Or it is the very best name!" Wren said.

"Well, it is definitely one or the other," Harpis insisted, laughing.

Jabruelle sat quietly in concentration for several minutes before looking at Wren.

"I don't get it, that name doesn't make any sense," he said in confusion.

"It never has lad," Wren answered.

Waiting for them all to finish, Harpis took the opportunity to address Mahala's other concern.

"No, a terrible idea would have been a suspicious lone man trying to sell this guise. A married pair of violinists and their only son traveling south to try and make their living entertaining in the city, is much more believable!" he said.

"You are not old enough to be his father," she said, pointing at the barely out of adolescence acolyte.

"You are only, what, five years older?" she asked.

"Despite being only twenty-four, he does easily pass for forty," Wren said with a shrug.

After a moment, Mahala sat straight in her chair.

"Wait, are you assuming I am old enough to be his mother!" she hissed, pointing again at Jabruelle.

"I don't make a habit of assuming. I make a habit of knowing," Wren replied.

Chapter 25

Anarchy

Bravit retrieved several bottles of wine from inside what had once been Benali Tuath's quarters before its conversion into his and Mahala's rooms. Excitedly, he made his way up the stairs to the balcony overlooking the northern seas. He was interested in hearing more about the ancient, enchanted mask that had played a role previously unknown to him in the life and death of his old friend.

He reached the balcony huffing from his haste and walked over to where Stone Mage Vennil and Stone Sage Mara sat around a small brazier with a roaring fire in it.

"Apologies for the delay, but I was able to find several of Mahala's better bottles of wine for your enjoyment. I will just have to replace them before she returns!" he said, joining them.

"Not a problem at all, Bravit. Have our thanks again for housing so many of us here at The Hall," Vennil said, filling Mara's glass and then his own.

"It's no trouble, really. We have had fewer and fewer students of journalism, and the recent events have sent nearly all of our musical pupils back to their homes in fear," Bravit said.

He was about to prod his guests to continue their story of Stone Magus Breyva and her Apotheosis when he realized the two were staring past him. Turning to look back at the door, he saw two oddly dressed women brandishing filet knives and a pair of pale-skinned, dark-haired men with swords.

"Having a nice evening, are we?" one of the men asked, walking towards them menacingly.

Bravit cleared his throat, and the sage and mage looked at him.

"Plug your ears if you please and do your best to help me when I finish," he told them quietly before standing from his chair and picking up his drum by its shoulder sling.

"Care to join us for a performance?" he asked, slipping it over his head.

"You can scream whatever song you like until your breath runs out, minstrel. Then we will paint this building with your blood," one of the women said in an odd accent.

"Ah, that would be maestro, not minstrel," he corrected. Then, grabbing his mallets from the table, he began striking out the notes of *The Dissonance of Bacoj* from his drumhead with them as if he were blocking and striking their weapons with a ten-pound hammer.

Within moments the attackers were writhing in pain on the balcony's stone, and he stopped his song. One of the women rose to her feet and slowly stalked towards them, bleeding from her ears. Bravit heard murmuring behind him and turned to see Vennil on a knee with his palm to the ground. A moment later, a dwarf-sized stone elemental sprung from the stones between the woman and them and bludgeoned her until she was a formless pile of meat while Vennil shouted in rage.

The other woman attempted to throw her knife their way and suffered a similar fate at the hands of the elemental while the two men lay unconscious next to their swords.

Bravit tried not to join in as he heard Mara vomit wine and her dinner over the edge of the railing. The three of them sprang into action a moment later when screams came from the quarters where the trainees and apprentices were staying.

After flying down the two sets of stairs and across the performance hall into the dormitory wing, Bravit could hardly breathe. He was increasingly sore from his drum bouncing against his belly, but he charged on undaunted.

It became apparent that their haste was unnecessary as they rounded the corner and looked down the long dormitory hall. Two trainees lay lifeless in puddles of their own blood on the floor. Their necks slit from ear to ear. The rest of the hall was blackened and charred with several piles of ash and bones between them and a teenage girl sitting on the floor cross-legged and crying with her eyes closed at the other end. A life-sized mountain cat made entirely of flame stood angrily before her.

227

Bravit began to sing a soothing gift-woven song to the poor girl as Vennil and Mara slowly approached her.

Mara wrapped her arms around the girl in a hug while Vennil knelt at her side.

"You must let go of the fire, sweetheart. It is safe now. We are here to help you," he whispered.

A tense moment later, the girl opened her eyes as the fire elemental faded.

"My dear, you had yet to create your cynosure, let alone been taught how to control an element, and here you are with the elemental conjuring required to become a mage standing guard over you. What happened?" Mara asked.

"I saw them kill my friends. It was so scary, all I did was keep screaming and screaming, and the flame of the lantern burst out and engulfed the hallway and killed them. I am so sorry," she said, starting to cry again.

Mara comforted her and took her out of the hall and into one of the rooms.

"I doubt this is an isolated incident," Bravit said to Vennil, who nodded his agreement.

"We must send word to Tuath city and beyond," the stone mage said as they tended to the other students and trainees.

*****

Over a decade ago when he was still in his seventies, Uridyll had accepted the fact that no matter what he did, an inability to sleep on a regular schedule accompanied old age. Usually, he would have roamed the grounds of the college hoping to encounter a student late at work studying or a colleague trying to finish some research in the light of nearly spent candles.

It was those moments of intimate tutelage and shared exploration of the elemental sciences that he relished most during his time as Arch Mage. He cherished that influence over the future of a single person's experience in the craft he had long loved. In the week since his resignation and the emptying of the college, the silence of its walls felt more like a prison than an intellectual sanctuary.

So it was that for the third time in as many days, he found himself making his way across the peninsula of the city in the

228

darkest, earliest hours of the morning. The cold of late autumn aided in the misery of his old joints. By the time Uridyll reached the door of the archives, he had decided tomorrow he would simply bring some of the texts back with him so that he might continue his research in his quarters by a warm fire.

He closed the archive doors behind him and tried not to cringe at the booming echo. He hadn't bothered cleaning up his notes or putting back the scrolls and tomes he had stacked on a desk in the back of the main wing. Abandoned as they were, he assumed he wouldn't be offending or angering any record keepers, and his work would be undisturbed by others.

Taking his oil and striker from his robe, he lit the line of candles at the far edge of his table and began thumbing through several texts in their growing light. He had decided that even if he wasn't to use his gift in the struggle of his people, he could at least use his mind to research some of the old ways and contribute his findings to Lorkin if they looked beneficial.

The crash of broken glass falling on the tile floor nearly startled him to death, and he quickly doused the flames of his candles and went still. Then, he heard the soft shuffle of at least three pairs of feet approach from different directions.

"I thought you said this place was supposed to be shuttered since we raided the harbor," he heard a feminine voice angrily hiss.

"That's what the drunk I bribed at the inn earlier said. They didn't want to waste the militia guarding a bunch of books," a man answered in a distinctly Kaltese accent.

"Then why does it smell like recently burnt candle wicks in here?" another feminine voice asked from nearby.

Uridyll struggled to remain still as there were crashes from the intruders knocking over several bookcases.

"Follow me to the back. That is where the older texts on magic are. You can pick through them before we destroy this place. Hurry though, we need to paint our warning on the front doors and be gone in the next hour," the man answered from the center of the wing.

Uridyll realized he could either confront and surprise the would-be thieves or likely be overtaken by them in the darkness. His old limbs trembled as he held his striker over the candle closest to him, and he drug sparks from it as hard as he could. The candle leaped back to life, and he heard the gasps of those around him.

"I need you, old friend," he whispered to the flame, which became a swirling vortex that spread into the form of his giant familiar, the blazing owl's wings outstretched overhead, illuminating the entire archive.

"Be gone or suffer my wrath!" he shouted in a voice that bellowed off the walls and ceiling.

He caught sight of a short-haired foreign woman, frozen in fear and surprise before turning towards the commotion of the fleeing man. He guided his familiar to chase, but as it started to obey, he felt a sharp pain in his back and a cool sliding sensation in his chest. Clutching at his breast, the sword blade protruding from it pierced his hand. Then, as his mind started to slip amongst the pain, he watched his familiar crash like a comet into a row of bookcases.

*****

Isra Rashida rubbed her head in frustration, setting down another formal written message, one of a dozen delivered over the past two days from all over Tuath and Mer. The former governor, and now minister, sat back and sighed. She spared herself a laugh at the most recent report that the Tuath family mansion high above Tuath bay was set ablaze the night before. Not more than two years ago, such an act would have been a slap in the face to the ruling family, but the family was no more, and now their home joined them amongst the ashes of history.

"Fitting," she said to herself and the paper when one of her staff entered the squat council chamber and waved in another messenger, who, per her protocol, was escorted by two militiamen.

"Yes?" she asked in a tired voice to the Tuathian man across the table.

"Sorry to disturb you, Governor. Sorry, I mean, Minister Rashida," he said nervously.

She set down the message and tried to give the man a calming look.

"No insult taken, please, what word from Tuath?" she asked, wondering what other ill-fated attack had occurred in her state.

"There was an attack on The Hall. Eight armed men and women assaulted them two nights ago," the man said.

Isra hung her head for a moment, knowing that so far north, there were no protective militia patrols to purposely hide any indication of the magically gifted folk hiding there.

"How bad was it?" she asked, not wanting to know the answer.

The man smiled and leaned on the table.

"They got more than they could have bargained for! Bravit knocked four of them to their knees with the magic of his drum, and Stone Mage Vennil crushed them to death with his familiar. Four others went after the trainees, and a young girl summoned an inferno that claimed them all!" he said excitedly before becoming serious.

"Two young trainees were lost, though. Their victory was complete but not as timely as could have been hoped," he said sadly.

"Well, this at least is better news than I have received in days. When you reach Tuath, please see to it that my condolences and appreciation makes it to The Hall," she said, and the man snapped to attention and left with the militiamen in tow.

Isra was about to finish writing her correspondence to the mayors, urging them to stay calm amongst the terror being wrought across the northern cities and states when the attendant came back in.

"Minister, I think you should come to see this," she said.

"What now?" she asked the ceiling as much as the other woman.

"The archives have finally finished burning," she answered.

Rashida rose from her desk and followed the woman out of the council chamber.

As they made their way down several streets towards the middle of the city peninsula, the smell of smoke still hung thick in the air and soot had stained many of the surrounding buildings, and ash still blew like snow from the rooftops.

The stone structure of the archives was still intact, but the tiled roof had mostly fallen in, save for the very back. Several militiamen came to join them and walked them through some of the wreckage and rubble until they were in the center of the charred archive with the fire-made skylight open to the sun above.

231

"I can't believe this building burned for three days," she said, looking around in awe of the damage.

"It is worse than that, Minister. We have lost more than the texts," one of the militiamen said, leading her to the back where the roof still hung dangerously overhead. The corpse sprawled over the table was barely recognizable as human, but the orange color of mage robes still clung to the burnt fabric in a few places, and the stone of the fire striker had cracked but otherwise survived the wild conflagration.

"There was only one mage left in Mer," the militiaman said, his voice cracking.

Isra's shoulders sagged, and she braced herself on the stone table. She had not known the kindly old Arch Mage long, but he had been a valuable advisor and confidant during her first days in office after Aanaman and the others had headed south. She looked up with tears in her eyes and barely stopped herself from wiping ashes across her cheeks.

Chapter 26
Devotion

Harpis was happy to hand the reins of his horse off to the militiamen that greeted them upon reaching the lakeshore where the largest branch of the Fjall river emptied into Lake Gitche. Spending the past few years in the farming state of Ravnice had gotten him accustomed to riding, but the entire day spent on horseback from the city had his legs aching.

He bent to stretch his back and noted Ezera, Jabruelle, and Mahala doing the same. Wren climbed down from his modified children's saddle, using the stirrup like a ladder.

"Whenever you youngsters are ready," the gnome chided them.

"We sadly do not have the benefit of the size and weight of a toddler, which would make the bounce in the saddle less painful, dear friend," Harpis replied sarcastically.

Straightening, he took a moment to look around at the construction and fortification that had impressively been completed in just a few short weeks. To his right, along the southern coast of the lake, sprawled the tent city that accommodated the nine thousand militiamen. Together with the dwarves, they made up the first unified army of Quaj. Men and dwarves alike were busy building a wooden perimeter and patrolling around the tents.

The patrol that greeted them told them to head to the river's edge. Chancellor Reaper, and the others were gathered in planning as they had been every day since arriving. As they walked to where the lake and river met, a squat wooden building came into view with dwarven guards standing at the door.

Once inside, they met the contingent from Mer, who

encircled a giant rough wooden table covered in maps of Kalt and Ravnice, overlayed with rocks that had symbols painted on them indicating various forces on both sides. Harpis waved in greeting to General Shieldborn and the newly appointed Field Marshal Elliswerth, who he had not seen since the battle of Tuath. He then went to Aanaman as the others filed in behind him.

Aanaman gave Harpis a somber look and motioned for them to take seats at the table.

"I am glad the five of you are here now, but unfortunately there have been some new developments that have accelerated our timeline and will likely affect your plans to the south as well," the chancellor stated, facing them.

At the same time, Lorkin, Shieldborn, and Elliswerth whispered on the other side of the table.

"There have been almost two dozen hit and run raids across Tuath and Mer, in the cities and smaller towns and villages. Some were unsuccessful, like the attempted assault at The Hall. Others, like the burning of the archives, were not stopped. Inconveniently, all have been successful in causing terror and doubt amongst the northern states. This severely strains our ability to keep this coalition together and stop our men from returning home in droves over concern for their families. Just today, I learned that the retired Arch Mage was among the casualties at the archive as well," he said bitterly.

Harpis exchanged sad looks with Ezera and Wren at the news of the grandfatherly Arch Mage's passing and the destruction of the archives that contained Turin's hidden missives.

Ezera wiped a tear from her eye and looked sympathetically at Lorkin.

"Lorkin, I am so sorry, Uridyll Vatra will be missed by many of us, but none more than you I fear," she said, bowing her head.

The dwarf gave a curt nod in appreciation, and everyone looked at Wren who was loudly drumming his fingers.

"It would seem that we are now to set a course wholly our own, no longer chasing after the plots of Turin Deadeye. Lorkin, you have my condolences, my friend, no one was more deserving of the rest found in the long final sleep than the good mage," the gnome said.

Harpis sat back in his chair, almost unable to accept that the last strands of Turin Deadeye's influence were lost to the flames.

Wren faced Ezera, rubbing his chin in thought.

"I'd bet my left leg that Svenus Kalt is helping them orchestrate these raids across the north. He has always had a mind for using fear to accomplish his means, and I don't think our foreign invaders would have thought to use such tactics to keep our attention and resources spread thin," the gnome assessed.

"Perhaps our efforts in Kalt may have much more specific and urgent needs. If we can't put an end to Svenus or whoever else is responsible for the planning and execution of these attacks, we won't have the luxury of time to spread dissent from within as planned," Harpis reasoned.

Aanaman held up a hand to stop them.

"I don't disagree but let us walk you through where we stand, and from there we can figure out the best use for your clandestine mission," he said, turning back to the table.

"Gentlemen, if you would," he said, motioning to Elliswerth and Okliff Shieldborn.

Elliswerth stood and looked over the maps on the table before addressing them.

"We are in a race against our enemy for the will and commitment of this island. If we lose, we will be unable to stay united in its defense or push the Tormenta from our lands," he said.

The field marshal paused to glance at the maps before continuing.

"With the dwarves and militiamen from Mer, Ravnice, and Tuath, we have a ten-thousand strong army which we believe will be enough to make our way into Kalt. First, though, we must get that army across the Kalt river. If they meet us at the trade bridge and they feel we will be able to get our forces across it, they might use their priestesses or other means to destroy the bridge. That would force us into fording the river while under assault from the far side, resulting in hefty casualties," Elliswerth concluded.

General Shieldborn walked around the table to reach the spot on the map where the bridge was and jabbed his finger at it.

"Our strength is in the armor and tactics of dwarven folk. We have experience in large-scale land warfare, and we are training the human soldiers of our army in them as much as we can before we move out. Dwarven officers will be amongst all groups to aid in the execution of large unit maneuvers and signaling. the

235

Tormenta are talented combatants, but we expect they won't have operated at scale on land. If we can meet them on an open battlefield, we should be the superior army if we can keep their storm priestesses from striking with impunity," he huffed.

Lorkin joined the general and spoke in a heavy voice that was still mourning the passage of Uridyll.

"We have been developing tactics and small reaction forces that will have the sole responsibility of engaging and impeding the storm priestesses using crossbows, mages, and clerics. In addition, we are working on plans to mitigate the loss of the bridge and its bottleneck. Unfortunately, the elves have already denied our request to march through their state, so we are stuck crossing the river there," the newly appointed Arch Mage said.

Elliswerth nodded in thanks at the dwarves and pointed towards Lake Gitche on the map.

"Now, the Kalt River is only waist deep near the trade bridge and maybe a hundred feet across. The bridge will be an obvious target for their magic, especially once we try to cross it. Ten men can stand abreast on it, so we will have to be creative in using it if we use it at all. All these and more are problems for us to figure out," Elliswerth finished, returning to his seat.

Aanaman walked to the doors of the command room and opened them.

"I will now ask for some of you to leave, as this last bit is quite sensitive," he said, and the room emptied save for General Shieldborn, Aanaman, Harpis, and Wren. The dwarf waved for them to join him on the other side of the table with Aanaman.

"You have six days to get into Kalt and do what you can about Svenus. Your priority is doing what you can to end the attacks putting pressure on us in the north. After that, learn all you can and do anything you deem prudent. Before dawn on the sixth day, we will make our move to cross the river. Be on the other side if you can. You will use the commotion to join back up with us. We will instruct our forces right before we march to look out for your uniforms," the dwarf said.

Aanaman walked over and embraced him.

"Harpis, I don't envy the three of you the dangers ahead. You have my blessing to do whatever is necessary while in Kalt and on the battlefield. If we cannot break them and get them on the run in seven days, we risk years of war if not divisiveness and defeat. Get what rest you can this evening. You leave before dawn on fresh horses. Though the elves refused our army, they have agreed to see you through their lands and into Kalt tomorrow night. Stay safe and keep an eye to the north and an ear to the ground the morning we attack. Kilannry should be making quite the entrance," he said with a smile.

Wren turned to him with uncomfortable worry in his eyes.

"Remember what you learned at Lodestar, remember what Arken taught you there and what I have taught you since."

*****

There was not a single cloud hanging over the Fjall mountains, and the reflection of the sunlight in the snow that capped them was nearly blinding. The frigid temperatures on the mountaintops would have had most folk shaking themselves to death, even without the constantly howling wind.

The elements did not bother Spavati though. They did not bother any of the Tormenta. Where most would be shivering with their teeth chattering while draped in furs, she and her priestesses stood rigid in anticipation as a single scout climbed to them.

"It is the place you spoke of High Priestess. I crawled below one of the windows cut in the mountainside and heard them conversing. They mentioned The Sleeper several times," the crossbowman said

He pointed to the slope below them where the winds pulled the smoke rising from stone chimneys poking above the snow.

She dismissed him to join the other warriors keeping guard over them and motioned for her priestesses.

"It is time, sisters," she said.

The other twelve women slowly formed a circle around her. Twice as many male curates knelt in the snow in a ring outside of them and began murmuring in prayer.

Spavati undid the belt of her robe and let the blue cloth fall to the snow at her feet. The other women did the same, and curates obediently came to them to take their boots and robes.

She slowly spun a circle, exchanging hungry looks with the other women.

"Today, we take up the task that generations of The Siren's storm priestesses have before us. We will extinguish the Maelar

237

and their vile worship of death from this plane!" she shouted, knowing the occupants of The Sanctum could not hear her above the wind.

Her priestesses joined hands, and she closed her eyes, beginning the chant of conjuring, leading them into a slow crescendo that grew louder as they repeated it for several minutes. She could sense the flickering and winking coils of lightning ripple across her bare skin and gather above her upheld hands. Then, opening her eyes, she saw the arcs joining the slowly growing pillar of electricity above her from the clasped hands of her priestesses.

Finally, feeling as though the summoning would tear her apart, she let out a feral scream. She watched in ecstasy as the bolt, now as wide as a tree trunk, slammed into the mountainside. Its force blasted the outer wall of The Sanctum open like a cracked egg. The thunderclap from its strike shook the snow from mountaintops as far as she could see. She watched in fascination as avalanches sent massive sheets of snow and ice crashing down like the angry, white-crested waves of The Siren's storms.

Her priestesses then began individual summonings. Bolt after bolt snaked into the exposed temple until they had no strength left to continue. Only then did she beckon for the crossbowman to check for any survivors.

*****

Enky was so engrossed watching his marionette in the frame on his desk that he did not notice he was not alone until he felt strong hands grab his chair and spin him towards their owner.

"Hello, Sunshine. Nice to see you!" he said with his typical snark. However, he immediately became serious when he saw the troubled look on his oldest sister's usually bright and calm face.

"What is it?" he asked.

"Show me my sister," she requested in a pleading voice.

Usually, he would have joked and asked which sister, but her tone and obvious concern was enough to tell him she meant her twin and not either of their younger siblings.

He climbed onto his desk and stood on the tiptoes to maximize the reach of his four-and-a-half-foot height. He grabbed a gold frame from high up on his wall and climbed down to sit.

His sister moved behind him so she could watch it as he did. He murmured a command, and the scene changed from a woodland oasis to dark swirling mists under a starry sky that revealed the nude form of their sister laying amongst the apparition-like tendrils of fog that encircled her. He was about to turn around and ask what she had expected when he saw both of her sleeping eyes snap open for a moment and stare right at him.

In a shock, he let out a childlike scream and dropped the frame to the ground, where it shattered and disappeared.

"Is she awake!?" he asked, spinning.

"Not quite, but nearly," she said quietly.

"But how?" he asked, afraid to hear her say the answer they both already knew.

"The devotion necessary for her ascension has almost completely faded from the mortal plane, Enky. Show me her temple on Nysia, please," she asked with sadness in her blue eyes.

He leaned over and grabbed one of the lower frames and handed it to her as he whispered to it. She clasped it gingerly in her pale hands. Together they watched as nude women donned blue robes and headed away from the smoking crater that had been The Sanctum. Her grasp trembled for a moment before she let out a scream of rage, and the frame shattered in her hands, its pieces fading before they hit the ground.

The uncharacteristic outburst from the goddess that embodied calm, and kindliness brought a fear to his stomach that he had not felt in ages.

She looked down at him, seething. He tried to match her stare but ended up looking away towards his gateway to The Nexus when his younger sisters entered his tiny domain. The oldest did not flinch or acknowledge them at first.

"Though they may have been her priestesses," she said, pointing at the fiery red-haired goddess of storms, "I know that the only reason they are there is you, Enky!" she said through clenched teeth.

For the first time in millennia, Enky was unsure how to respond. The younger twins, too, he observed, were caught off guard by their sister's rage.

"As if your plot regarding our brother wasn't problematic enough, you have brought Nysia and Maelara closer together than they have been in two ages. Should Lilynth walk the mortal plane

239

again, our mother may banish us all to join her. Yourself included!" she warned.

Chapter 27
As Instructed

Kisa's feet ached as she finally headed back towards her command tent on the northern end of the camp. She had spent most of the day observing Tormenta women and men who were hopelessly attempting to train Kalt militiamen in combat. Once dusk arrived, it had been another three hours of debating with Tormenta officers and those appointed by Svenus while they argued over how best to defend the bridge and river.

She was pleased to have received word from the forts being constructed to her north that they should be complete in the coming days. The workers would then descend on her current position to build a much larger fortification to look over the stout stone bridge that spanned the Kalt river.

Even without work having begun at their camp, she felt secure in their position. The two thousand Tormenta and two thousand militia she had at her immediate disposal could hold back a much larger force due to the bottleneck the bridge created. If a battle was joined in earnest, she could also send word to the fifteen-hundred troops stationed at the string of forts and have them cross the river to flank and hit the rear of any attack. She had wished there were more storm priestesses with them, but she had Galonica and her clan's four other priestesses, plus several more from other families.

She was not confident yet in the ability of the force to fight with much semblance of unity. However, she did take comfort that they had established their communications to the forts and the city. Also, they were at no risk of running out of supplies thanks to regular rotations of wagons from the city. Reaching her tent, she looked up at the moon before hanging her head and sighing heavily at the dawn that was only a handful of hours away.

The flap fell behind her. The disappearance of moonlight left her fumbling in the dark, looking for a candle, when suddenly her tent was basked in golden light of an uncovered lantern. She leaped back and held a dagger threateningly before relaxing when she saw the smirking face of Oluja's second captain. The woman set the lantern down on the small table near her bed.

"Good evening, General Hadjuk," the woman said sarcastically.

"What do you want, Verisna, and can it wait for tomorrow?" Kisa responded.

She grumpily put her hands on her hips while she waited for the other woman to respond. Verisna was second only to herself amongst the forward deployed forces, and Kisa knew Oluja had sent the captain to keep an eye on her.

"I am afraid tomorrow is no longer your concern, Kisa," Verisna said, standing.

Kisa drew her dagger and crouched. If Oluja's pet wanted her position, she would not go quietly. She opened her mouth to call for her guards, but before she could speak, she felt a flash of heat on the back of her head, and everything went dark.

*****

Lazar rubbed his knuckles after gagging and binding the unconscious Kisa and watched while Verisna slapped the other woman awake. When she finally came to, Kisa Hadjuk glared in fearless, defiant rage at the other woman, grunting as loud as she could around the gag.

Verisna walked up to Kisa and grabbed her by the chin.

"You know, I always thought it would have been best for our people if you had been put to death all those years ago for your disgraceful escapades in Kalt. So many others, me included, were incensed that your family name had saved you from that fate. How fortunate now that I get to finally end your life for creating that despicable half-breed and, worse yet, letting it live. Take solace, Kisa Hadjuk, that your death will serve our people better than your life ever did," she finished, smacking the bound woman, and spitting at her.

Lazar was no stranger to violence and killing, but even he had been entirely unnerved by the vicious and ruthless nature of Tormenta women. Having watched several of them silence and then gut a house full of armed militiamen like they were fish at a market, he did not need to watch what Verisna was likely to do to the bound woman.

"I am to take the horse and sprint towards the river before turning north, correct?" he asked.

"Correct," Verisna said, walking towards him.

"The guards there have been killed, and I will corroborate the murder scene here saying I was meeting with Kisa when an enemy assassin burst in and stabbed Kisa in the back with a dagger before I was able to fight him off. I'll pull her gag once I've stabbed her. You flee as soon as you hear that and yelling something about Ravnice should do the rest. Now, break my nose," she said.

It was one of the strangest things he had ever done, but he knew disobeying meant his death, so he reared back and punched her square in the nose. She turned away, spitting blood before pulling his dagger from his belt and dragging it across her forearms and shoulder in shallow cuts.

"The horse is behind the tent, go now," Verisna ordered.

He slipped out of the tent and into the moonlight and winced as he put his splinted, but still healing, ankle into the stirrup and pulled himself into the saddle. A moment later he heard the gurgled scream from inside the tent and kicked the horse into a sprint towards the river while he heard Verisna scream for guards.

He had only a chance to shout a few curses towards Kalt as if he was a northerner by the time he reached the edge of camp and spotted several dead Tormenta. He urged the horse faster and clung tight as it galloped towards the river. As he reached its banks, he felt the cold thuds of crossbow bolts hammering his chest, and he fell from the saddle trying to suck air into his lungs that were quickly filling with blood.

He felt several boots kick him and push him so that he was laying on his back, and he looked up at the angry face of a Tormenta woman.

"This is for leaving my sisters to die!" she hissed before she pulled the blade of her filet knife across his throat.

*****

Ezera followed Wren and the other gifted members of the coalition further east along the coast of the lake to a spot he thought would be suitable for them to do some training and practice. She couldn't help but cringe as they passed a group of men being drilled by a dwarven officer who was jumping up and down in anger.

"Gods forsake the lot of you! You soft, sun-loving, surface-dwelling imbeciles are soldiers now. You're not militiamen anymore. Stop acting like glorified bouncers and follow my commands!" he shouted.

She turned to see Lorkin chuckling with the detachment of fifty dwarves who were to be at their disposal and for the protection of the spell casters. They were some of the best warriors of the dwarven army. All carried a crossbow and wielded the same enormous flat broadswords and heavy rectangular shields.

Once they were a good way away from the berating, Lorkin motioned for their guards and two apprentices to back away, which they did while remaining within eyesight and earshot. The dwarf then turned to Wren.

"Death Herald, you're the only one in the present company to have seen and felt first-hand what these storm priestesses can do. How do you think we should try and mitigate the risk they pose to our conventional forces?" he asked.

Wren walked to the front of their small gathering with his back to the lake.

"Once we have revealed that we have gifted as well, the storm priestesses will be targeting us first. I believe we can use that too, for one, to draw out their spell casters but also to take their focus away from the bridge," he said.

Looking down at the scythe now in his hands, he brushed his deep purple robe nervously for a moment before speaking again.

"Fire Mage Lyrnah and Water Mage Helki will spring our surprise. Mind you, we must assume they'll feel the pull of summoning just as we do. I will deal with the first one that responds, as I did the other day. It is not something I can or would endeavor to practice here today. Once I do, Ezera will extend her bulwark around her and I, to hopefully absorb the second lightning strike. There will surely be an assault to follow," Wren explained.

Lorkin then called for one of the soldiers, and a young dwarf was soon standing before them at rigid attention.

"Stand easy, lad," the Arch Mage said before turning to address them.

"As Ezera knows, a cleric's bulwark can stop all sorts of things, it can be a barrier against physical things or magical ones, or both if the caster is gifted as Ezera here, but that would be immensely taxing on her. As such, she will shield Wren and a small group from our guard detachment from magic. They will shield them from arrows, bolts, and other attacks," he said with a nod at her.

"Now, you two mages have yet to experience any sort of battle, so let me show you a few things. I will summon my elemental, and our fearless warrior here will give it a few bashes of his shield, do your best to knock off some of its stone if you would please," Lorkin said before kneeling in front of them with his hand on a stone from the lake.

After chanting softly, the black lake stone grew until it was the size of a cottage and in the form of a great mountain bear. The warrior shook his head in wonder and then started beating the bear's foot with the shield until a fist-sized chunk broke off, and they all looked at Lorkin for a response.

The dwarven Arch Mage released his hold on the stone and opened his eyes as it returned to being just another rock with a tiny, broken-off piece.

"Our familiars can withstand punishment both physical and magical. You'll be aware of it while you hold the enchantment with your element, but it will not unravel your mind, even when destroyed. The only danger is if you are wounded. Remember that and sacrifice your familiar to protect yourself if necessary. You can always summon another from water or fire," he said sternly to the other two mages.

"There were essentially three ways mages killed other mages in battle," he said sadly, pausing for a moment.

"We killed with an item we had enchanted before, we killed by defeating their elemental with our own and then using ours to destroy them, or we used our ability to control the flow of our element," he finished somberly.

Wren then walked into the middle of them and used the butt of his scythe to draw a rough picture of the river, bridge, and

245

surrounding area.

"Lyrnah and Helki, you will be here at first, with half of our guards to spring the trap. Once I feel one of them casting, I will deal with them. As soon as you are done, rush and join Lorkin and me under Ezera's bulwark and summon your familiars. I will then call out targets for you," he said, drawing several more lines on the dirt map.

"We will use these four numbered sectors to help you guide your familiar to the right target so we can engage as many priestesses as possible. We guess that they have somewhere between forty and fifty. It would seem reckless for them to all be deployed to the front so we can hope for less. Between the chaos of battle and the fear we will hopefully instill in them, the ideal outcome is we very quickly have the priestesses and the rest of their forces on the run back to Kalt city as quickly as possible," he finished.

Lorkin motioned for the other mages to join him, and they began working with their familiars. Ezera walked to the water's edge, and Wren followed her, standing at her side in silence as they looked over the pristine surface of Lake Gitche.

"This will be an ugly and terrible thing when it happens," the gnome said, shaking his head.

"Hopefully not so ugly as you think. Maybe the Tormenta will turn tail and run quicker than you guess," she replied hopefully.

Wren looked towards the mages and then around them before speaking softly.

"They may want to, but they won't be allowed to," the gnome said quietly, refusing to look at her.

"What do you mean old gnome? Is this why Harpis and the others are not here?" she asked with concern.

"We break them there on that field, Ezera, or we risk a prolonged siege at the city and many more deaths on both sides," he said, running his finger along the blade of his scythe.

"Are you saying we will not let them flee or surrender?" she asked in shock.

When the gnome looked up at her with tears on his cheeks, she almost wept herself at the sorrow in his eyes.

"This guilt will be my own burden. I will not let decades of war tear this island apart again. Not after spending centuries trying to undo the wounds of the last one. Not after the losses of friends and family I have endured. Ezera, I will not allow it," he said firmly and then walked back towards the mages.

*****

Returning to his tent in the late afternoon, Wren was tired. He felt old, older than he ever had. Something was different, but he couldn't exactly tell what. Summoning Xissay and using his gift to sense the others in rehearsal for the coming battle, the magic felt closer. Usually, he envisioned using his goddess-given abilities like taking water from a well.

When he was young and barely trained, it took a long while and much work at the crank to pull a bucket of water from the well. Then, after centuries of practice, especially after he was named Herald, it was more like the well was almost full to the top, and he merely had to dip his hand. Today, it felt like the water was brimming to the edge, and he was floating on top of it.

He lit a candle and pulled out a bottle and an ancient necromancy tome from his pack. He read the words and description of the ritual to come several times over before simply laying his small hands on the words. Staring into the dancing flame of the candle, he allowed its hypnotic swaying and the tingle at his mind from the whiskey to pull him into a meditative state.

"Herald?" came the call from an unknown voice outside his tent, and he cursed, slamming shut the tome and placing it back in his pack, he turned towards his tent flap.

"What is it?" he asked the dwarf.

"Someone has come looking for you, sir, a Quaji man, asking for you by name. Well, he asked for Harpis first, but we couldn't find the bard. Sorry to disturb you," the guard apologized.

Wren licked his fingers and pinched out the candle flame with a hiss before exiting his tent and motioning for the dwarven messenger to lead on.

He followed the guard to the command building and stepped inside. He smiled at the sight of Tawito, and the short Quaji man came and embraced him.

"Greetings, fellow friend of Turin Deadeye," the man said.

"Well met again, Tawito," he returned.

247

Wren then looked around the table as Tawito took a seat across from Aanaman, General Shieldborn, Field Marshal Elliswerth, and an older Tuathian man he had not yet met but assumed to be the new admiral.

Aanaman motioned for Wren to join them.

"He would only give us his name until we found the bard or yourself," the newly appointed chancellor said.

Tawito smiled at the man and turned to Wren.

"I received Harpis' message and came as quickly as I could prudently do so," the Quaji stated.

"How did you evade the Tormenta, they are assuredly patrolling the city ports and around the island?" the admiral asked.

Tawito smiled and threw Wren a wink.

"My people sailed these seas long before your various folk wrecked and settled here over the centuries. Amongst the rocky spine of Quaj, there are tiny hidden portages and several safe paths through the mountains. I was headed to Ravnice along the Fjall river when I spotted this great big army and assumed my friends would be in and amongst such an enterprise," he answered while glancing around.

The Quaji then spoke directly to Wren.

"My people have coexisted with the Tormenta for millennia, though that was before their tribes united and ventured north from the icy southern seas in force. I come to offer the assistance of my people in exchange for once again returning to this island that was our home," Tawito finished seriously.

Wren sat back and looked across the table to Aanaman and the others.

"That is not my decision to make, Chancellor Reaper, care to weigh in?" he asked the man from Ravnice hopefully.

"What kind of assistance, and what is the real cost then? I may temporarily be chancellor, but I cannot cede this entire island back to your people, moral and deserved as that might be in some respects," Aanaman questioned.

"Fate is a funny thing, no? She is tidy if nothing else. It is perhaps no coincidence then, that what my people ask for is wholly within your purview to give. My people, we worship The Wild. The seas and their coasts are things to curse and struggle against. When we first settled this island, convening tribes and people across the Nysian islands, it was right here, at Lake Gitche.

The name means huge water in old Quaji. We have two words for water, you see, one for the angry seas and storms, another for the sustaining rains, rivers and lakes," Tawito said, walking over to Aanaman and pulling a map of Quaj Island in front of them.

"How much would you cede Aanaman Reaper?" Tawito asked the former governor.

"What is the gain?" Aanaman countered.

Tawito crossed his arms and smiled roguishly.

"You have quite the army here and a ramshackle fishing fleet parked in the lake. When you are ready to march on Kalt, my people will swarm the harbor and deal with their ships. We can meet on the wharf for a celebration dinner!" he exclaimed.

The admiral slammed his hand on the table, startling everyone.

"Deal with their galleons? I have seen the Tormenta battle at sea. Even our brigantines were no match for them. Neither was the navy of Mer," the man nearly shouted.

Field Marshal Elliswerth interrupted before Tawito could respond.

"My apologies for not formally introducing everyone. Tawito, this is Admiral Galanis, in charge of our coalition naval forces," he explained.

Tawito raised an eyebrow at the statement and shook his head with a chuckle.

"Well met, Admiral. I am not surprised, you see. You cannot fight the sea monsters. They sail with big ships. You swarm them like many ants up the legs of a man standing in their home. The man is larger, but he will succumb to the ants if he does not flee. That is a lesson we taught the Tormenta long ago, and why we have largely left each other alone since," he answered the admiral before turning back to Aanaman.

Tawito took a stick of charcoal and drew a long line on the map from the northern shore of Lake Gitche to the Tuath river to the north.

"Allow my people to resettle the western shores of this lake and give us the plains between the Fjall and Tuath rivers. Do that and allow us passage through the port of Ravnice into the mouth of the Fjall River, and we will help you push The Siren's witches from our island," he said, pointing from Aanaman to himself and then the dwarves and the rest of the room as each of them slowly

249

nodded in agreement after exchanging looks of their own.

"Now, as I made my way in here, I noticed that there had been quite a lot of interesting work done to the larger sailing vessels you have docked here in the lake. Would you care to show me the naval forces I will be working with when we meet in Kalt's Harbor?" he asked Admiral Galanis.

Chapter 28
Back Home

Sudbina relished the swamp of unfamiliarity and presumption that Kalt became under Tormenta occupation. It was within the resulting sea of anonymity, where folk rarely looked up or implored this or that, where Sudbina experienced confidence she had never known before.

She would need confidence and more to make it through the task at hand. Even then, she knew this night to be her last among the living. Until now, she would never have dared the attempt, knowing full well it would assuredly fail. That was until the fascinating distraction of the Tormenta decided to call her city of birth their new home.

She had fantasized for a decade about having the chance at this moment. Even then, the past few days in Kalt, observing her prey and stepping through her actions had felt like an eternity. Then, winding the white horsehair she had sewn into her black wig around her finger, she smiled thinly and resolved herself.

In stolen Tormenta-blue leathers, she marched purposefully through the guards that would have customarily halted her. Next, she angrily flung open the door that would usually be locked and have stopped her. Lastly, she stared down the armed men who would have skewered her without question for simply being where she was without welcome.

"I have a message from Queen Oluja Vetar, for his ears only," she stated angrily in a voice that tried to match the accent she'd heard in Zolga's speech.

One of the men snapped up from where they sat rolling dice at a table, and softly knocked on the door before her. A moment later, he opened it, and she walked into his office. Then, unbuttoning her tunic to her navel, she shut the door behind her and waited for him to look up.

He set down the papers he was writing on and looked up with an expression of confusion.

"What might I do for your queen?" he asked.

Discarding the accent, she focused all her effort on weaving allure and seduction into her raspy flirtatious voice.

"This is regarding what the queen would like done for you," she answered.

Tilting his head to the side, he crossed his arms and looked her up and down, his gaze pausing for a long moment at her exposed navel.

"Oh?" he asked, amused.

She knew she had him. She knew the thought of having tempted the vicious untemptable dominance of a Tormenta woman was a tantalizing fantasy his ego would cling to above all reason. She walked up to his desk and slid her fingers slowly along its edge.

"You will spend tomorrow evening in her quarters. Tonight, I will teach you what it is like to be ravaged by The Siren's storm so that you do not disappoint her in the first moments of frenzied rapture," she finished, sliding onto the top of his desk.

Laying on her back, she put her heels firmly on its top with her legs bent and spread.

"Is that so?" he said, a grin spreading across his face as he walked to the side of the desk, intoxicated by the look of hunger she forced upon her face.

She closed her eyes as she felt him slide his hands under her calves and towards the back of her knees. The passionate hysteria of satiating a lifelong ambition washed over her like a hot bath. He pulled her closer to him. When her eyes opened, he was startled by the rage that burned within them. His gaze did not move from hers as she slid her hand into her boot and pulled out Harpis' whalebone dagger. They grew wide, though, and he staggered back a step when she plunged it into his crotch.

She knew she was about to die. His screams of anguish would alert the others outside, and they would come and end her miserable life. In one last act of violence, she kicked the protruding handle of the dagger as hard as she could with her boot heel, and it dug several inches further into him. She watched in

252

amazement as no sound came from his mouth, opening in a silent scream. There was no noise either when he fell back into the wall and slid to the floor, a spreading pool of blood around him.

She stalked forward and knelt before him, and slowly pulled the wig from her head.

"I am Sudbina," she said as if those three words explained everything.

"I am the offspring of your favorite whore in Kalt's cheapest whorehouse, and I am your undoing," she said, watching his eyes widening.

She hoped that despite the silence around him, he had heard her. A few delightfully long moments later, she watched as the light faded from his eyes. She placed the wig back on her head. Slipping out into the darkness of the night through his window, she pondered a thought that had never occurred to her until this very moment. What would her purpose be now that he was gone?

*****

It had taken longer to get into Kalt and find a room for the three of them than Harpis had hoped. The impending attack was only two days away. He had made sure to find a tavern as close to the lumber yards as possible, hoping to hear news and information relevant to the task at hand.

The tavern keeper readily accepted them, and the man had asked if they'd play some music tonight, offering dinner and ale free of charge. The lack of information or even patrons they encountered the night before had been disappointing. The people of Kalt were either shuttering themselves in their homes or out at the front, per their proprietor.

"Let's go earn our dinners and some ale and hear what we hear," Harpis said, rolling his eyes at the scornful look Mahala threw at him.

"Look here, wife, try and keep from making a scene this time," he said, dodging the wide left hook she threw at his head.

"It is bad enough suffering through you calling me that in public, I'll not endure it in the privacy of our room!" she growled.

"Maybe keep your gift out of the music to avoid unnecessary attention," he said as Jabruelle followed her out their room door, doing his best not to laugh.

253

Watching them descend the stairs ahead of him, Harpis did his best to keep calm and not be overwhelmed with the knowledge that their lives and so many others were in his hands. The words of Arken Hester rang loudly in his mind.

"Do not get caught, but if you do, die for our secrets rather than live by giving them," the old Quaji spymaster had said. Harpis shook off the sadness at the fact that the man was no longer around to make good on the promise of hunting him down if he failed to live up to The Syndicate's decree.

Reaching the bottom of the stairs, he was nearly overwhelmed by the crowd that filled the tavern from wall to wall. The three worked their way to the corner where stools sat for them, and he couldn't help but notice evident anger and stress hanging about the raucous customers of the tavern.

"You sure you don't want me to calm these folk down?" Mahala asked as they took their seats.

He shook his head, denying her request, and pulled his instrument out and placed it to his chin, and with a look to her to see if she was ready, led them through a selection of calming and cheerful tunes, devoid of their magical gift. When they finished, a particularly loud and drunk patron shouted at them from feet away.

"Play something I can drink to. I'm in no mood to celebrate or dance!"

Harpis calmed Mahala with a wink and began plucking his strings, singing several shanty songs he had learned in the fishing village where he had spent his youth. The last one was familiar to Jabruelle as well, and Harpis smiled as the younger man joined in instead of simply tapping his foot along with their songs.

When they finished, the owner gave them a small table as the crowds thinned. They happily supped on fish stew and dark Kaltese stout.

Hearing a loud slap of a fist against a table, he turned around to see the man who had shouted at them earlier, barely audible as he slurred.

"I can't believe those witches from the sea killed Svenus!" the man yelled at his companion.

"One of them walked right in, said she had a message from the queen, stabbed him in his balls with a filet knife, and jumped out the window!" he went on.

His companion shook his head in a similar drunken rage.

"The gall of the storm whores, leaving a whale bone-handled knife stuck in him like that with a carving of their damn goddess in its handle!"

Harpis dropped his spoon in shock and stared across the table at a wild-eyed Mahala and Jabruelle.

"We should be going," Mahala hissed under her breath, and Jabruelle nodded his eager agreement.

Harpis took a moment to scan the tavern. Though he knew he would not, he hoped to catch a glance of the temptress that had stolen his knife just weeks ago.

"Do not hurry. Finish your food, and we will retire for the evening and slip out when this place has emptied."

*****

The day after learning of Svenus' fate, Oluja stared out over the wharf with angry resentment. She looked down the waterfront at the increased presence of Tormenta guards as crews dedicated almost half their remaining personnel to standing watch over their galleons as tensions in the city nearly boiled over.

Normally, she would have lounged, projecting confidence and quiet savagery as she addressed her captains. Not this time, though, not now. She spun around and grabbed the chair, pushed in at her desk, and threw it into the far bulkhead where it shattered.

She looked over six of her seven captains with sneering contempt before turning to the two male messengers.

"Speak," she commanded.

"Highness, one of our advance scouts has indicated that an army of almost ten thousand is approaching from the north. They will be at the bridge in a day or two at most," the first messenger answered before leaving as Oluja waved at him dismissively.

Glaring at the other man, she waved for him to report.

"Highness, Captain Verisna said to tell you that her mission was a success," when she did not immediately respond, he turned nervously to leave, but she reached out and grabbed his tunic.

"Tell Verisna that at the first sign of the battle swaying from our favor, she is to retreat here with as many of my raiders and crew as possible. Use the Kalt forces as fodder, use the other Tormenta clans, if necessary, but she is to get our people here if defeat looks likely. Take a large escort back with you," she ordered, letting him go.

She then turned calmly to her captains.

"You will find out which of our people was foolish and ignorant enough to kill Svenus Kalt and have them put to death in the middle of the wharf, slowly. Maybe that will regain us some complicity from the people of this cursed city," she said, walking to stand before her commodore.

"Pick three of our senior officers, appoint them to captain Kisa's ships. Send her captains to me if they argue. I want all ten ships ready to set sail at any moment. Signal the same to Morel if you catch sight of one of her ships passing along the coast," she ordered.

"We have supplies enough on Lodestar to last us through the winter and lumber enough to double the size of our fleet. Those were the things that made this city useful to us, the only other immediate advantage we had here died last night, and the people of this city are as likely to turn on us as they are to fight for us," she explained, finally dismissing her officers.

*****

Sudbina had made her way to the farthest reaches of Kalt city from the lumber yards. She had been staying in a small inn there for a couple of nights, thinking on what she would do in a life now unburdened by vengeance. She ran a hand over her freshly shaved head before trying to rub stress from her neck. Since plunging a knife into the loins that had made her, she thought it wise to play the part of the young man, at least until she made her way out of Kalt.

She had spent this evening like the last, sipping ale in the back corner of the inn, out of sight from the entrance and main dining area. Tonight would at least be somewhat different. She had overheard more than one patron during the day excitedly talking about how musicians had come to stay at the inn and were to play that evening.

When she heard a gravelly voice from around the corner announce the music would soon begin, she thought she might as well enjoy the evening's performance.

She froze in her tracks, and her cup of ale slipped from her hand, shattering on the wooden floor as a familiar voice introduced the group as The Sea Goats. She rounded the corner, and her eyes met those of Harpis. The music came to a screeching halt, and he stared open-mouthed at her.

Unthinkingly, she turned to the bar and asked for another drink, returning to her corner as quickly as possible without looking back at him. She was in a near panic when she heard the music resume and calmed some. The simple act of being recognized tormented her fraying calm nearly as much as the man himself. She did not know the others with him. Part of her wanted to run, and another wanted nothing more than to let him confront her.

Her last two conversations in weeks had been with a horse and a man she had waited a lifetime to kill, and in both cases, they had been rather one-sided. After an hour spent in agonizing anticipation while consuming several more ales, she straightened in her seat when the music stopped, and a moment later, Harpis and his two companions rounded the corner.

He did not say a word, simply nodded towards the stairs and headed up them. After leaving payment and an excessive tip, she cautiously headed up after them, unsure if she would be attacked or subdued. The second door past hers was ajar, and she slowly walked up to it. Then, slipping inside and closing it behind her, she looked from the others to Harpis.

"Careful around this one, she has a blowgun on her person or in that satchel on her shoulder that'll put you into quite the slumber," he warned, raising an accusing eyebrow.

All she could do was shrug in apology before turning her attention to the petite brown-haired woman.

"I am Sudbina," she said, grabbing and kissing the woman's hand. The other woman seemed confused as she pulled her hand away and scowled.

Turning to the younger-looking man, she extended her hand, and after he shook it, she slowly let go of his fingers before sliding her own from his ear to his chin, watching him blush.

"Sudbina, meet Mahala and Jabruelle," Harpis said, pointing in turn to the others.

"You don't happen to know the whereabouts of my knife, do you?" he asked.

She walked over and sat next to Harpis with a disarming

smile before placing her hand on his thigh.

"I do, or I did anyway, but I do not think that you would want it anymore," Sudbina said, sliding her hand quickly from his thigh and tapping him on the crotch before laughing as he winced.

Mahala walked until she was standing before Sudbina and then looked at Harpis.

"This is the spy that brought you the first bits of information about the Tormenta then?" she asked.

Sudbina gave her a quick wink, and a bow as Harpis nodded in confirmation before answering.

"She also apparently has sent this entire city and its people's relationship with the Tormenta into more chaos than we ever could have hoped to accomplish," he said, staring at her as if she was an unfinished puzzle.

"Can we trust her?" Mahala asked narrowed her eyes.

"I trust Sudbina completely and not at all," Harpis answered with a shrug.

"It seems we are the only ones who know each other's true intentions here. We would be the most hunted people in this entire city if folk were to know our identities," Sudbina said, staring at her own hands and then back at Harpis.

He sat still for a moment and then gave a long look at Jabruelle and Mahala before turning back to her.

"Sudbina, the morning after tomorrow will be the most tumultuous and important that this island has seen in over a century. Come with us and aid in its culmination," he asked.

She had no intention of even leaving the inn until an hour ago, and he had not been very convincing in his request. Still, somehow once he had made it, she couldn't ignore the coincidence of their meeting, or the feeling of fate in accompanying them into the heart of the chaos to come.

"Sounds like fun," she answered, grinning.

Chapter 29
Crossing Over

Wren hadn't felt such nervousness and excitement since his first mission away from Turin's watchful eye nearly two centuries ago. He had learned hard lessons that day and in the days that followed at the hands of merciless torturers. Though their lives were shorter than the other races, he had to hand it to humans, their knack for developing cruelty far outstripped those of the longer-lived.

Still, there were benefits to spending months being cut apart and put back together, kept from death by the perverted shell of what had once been a cleric of Daybreak. He had become resilient, a better spy, and The Sleeper's most devoted and gifted follower. War does that to all people, he supposed, making them a perversion of their former selves. He hoped Harpis and Ezera wouldn't forsake him for the monster he would become today. Moreso, he hoped they would never join him amongst the ranks of the cruel.

He crouched with Ezera and the mages near the bridge with their guards. Their entire army had arrived in the darkness of early morning. Soon, the grey of dawn would creep in and reveal the battlefield and its players to each other.

The army had not been particularly quiet when they arrived. Purposefully so, they wanted the enemy formed up and ready to receive their assortment of surprises. To his right, he knew that ten thousand coalition forces stretched almost three-quarters of a mile in maneuvering formations fifty soldiers wide and ten deep. General Shieldborn would normally be standing proudly out front. However, the scale of today's fight dictated he stand further back, uphill from the battle, with several officers carrying signal horns to guide the tremendous dance of death like a concert conductor.

Each formation had a dwarven augment to aid in responding to the orders and to keep the recently trained troops from running. The bulk of the dwarven presence though was closest to the bridge. The formation to Wren's immediate right was entirely made up of five hundred dwarves.

He and Lorkin tried to calm the other mages while they waited. There were rustles and clinks of armor here and there on both sides of the river. Other than that, it was eerily silent on both fronts as the coalition awaited the thunder that would indicate the battle had begun. Hopefully, they would win the day, and they would meet up in Kalt city with the Quaji forces and their own ships sailing from the lake by tomorrow morning.

*****

Zolga stood with Galonica outside their tent as all around them Kalt militia and Tormenta raiders were making their way quietly to within crossbow range of the river's near side. They, and the rest of Kisa's forces, were more than yearning to avenge the death of their duchess at the hands of the Quaj northerners. Scouts had reported hours ago that the army had started arriving across the river and the anticipation of battle was almost overwhelming.

Within minutes of the enemy's arrival, they had lit signals and the furthest woodwork fort along the river had received the message to send their forces south. The fifteen hundred militia stationed at those forts had just finished trickling in and joining the others.

"Who'd have thought it? The Siren's warriors of the sea fighting a massive land battle," she said, looking towards the armies she couldn't yet see.

"I don't think The Siren has much to do with this, Zolga. At first, I thought High Priestess Spavati was being paranoid, but I am beginning to wonder if Queen Oluja's ambitions might be the downfall of our people," Galonica replied.

Zolga shook her head in silence before resting her hand on the pommel of her rapier.

"Our raiders can outfight the militia of this island ten to one. So even if the scouts are correct in guessing the enemy has almost twice our numbers, we will gut them on their feet, two at a time like baitfish, and you and the other priestesses will cook them alive," she whispered confidently.

Galonica shrugged and looked at her with more concern than she expected.

"Stay with me here, Zolga, protect me while I rain down the rage of our goddess on our enemies from afar."

"Will you not join the other priestesses at the rear of the formations?" she asked.

"You and I. Here. Together. With Kisa gone, we have each other above all else," she said.

Zolga smiled at her longtime friend, and sometimes lover, and drew her rapier. Then, looking up, she noticed that the clouds above were starting to glow as the sun began its crawl from the horizon and the darkness began to reveal the blotchiness of predawn.

"Is that thunder?" Zolga asked, hearing a faint rumbling from the northwest.

Galonica looked from the clouds above to her feet.

"The ground is shaking!" she exclaimed.

*****

Harpis, Mahala, and Jabruelle stood together within earshot of the rear ranks of the Tormenta and Kalt militia with instruments in hand and bright white tabards and hats. Except for Mahala, she had given her hat to Sudbina along with a white tablecloth they had cut a hole in and covered the edges in charcoal to make it appear like their own tabards.

It had taken Sudbina mere moments to sway one of the Kalt militia commanders into allowing The Sea Goats to join their camp at dusk the day before. It had taken that commander much longer to convince his Tormenta overseer that they could be there during an uncomfortably tense exchange.

The result was that they were allowed to play battle music to raise morale, so long as they did not get in the way.

"Did either of you see where Sudbina went off to?" Harpis asked.

Looking around in the receding darkness he suddenly felt and heard rumbling.

261

"Can the storm witches summon an earthquake too?" Jabruelle asked in fear.

*****

As soon as the others had fallen asleep, Sudbina started picking her way around the tents that bore the same sigil she had seen on Zolga and Galonica's attire, hoping she would find her prey still living. She had nearly given up in frustration and returned to Harpis and the others when she heard two voices quietly talking nearby at another tent. She went still next to the tent pitched behind theirs, listening to their exchange.

Laying on her belly, she felt the rumbling before hearing the accompanying thunder and decided she would probably lose her opportunity if she did not act now. She slid her blowgun from along her calf, tucked a spare dart behind her ear, and let fly at the voice to her right. A moment later, when there was a thump, she waited patiently for the other woman to speak.

"Galonica? Are you alright?" Zolga asked in a frustrated whisper in the distance.

The height of Zolga's voice told Sudbina the other woman was kneeling, and she loaded her second dart, and after another puff, she heard a curse followed by the thump of a second unconscious body. The shaking of the ground grew, and she began hearing screams and shrieks to her left as she pulled the two women into their tent.

*****

In the grey light of dawn, Wren could make out the tense face of Fire Mage Lyrnah next to him. He held his hand up to hold the Tuathian woman for another moment as he felt the shaking of the ground grow. Then, when he began hearing shrieks of terror and screams from the barely visible far side of the river, he dropped his hand and nodded.

Lyrnah pulled the hood from the lit lantern they had carried the entire way, dumped oil from a skin in front of her, and threw the lantern into it. The resulting flash of fire quickly grew at the mage's bidding into churning maelstrom shaped like a winged pegasus. It sprang into the air a second later, soaring across the

262

river to the edge of the enemy formations, and began sweeping dives. Each swoop brought forth fresh shouting and yelling as Tormenta and Kalt fighters alike started fleeing in terror away from the fire elemental and towards the thunder.

Wren smiled as a Tormenta bolt sizzled through the elemental to no effect. However, upon feeling and seeing the enemy magic, Ezera looked at him in concern.

"Not yet, lass, after our storm arrives" he said, pointing towards the other end of the enemy lines.

There were gasps up and down their own formations as the ground shook like an earthquake and the growing light of dawn and horse-sized flying lantern revealed the surprise only he, Aanaman, Kilannry, and General Shieldborn had known.

Almost a thousand cattle were stampeding at full speed, driven by Ravnice's Captain Kilannry and a hundred riders screaming and whipping them straight at the northwestern flank of the enemy. The sight of bulls and cows flinging enemies around like rag dolls brought a sadistic smile to Wren's face.

"Where in this gods forsaken world did they come from?" Ezera asked in amazement.

"Aanaman withheld the autumn livestock drive to Kalt when all this started and had them kept at several farms north of here. Kilannry had quite the whiskey-induced clever idea to push them across the shallower part of the river to the north and drive them into the enemy to help us get across safely!" he shouted at her above the din.

He looked back at the mages and commander of their small guard unit, who were all staring at him in anticipation.

"As soon as they get across," he said with a nod.

A moment later, the riders came sprinting across the bridge and blew past them, and he waved them forward. The dwarves rushed to the far edge of the bridge with the gifted right behind them, and he watched Ezera close her eyes and stretch her arms above her in concentration. Wren pointed at Lyrnah and then at Water Mage Helki, who plunged his hand into the river water. Almost as soon as he closed his eyes and began murmuring, a wagon-sized crab made of river water began scuttling from the bridge towards the far end of the battlefield.

The fire elemental flew just above it, and the result was a wall of steam growing along the river that eclipsed any view the enemy might have of their forces. As the wall of fog grew down the water's edge, signal horns began blaring from behind him, and Wren knew it was time. Lorkin smiled at him and grabbed a river stone.

Wren climbed on the stone wall of the bridge to get a better view. Looking across, he could see that the Tormenta and Kalt forces had regained some semblance of order and were forming in lines that began advancing towards the river. As soon as he noticed their own front lines appearing from the fog after crossing the river, he felt the telltale tug of not one but many Tormenta storm priestesses conjuring. He spotted a group of almost two dozen robed women behind the back lines at the center.

"Sector two at the rear, they are almost all bunched together, don't wait for me to call out, just go!" he shouted.

Closing his eyes, he called on the same method he used in taking the life of his second Tormenta victim as he had the first over a week ago. Scythe in hand, the battlefield greyed for a moment to his vision, and he saw a handmaiden already obeying his command, pulling the soul from one of the women.

When color returned to the carnage before him, he cringed as several bolts of lightning slammed into Ezera's bulwarks and crashed around them.

"Still all right, lass?" he asked, and she nodded and grimaced.

Looking at the gathered Tormenta, he saw Lyrnah's elemental slam into the ground, lighting several priestesses on fire before dissipating. A new thunder shook the ground too, as Lorkin's stone bear and Helki's crab crashed across the battlefield and through the lines as if the fighters weren't there at all before slamming into the group of priestesses.

He snapped his fingers, and Xissay appeared wide-eyed, screaming in joy at the spectacle she saw before her.

"The blue-robed ones first!" he shouted, pointing at the battlefield, and she sped off gleefully.

He shook his head as he watched the poor excuse for a battle turn almost immediately.

Without the lightning bolts of their priestesses raining down from behind them, the barely organized militia and Tormenta quickly lost the stomach for battle. He witnessed a large group leave the rear ranks and took a calming breath for what was to come. The priestesses had scattered with the retreat of the rear

Tormenta formations, and he put a hand on Ezera and then the mages so they could release their magic.

Hearing the repeated double blasts of the horn that signaled for the ground advance, he clasped his scythe in both his hands and looked to Ezera.

"I love you and the bard like family Ezera, you tell him that won't you?" Wren pleaded.

"I will," she replied, somewhat confused.

*****

Harpis and Mahala had stopped playing the cringing gift-woven notes of *Clario's Cacophony* after seeing the priestesses assaulted by elementals and Xissay. Jabruelle stood next to them, a spectator to the savage disarray. Harpis had seen violence on a large scale in Tuath. He had done everything he could to bring that battle to an end as quickly as possible, and it had cost Wren and him both years of their lives.

What he saw before him was pure chaos. It was over almost as soon as it began. Nearly a thousand Tormenta had abandoned the field within a few moments, fleeing towards Kalt city. Mahala and he felt no more gifted summoning from their side of the river, and the elementals had gone, but as he watched the two armies meet, he shook his head.

The tactical superiority of General Shieldborn was on full display as the dwarven formation at the bridge end of the battlefield turned northwest and began slow stepping. Their shield wall pushed the poorly coordinated Kalt militia at the front along with the rest of the coalition forces like a wedge of cheese against a grater to devastating effect.

More and more Kalt men and Tormenta began to flee, and it did not take long before he heard drums and horns formally signal a full retreat. At that moment, he felt not the pull of a gifted summoning but something closer to the change in air pressure when a storm front approached on open waters. He and Mahala exchanged concerned glances before screams of sheer terror drew their gaze.

*****

265

Wren heard the signals of retreat from the other side and knelt on the bridge wall. Holding his scythe across his thighs, he began the prayer he had read and reread a hundred times over these past few days. He prayed to his goddess, each time, the seduction of her true name pulled him deeper into the grey.

"I am coming, Lilynth, at long last I am coming home," he said in a whisper.

*****

General Okliff Shieldborn had seen the horrors of a hundred battles, and still, he clung to the rail of his command tower to keep from falling off in shock. He had just watched the rising sun of dawn move backwards several inches the wrong way towards the horizon. The entire battlefield lost the golden hue of the morning hours and returned to the grey of predawn.

Unnatural, guttural screaming drew his attention further into the ranks of the retreating enemy as wispy white tendrils of mist began to solidify into apparition-like arms, hands, claws, and tentacles. The appendages appeared in a line almost half a mile long amid the enemy. The backmost kept retreating at full speed, spurred on by the nightmare behind them. He watched open-mouthed as the rows before them were unable to flee, barely moving as the ground seemed to teem with grasping and snaring phantasms.

"Goddess below us, Wren, what have you done?" he asked out loud.

Over half the enemy forces were trapped between the clinging specters and his army, and their attempts to run through their snared companions resulted in a crushing stampede of death.

Shaking his head, he looked down to his signal officers.

"Signal a break ranks and charge. We crush them here!" General Shieldborn shouted.

*****

Wren finally let go of his conjuring, and he watched as the ghostly grasp of those in The Great Dream finally let go of the fleeing men who killed more of their own as they trampled in terror than could have been cut down by the charging coalition army. He no longer had the strength to hold up his head, and it sagged forward in time for him to see his scythe fade and his robe sag around impossibly thin and frail legs. His hands looked like bones wrapped in parchment paper.

The sound of a familiar voice screaming his name gave him the strength to lift his eyes once more, and tears rolled down his ashen and lifeless face.

"I am so sorry sweet Xissay, dead as you may already be, I've stranded you in The Dream a second time," he whispered.

*****

Harpis turned from the haunting visage of the enemy forces trampling themselves to death among the phantoms conjured by his friend to the sorrowful screaming comet he knew to be Xissay flying back towards the bridge. She nearly reached the slumped form of the gnome before fading into sulfuric smoke with a last mournful wail. The sound of battle faded, and he hardly noticed that the coalition army had advanced almost all the way to them.

Without thinking, he grabbed his violin and began a song he had sung but once. He sang the name of a goddess for the third time in his life. He was there, again, before her in the mists of her dream and under the stars where she slumbered. This time though, she was not asleep, nor was she the size of a mountain. Instead, she sat before him with the silhouetted physique of a human woman. Lilynth clung to the diminutive form of the robed gnome as if holding a babe, looking down at Wren with a smile.

When her black eyes looked up at him, Harpis felt his strength fade, and he dropped to his hands and knees. He opened his mouth to speak but was interrupted by the crash of her voice echoing around him.

"No bard, I've waited for the gnome long enough," her voice boomed with an undeniable finality.

The blackness and the grey faded. Harpis found himself on all fours looking down at the grass, his violin next to him.

He put his head on the ground, and he wept.

Chapter 30
Following Through

Harpis had hardly noticed the passage of time or even his surroundings since Wren's death. He had bitterly argued with Jabruelle and Ezera about taking Wren to The Sanctum himself, but eventually, logic won out. He knew in his heart Ezera was correct in informing him of the guilt he would feel in not finishing what his friend had started. Jabruelle swore to him that he and the other necromancers would confer the burial rites a second time when Harpis could make it to the mountaintop temple. The acolyte had then immediately left with Wren's body and an armed escort, headed for Fjall.

It was almost evening when the coalition army had finally reached Kalt city. Those Kalt forces not killed by the crushing surge during Wren's summoning had almost immediately surrendered. the Tormenta that were left fought and died to a one in a woefully one-sided and short-lived clash against dwarven shields and under a rain of thousands of arrows and bolts.

According to some of the captured Kalt men, almost half, roughly one thousand, of the Tormenta with them had turned and fled immediately. As Kalt city came into view before them, they noticed white tablecloths and sheets hung from windows and over roughly constructed barricades.

"What is that?" Ezera asked as she rode next to him with Mahala.

He looked at the three pillars of billowing smoke from the other side of Kalt city.

"I would guess burning ships. The tar used to keep out leaks and bugs makes smoke as black as night," he said.

The army marched through the city without incident to the

fortified wharf. It was an odd thing, too, Harpis thought. They were cheered and celebrated by many of the Kalt citizens from their windows as they walked.

"Perhaps Kalt was not as complicit as we thought in all of this," he stated, and the two women nodded their agreement.

Arriving at the sea wall, they looked over several still-burning galleons tied to the docks. He turned in his saddle to a woman looking out her window above them.

"What happened to their ships?" he asked, pointing.

"When folk saw the Tormenta abandoning us and that our militiamen were not with them, they started throwing oil lanterns and torches at their ships as they tried to disembark. Seven of them did make it out of the harbor, though," she said, spitting in the direction of the wreckage.

*****

Spavati stood on the galleon's steering deck with the captain and several of her senior priestesses. Off in the distance, she could see the drifting smoke from the Kalt harbor and let out a sigh of frustration.

"High Priestess, what are your orders?" the captain asked her.

Looking back in the direction of the island's mountainous western shore, where she had carried out her fated task, she felt like they had accomplished more than enough.

"I'll not have us sailing into a trap. We will make for Lodestar," she replied.

*****

Sudbina sat patiently in her chair, staring at the two prisoners that lay bound and gagged in the bed before her. Then, seeing Zolga finally stir, she walked over to the bedside and brushed her hand on the woman's cheek.

"Good morning, beautiful," she said sweetly.

Zolga's eyes shot open, and she struggled against her bindings and tried grunting through her gag. The commotion of her struggle woke Galonica next to her. Sudbina tried not to laugh as the two squirmed and eventually sat upright next to each other on the edge of the bed.

"Now, I am going to take that gag out of your mouth Zolga, no biting," she said, wagging her finger in front of the woman's fierce blue eyes.

She cut the gag and poured water from a skin into Zolga's mouth and waited for her to finish coughing and hacking.

"Where are we, Sudbina?" Zolga asked angrily, looking around at the room.

"We are in a room above one of the inns that line the Kalt wharf," she answered the woman with a grin.

"Then we were forced to retreat?" she asked.

Glancing at Galonica bound next to her, she became more frustrated.

"We will not surrender, Sudbina. We will fight them even at the city walls."

"Oh, there is no need for you to surrender, dear Zolga, your people have already fled our shores, and the city has been taken," she explained.

"Torture us if you like, but you may as well kill us. We will never give any information to you or anyone. We would rather die," Zolga growled.

"Oh, don't be so morbid, Zolga. I would rather die myself than allow anything to happen that might mar your pretty faces or shapely bodies," Sudbina said, pushing her lips out in a pout before licking them and looking the Tormenta up and down enthusiastically.

Zolga and Galonica both stared at her in dumbfounded confusion.

"If Zolga will swear on your goddess, and Galonica, if you nod your agreement that you will not blast me to ash with one of your little lightning bolts, I will ungag you. And if you both then promise to be nice, I will release your bindings and have some food brought up to you. If you do feel inclined to send me to The Sleeper, the dwarves on the other side of this door or their friends downstairs that helped carry you here will happily turn you into pin cushions. They told me as much, very excitedly in fact," she finished.

*****

Harpis was sad to see Mahala leave, but she had made it clear

270

she had seen enough of death and killing for a lifetime. After spending the entire day with Sudbina speaking to the captives, he was exhausted but thankful his day had a purpose to it aside from waiting, drinking, and mourning.

Harpis sat at the tavern table the night after Kalt surrendered and sipped his glass of spicy southern rum, pulling a face and shivering. Tawito laughed at him and took a long pull of his own while Ezera shook her head at the both of them, her blond tresses tumbling about her shoulders. The Quaji had arrived late that afternoon with over a hundred ships and boats of different sizes, from catamarans to canoes and sailing vessels.

"I've sent several of our fastest ships to Lodestar to scout the island. They can outrun Tormenta galleons if necessary. We should receive word in a few days as to the disposition of our enemy. Time enough for Aanaman and your ships to arrive here so we may decide on how to deal with them," Tawito said.

Ezera raised her glass and waited for the two of them to do the same.

"To The Syndicate," she toasted.

"To Wren," he added, his voice cracking.

"To there not being less of us each time we get together," Tawito finished, and they downed their drinks.

Harpis reached to the middle of the table, tore a chunk of bread and dipped it in his soup before taking a bite and chewing thoughtfully.

"Tawito, how did you end up uniting the tribes and convincing them to come here?" he asked the other man.

"I am glad you have ventured across Moodi Shen, or you would not believe me. Now, I took your offer to the three chieftains, as you asked, but I was not confident in them favorably or jointly responding. Happy as a clam was I to find out that the oracles of the three tribes had met with the crazy troll and shared in a vision they claimed to come from The Wild herself. They said that our people would be reunited around Lake Gitche," he said with a laugh.

After taking another swig of rum, Tawito shrugged at him and finished.

"You see, when I brought them the offer from Aanaman, they saw it as a prophecy foretold!" he said.

*****

It had taken Jabruelle two exhausting days to get to Fjall and then navigate the tunnels to The Sanctum. With the corpse of his mentor swaddled across his shoulders, he began the long, muscle-aching trek up the spiral of hewn rock towards The Sleeper's temple. There was more cool air rushing down from above than he remembered, but he attributed it to a more blustery than usual winter wind.

Nothing, not even the widespread carnage in Kalt or the death of the old gnome, could prepare him for what he beheld when he reached the top of the stairwell. Shivering at the wind and cold, he stared in silence at the crumbled slabs that had been the doors. The beautiful mosaic to his goddess that had adorned it was now a shattered ruin. Walking through the portal into the remains of the temple, he knelt to the stone floor, tears streaming down his face as he spotted the now-frozen, fragmented body parts of his fellow necromancers.

He walked into the now exposed sepulcher and sighed at least that The Dreamer's Door, the well that led to The Great Dream, was still intact on its stony plateau. Reaching its edge, he undid the cloth around his shoulders and laid the bundle that held Wren's body next to it. He looked from the gnome's shroud back to the demolished rocks and hewn corpses of his brothers and sisters. A holy purpose filled his heart and mind, the last act of dedication to his goddess and her devotees.

Leaving Wren's body by the well, he walked somberly to the kitchens and grabbed a fire poker next to one of the ovens. Next, he went to the dormitory hall and tied several blankets around himself for warmth, tearing another into pieces and wrapping his hands.

It took him almost the entire day to chip away at the ice and frozen blood, freeing at times whole bodies and at others only appendages and hunks of flesh from the clutches of winter.

Each time he was successful, he would take the pieces of the fallen to The Dreamer's Door, say a prayer to their goddess and send it tumbling soundlessly into the abyss. After countless hours, he could not feel his bleeding hands and his face hurt from crying and sobbing, but he steadied himself for his last act of dignity.

He slowly said the words for a final time, dedicating the

fallen Death Herald to their goddess and sent the gnome's corpse into the darkness of her dream. He sat at the edge of the well for long moments in silence, only his shivers indicating there was life yet left in The Sanctum. Everything he had loved and lived for was gone from the mortal plane. The only home he had ever been welcome in was barely more than rubble.

He stood on the edge of The Dreamer's Door and looked down into the darkness that to him looked more comforting than the harsh world raging around him.

"So dies the last necromancer," he said without remorse and leaped from its edge.

He closed his eyes and felt the rush of air past his ears for only a breath when a female voice screamed inside his mind.

"No!" it shouted, and he saw the black pools of The Sleeper's eyes.

He reached out to stop his fall as she commanded, and he opened his eyes in surprise as he grasped at what felt like a wooden handle.

He laughed and cried as he hung not five feet from the well's edge, clinging to the necromancer scythe he had for the first time pulled from The Great Dream, its blade dug into the rim of The Dreamer's Door and holding him fast.

"As you wish," he whispered in a voice that echoed around and below him.

Chapter 31

The Siren's Scream

Three days after the battle at the river, Harpis had spent the better part of the morning with Ezera drawing out maps of Lodestar and detailing its tunnels. The two told all they knew to Aanaman, and the others gathered at a wharf tavern converted into a temporary command building. The coalition army would remain in Kalt only long enough to achieve an outcome at Lodestar and then transition the city back to its citizens.

The maps they made and discussed were to aid in taking Lodestar in a complete sweep by a mostly dwarven landing party. That was only a contingency, though to what they hoped would be a more peaceful resolution. They planned to engage the Tormenta, overwhelm their attack galleons, and force a surrender of those left on the island.

Finishing and conferring with Ezera on the tunnel structure within the island's crater, General Shieldborn had taken the maps and went with Field Marshal Elliswerth to plan what they all hoped was an unnecessary assault.

"Admiral, Tawito, if you would please, let's go over our plan one last time," Aanaman requested.

The Quaji walked from his seat at the table to the charcoal-drawn map of Lodestar and Kalt's coast drawn on the wooden wall of the tavern.

"It will take our ships about four hours to make it into the waters within sight of the island. The most recent reports from our scouts are that perhaps ten or eleven galleons are sailing patrols around the island, all within view of it. We can't be certain, but it appears as if the Tormenta are loading their other ships to leave. Lodestar's harbor can only accommodate two at a time. It will take them at least until tomorrow to vacate the island. If you do not want to spend the decades to come facing their raids and further attempts at being conquered, today is our one chance," he said, sitting back down.

Admiral Galanis stood and walked to the map.

"The Quaji will sail at the northern coast of Lodestar, drawing the galleons out to them. They will then start chasing and leading the galleons outward from each other through consecutive spirals. We have outfitted the surviving three naval ships from Mer and two from Tuath with enough rigging and sails to keep up with the larger Tormenta vessels so that we can catch and engage them one at a time once they are separated and spread out by the Quaji," he said, nodding at Aanaman.

The chancellor stood and faced Harpis, and he was almost nervous as he looked at his friend and former governor.

"Harpis, Ezera, you are the only two who know the island. The Tuath brigantines have been armored and outfitted with several dwarven ballistae, but we want you on our flagship with the admiral to shield it from the lighting of priestesses. Lorkin, Helki, and Lyrnah have agreed to serve on the other," he stated.

He and Ezera nodded in unison before exchanging a look of vengeance.

With a nod from Aanaman, Tawito and the admiral left to prepare for their departure. Sudbina then walked downstairs from the rooms above, followed by the two Tormenta and several dwarven guards.

Sudbina walked over to join Ezera and him while across the table, Zolga and Galonica took their seats.

Aanaman was the first to address them.

"In hopefully one of my last acts as the chancellor, I would like to make the two of you an offer," he said, looking from one to the other.

"But first, please take this back as a token of our honest intentions," he said.

When he finished speaking, Arch Mage Lorkin took the scale patterned, blue-dyed leather tome from his robe and slid it across the table to Galonica. The priestess stared at it in shock.

"How did you get our people's most sacred text!" she shouted.

Harpis buried his head in his hand as Sudbina gave them a

275

wave with her fingers.

"I took it when I escaped from being locked in a cabin on one of your galleons," she answered.

Zolga sat back in her chair and stared in exasperation at the ceiling while Galonica placed a hand reverently on the tome.

"What is it you will have us do? Our people will never surrender, even if we ask them. Surely you realize that?" she asked.

Aanaman held his hands up in peace, acknowledging her statement.

"We just want you to try and save their lives. We will not ask for their surrender, and we will not imprison them. I only ask that if we succeed in forcing them to hole up on Lodestar, you two deliver our terms to whoever is left in charge and return to us with their answer. The tome you may keep, of course," he finished.

*****

Harpis had spent the entire voyage motionlessly clinging to the bow rigging. He stood on the ropes, hanging out over the sea that slipped towards, under, and past them. Then, after half a day on their due southwesterly course, he finally spotted the smudge of Lodestar on the horizon.

Before long, he was able to make out more than just the island, and he smirked at just how true to his word Tawito had been. Twelve Tormenta galleons were sailing in wide circles like hawks mobbed by a murder of crows. Flighty catamarans were weaving and fleeing from the larger vessels while countless small boats from the hundred-strong Quaji fleet harassed the blue-sailed giants from behind.

He could tell the Quaji had spotted their smaller flotilla as most of them continued their swirling dance in the same direction, pulling the galleons engaged with them to the west while two of the ships were herded south towards with their approach. Harpis spared a look behind him at their single-file formation.

Behind his ship was the second of their specially outfitted brigantines, complete with dwarven plate armor on their hulls and multiple ballistae on their main decks. They were crewed by less than thirty and had only a handful of others onboard to operate the weapons or hurl spells. Typically, the Tuathian ships could sail fully loaded with a crew of nearly one hundred and transport twice that again. Despite minimal personnel and no need to carry many supplies at all, the hulls rode low in the water, and the wind in the extra sails strained the masts against the weight.

Ezera walked up behind him, holding fast to the ropes with the unfamiliarity of one who did not grow up on the waters.

"How do you think we will fare today?" she asked, staring out at the scene before them.

"Well, the Quaji look quite capable of imparting a death of a thousand cuts where necessary. I just don't know that we have time for all that if we are to catch them still on the island instead of chasing them to the edges of Nysia," he answered.

"Don't forget the rest of our armada," she said.

He looked again behind them at the two dozen larger merchant and fishing vessels that could sail the open seas and had initially made the escape to Lake Gitche.

"If the rest of our valiant navy can provide even a modest distraction, I'll be more than happy. Come, the moment is at hand, and I would prefer to watch Tormenta harmlessly flicker off that bulwark of yours instead of being blasted from the bow," he said, motioning for her to follow.

*****

Spavati stood at the edge of the crater next to Oluja, nervously watching the deadly pageant play out in the waters around Lodestar. Early on, when Tormenta lightning had struck several Quaji ships, there had been cheers erupting from thousands of Tormenta gathered on the shoreline below who were waiting to board ships. The going was slow, though. Loading the elderly and children and supplies onto ships one or two at a time was tedious work.

Now the High Priestess and her sixteen surviving storm priestesses stood atop the lip of the crater with their queen in anxious silence. Throngs of Quaji vessels had already swarmed five of their galleons. Tormenta did not surrender. So, she knew that when those ships lowered their blue sails and dropped anchor, there were no longer Tormenta left living onboard.

A sixth and seventh were headed inevitably into similar situations. One of those two looked sure to fall to a mass of smaller vessels, and the other was trying to dodge the ramming of three medium-sized ships that were covered in sails and riding so high in the water they looked as though they'd fly.

"Oluja, our attack galleons will not be able to keep this up long enough for our people to escape," she said, not bothering to use the woman's title.

Queen Oluja Vetar did not even turn. Her shoulders sank a bit more, and she continued to look from the ships loading in Lodestar's tiny harbor to the massacre of their people at sea. Both women winced, and there were collective gasps from below when a flaming Pegasus flew from one of the brigantines and scorched giant holes in the sail of one of the galleons outrunning the Quaji before its sides were torn open by an immense elemental crab made of seawater.

"How are we so outmatched?" Oluja said, finally speaking.

Spavati heard the desperation in the other woman's voice and knew it was time.

"There may be a way to force them from the island and save some of our people. Would you join me below in the center of the crater and help me summon our goddess's greatest gift?" she asked.

"I am not gifted, Spavati. How could I?" Oluja asked her.

"The power of our queen's strong and commanding voice echoing off the walls of the crater below will give strength to the priestesses above us who will join in the summoning," she replied to the queen.

When Oluja nodded silently in agreement, she motioned for the queen to follow and then smiled at the priestesses spreading out evenly in a circle atop the crater mouth.

When the two of them made their way down the slopes and through the tunnels into the crater, an odd calm came with no longer witnessing the destruction at sea. Walking to the circle of more recently disturbed soil in the center of what had once been a courtyard, she turned and held Oluja's hands.

"Our people will never forget what we do here today, Oluja. The entire world will shake with The Siren's Scream!" she shouted. Then, on cue, her priestesses began a slow chant and the very air hummed with energy. After long minutes black swirling storm clouds began appearing high above their heads, and slowly but steadily, a storm grew as they continued to channel their summoning.

"Witness the true power of the storm, Oluja!" she shouted.

The queen stared up in awe at the lightning that began rippling across the expanding clouds. At that moment, Spavati drew her filet knife from her boot and cut the queen's throat.

"This summoning is of the old ways. It requires sacrifice, and you owe our people that at least," she screamed into the dying woman's ear before letting her slump lifeless to the ground. She cupped Oluja's spilling blood in her hand and ran it through her hair, its white streaks now glowing red in the flickering lighting.

Throwing her hands in the air, she joined her priestesses in their chant.

*****

Harpis and Ezera both felt the unbound and monstrous surge of summoning from the island. The entire crew had begun to point and murmur about the swirling black storm growing over Lodestar on what had been a clear and sunny afternoon. They returned their attention to the more immediate threat by frantic whistle blows from the steering deck. They held tight as their brigantine was steered into a leaning turn to bring it to broadside the galleon that had been forced straight at them by Quaji pursuit. The larger ship was turning in kind, and Harpis held Ezera around the waist with one arm while his other clung to the mainmast so she could focus on her bulwark.

Despite knowing she would keep them safe, he still flinched when a bolt of lightning from the galleon slammed into the bulwark in front of his face, resulting in shimmers and a feeling of static. the Tormenta ship was barely a hundred feet from them, and he could see the angry faces of Tormenta women behind the sprays of seawater as the two boats slashed through the waves and forced choppy crests between them.

Another quick whistle and all four ballistae let loose their barbed spears, and they sank together only a few feet apart, digging deep into the side of the ship's bow that faced them. The chains shackled to their shafts pulled tight for a minute, but members of the crew quickly flung the release latches, and the thousand-pound stones chained and shackled to the ballistae bolts were released from where they had hung to the brigantine's hull.

279

In half a breath, the chains went taught and the stones swung beneath the Tormenta galleon, pulling its bow into the waters. The giant blue sails and the ship's momentum did the rest, ripping the entire front of the vessel off as it bobbed bow first for a moment in the sea. The sickening sounds of ripping and popping wood mixed with the screams of the Tormenta while the ship sank.

Their own ship listed heavily, forcing them to cut two of the four stones from the other side just to keep from capsizing.

The sea was almost theirs, but the storm over Lodestar was now growing beyond the island. Lightning was beginning to roil amongst the clouds before cascading into the waters closest to the island.

He felt the brigantine turning, and he looked up at the helm with his hands in the air.

"The rest of the fleet is running from the storm, Harpis. I am doing the same. We can come back when it is gone," the man shouted down at him and Ezera.

"When the storm is gone, they will be too!" he shouted back in frustration.

"Harpis, they're defeated. Zolga and Galonica can help us find them in the days and weeks to come, and maybe they'll see reason enough to negotiate a peace with Aanaman," she said.

He looked up at the storm, thinking of his father and Wren and how The Siren had taken them both from him.

"No," he said, gritting his teeth," this ends now!" he kissed Ezera on the cheek and sprinted up the stairs to the steering deck.

He looked over the back railing to ensure their scout boat still hung from the stern.

"Hold this course for a moment longer. Lower the schooner and then cut me loose and run!" Harpis shouted over the thunderclaps that were growing in volume and regularity.

Chapter 32
Ultimate Sacrifice

Harpis was weary from the strain of holding the rudder against the current and the whipping winds of the Tormenta storm. At last, he guided the small vessel crashing into the shoreline away from the harbor. Looking up at the billowing blue robes of the storm priestesses who stood atop the crater screaming their chant, he began climbing his way up, hoping they wouldn't notice him.

As he got closer, he could see the two nearest him had their eyes rolled back in their heads and could feel the surging static around their upwardly held hands. He had only tried the song from Mia Kespeare's tome a few times in the Kalt tavern with Mahala before she left. Hopefully *Maev's Mimic* worked as he intended. He had to believe the name he'd read in the chapter titled *The Proceeding Quiet* from the Tormenta's religious text was what he thought it was. Why else would the first line say the holy words of the chapter were never to be uttered out loud, only in the temple of the mind?

"If this is how I die, at least I'll share a laugh with Wren and my father in The Great Dream about it" he said in a voice that was unheard over the din of the storm.

Crouching behind one of the enthralled priestesses, he cleared his throat and began following their chant. It was only a few verses long, and after a few rounds with them, he began altering the notes as he went to match the tonal changes of *Maev's Mimic*.

After one more round, he could feel a change in the voice nearest him, that she was now singing as he did. He slowed the pace of his chant for a single word and heard not only the priestess in front of him but several others around him falter as well. Then, his confidence growing, he began singing as loud as he could and started feeling the electric thrum of their spell as he dictated the words through each of them.

With one last glance at the swirling clouds and lightning above, he shouted the climactic end of the last verse to The Siren with what he hoped to be her true name.

The final syllable of Zavesti rolled from his tongue, the mouths of the priestesses around him and the High Priestess, but it refused to fade. His eyes opened in horror as he and the Tormenta priestesses kept screaming the last vowel of her name. It grew louder until he had no breath left in his lungs and his throat felt like he had swallowed shattered glass, and still, they screamed together.

He gripped the edge of the crater, unable to close his mouth as their scream melded into the howling and shrieking of the wind around them. One by one, the priestesses around the rim began to collapse. Instead of abating, the scream became louder. Finally, when only he and the High Priestess were left, he began to cry at the pain in his throat, feeling the wet of blood dripping from his ears.

He watched, awestruck as the High Priestess fell and the scream hit its crescendo as a pale, red-haired woman appeared standing above the fallen form of the blue-robed High Priestess. The figure clutched her ears and screamed louder than the tempest around him, and everything became quiet and black.

*****

Even halfway to the horizon Tawito and his crew cringed and covered their ears at the wailing from Lodestar Island. After the screaming hit its highest pitch, there was an impossibly deafening thunder followed by a downward gust of wind from above the clouds. The burst was strong enough to force the billowing black storm clouds to rush towards the island, down the slopes of the volcano and into the ocean.

What followed was a massive tremor in the ground beneath the seas and a rising swell of water rushing outward, and he quickly turned to the helmsman of his catamaran.

"No chance we outrun that goddess sent wall of water, turn us into it now!" he shouted.

*****

The floor of a dormant volcano crater in the northern reaches of the Nysian seas shook for the first time in two ages. A long crack appeared across its surface, widening to several inches when the whole island shook again. In the darkness, two amber eyes shot open. They glowed and smoldered with abandon in the sunlight.

From below, the fingers of two ghastly white hands appeared gripping the crack on either side before tearing the ground apart with a sundering rage. The nude sculpture of a perfectly muscled and hairless man pulled itself from the darkness of its tomb-like prison.

Climbing out of the crater, it strode straight for a river of lava that had begun flowing from the side of the volcano. It walked with unwavering determination right into the reddish-orange rivulet of molten stone until only its head stood above the surface.

It began striding out where the glowing liquid stone cooled and hissed, exploding, and steaming where it reached the ocean. There it stood on a tiny island of freshly cooled lava rock, newly clad in plate armor of black polished volcanic glass. Holding a spear that was nearly as long as its eight-foot height, the weapon seemed to endlessly drip blood from its tip, the figure smiled and pointed the weapon directly at him.

Enky dropped the frame he was holding to the floor where it shattered before reappearing on the wall, and he watched the armored god wade into the sea after pulling a black helm from the cooling lava.

He nervously looked to his portal to The Nexus, expecting at any moment for his sister to appear and scold him, but after long, painful moments of silence, the stone remained. He was sad, and he was alone, and he was fearful of what he had just witnessed.

Wrinkled frail hands came to rest on his shoulders, and he nearly jumped out of his skin in surprise. He bolted out of his chair and turned towards his back wall, fear turning to joy as he ran forward and embraced the silver-haired visage of Qisme.

"Mother, I did not mean for it to turn out this way. My plots have come undone. My sister's scream woke your son," he exclaimed, burying his face in her wispy robes.

283

"Of course, you didn't, Enky. You never do, but they always will. Mischief by any other name is mayhem all the same."

*****

Ezera had sat at the chair beside the bard's bed since Tawito had brought him back from Lodestar. The Quaji refused to describe what he saw in the moments spent collecting Harpis from the island.

There was a soft rap at the door before it was cracked open, and Sudbina poked her head in.

"How is he doing?" she asked.

Ezera looked down at the slumbering bard for a moment before shrugging helplessly at Sudbina.

"All he has done is sleep. I cleaned the blood from around his ears, and I have prayed to Daybreak for the gift of healing several times, but I sense no wounds to cure," she answered honestly.

"Care if I bring in a visitor? She knows the magic that was cast that day," Sudbina asked from the doorway.

Ezera nodded and then tensed as she watched with some trepidation as Sudbina led the storm priestess Galonica into the room.

Galonica looked down at Harpis and shook her head in confusion.

"Where was he found?" the priestess asked her.

"Tawito says that he was laying below the slopes of Lodestar's volcano after the storm. I haven't been able to get much more out of the Quaji than that," she said.

"The storm you speak of is of the old ways, summonings that have long been forbidden due to their necessary reagents," Galonica explained.

"What sort of reagents," she asked.

"At least one life, if not more. Still, it doesn't make sense," she answered with sorrow in her eyes

"What doesn't make sense?" Sudbina questioned, walking to stand near her and stroking Harpis' ear.

"Conjuring The Siren's Scream, the storm you said you saw swirling over Lodestar, was done in centuries passed as a last resort for survival. It is supposed to cleanse those not of Tormenta blood from the land or seas beneath its clouds, and yet the bard

284

made it through, all the way to the volcano where they channeled it from," she said softly.

Galonica then placed her hand on the bard's chest and chanted softly.

Feeling the pulse of magic, Ezera leaped to her feet from the chair and shoved the Tormenta priest against the wall.

Sudbina pulled them apart and shot Ezera a glare.

"What was that for," the enigmatic woman asked.

"She was summoning storm magic!" Ezera said in an accusing voice.

Galonica held her hands up in peace, and Ezera retook her seat beside the bed.

"Our people long ago mastered the ability to identify Tormenta bloodlines. We were a bitterly divided and wildly untrusting people for many generations while the tribes fought each other. It was a necessary thing to know if another Tormenta was of your family tree or another tribe's," she explained.

"May she?" Sudbina pleaded.

Ezera waved for Galonica to proceed, and the priestess again placed her hand over his heart. After only a few moments of murmured channeling, Galonica straightened and opened her eyes wide in surprise.

"He is of the Hadjuk tree, not just of that family but from its central branch," she said in awe, taking a step back and staring in disbelief at Harpis.

"What does that mean to us then?" Ezera asked, raising her eyebrow at the look of delight on Sudbina's face.

"He is the direct descendant of Duchess Kisa Hadjuk, a distant cousin to me. If he were a woman, the Tormenta would consider him royalty," she said in amazement.

Sudbina bit her lip as if the irony itself aroused her and looked expectantly at Galonica. The priestess lightly touched his cheek and put her finger under his chin, inspecting his face and hair.

"I was barely a woman when I watched a half-breed babe get handed to a poor Kalt fisherman. What cruel fate that the exiled product of Kisa's lowest moment was that which ultimately defeated us," she said, turning to Ezera.

"His mother, Kisa, died the night before the battle of Kalt River, murdered by a spy from the north," she finished in a whisper.

285

All three women shrieked in surprise and backed against the wall when Harpis opened his eyes and sat up in confused terror.

"How are you feeling," Ezera asked him.

Harpis shook his head and stuck his finger in his ear before opening his mouth to speak. Though she saw his lips form the question 'what?', all she heard was the raspy rattle of wind escaping his throat.

Confusion and surprise were replaced in his brown eyes by fear and sadness as he looked from one of them to the other. Sudbina clasped her hand to her mouth and gasped.

"I don't understand. I sense no mortal wounds to heal," Ezera said desperately, looking to Galonica for answers.

The priestess had none to offer, and Sudbina led her from the room.

Ezera watched him trying to ask the same question over and over, and she began to weep as the wheezing became more frantic and the words on his lips indecipherable. Then, grabbing a parchment, ink, and quill from the nightstand, she shakily wrote on the paper, brushing her tears from its surface.

She could not imagine the physical pain the bard was already in, nor the disheartening fact of losing his voice and hearing. Still, she knew it would not be right to keep the fate of his heritage or his family from him.

*****

Zolga tightened the single rope holding the boom of their sail in place to catch as much wind as possible and returned to guide them into the harbor of Lodestar. Behind them was the backdrop of the entire Quaji fleet and both brigantines. Before them, the four remaining Tormenta ships were anchored in a line across the small harbor, and the throneship tied off to the docks.

As they got closer, the stern-faced, crossbow-bearing raiders at the rails of the galleons relaxed and waved them past. Then, rounding the enormous throneship, Zolga saw Duchesses Zeln and Lorent standing in their fur-lined cloaks waiting for them.

"Come to join us in our final fight against the land-born?" Zeln asked with discontent. The still-teenage Duchess Lorent stood obediently at her side, staring at her feet. Zolga was about to question the duchess on how it felt living a coward's existence

286

these past weeks, but Galonica stepped from the boat to the dock and stood defiantly before both Duchesses.

"There is no need for further Tormenta deaths!" the priestess shouted.

"If you suggest a surrender, I will have you killed here and now, Galonica! Whether you are our last priestess or not, I will not suffer a traitor," Zeln sneered.

Zolga sprang from the boat and put her rapier tip at the woman's throat, holding it there as several crossbows cocked around them.

Galonica shot her a calming look before turning back to the gathering crowd.

"No surrender. The leader of the land-born has offered us peace."

Zolga looked around as many of those near them muttered and exchanged surprised glances.

"Is it true what you claim? I am the only priestess that lives?" Galonica concernedly asked the two Duchesses.

Zeln merely crossed her arms and continued to scowl, but Lorent nodded her head.

"It is true," the younger woman said sadly.

"Then the fact that I hold this, means that I am High Priestess of the Tormenta tribes," Galonica said, raising the blue leather tome above her head.

Zolga was surprised that none dissented her friend's claim.

"Sudbina stole this while with our flotilla. She returned it to me after she used magic to subdue Zolga and me at the battle at the request of their leader. It must be clear to all Tormenta, priestess, curate or not, that The Siren no longer blesses our attempted conquest. I have witnessed its failure at every turn. Yet, in my heart, I know we would have continued that course without her favor," the priestess concluded.

Zolga lowered her sword tip and shouted at the top of her lungs while staring down Duchess Zeln.

"The land-born ask that we return with a leader chosen and elected by our people to discuss a treaty. I can tell you that they are happy to return the surviving galleons they captured yesterday and may even allow us to continue occupying this island. That, to me, sounds like an offer worth hearing and a far better fate than starving to death, trapped on this island," she finished.

*****

For the third day in a row, Harpis sat in the booth he had often shared with Wren at the back of The Siren's Scream. Across the table was an untouched glass of whiskey. Next to him were several empty ale mugs and his own glass. Though exhausted, he dared not sleep.

When he slept, there were only nightmares. He couldn't take another night reliving his father's death, or Wren's, or those of countless others lost over the past three years. There was no longer strength within him to withstand another journey through a fantasy conjured by his sleeping mind of the mother he had never met.

The life that had been built over the past years was no more. The Syndicate that had given him purpose was destroyed, and the music and gift he had grown to love were now unattainable comforts. Everything that had separated him from the drunk fishing hand stumbling around the Kalt wharf was gone.

He reached for the glass of whiskey in front of him only to have it snatched from the tabletop before he could grasp it in his shaking hand. He glared up at a stern-faced Kalna as she slammed a written note onto the table in front of him and pointed at Wren's usual seat.

What would Wren say about feeling sorry for yourself?

Harpis angrily crumpled the note into a ball and threw it. He opened his mouth and tried to scream in rage at her, though he knew she wouldn't hear anything but the rasping breath that he could feel struggling past his goddess-burnt vocal cords.

Kalna threw the whiskey from the glass in his face, and as he coughed at the liquid that had made it into his mouth, she slapped him hard across the face.

As he felt her angry stomps recede across the wooden tavern floor, he lowered his face into his hands and tried to wipe the stinging salt of tears and the burn of whiskey from his eyes.

Chapter 33
Reformation

Zolga stood on the Kalt wharf holding Galonica's hand while they waited for Governor Lorent to finish her conversation with Aanaman and several other land-born. Since arriving at Lodestar the day before to present Aanaman's request, there had been quite a lot of firsts for her people. Watching the galleon bobbing peacefully with the rising tide, she could not help but smile.

"Look at that, Galonica, a Tormenta ship moored in a harbor that it is not in the process of invading or having already conquered. I don't know if I ever thought I would see such a sight my entire life," she laughed.

"What will the fearsome raider Zolga do with her trident and rapier now that our people have a harbor to call their own? I bet you'd prove useful in one of their stables. You can even bring your own pitchfork," the priestess replied with a chuckle.

"Well, I certainly couldn't use this," she said, drawing her rapier and examining its slim blade.

"No, I suppose not. It wouldn't be very effective at spreading hay. However, it was very effective at quieting one nasty former duchess," Galonica replied.

"I am not surprised that when given the opportunity to elect anyone as their leader, our people decided to pick between the only two royals left. I am just glad that they picked Lorent and not Zeln. Gods, you probably would have been elected if you had wanted, High Priestess Galonica," she said with a smirk, sheathing her weapon.

The other woman let go of her hand and gave her a playful shove.

"I'd rather be stabbed to death by your rapier or pitchfork!"

she said.

Governor Lorent finally began walking their way, and Zolga stood respectfully with her hands behind her back. She raised an eyebrow at Galonica. Her friend rolled her eyes before moving to stand with her, hands clasped, and head bowed slightly.

"She's barely a woman," the priestess said cynically.

"Good thing she has the guidance of the wise and ancient High Priestess," Zolga said.

"She has the old and crafty Zolga to command her raiders too. After all, she did ask both of us to be her advisors," Galonica responded accusingly.

Zolga did not get a chance to respond as the governor came to stand with them.

"Thank you both for coming with me," she said with a slight bow of her own.

She glanced back at Aanaman walking back into the coalition headquarters before looking up at their galleon.

"I did not expect such intelligence and leadership from a male. The people of this island are quite intriguing, to be honest. They are also far fairer than we would have been if our recently deceased queen had been successful in her campaign. Come, we will take their formal offer to our people. I told Aanaman that I want to weigh their response before formalizing our agreement," Lorent said, stepping towards the steps down to the docks.

Zolga grabbed the young woman by her arm, and Lorent looked at her almost fearfully.

"I know you were barely a duchess for a year before yesterday and have now been elected by our people to represent them. However, you must remember, Governor Lorent, you do represent all of us. If you accept what the chancellor has offered our people, then our people have accepted it. If you want our opinion, we will give it to you now, but you must decide before we leave," Zolga said and looked to Galonica for support.

"It is for the sake of our people that you show both them and the land-born that you are our leader, with the authority and ability to act as such," Galonica agreed.

Zolga released her grip from the woman's arm, and Lorent gave them both a determined nod.

"All right then. I do want to accept Aanaman's terms. He wants us to join the nation they are forming with the states of this island and the Quaji tribes. They are willing to give us Lodestar Island as a permanent home and harbor for our people and ships. They are going to hand over all Kalt family-owned properties and business assets to our shipbuilders so that we may repair our vessels and make new ones," she said.

"What do they want in return?" Zolga prodded.

"They want us to not only repair our fleet but help them build and operate one for the new nation. the Tormenta will protect the waters and sea trade of the unified peoples. We will share in the military defense of this new nation's territories and participate in its governing councils. For that, they offer peace and goods to keep us supplied on Lodestar. More specific details on what all of that will entail are to be decided at the next council meeting, which you two will attend with me in several months," Lorent said with confidence.

"Oluja may have unified the clans, but it sounds like you may have finally delivered the promise of bringing prosperity to our people, Governor Lorent," Galonica responded.

"I do believe our people made the right choice in trusting you," Zolga agreed.

For a moment, the nineteen-year-old governor acted her age. She gave them both a smile, hugging them awkwardly and then resuming the fierce dignity of the Tormenta as she walked back towards Aanaman's offices.

*****

Aanaman walked along the western coast of Lake Gitche with Tawito. They had left Kalt three days ago, parting ways with Ingar and most of the dwarves as they turned towards Fjall. A small contingent had traveled back to the lake as Aanaman's personal guard despite Kilannry's argument. A few paces ahead of him, Tawito stopped, and he joined the Quaji as the man stared out across the lake.

"Here. This is where we will rebuild Quajillian, the old capital of our island empire that sat on this very lake. The three Quaji tribes have made agreements to be jointly ruled within their state by the triumvirate of chieftains. However, they have asked me to represent our diplomatic interests in external-facing matters, such as our role as a state in this nation you plan to propose," he said.

Aanaman bent and picked up a flat stone from the lakeshore and skipped it out across the serene water.

"How many will come back, do you think?" he asked.

"Most of the people from my atoll, the Urylap tribe, and most of the Aylap families as well. I believe close to a third of the Jawylap will stay on their atoll and probably spread to the others. Several of their families had been living out there long before you folk came and populated our main island. I would say close to forty thousand Quaji might return over the next year. I thank you again for honoring Harpis' request," Tawito said.

"Well, without help from your tribal fleets, we might not have had land to give back, so I thank you as well," Aanaman replied.

"What will you call this nation, Chancellor Reaper?" the other man asked.

He shrugged unknowingly and watched in silence as the ripples from his stone broke the tranquil waters.

"I don't know. I am afraid to put it to a vote as well. There would be endless fighting on whose idea should have precedence," he laughed.

"Savja," Tawito muttered, looking over his shoulder towards Ravnice.

"What was that?" Aanaman inquired.

"Savja. It is the old Quaji word for southernmost. Fitting, I'd think, for a nation of Quaji tribes, Quaj islanders, and the Tormenta. After all, between Quaj, Lodestar, the Atolls, and Huval Island, the only thing you find when you go further south is ice," he chuckled.

"The nation of Savja. I like the sound of that," he agreed.

"Well, Tawito, I hope you don't mind if some of the Savjan army will stay here on your new border with some of the dwarven forces and continue to build and fortify our military hub," he said.

"I don't mind at all. How do you plan to proceed with these states and the standing army, Aanaman?" the Quaji asked.

"For now, we will keep six standing battalions of a thousand men and women. One battalion each will forward deploy to Tuath, Mer, Ravnice, and Kalt. Two will be kept here for deployment as necessary, plus we'd count the dwarves as a seventh. General Shieldborn plans to rotate the companies within them from the cities and back to here to keep them drilled and trained and to commingle the personnel as much as possible," he answered.

"I assume Elliswerth will take up his posting as Field Marshal here once he finishes transitioning Kalt back to control of its citizens and the lumber yards and offices over to the Tormenta. What of yourself and your Minister Rashida?" he asked, grinning at the frustration on Aanaman's face.

"Oh, you'll have to ask my political advisor, Ingar Hammersmith, after he gets done figuring out how this whole thing is supposed to work," he answered sarcastically, pointing towards Fjall city.

"In that case, I look forward to being part of the next council meeting," Tawito said, patting Aanaman's back and turning to head towards the growing Quaji encampment.

"Tawito, you haven't heard anything about where Harpis is, have you?" Aanaman asked hopefully.

"I am sorry, my friend. I spoke with Ezera the other day. No one has seen or heard anything about him these past weeks. If I catch wind of anything, I'll surely send word your way," Tawito replied.

*****

The stairs to the second-story apartment creaked in protest with each step Jabruelle took. Opening the door slowly, he looked over the small apartment. He had previously been to the gnome's home on several occasions at the former Death Herald's invitation. He peeked into the bedroom nook across from the stairwell and noted that he would have to find a human-sized bed in the morning. Taking in the room, he sighed sadly to himself and went to the small wooden table with a whiskey glass, shot glass, and a half-empty bottle.

The anguish of entering the mausoleum-like shrine to Wren's humble existence might have overtaken him a few weeks ago. After performing The Sleeper's funeral rites to the frozen body parts of his former mentors, peers, and friends, he was not sure he could feel further sadness. He gingerly lifted the bottle and poured some into both glasses before grabbing one from the small cupboard.

He poured himself some of the Reaper vintage and looked from the empty fireplace to the thankfully human-sized comfy

293

chair.

"To you, Herald, and Xissay of The Great Dream. May you both find peace in slumber beside our goddess," he finished, raising his glass in a toast.

Placing his empty glass next to theirs on the table, he decided he should head downstairs and grab some of the linens from the preparation room so he could have something besides gnome-sized bedding for the evening. He was thankful for Aanaman allowing him to live in the building. He would stay until the dwarves had finished walling in the salvageable portions of The Sanctum in the coming months. Ingar had told him it would likely be much smaller, essentially a tunnel from the top of the stairwell into the sepulcher.

That was fine, he figured. It would take him years to find more to join him in worship if the past months trying to do so had taught him anything. Then, grabbing a pile of linens from the workbench, he stared for a moment at the oil-covered corpse of a dead cat that lay on the floor against the far wall.

"Sleeper, hear my call," he whispered.

After much effort, he was able to pull his scythe from The Great Dream. Holding it and concentrating, he focused hard, and the wispy grey of the between dulled his surroundings. Finally, after several long moments of murmuring, he opened his eyes and glared at the unmoving feline corpse.

"Let's just hope I don't have to try committing suicide again to increase my goddess-given gifts further," he said to the dead cat before shaking his head and making his way back upstairs to sleep.

Epilogue

Harpis' arms and shoulders screamed at him as he quickly heaved his oars into the water several times to get ahead of the cresting wave before letting the swell carry him the rest of the way back to the shore. He had been out to sea in the freezing waters off Kalt for half the day and caught nothing but a headache from the long-ago finished rum he had brought with him. The salty spray from the waves breaking on the shore around him felt like embers hitting eyes already burned from the howling wind and midday sun.

After dragging the small boat out of the reach of the rising tide, he stood, bent at the waist, trying to steady his breath for a moment. He found himself staring at the violin case that lay behind the vessel's lone bench seat. Then, unclasping the hardened leather lid, he pulled out the ebony-wood instrument. He ran a hand softly along the pearl inlay before grabbing the bow and dragging a long solitary note from the strings with it.

He heard no sound for the twentieth time in as many days, and tears began rolling down his face. All he could sense was the light vibration of the wood and strings, and those were soon lost when his body shook with silent sobs. Sliding the violin reverently back into its case, he took it and the empty skin with him on the hours-long walk to the tavern in the small town halfway between Kalt city and the village where he was born. There was rum there, and almost as importantly, there was not a soul who recognized the voiceless Harpis Akkeri.

*****

The black-armored giant trudged out of the sea and onto the sandy coastal shore. Several paces out of the waves, it stood unmoving, its blood-dripping obsidian spear scorching the sand where the red liquid fell.

Fishers and their families on the beach froze at the spectacle of his approach. Before long, a group of armed men and what appeared to be a chieftain arrived on the sand. They confronted the titan that was half again as tall as they were. Without a word, the dark spear flew from its hand. The weapon went through the chieftain's heart before disappearing and reappearing once again in the armored gauntlet.

It turned its head, pausing as it looked down at each of the men before it, and to a one, they fell to their knees in worship.

Enky lowered the frame he was watching to the desk before him.

"I forgot just how terrifying you were, little brother," he said regretfully.

Staring curiously at the visage of Sudbina in the frame that always sat atop his desk, he allowed himself to grin.

"Perhaps there is something we might do about this calamity after all."

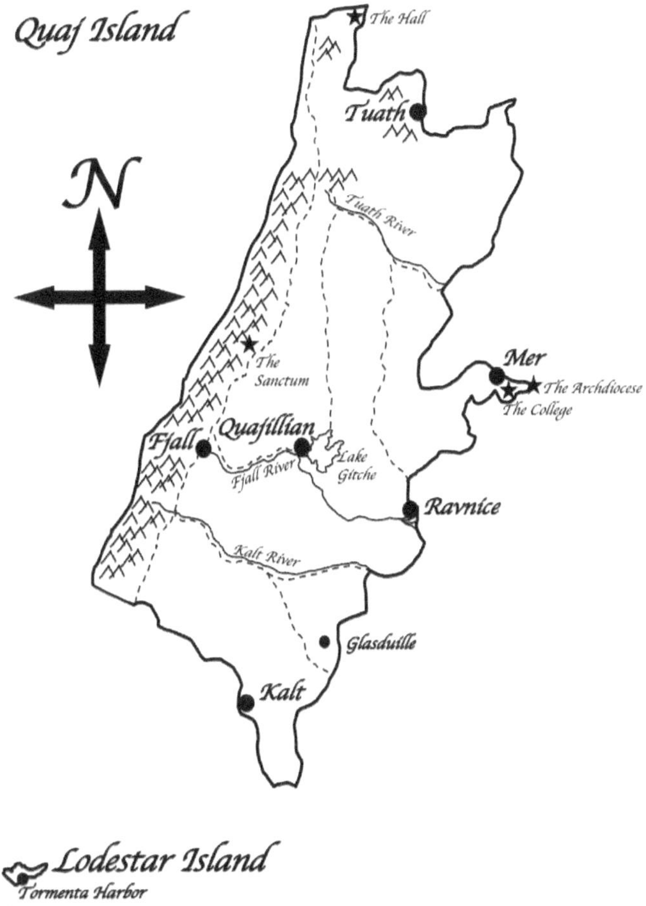

Quaf Island

★ *The Hall*

Tuath ●

N

Tuath River

★ *The Sanctum*

Mer ●
★ *The Archdiocese*
The College

Fjall ● **Quafillian** ●
Fjall River   Lake Gitche

● **Ravnice**

Kalt River

● *Glasduille*

● **Kalt**

Lodestar Island
Tormenta Harbor